**Acc**

This second bc ... mark of good plot—it leaves you wanting more. The excellent character development makes you love some characters and want to strangle others—a trait of a good storyteller. But either way, you can't help but get involved in this rich love story. Davis has done an excellent job of research, from her realistic descriptions of life in the hills of West Virginia to the accurate names and locations of the streets and places in Pittsburgh, Pennsylvania. The language of Appalachia in *Jason's Journey* rings true, without being overly sentimental, not an easy task. West Virginia should be proud of its daughter, storyteller, historian--Addie Davis.

— **Dr. Thomas K. McKnight**, Professor of English at Southwest Virginia Community College, Richlands, Virginia

*Jason's Journey* is every bit a match in quality and maybe more for *Lucinda's Mountain*, Addie Davis's successful first novel about life in McDowell County, West Virginia, around mid-century. Thoroughly realistic, the novel exhibits convincing detail, about life in mountain communities of central Appalachia, marriage and family, courtship and folkways, education, medicine and health, politics, social classes (in Pittsburgh and West Virginia), and religion, especially challenges to belief in the face of inexplicable suffering, and last but by no means least transportation, the effect of the condition of the roads upon the plot of the novel. All of these topics provide a backdrop for the overarching theme of the novel, a love triangle centered around Jason McCall, his wife Janet, and Lucinda Harmon, the main character and title figure of the opening novel. Here the emphasis is upon Jason, a doctor from Pittsburgh, and his journey to the heart of Appalachia, which is only one of several he undertakes in the novel, as he makes his way through mountain cultures, a tour in the army in time of war, and especially a spiritual odyssey into rocky ravines of love in all its forms. Tears of characters are abundant but never false. Davis carefully avoids stereotyping of characters and scenes where writers less skilled might flounder and fail in similar settings. This is a page turner full of surprises. Davis shows how Appalachia is like every other place in her handling of human emotions, but different. In the rendering of that difference lies the excellence of her craft.

— **Robert J. Higgs**

*Jason's Journey* is an endearing combination of local color and period romance. Southern West Virginia in the 1950s has never seemed more nostalgic and appealing. Sure to make many readers, not only those from the region, long for now... no matter where it may be.

— **Gregory D. Horn**, Assistant Professor of English, Southwest VA Community College

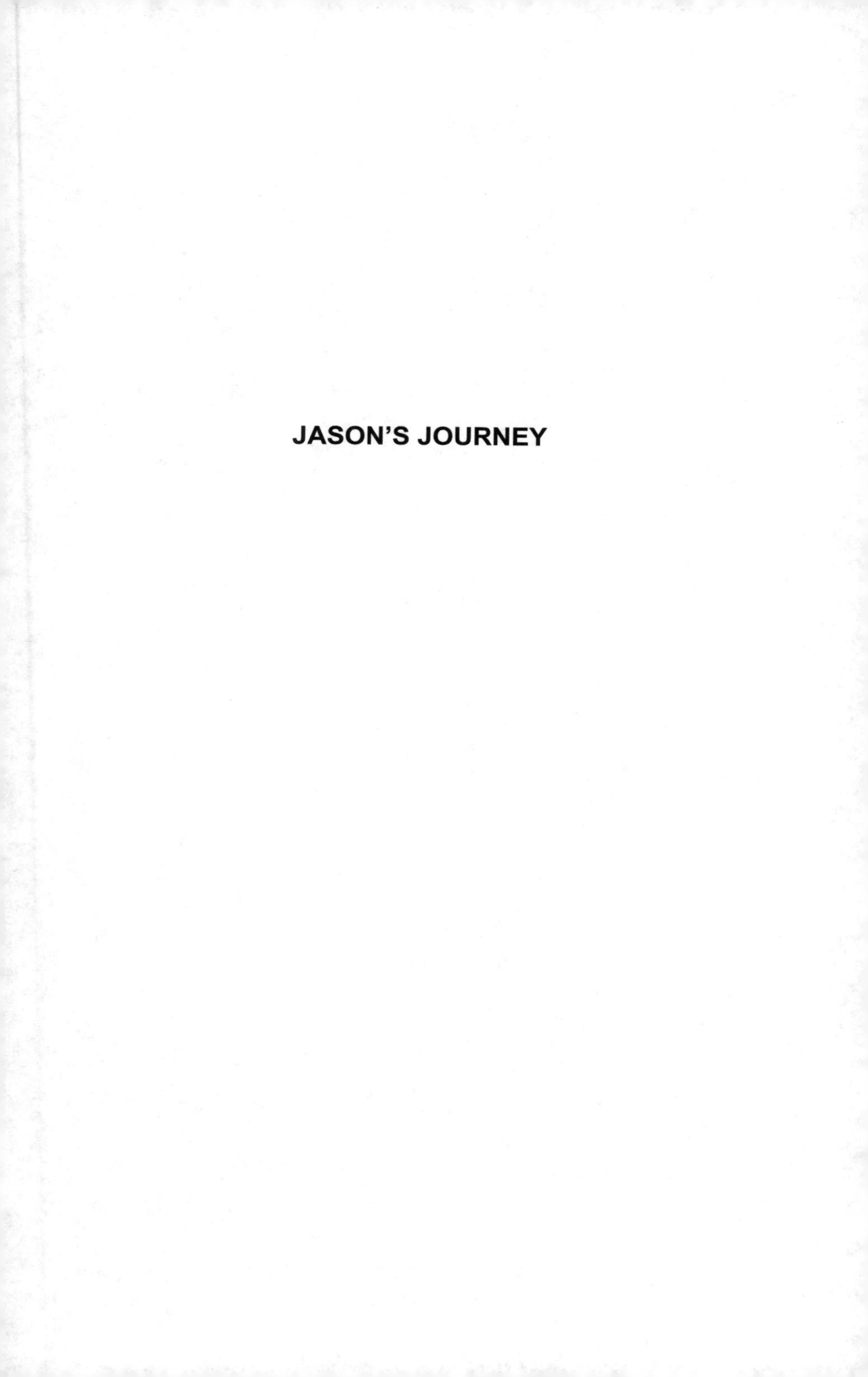

# JASON'S JOURNEY

# JASON'S JOURNEY

Adda Leah Davis

Mountain State Press, Inc.

Charleston, West Virginia

International Standard Book Number: 13: 978-0-941-092-54-8
10: 0-941092-54-2

Library of Congress Catalogue Number: 2008928281

Cover Art by Rhonda Whited

Book and Cover Design by Mark Phillips

Mountain State Press, Inc.
2300 MacCorkle Avenue, SE
Charleston, WV 25304

1 2 3 4 5 6 7 8 9 0

Printed in Canada

## DEDICATION

To all the fellow travelers who have walked with me through my life's journey of learning. They are all my friends.

***Knight's Journey***
By: Adda Leah Davis

A gallant knight went traveling
On a steed called daring deeds
Scaling mountains filled with challenge
Wading every tumultuous stream
Then came cupid's fateful arrow
To pierce through his armored vest.
Rending cultural views asunder
A challenged heart to be the test.
Then in various cultured clashes
His rapier thrust, cut, and slashed
Though his foil's point was covered
He held his superior lance as staff
He wended his way by learning
About the faith, the ways, and more
Of his fair maid's shining mantle
That with grace was simply worn.
With patience, he hoped to win her
Hoping and steadily biding time
Until age and culture melded
And both cultures could be entwined
Time, however, waits for no one
Age and trials steal from youth
Blurring visions with poor judgment
Almost blinds the glaring truth.
Many trials and many journeys
And gallant knights become serene
Until the peaceful calm is shattered
Long hidden secrets then are seen.

## INTRODUCTION

As I write this introduction in the home of my daughter located in the eastern foothills of the incredible Andes Mountains on the extreme western edge of the vast Amazon basin of South America, I am reminded of the two places and times that will forever be entwined in my memories. McDowell County in West Virginia and the Pastaza Province of Ecuador. Even though they are immensely different geographically and culturally, they share a common bond in my life. I have had the opportunity to practice medicine in both places. And they both challenged and rewarded me culturally and spiritually.

The story you are about to read is the second book of a trilogy. If you haven't had the opportunity to read the first, *Lucinda's Mountain*, don't worry. There is no great harm in reading this one first. At least I hope so, because that is precisely what I did. What I do know for sure is this. You will not be able to read the one without reading the other. In the first two books of this trilogy, the lives of Jason McCall and Lucinda Harmon are like a double-stranded helix of DNA, intimately connected, forever entwined, but frustratingly parallel.

What Adda Leah Davis has accomplished in the first two books of this trilogy is remarkable. *Lucinda's Mountain* is the story of a young woman growing up in the isolated hills of West Virginia in the "free state of McDowell". It bears the marks of an autobiography. She is clearly writing from personal experience. What amazed me personally about *Jason's Journey* is the hauntingly biographical nature of the novel which reminded me of my own experiences as a physician coming from the "outside" to practice medicine at the Tug River Clinic in Gary. I found myself reliving my own journey, medically and culturally. The author has clearly captured the essence of what it is to live in McDowell County as an "outsider".

I remember wanting to learn everything I could about McDowell County in the late 1970s. Mike Hornick, the unofficial historian of Gary, West Virginia, was my primary mentor. He unselfishly loaned me his personal collection of photographs and historical poetry about the birth and life of the mining industry and mining communities in McDowell County. My patients were my mentors as well, introducing me to the idiosyncratic descriptions of their illnesses and conditions. I learned the meaning of the term "fall sores" and the translation of the statement, "Doc, I lost my nature".

The local morticians educated me as well when they called me to remove the lungs of a deceased miner to be sent to the "state lab" to confirm the presence of coal-worker's pneumoconiosis so that his widow could receive her "black lung" benefits. Our neighbors included my family and me as their own family members in their social gatherings. We established close friendships that are part of our lives even today. We were invited to immerse ourselves in the lives of the wonderful people of McDowell County. And now, Adda Leah Davis has become my mentor as well.

*Jason's Journey* will place you squarely in the life of Jason McCall, a young physician practicing medicine in a location culturally different from his own and technologically isolated from his training. Don't worry about the authenticity of the medical details of the book. It is not about the practice of medicine. Rather, it is the story of how a young man becomes immersed in a culture distinctly different from his own and the tensions it creates in his own family. It is a journey of human drama, deeply personal interactions, and spiritual discovery. It is a story about how we, as human beings, react and hopefully grow when confronted with circumstances that take us by surprise or frustrate us personally. I am suspicious that this trilogy's deeper, hidden meaning is an allegory about how McDowell County itself has related to culturally distinct outside influences.

As I read this book, I relived our early days in McDowell County when we moved there with our twenty-one month old daughter and two week-old son. I remembered the old John Denver ballad of what it was like in my twenty-seventh year "comin' home to a place I'd never been before". If you have never had the opportunity to find yourself immersed in a culture distinctly different from your own, then sit back, relax, and enjoy the experience as Adda Leah Davis takes you along on *Jason's Journey*.

**Ross M. Patton, M.D.**
Professor, Joan C. Edwards School of Medicine
Marshall University,
Huntington, WV

# JASON'S JOURNEY

## CHAPTER I

"Another damn flat," groaned Doctor Jason McCall as his car suddenly became difficult to steer. He pulled to a stop in the only wide place by the side of the road, opened the door, and rolled up his pant legs in preparation for the mud he was certain to encounter. The first step seemed to be on solid ground but the next found him ankle deep in a water-filled hole.

"I hate this damn place. Now, I know why coal companies have so much trouble getting doctors to work in a program like this," said Jason aloud as he raised the trunk lid to get out his jack and spare tire.

Jason often wondered about his own motives for joining this Rural Medical Initiative Program. "I know these people need doctors and it is a challenge but I certainly didn't know what I was getting into," grumbled Jason and all during the process of changing the tire, he pondered his reasons for joining the program.

"It certainly isn't the money and couldn't have been this area of the country, so what?" Jason questioned himself.

When he'd first arrived in McDowell County and the town of Bradshaw, West Virginia, he was so caught up in the challenge of a new venture he didn't question anything. Now, since he had become more deeply immersed in the affairs of the town and the surrounding mountain farms and communities, he often wondered if the sense of challenge was enough.

Driving alone in the car, Jason often spoke his thoughts aloud. "I suppose I just love challenges. Or, perhaps because Bob Mills, that agent for the coal companies, who visited the University looked as if he didn't think any of my class would accept his offer," said Jason with a wry smile. He remembered looking around at his classmates and not seeing many takers.

Doctor Silas Weimer, his instructor, had rolled his eyes

and hunched his shoulders as if saying, "There it is, then. We don't have a fourth year student willing to take that kind of chance."

Mr. Mills had smiled grimly as he turned to leave but Jason had stopped him.

"I may be interested, Sir. I have a lot of questions, however," said Jason as the students began to file out of the room. Thinking back to that day Jason realized that he had been more intrigued by the challenges presented than any thing else.

Jason had always been drawn to challenges. From a very early age he had been an avid reader with a vivid imagination. Perhaps reading about conquering heroes fired his imagination. Whatever it was, Jason McCall always wanted to know "what if" about everything. He had always taken on the tough tasks, the ones that nobody else dared to tackle, and this program he had volunteered to be a part of had been and still was a challenge.

McDowell County was a picture postcard of rugged, beautiful, and untamed terrain. It was a place of stark contrasts with houses clinging to timbered hillsides above the Dry Fork and Tug Rivers while in the narrow ravines, bustling towns huddled along the banks. Yet when one crested the top of the many ridges like the ones along the top of Bradshaw Mountain the scenery was beyond compare. It wasn't just the lofty peaks soaring high into the clear blue skies, but also the neat and productive farmsteads scattered along the fertile hogback ridges, visible from one peak to the next. These homesteads were miles apart, but as the locals would say, in "hollerin distance" of each other.

"Being a doctor here in McDowell County is certainly daunting and demanding. However, I'm still not really positive as to why I was so eager to join up," mused Jason McCall frequently as he made daily house calls in the towns and on top of the mountain ridges.

He had been working in the program for an entire year and it had been a time of sacrifice. He missed being able to attend a play, a lecture, art shows, and most of all, his weekly visits to the library. Jason was steeped in classical literature and often harkened back to the words of some of his favorite authors, such as Steinbeck, Shakespeare, Hawthorne, Hemingway or the poetry of Poe, Frost, or Mansfield, when struggling with some dilemma. "These people don't know the power of the written word. I don't think many of them can even read," Jason surmised as he made his solitary treks up and down rutted, muddy, and unpaved roads on the ridges and the pot-holed paved roads of the towns and Route 83.

Loneliness had slowly crept upon Jason but now it seemed to have reached its zenith. He realized he needed a social life but didn't know what to do about it. He had not met any women with whom he felt he could build a relationship. Being celibate for almost the full time was causing him to miss female companionship, but there again, he did not know how to remedy that either.

After an embarrassing first sexual encounter in high school, Jason had been wary of intimacy until he was in college. Being in constant contact with members of the opposite sex he soon lost his reticence. He was never promiscuous, however, but tended to date a girl on a regular basis instead of, as his friends joked, "shopping around." Since being in McDowell County he had dated very little and had abstained from intimate contacts.

Not long after he first arrived in McDowell County, he met a doctor's daughter in Welch who he thought would help to ease his loneliness. She was attractive and certainly had an eye-catching body and he thought she might be interesting. After the first date, however, he realized she just didn't appeal to him. They had nothing in common and he never called her again.

Later he met Marcia Roberts who had come home to Bradshaw from college. They had a couple of dates but before the relationship really got underway she had to return to school and he forgot all about her. Jason drove along thinking that he would like to meet a nice girl, "I really don't have anybody to talk to and I've read so many books that I need a break," thought Jason as he shifted into a lower gear to go up Bertha Horn hill.

For a while his mind stayed busy as he thought about how treacherous this hill was in the winter and how often cars ended up in the deep ditch on the right side of the road. The official name wasn't Bertha Horn hill but people on the top of Bradshaw Mountain named hills after the people who lived at the foot of the hill or the top of the hill. In this case, Bertha Horn ran the Post Office, which was at the bottom of the hill.

He crested the hill and drove on around the curve and passed the road that led around Stateline Ridge No. 2. This in turn led to the Marion Kennedy and Randolph Viars farms. Both men were in good health for older men but he had made house calls to both places. The last trip had been to see Marion's wife, Mertie who had a touch of pneumonia. Jason was thankful he had been called in time.

Jason drove around the curve below the Vance Cemetery, thinking, "I must be crazy. I've gotten myself in a mess. I'm living here in McDowell County with bad roads, backward and uneducated people, not one decent restaurant in the whole area, and I've not had a date in months. Damn, I'm lonesome," mumbled Jason aloud.

Such thoughts were immediately put to rest by an alluring and potent distraction. About 100 feet ahead walked a most attractive and arousing diversion. The sun glinted on the waist-length fall of honey blond hair swinging in rhythm with a very attractive derrière, as shapely legs propelled this provocative vision down the road.

"She'll probably look like a dog in the face," Jason said as he slowed his car to a crawl on the other side of the road from her. He rolled down his window and leaned out; "Would you like a ride, M...?" began Jason, but didn't continue, as the startled face of a very young girl turned to look at him.

Never in his entire life had Jason seen such beauty. The bluest eyes he had ever seen looked first alarmed but then softened. A slight dusting of freckles powdered her nose and cheeks and when she smiled two dimples appeared on each side of softly curved lips, which revealed even white teeth. Jason was stunned. Suddenly the smile and dimples disappeared and the girl's face became expressionless.

"No, thanks! I'm only going to the store," she replied, while pointing on out the road. Just ahead stood a small building covered with tarred red-brick siding with a sign across the gable end stating that it was Vencill's Grocery.

Jason slowly shifted into gear and drove on but watched in his rear view mirror until she was lost from view. Then he drove on down Bradshaw Mountain, wondering who she was, and more than that, how old she was. "I bet she gets a lot of attention, no matter how old she is," thought Jason, bemused. As pretty as she was, Jason knew that most men would react just the way he had. Men would look at her face and want to know her. They would look at the rest of her also, especially the provocative movement of her hips with every step she made.

"I wonder if she is aware of the effect she has on men?" said Jason aloud as he swung too sharply around the steepest curve going down Bradshaw Mountain. Swiftly gaining control, Jason grinned. "I think I'll try to find out who she is," Jason said, gripping the steering wheel as he swung around another curve.

"It shouldn't be hard to find out. Everybody knows everybody else on this mountain, and she was going to Vencill's Store, so she must live along there somewhere," Jason mused aloud as he drove on into Jolo, wondering why he'd never seen her before now. He'd been on every hogback ridge from Bartley Mountain to Bradshaw Mountain and thought he had probably seen every person living in these hills but now knew he had missed one.

Jason had a house call to make at the Lovice Hardy home in Turkey Branch, a hollow leading away from Route 83, and had to get his mind back to where it should be. Tilda, Mrs. Hardy's daughter, was having epileptic seizures. Mrs. Hardy was very troubled about Tilda, because her violent seizures often caused falls.

"I can't do my work for fear she'll fall into the fire or off the porch. She could break her neck the way she pitches around," complained Mrs. Hardy worriedly.

Jason now knew more about Grand Mal Epilepsy and had ordered some Dilantin to try with Tilda. He eagerly climbed out of the car, anxious to see if the medicine would be of help. He was always so very pleased and proud when he felt like he had really helped someone.

Tilda was an intelligent thirteen-year-old who had been kept home from school for over a year because of her illness. Earlier Jason had discovered that Tilda had only begun having seizures when her menstrual cycle began. He called Dr. Weimer, his old professor, to be sure of the best way to treat her. He also questioned Dr. Weimer as to whether her hormone levels would affect her emotions in such a way as to cause epileptic seizures. Dr. Weimer's thinking was that emotions did not cause the onset but could possibly acerbate the condition.

"Mrs. Hardy, once she gets this medicine into her system, the seizures may become infrequent or stop altogether. If that should happen, then Tilda could return to school."

Mrs. Hardy looked doubtful, but Tilda gasped in pleasure and, with shining eyes, questioned, "Oh! Could I, Doctor? I've hated seeing my friends pass on the way to school while I had to sit here like an old woman."

"Well, Tilda, let's give you about two weeks and see how the medicine does, then we'll see about school. What do you think, Mrs. Hardy?" asked Jason, closing his bag and rising from his seat.

"If she quits having them fits, I reckon she could try it, but I swear, I'll be scared plum to death. Course, I just won't let her go if she even feels dizzy," stated Mrs. Hardy worriedly.

"That's settled then. I'll be back in two weeks or before then if you need me. You can always bring her down to the office, which would probably be better anyway," Jason said, as he walked out onto the porch.

When he was back on Route 83, he once again began

thinking about that really pretty, no, beautiful girl. "She's probably about fourteen and I shouldn't even be thinking about her at all," said Jason, scolding himself aloud. He switched his thoughts to Tilda Hardy which kept his mind occupied all the way back to the office in Bradshaw.

In the following weeks Jason frequently thought about the girl he had seen and amazingly forgot about her "sexy" walk or at least did not think of that as much as he did about her beautiful face. "Maybe, she is visiting someone up there," thought Jason.

When Friday rolled around and Maggie, his nurse/ receptionist was ready to go home for the weekend, Jason asked, "Maggie, do you know a girl with long blond hair, blue eyes, and dimples who lives near Vencill's Grocery on Bradshaw Mountain?"

Maggie stood in deep thought. "I don't know, right off hand. Let me think about it. I might be able to tell you by Monday," she said with a laugh before asking, "Somebody caught your eye did they?"

Jason grinned as he said, "You could say that, I suppose." He picked up his bag and followed her out the door.

Two weeks later, Jason officially met Lucinda Marie Harmon. It was a hot day in August in 1950, and the meeting was nothing like he had visualized. He was going down Brushy Ridge on the top of Bradshaw Mountain to make a house call. His patient, Mrs. Artemis Lester, whom he ended up calling Aunt Sarie, had an incurable cancer and he went to treat her once each week. As he drove up a little hill and around a curve, there, right in the middle of the road, walked a girl.

"God Almighty!" gasped Jason as he blasted on the horn and jerked the steering wheel as far to the right as he could without hitting the high bank on that side. The girl looked around startled and gave a hurried leap to the lower side of the road. Since the road was so narrow and rutted the right fender went scraping along the side of the bank anyway. He groaned as he heard a horrible scraping sound while righting the car to pull back into the middle of the road. He stopped, flung the door open, and marched back to the scene, ready to give that stupid girl a good tongue lashing.

"What do you mean by walking in the middle of the road? If I'd hit you, it would serve you right," he shouted from a red face and eyes sparking with anger. Then he stopped and stood staring in amazement. This was the same beautiful girl he had seen several weeks ago.

She had jumped to the side, but not soon enough to keep from being covered with splotches of mud and dirty water. Her amazingly beautiful blue eyes were spitting fire as she yelled, "What's wrong with you? Don't you know how to drive?"

When he started laughing hilariously, big tears began to roll down her cheeks and he was instantly consumed with guilt. Taking his handkerchief from his pocket, he reached out to wipe the mud away, only to have his hand slapped. She scrambled away from her precarious position on the edge, still clutching her bag of groceries. Trying to get to more stable ground, she lost her footing and fell into the mud puddle she had been trying to avoid.

Fighting anger, tears, and the sticky muck, she began struggling to her feet. When she put her weight on her right foot she turned deathly white, yelped in pain, and then fell again. The already wet paper bag had been joggled once too often and took that opportunity to split apart and disgorge all her groceries.

"Now, see what you've done," wailed the girl, now really crying.

Jason apologized profusely, lest she wouldn't allow him to check her foot. When he bent toward her she tried to back away as if in fear.

Jason said, "I'm not going to hurt you. I'm a doctor. I've been treating Mrs. Artemis Lester who lives on this road," and the girl relaxed slightly but was still wary.

On examination, he found she had sprained her ankle. Rising to his feet he said, "You can't walk on that foot. It needs to be bandaged. I'll have to carry you to the car."

He bent down in preparation of lifting her but she quaked

in alarm. “You can’t carry me…I don’t know you.” She was so pale that the mud became more noticeable.

“How do you plan to get home? I promise I won’t hurt you,” Jason assured her and she finally relented. Scooping her up, he carried her to the car. She felt so soft and fragile in his arms and looking down he realized she was scared. He shook his head in puzzlement while gathering up her groceries which were placed in the trunk, already cluttered with chains, cinderblocks, an extra tire and an inner tube.

As Jason started the engine and pulled out he looked over and asked, “What’s your name and where do you live? I haven’t seen you on the mountain before, except for the day you were going to Vencill’s Grocery,” finished Jason as he looked expectantly.

The girl turned her blue-eyed stare in his direction and smiled a heart-stopping smile. “My name is Lucinda Harmon. I’m Burb Harmon’s daughter. We live on the left hand fork of this ridge at the bottom of Luther Horn hill.” She gestured with her hand as he approached the forks in the road.

Jason smiled at her and asked, “Where have you been hiding, Lucinda Harmon?”

“I haven’t been hiding. I’ve been going to school. I just graduated from Iaeger High School in May,” Lucinda stated proudly.

Jason breathed a sigh of relief, “Good, I’m glad.,” said Jason and at her bemused look he said, “I mean, I thought you were twelve,” explained Jason as he drove down the road.

When he pulled up in front of a hewn log house enclosed by a tall pointed picket fence, he realized that, by his standards, these were very poor people. He got out and rounded the car to help Lucinda but encountered Nancy Harmon, her mother already at the car door. He assisted this energetic and friendly woman in getting Lucinda into the house, expecting questioning or perhaps a “dressing down” as Maggie called it when someone was upset with another person.

Mrs. Harmon, however, accepted his explanation. “Well, things happen when we least expect them, I reckon. It could have been worse. She'll be back on her feet in a day or two," stated Mrs. Harmon with a smile.

He learned that Burb Harmon, Lucinda's father, worked in timbers, and was a man who ruled over a large family. "We've got eight younguns but most of them are already married. Lucy here is just sixteen years old but she's already graduated from high school," boasted Mrs. Harmon proudly.

"Well, you'll soon have her off your hands too. I'll bet she has plenty of boyfriends, doesn't she?" questioned Jason, looking at Lucinda.

"Lord no, she ain't got no boyfriends. Burb Harmon would run any boys off with a shotgun. She's our baby and we don't aim fer her to marry young and have such a hard life as her sisters is having," blurted Mrs. Harmon.

As he left, Jason thought, "Well, she sure is beautiful and I wouldn't mind getting to know her better. I don't want to be faced with a shotgun though." So he tried to put her out of his mind. The attempt was fruitless, however, since he kept seeing her angry blue eyes and lovely face spattered with mud. He also remembered the soft curves he had held in his arms while carrying her to his car.

Jason did not realize it then, but that meeting was the beginning of a journey; not a traveling journey but one of discovery and learning. Jason didn't want to accept the fact that he was interested in a mountain girl who was as far removed from the girls he had always been interested in as daylight from the darkest night.

When Mrs. Harmon said that her husband would get a shotgun after someone wanting to date Lucinda, Jason was astonished. The idea that some man would bring out a shotgun to keep his daughter from dating was preposterous to Jason. Such thinking was almost a culture shock, and Jason wondered how many more beliefs, practices, and outdated ways of thinking he was going to encounter.

# CHAPTER 2

Jason thought he knew all about the culture which he had chosen to enter. Now, he understood that there was far more about these people in the mountains and the coal towns than what could be seen on the surface. He knew the many faces of those he encountered but he didn't really know the people.

It was difficult, if not impossible to get some people to go into a hospital and Jason felt that he knew some of the main reasons. The trip to Welch was long and not many people had cars. Many of these people were uneasy with strangers and were very wary of trying new things. The money to hire someone to take them to Welch was more than many of them usually had. Then too, there was this belief in faith healing, but Jason was not sure how many people depended on that.

Jason knew a man in Jolo who had told him of a church on Middle Fork Road where snake handling was practiced. The man, Mr. Chatman, had said that some of the people even drank poison during the service. Jason asked, "Has anyone ever been bitten?"

"They shore have," said Mr. Chatman. "Not just once but a whole bunch of times." Mr. Chatman seemed to delight in talking about the happenings in that church and went on to tell a tale of horror.

"Preacher Tatum's girl died," he said. "The church refused to take her to a doctor because they believed their faith would heal her. They prayed for her for two weeks, but she died anyway," Mr. Chatman continued.

"The neighbors said it was terrible how that poor girl screamed." Mr. Chatman spit ambeer between his parted fingers into the spittoon beside the door.

Getting into the story in a big way Mr. Chatman arose from his chair and dramatically spread his arms wide. "They questioned Preacher Tatum and you know what he said?" asked Mr. Chatman conversationally.

Jason didn't respond but sat waiting and Mr. Chatman

continued, "He said she didn't have enough faith. Can you believe that?"

Jason had listened aghast to Mr. Chatman's story and blurted, "That is criminal. Surely, there must be a law against that kind of practice."

But according to Mr. Chatman, some neighbor had called the State Police and by the time they had found some legal way they could intervene, the girl had died. "They said something about freedom of religion," Mr. Chatman said, scowling.

This didn't make sense. In Jason's mind, no matter how much faith the father had, neither he nor anyone else had the right to impose their faith on another person. That poor girl was a victim in his mind and those who failed to get a doctor for her were certainly liable.

Jason slowed down every time he passed The Church of Jesus Only on Middle Fork Road after he found that this was where that practice was observed. He promised himself a visit to their services some night to see what really went on. Surely people knew better than to drink poison. Being a doctor he knew that strychnine in occasional small doses wouldn't kill anyone and suspected that these people had learned how much was safe.

Jason knew that most of the people in the area did not believe in snake handling. When he drove by, there were very few cars parked nearby. Maggie Barker told him when he first arrived in Bradshaw that most of the people were honest, hard-working, and religious people, but she had said nothing about religious practices.

Jason did not know how many attended church but in most conversations some mention of the fear of the wrath of God would be brought up. He soon realized that many of these people did not value money and things as the road to happiness, nor did they feel that some other place or way was better than what they had at home. These people seemed, happy, safe, and content with their lot in life. Jason wondered about this since they didn't have many of the comforts available.

In one conversation he had with Aunt Sarie Lester she explained their attitude. “Here in these mountains, we thank the Lord for legs to walk with sted of fretting cause we have to walk,” she said in staunch support of mountain ways.

Often, since coming to McDowell County over a year before, Jason had heard, “In the Lord’s time I’ll get a car if that’s good for me and I’m willing to work for it.” This seemed to be the prevailing sentiment about any endeavor or difficulty and Jason could readily see why they seemed so content and happy.

“Hmm,” said Jason as he thought about this attitude. “I’d be happy too if I believed that failure to get something or do something just meant that the Lord didn’t think it was good for me and caused me to fail. That way I would have someone else to lay the blame on when I failed.”

Jason had been raised in the Presbyterian faith and attended Sunday school on a regular basis when he was young and church as he grew older. Jason knew most of the Bible stories but he really didn’t pay much attention to the sermons he heard on Sundays. Thinking back he could not recall definite beliefs being talked about. Mostly, he remembered that one must attend church, pay his tithes, and do good works if one wanted to live with Jesus in eternity. Jason had never questioned anything that happened at church. Going to church on Sunday was just something he was raised to do and so he was faithful in attendance.

Here in McDowell County he had encountered a different reaction to religion and church attendance. These people seemed to really look forward to meeting their neighbors and kinfolk every Sunday and in some churches Saturdays also. This was not just a habit they had gotten into. They really wanted to attend church and many of them had this Calvinistic view of predetermination.

Jason thought about that childbirth case which had to be sent on to the hospital. Edema and a weak heart made the patient at too much risk for a home delivery. On one occasion when Jason said, “Women with these kinds of problems should not become pregnant," his patient answered sharply that she would have every youngun' the Lord intended for her to have whether she had good health or not.

Here was another instance of predetermination of lives and Jason wondered if these people believed that everything was predetermined. Surely they didn't think they had to kill, steal, and commit other crimes. On further thought, he felt that they probably did not think everything was predetermined, or at least not knowingly. This was a very law-abiding area except for the Saturday night drinking which led to fights, and of course, there were the illegal moonshine stills.

Not long ago Jason had been sent for by a family who lived on Crane Ridge on top of Atwell Mountain, which towered above the community of Atwell. After treating the child who had whooping cough he began the slow trek along the top of the long plateau of the ridge. He drove aimlessly, stopping here and there to look down over the mountain. The view was breathtaking in its wild, uninhabited stands of timber and meandering creeks. Going around a wide curve he came upon a cemetery and then just beyond it was a small starkly white church building almost hidden among a semi-circle of trees. Mighty oaks and locusts seemed to shade and guard or protect the building in its solitude. Curious Jason stopped his car, got out and walked slowly up to the building. He wanted to see the name.

"Maybe it's another 'snake-handling' church," thought Jason as he drew closer. The building was turned so that the gable end faced the road and also became a small porch before the front door. Above the door he read "Mount Zion Primitive Baptist Church," with no Pastor's name or contact information.

"I wonder how people find their way here," said Jason as he walked around the building and found the outside toilets built on separate sides of the church and secluded in sheltering trees. He stretched up at the side window trying to get a glimpse inside. He wasn't quite tall enough and moved a rock under the window and peered inside. He was astonished.

"You talk about being as poor as church mice," said Jason as he got down and dusted off his hands.

"There's not a picture, books, lights, or anything else in there. Maybe they don't use it anymore," he muttered to himself as he went back to his car.

Back in the office he told Maggie about the Pruitt child with whooping cough and Maggie said, "Oh! You mean Jesse Pruitt that lives back this side of Mount Zion Primitive Baptist Church. I know that family. They're fine people but most Primitive Baptists that I know are good people."

"They don't handle snakes do they?" asked Jason curiously.

"No, they're the No-Hellers," stated Maggie. When she turned and saw Jason's look she continued. "You mean you've been here a year and haven't heard of the No-Hellers?" she asked in unbelief.

"I thought you said they were Primitive Baptists. Now you're saying they are No-Hellers. What does that mean?" questioned Jason, his head cocked in interest.

"I reckon they believe everybody on this earth goes to heaven when they die," Maggie said with eyebrows raised in doubt. "I've never asked any of them but that's what I've always been told," finished Maggie as she picked up the next patient's chart and went to bring them in. Jason waited at his desk thinking that he'd like to know more about that church.

The following Saturday the Pruitt family sent for him again since the little boy wasn't any better and now his sister had the same thing. He went to the Pruitt's and treated both children leaving some medicine for both and then drove back toward the Mount Zion Primitive Baptist Church. This time the building wasn't silent or empty.

Jason stopped under a tree beside the cemetery and sat listening to the singing. He could not understand at first what the song was but soon he heard "It's that old time religion, old time religion. It's that old time religion and it's good enough for me."

Jason sat very still, moved by the perfectly harmonized

voices raised in praise. "Everybody must be singing," said Jason in awe. Soon that song was finished and another song was started. Again he had difficulty hearing any of the words and he quietly opened his door and eased out onto the road. Just as he did he heard loud and clear, "And glory crowns the mercy seat," and a female voice shouting "Thank you Jesus" broke in upon the song.

Such a feeling of peace washed over Jason that he found himself smiling. His heart seemed glad or something, which stayed with him through the remainder of the song. Just as it ended some boys came chasing each other around the building and stopped when they saw him. Since they were looking at him suspiciously Jason got back in his car and drove quietly off the mountain.

He made up his mind that he was going to visit that church and sit in on one of their services if they would allow him to. He didn't know why he wanted to do that. He only knew that he did. There was just something about the singing that seemed to draw him and he wondered why since he had always been used to choirs in church.

The opportunity to visit again seemed to never come up and as time elapsed, he tended to think he had imagined the amazing feeling he had experienced. He wondered what the difference was between Southern Baptists and Primitive Baptists. He also wondered what the name "primitive" meant when applied to a church.

He knew that children in the Southern Baptist churches would be in Sunday school classes during the services and certainly would not be allowed to stay outside and play. He guessed that the Primitive Baptists did not have Sunday school but they had services on Saturdays since it was Saturday when he'd had that experience. He'd ask somebody about that church if he thought of it later, he promised himself.

Regardless of, how hard he worked or what he did, thoughts of Lucinda Harmon entered his mind on a daily basis. But, no matter where he was called all over the top of Bradshaw Mountain, there was no glimpse or sign of the aggravating girl. Jason was beginning to wonder if he was going to have to create some excuse to visit the Harmon home. At the same time, he was amazed to think he still had this backward and uncultured girl on his mind. It was very frustrating, but for some reason, he still wanted to see her again.

"If I could just see her again I'd realize how stupid I am," grumbled Jason every time a vision of swaying blond hair and blue eyes came into his mind. He laughed. "Maybe it's because I've never seen a girl drenched in mud before."

Several weeks later, Jason finally decided that he would ask about the Harmon family in a casual way when he made his next visit to see Mrs. Lester. The old lady, beyond belief, was still alive and her mind was still clear. She had refused the morphine after one dose saying it made her fuzzy headed and kept her from knowing what was going on. Never having seen a case such as hers, Jason had asked how she stood the pain because she was only taking aspirin.

Her weathered, wrinkled face broke into a wide toothless grin that seemed to lighten her whole face. "Why son, the Lord has helped me. I couldn't have made it 'cept for His loving kindness."

"Do you pray?" asked Jason, knowing that she couldn't go to church because of her condition. "Well, I do a lot of talking and beggin. I ain't so sure I pray. But I called Preacher Hiram and had him and the other elders to come and doctor on me. That's what done it," declared Mrs. Lester with assurance.

Being of a curious nature, Jason questioned, "I've heard about faith healing since I've been down here. What is it these elders do and how do they do it?"

"Lord, son, they don't do nothing, 'cept lay their hands on a body and pray. The Lord does the healing. But that's what the scriptures tell us to do. 'Course now I wouldn't ask for something like that a-tall if the Lord didn't give me faith to believe. Anyway, when a body asks to be doctored on, as many elders as can will get together and come to the person asking for doctoring. If a body is able to get to the meeting houses they ask for healing there, but if they can't, the elders go to the houses of the ailing," revealed Mrs. Lester.

"How do you know you are healed?" questioned Jason.

"I can't say fer ever body but I just asked one time and I felt the power of the Lord run all over me and I never had a doubt that I had been touched by his mercy. You can see for yourself how well I've been holding out, can't ye?" asked Mrs. Lester from a smiling face.

"I know that you've amazed me with your strength and courage, that's for sure," stated Jason positively. Being from a more scientific turn of mind, Jason was dubious about the Lord's intervention in the natural illnesses of humanity. He had been raised in the Presbyterian faith and he had never heard of anyone who talked about or believed in this kind of healing practices.

"I really don't know much about the church I was raised in," thought Jason, as he tried to remember. Regardless, Jason realized that Mrs. Lester had certainly outlived the two weeks he had at first given her, in his mind. That had been in May and now, four months later, he couldn't see much change in her.

Jason shook his head in puzzlement. "Faith healing and quack remedies for cancer," he thought, yet made no comment as he deftly changed the subject by asking about her neighbors.

"I guess the Harmons and your other neighbors drop by often, don't they?" asked Jason.

Mrs. Lester sat thoughtfully studying, "My other neighbors have, but Nancy Harmon has been so tore up since Lucy left that she just about cries all the time, I hear. Poor thing! Her other girls stayed home till they married but I reckon Lucy had other idees."

"Where did she go…this Lucy?" Jason asked in amazement. Who would have thought she would have the courage to risk the unknown.

Mrs. Lester nodded her head as if in thought while looking at Jason with a penetrating gleam. "Off somewhere to get a job, Jeb said. I can't rightly remember where it was. She was always real smart. Made straight A's in school, Nancy told me. She said Lucy wanted to go off to college but there weren't no money to go on. She wanted to go way off in Kentucky somewhere to a college where she could work and pay her way but Burb Harmon wouldn't hear of it. He said girls didn't need all that edifying to marry and raise younguns' and besides it was too fur away and her only sixteen years old. Too much temptation for a girl that young, Burb said," stated Mrs. Lester derisively.

She slowly nodded her head as if deciding something, "I always felt that if a body wanted to do wrong they could find a way no matter where they wus," Mrs. Lester solemnly finished.

"Mr. Harmon must keep a close watch on his girls," stated Jason in reply. He recalled Mrs. Harmon saying what Mr. Harmon would do to any boy trying to hang around his baby. There are only two towns that are close and large enough to find work, so she must be in Welch or Grundy, Virginia. Both are good-sized coal towns but not thriving metropolises," Jason thought to himself, as he packed up his stethoscope and other equipment.

Shutting his bag firmly he squatted beside Mrs. Lester's chair. "I don't know about this faith healing but something has sure kept you going. So whatever you're doing, just keep on doing it."

Mrs. Lester looked up at him from a glowing face and gaping-mouthed grin, "I aim to Doc, but you come on back to see me. I like you. You jest call me Aunt Sarie, everybody else does."

Patting her hand, Jason rose. "Oh, I'll be back to see you, Aunt Sarie, probably next week, but sooner if you need me," said Jason, smiling fondly.

"Here, gimme a hug. I need a hug," said Aunt Sarie, reaching up her arms. "You look like you need a hug too. I'll try to find out which town Lucy went to for you," said Aunt Sarie, grinning mischievously.

With a knowing wink and a wicked grin, she pushed him

away, "Go on now, but you come back next week."

Puzzled and a little embarrassed, Jason made a hasty retreat wondering what he could have said to make Aunt Sarie think he was interested in Lucinda Harmon. Well, he was curious about her and more than that, he had been ashamed of himself over his reaction at the first sight of her, when he thought she was much younger. He admitted to himself that he had constantly wondered what had happened to her or why he hadn't seen her. Now, if he really wanted to see her he wouldn't have to search the whole area to find her.

"Am I really interested or just curious?" Jason questioned himself. She was just a kid, a beautiful sixteen-year-old hillbilly and clumsy besides. "I've seen a lot of bodies in this business, but those dimples, big blue eyes, that walk, and especially the way she felt in my arms is just hard to forget for some reason."

Jason thought about the best way to find out where she had gone to work as he began the trip out of Brushy Ridge.

At the bottom of Luther Horn hill he came up behind a logging truck loaded with what he estimated to be two-foot lengths of logs. Maggie Barker had told him that these were prop timbers which were used in the coal mines to shore up the roofs as the coal was taken out.

Jason studied the size of these timbers. "My God," he exclaimed in amazement since he was now actually looking at the size of the logs. He shivered as he thought about men crawling back under those mountains with only about three feet of space between the floor and ceiling, and that propped up with these small timbers. Back in those holes men would have to lie down to shovel coal. "It's no wonder that unions have such a strong presence in the lives of coal miners," stated Jason aloud.

According to Maggie, these timbers were part of how some of these mountain people made their living. Prop timbering and produce peddling to the coal camps provided a vital source of revenue for mountain people. They peddled poultry, butter, eggs, vegetables, fruits, and berries in the summer and fall and cut prop timber and wood for fires in the winter. Jason had plenty of time to reflect on this as his car crept along behind the heavily loaded truck. He had shifted into first gear and was barely moving and eating dust all the way. Finally he decided to pull over after he reached the top of the hill and just wait until the truck had gotten almost out of the ridge.

He sat thinking about a story Maggie Barker, his nurse/ receptionist, had told him of a Baker family from one of the mountain ridges who came into Bradshaw to peddle.

According to Maggie, they had come into town with the Deputy Sheriff as he made his weekly trip to the county seat in Welch. The mother, father, and daughter made up the group on this trip. They unloaded in front of Aunt Liz Hopster's Boarding House where peddlers usually set up. They arranged their wares there beside the street and did a thriving business for about an hour.

Then two boys with their dogs came down the street. Seeing all these nice fat chickens, the dogs made flying leaps right in the middle of the produce in an attempt to get to the chickens. The chickens, however, were in coops and the dogs couldn't get to them but that didn't stop their frightened squawking. Neither did it stop the man from kicking, nor the women from flailing the dogs with whatever lay nearby.

Soon a crowd had gathered and the dogs were hissed, while at the same time, the man and the women were encouraged in their endeavors to chase away the dogs. This led to the boys becoming angry because of the kicks their dogs were receiving. Their attempts to stop the man and the women from belaboring their dogs ended when one of the women not only walloped a dog, but slapped one of the boys who had grabbed her arm.

That's when the free-for-all started, because the boy's mother had arrived on the scene. She immediately reacted in defense of her son and sent the woman who slapped her son flying backwards into a tub of tomatoes. From there several people joined the fray. Hair pulling, punches, kicks, and blooded noses were in evidence before a constable was called to the scene. Maggie said that old Doctor Harrison made about $50.00 on that peddling day.

Jason laughed merrily as he started his car and drove on out of the ridge and down to Bradshaw, still in a happy mood. He knew first hand, that people still brought produce and chickens to town, since he had been paid with a live chicken and some vegetables just last week.

Jason knew he was not likely to see a scene like Maggie described because now people already had orders before the produce was brought in. Large orders were contracted to the three grocery stores: Jones and Spry's at the lower end of town and Walter Day's General Merchandise at the intersection to Route 80 on the road to Iaeger, and Island Creek's Company Store across the road on the other side of Route 80.

The farmers also sold over in the black camp called Eclipse, which was located across the Dry Fork River. Everything had to be carried over a swinging bridge since there was no other road to the black camp. Not many of the black people lived there now. Jason had heard that most of them moved after the explosion at No. 1 Bartley in 1941. They had moved to places like Gary, Keystone, Northfork, and Kimball where they felt life would be much easier, where they would be closer to stores, schools, and hospitals and where they would at least have a road to their homes.

The black community had its own school and its own churches, or Jason supposed they did since he saw very few of the people in town. When he met any of them in the stores or when they came to the office, he did not notice anyone being unkind to them but they certainly kept to themselves.

When Jason mentioned this to Maggie she said she hadn't thought about it. "I guess I've just assumed that they want to be by themselves."

"What if they sense that the town's people will only tolerate them if they stay in their place?" asked Jason.

"I don't know. To tell the truth I don't even know how I feel about them. I know I don't hate them and I don't want to see them mistreated, but…well, they've always lived over there. I think its better that way," said Maggie as if she was in deep water.

Jason felt this was not a good situation. People were people regardless of race or color. Yet, he also knew that there was segregation all over the United States. As a doctor he found racial bigotry intolerable. He could not understand it in this area where they worked together every day.

"They all bleed red when they get cut and when they come out of the mines all of them are black," mumbled Jason as he pulled in behind his office and turned off the engine.

## CHAPTER 3

Jason McCall was a doctor in a new program that hired medical students willing to work in the coalfields for two years of free training, or almost free. His hours were long, often stressful, and very challenging. But, in a medical school he would have had to pay tuition and be a closely supervised intern, and yet not gain such practical experience.

He felt he was learning more about being a doctor here among these people, than he could have ever learned in a hospital. If he wanted to be a surgeon, further training would be required. To have a specialty in any field would also require more schooling, but now he was gaining a wealth of knowledge right where he was.

Here in McDowell County he had no superior to turn to for answers when he had doubts. He was on his own and had to 'think on his feet,' as it were. He had really put that set of medical books to good use and he also made lots of phone calls to talk to other doctors about his diagnosis of certain illnesses. In this manner, he had diagnosed and treated illnesses that students in the teaching hospitals would only have learned about in lectures.

Everyday Jason was made more aware that practicing medicine in Bradshaw was very challenging. Jason was often frustrated by the lack of modern facilities and communication. He was fortunate to have a telephone with a private line since most of the phones in the area had two or three people on each line, especially on the mountains. Without that privacy on his line, he could not have called about the illnesses he encountered.

He had arrived in September, 1949 and had not been home to Pittsburgh since he came, which was more than a year ago. At first, he wrote about once a week and called almost as often. Now he just called his family about once a month, because he was so caught up in the various cases presented to him. Also, having to make house calls all over these hills, hollows, and mountains left little time to write or call.

He just had to call tonight though, and tell his brother, Frank, about his most recent payment. A woman named Jetty Daws came down off Three Forks Mountain with four dozen eggs, two cabbage heads, a bag of tomatoes, six or seven cucumbers, some green onions, and a live chicken. She said she didn't have any money but she had priced it all in the store and it came to ten dollars

That was the charge for an office call unless the patient was employed by the coal company. Then the charge was only five dollars per visit. He had to accept the payment but didn't know what to do with it all, especially the squawking chicken.

Before pandemonium broke out in the waiting room, Maggie Barker intervened. Maggie knew everybody within a twenty-mile radius of Bradshaw. She got a boy who was playing in the alley behind the office to take the chicken to Mrs. Harper, a widow lady who struggled to survive, as a gift. All the rest was given to his cleaning lady who said she would make soup and salads to share with him as long as they lasted. This suited Jason fine since he had gotten so tired of restaurants.

Many people came in and left owing part of the bill. Maggie said some people would pay and some people would never pay a cent. Since she knew more about the area and the people, Jason took her word for it, but he didn't know what the company did about unpaid bills.

Jason realized that his pay was assured regardless of whether the company made any money or not. However, he also knew that some of these people had a hard time just keeping their large families fed, and he felt really sorry for them. Therefore, when he received free samples of medicines from salesmen, he tried to pass them on to those patients. Island Creek Coal Company, for whom he worked, would probably make them pay somehow. The miners fees were taken care of in withholdings from their pay checks but the people who didn't work in the mines received treatment also and some of them didn't pay.

"Why in the world do these people keep having children

when they can't afford medical care for them," muttered Jason quietly, but Maggie heard him.

"The trains cause it," she said with a grin.

"The trains cause it! No Maggie, trains don't make babies."

Maggie cheekily replied, "I know that but when the trains wake people in the middle of the night...well...it gives them ideas."

They laughed merrily, but it didn't keep Jason from wondering if they knew about birth control. Maybe it was just the religious beliefs of many mountain people which kept them holding onto the old ways of thinking. According to many of his older patients, each child was a blessing of the Lord and every one a woman could have was welcome.

Yet if he talked to some of those welcomed children who had grown into adults he got a different story. "Pa wanted a passel of younguns so he'd have plenty of field hands that he didn't have to pay," one patient told him. Many of these children never saw a dentist, some did not go higher than the sixth grade in school, many were undernourished and poorly clad, and some had never been off the mountains on which they were born.

How did one combat this ignorance? No, not ignorance, thought Jason. These people were smart in their way. Like Aunt Sarie who had a keen wit, could read people, and had a wealth of knowledge about life. "They're just uneducated and backward since they have never been exposed to outside influences," Jason mumbled to himself.

Not many homes that he'd been in had any books except the Bible. They had catalogs, often called wish books, and some had battery powered radios, but no novels, no newspapers, and few televisions. A large majority of the homes had no electricity and no telephones, especially on the tops of the mountains, and therefore had no access to any other way of life.

Jason wondered what would happen to people like Aunt Sarie's family, when they would eventually be exposed to the modern world. Would they be able to cope? How would Lucinda Harmon fare going off to town to work? She had finished high school, which should help some, but still it would be difficult, especially since she was so young. Jason thought she must be very intelligent to have finished high school at sixteen.

Jason wished he could help her some way, then wondered why in the world he was still thinking about that little backwoods girl anyway. He thought the best thing for him would be to find a girlfriend and get Lucinda Harmon out of his head, blue eyes and all.

"She'll probably meet some man in town, think she's madly in love, and end up pregnant before she is seventeen," Jason muttered gloomily. Realizing that he didn't want that to happen to Lucinda, he decided that he would visit the nearby towns to see if he could find her.

As luck would have it, the following Friday he stood looking out of his apartment window as the big blue and white Trailways bus pulled into the station from the town of War, and there was Lucinda Harmon perched on the front seat behind the driver. She looked prettier than he remembered and he stood gazing intently. She turned her head and smiled at something the driver said and Jason caught his breath. He hadn't realized she had such a dazzling smile.

"Well, well, so my little aggravating daydream works in that direction. Maybe she is working in War rather than Welch," thought Jason. A nebulous plan to follow the bus next Sunday evening formed in his mind as he turned back into the room and picked up the shrilling telephone.

It was several weeks later before he actually followed the bus, and discovered that Lucinda got off the bus in War and boarded a waiting bus headed for Welch. He didn't have time to follow it that evening, but turned and drove slowly back to Bradshaw.

He then began planning a trip to Welch to surprise Lucinda Harmon even though he really didn't understand why. All this had been running through Jason's head as he drove down to Yukon and turned left on Route 83 to make his way to Bradshaw. As Jason pulled up in front of his room above The Five and Ten Cent Store, Mrs. Harris, his landlady came out the door. Jason shut off the engine, opened the door and reached in the back to get his bag, when he heard a thump. Looking up, he saw Mrs. Harris lying against the hood of his car.

Leaving his door open, he ran around the car just as Mrs. Harris began to slide toward the ground. He caught her and eased her gently to the earth, then quickly loosened her belt and grabbed his stethoscope from his bag. Placing it over her heart, he listened and, hearing a weak, erratic beat, quickly checked her pulse. He got a syringe from his bag and administered a shot of atropine just as Mr. Harris came out his door.

Seeing his wife lying on the street, he rushed to the car shouting hysterically, which gathered a crowd.

"Mr. Harris, I'll need your help. She needs to go to the hospital. It's her heart and we need to hurry, so help me load her into the back seat and get in with her," commanded Jason.

Jason would remember that trip as the fastest he had ever driven and the most afraid he had ever been. He had driven back up Route 83 through Raysal, Bartley, English, and Yukon before he reached Route 16 where he turned left on his way to Welch. The entire route was like a snake slithering up and down hills and Jason hoped that he wouldn't meet too many cars. The roads were so narrow in some places that a speeding car would have collided with anything in the road. Most of the way, he couldn't even make fifty miles an hour and was lucky to make forty. However, in a little over an hour, he pulled into the emergency department of Grace Hospital and jumped out.

He stayed there until twelve midnight before learning that Mrs. Harris had suffered a heart attack, but it was not as damaging as it could have been. When Mrs. Harris was stabilized, Jason walked a troubled and subdued Mr.

Harris back to his car and began a much slower trip back to Bradshaw.

As tired as he was, Jason tried to keep a cheerful conversation going. "Joe, you know she's going to be all right now. She'll have you cleaning windows again by next week," said Jason as he looked sideways at Mr. Harris who smiled tiredly.

"I hope she does, Doc. Another scare like this and I may never clean another window. When she gets home again, I'm going to tell her if she wants me to do all the work she'd better not scare me no more." Mr. Harris commented, looking sideways at Jason.

Jason slapped him on the leg. "You do that, Joe. Stand right up to her and tell her to do it herself," said Jason chuckling.

Mr. Harris looked startled. "Well, I wouldn't go that far. She'd whop me over the head with a frying pan."

Jason grinned. "Yeah, I bet she would. She likes to get things done doesn't she?" Mr. Harris nodded his head and remained silent.

Jason was tired, dirty, and felt in need of sleep which he planned to get as soon as he reached his bed. This didn't happen though, because he hadn't been in his room but about thirty minutes when Hassell Hagerman came knocking on his door.

"You gotta come, Doc. Betty's having her baby. Where have you been anyway? I've been down there waiting on you for over an hour. She's scared to death just to have old Armindy with her," said a worried Hassell, breathing whiskey-laden fumes toward Jason. Jason stood staring blankly as he listened, then he turned tiredly and picked up his bag. Then he put it down, went to the bathroom and washed his face in cold water, while deciding what he might need.

Jason knew that the Hagermans lived up a hollow from the Middle Fork Road, but he didn't know how far. He cursed softly as he gathered up what he would need and went out the door behind a staggering Hassell.

This trip was even worse. The road not only snaked, but it

ran over ruts, mud, rocks, and crossed the creek twice before they reached their destination. As Jason got out of the car, he saw a dim light shining through a window across a narrow creek, which Hassell called a "branch." He couldn't see well enough to really know how one got to the house.

Hassell said, "Here Doc, let me carry your grip cause this log can be slippery when it's wet."

Jason looked down just as a weak moon broke through the clouds to reveal a round log not a foot wide, which was thrown across the creek. "I'll fall in that damn creek," thought Jason and determinedly stepped up on it, thinking, "If Hassell can cross it drunk surely I can make it sober." He made it across and followed Hassell up a stone step and into the front room.

The first room had a bed, a chest of drawers, and a chair, which was occupied by the fattest woman Jason had ever seen. Betty Hagerman was in the bed, which was none too clean, seemingly asleep but not for long. Just as Jason put his bag down on the foot of the bed, Betty reared up and screamed as she thrashed about. Jason grasped her shoulders and pushed her back on the bed and began talking to her. When she realized he was the doctor, it seemed to give her some relief. Turning to the woman in the chair, she said, "Armindy, you can go on home now. The doctor will deliver my baby."

Armindy made several attempts to rise but didn't make it until Hassell and Jason grabbed her arms and gave a heave. She shuffled slowly towards the door, saying, "I can stay if you'uns wants me to. I've helped birth many a babe in my time."

Jason wondered how, with the trouble she had getting out of the chair. When Hassell didn't go with her or offer her a light, Jason thought she would break that log and fall in the creek. He told Hassel so, but that young man shrugged it off, saying, "Armindy can wade that little ole branch. Besides, if I tried to get her across on that log, we'd both fall in. She weighs a ton."

This would be the fifteenth home delivery Jason had

performed since coming to Bradshaw and, after examining Betty, he felt everything would be fine. However, it seemed as if it would be a while before the young Hagerman would make an appearance.

Jason turned to Hassell, "Could you make me some coffee? I've already taken a patient to Welch and had just gotten back when you came. I could certainly use some coffee."

Hassell looked bewildered and mumbled grouchily as he started into the other room. "I don't know if I can or not. Betty ain't washed the dinner dishes today. We ain't got many cook vessels."

Jason knew he'd never make it without coffee or something to keep him awake so he followed Hassell into the kitchen. There he found a coal and wood burning cook stove, a table and two chairs, and a shelf on the wall with groceries stacked on it. In another corner was a wooden block with a water bucket and a dipper. It was a daunting aspect but Jason was determined. He picked up the coffee pot on the back of the stove, emptied the coffee grounds out the back door and came back in to get water to rinse it out. Before he could fill the coffee pot, Betty let out another yell and he handed the pot to Hassell and told him to make the coffee.

An hour later, the coffee was done and Betty was showing signs of delivering any minute. Jason was so busy he didn't even smell the coffee until he held the lusty baby girl in his hands. The smell of that coffee hung in the air while he snipped and tied the umbilical cord and cleaned the baby. He yelled for Hassell to pour him a cup as he waited for the afterbirth.

He heard Hassell clanging and banging around in the other room as he cleaned the baby, who was squalling loudly. As soon as the afterbirth was taken care of and the baby was safely in its mother's arms, Jason headed for that coffee. He found Hassell sound asleep with his head on one corner of the cluttered table and the coffee almost boiled dry.

After scrubbing his hands and arms with alcohol, he looked for the cup of coffee Hassell was told to pour. Not finding it, he looked around and found an empty cup on the block of wood beside the bucket and dipper. He poured out the thick black coffee and took a sip. Grimacing and sputtering he ran to the door and spit it out. He added about a half cup of water and did drink some of it. He had to drive home and he was dead on his feet.

Jason shook Hassell, who jumped to his feet looking wildly around as if being attacked. Seeing Jason, he slumped back down to the chair, "Has she had it yet? I went to sleep." Jason wondered how many more children Hassell would help to enter this world. Then sleep as they appeared.

Back in Bradshaw, a very weary Jason climbed the stairs to his room at five o'clock A.M. and fell atop his bed and was instantly asleep.

## CHAPTER 4

Jason Henry McCall was born March 24,1924, in the city of Pittsburgh, Pennsylvania. He was born in the master bedroom of the Wentworth mansion situated on a corner of Beechwood Boulevard in the area of Frick Park.

The various ethnic groups coming to Pittsburgh had settled together in close knit communities. The area around Squirrel Hill was exclusively Jewish. The Homestead area was settled by people of Polish and German descent. The Oakland/Frick Park area was inhabited by English and Scotch/Irish descendants. When studied from that perspective, Pittsburgh appeared to be little cities within a bigger city--"A wheel in a wheel in a wheel."

Jason was born in the same house in which his mother, her father and grandfather had been born. Elizabeth Wentworth McCall, his mother, could trace her lineage back to fourteenth century England. She was never so gauche as to deliberately bring it up, but if there was some way it could be referred to in the conversation, she unfailingly did so. According to Elizabeth, the Wentworths had always lived in the top echelons of English society. Even though she could not historically claim close ties to nobility, she still boasted of her family's noble ancestry.

Jason thrived and grew into manhood in this same house and dearly loved every aspect of not only the house but the entire estate. The only thing to mar this halcyon existence was his early recognition of his mother's pretensions.

"Mother, you are such a snob," Jason first teased Elizabeth, during his growing up years. This bemused teasing later became resentment, and then anger, as his mother coerced him to form various relationships which were unwanted. He was to make an open break when he fell in love with a woman from a totally different background. When his mother was made aware of this alliance, her attack was not only snobbish but devious and vicious in its determination.

As Jason grew up, he tried to understand Elizabeth's desperate need for recognition and acceptance for herself and her children. It was then that Jason began to delve into his ancestry, particularly on his mother's side of the family. He needed to look beneath the sanitized version so proudly brought to the fore any time Elizabeth felt her ancestry was in question. The bronze family crest was prominently displayed over the entrance foyer of the Wentworth mansion. Jason wanted to know the real-life family tree. Who were these people his mother boasted about and immortalized?

Jason, however, did not go back fourteen generations, as his mother claimed to have done. When he discovered a distant grandfather, Lord Clively Wentworth, who had fallen out of favor with the reigning king, he became very interested.

He found that this grandfather had so many children that none fared well. Now, Jason was hooked on his findings and wanted to learn all he could. He quickly realized that, even way back then, the Wentworths had kept to all the social etiquette of that era which had once been their due. Further research revealed that this Wentworth's eldest son, Harrison Clively, had two sons, Harrison and Bascom.

Bascom was killed in an accident before he reached his majority. This left Harrison Clively Wentworth, Jason's great, great, great grandfather to inherit the title but little else. Still, by selling off much of his land and carrying a heavy burden of debt, he managed to keep his place in the society into which he was born, until it was no longer possible. Eventually, his creditors became so demanding that Harrison Clively sold most of his holdings. He lived an ostracized and meager existence until his death, leaving his son, Harrison Clively the II, an inheritor of a meaningless title.

Harrison the II sold what was left and migrated to America with his family, leaving all his unpaid debts behind. Once in America, where they were unknown, the family automatically sought to be a part of the elite society in Pittsburgh, where they had settled.

Harrison the II was a shrewd gambler and business man, and after a fifteen- year stay in Pittsburgh, had accumulated enough wealth to buy property and build the Wentworth mansion.

There, Elizabeth's McCall's grandfather, Harrison Clively Wentworth the III, was born. Unfortunately, this Harrison also liked to gamble but wasn't very adept. Each year he grew more daring and began to amass enormous debts. This would leave Elizabeth's father, Harrison Clively the IV and last Harrison, to inherit the estate and the debts when his father was mysteriously killed one cold winter night. Shocked beyond belief, the younger Harrison stayed away from gaming halls for many years, since most people believed his father's death was linked to his gambling.

Harrison the IV was working in the shipping department of Pittsburgh Steel, but in a minor position, when he met and married Katherine McClain along with her substantial dowry. Katherine's father operated a steel mill and took Harrison the IV into the business. Harrison proved to be an astute and able student of the business and was soon vice-president. After his marriage, he was able to settle the debts against the Wentworth estate before Elizabeth was born.

Katherine, his bride, was very conscious of society's strictures and, therefore, always made it a point to refer to her husband's descent from Lord Clively. With this persona, as well as her own inherited wealth and position, she and Harrison were naturally invited to all the elite functions of Pittsburgh society.

After all this research, Jason began to understand that class, family, and traditions were ingrained into his mother's very being. It wasn't difficult to learn Elizabeth's story since his grandmother, Katherine, reveled in talk about the past. From the many talks he had with his grandmother, Jason became well versed in that side of his family history. Jason loved watching his grandmother's eyes glow as she described Elizabeth's childhood and youth...

"I saw that she had everything that any of her friends had. If all her friends were going to a private school, I saw that Elizabeth did also. I also made sure she was invited to the same parties as all the children of the best people in Pittsburgh. Elizabeth was prettier than all her friends anyway, and her father is descended from royalty," Katherine gloated. Jason tried to be more tolerant of his mother's snobbery after he realized that it was natural for her to be proud of the heritage presented to her so meticulously by her mother.

Elizabeth, who always held herself very erect, sat with good posture, and was always coolly poised, left the impression of aloofness. Those who grew to know her realized that she was unknowingly a true bigot at heart.

Harrison the IV left most of the rearing of Elizabeth to Katherine. When he did take the time, he was very good to her and sometimes took her to parks on the weekends. One time, he took her on a boat ride down the Monongahela River almost to McKeesport and that became one of her most cherished memories of her father.

As Harrison the IV reached his middle fifties he began staying out late at night and often came home a bit unsteady on his feet. Katherine, who had always feared the gambling trait was inherited, wondered if her husband was starting to follow in his father's footsteps.

After several of his late night ventures, she began to question, "Harrison, are you gambling? You know what happened to your father in places like that."

"Katherine, I've never been in a gambling casino in my life and I don't intend to start now. I go to a club with several of the men from the factory. I have to have some friends. You go to your bridge club with your friends, don't you?" defended Harrison.

Katherine did not say any more but she became more and more suspicious because she often found him creeping quietly into the house in the wee hours of the morning and then not going to work the next day. She knew the business would not prosper if he started missing work and she was worried.

Then one day while cleaning in his study, she lifted the blotter pad on the top of his desk and found numerous bills for large amounts which had not been paid. She confronted

Harrison and after a long and vociferous denial, he finally admitted that he had been gambling heavily.

"But not in gambling halls," insisted Harrison, as if private games were somehow more acceptable. Seeing that Katherine was not of the same mind, he promised to stop gambling. He fully intended to keep his promise, but soon realized that his salary alone was not enough to maintain their prevailing lifestyle and pay the past due bills. So, after a short time, he began making business trips, which Katherine later discovered were really gambling trips.

Katherine had quickly realized that she would have to do some economizing or her friends would find out about Harrison's unwise practices. She could not bear the thought of Elizabeth being stigmatized and shunned by the society into which she was born. She was agonizing over this when Elizabeth met and wanted to marry Henry McCall.

Elizabeth had been allowed to accept Henry McCall's proposal of marriage because it was thought that he too had a lineage similar to her own. Henry had not descended from nobility but from moguls of industry. Ancestry, however, was not the factor that had influenced Elizabeth's father when he agreed to the marriage. He had a much more pressing reason.

Starting before Elizabeth finished high school, Harrison had gradually accumulated massive debts and it was getting steadily worse. Therefore, his decision to allow Elizabeth to marry Henry was based on the wealth and lineage he assumed was Henry's. Not until all the announcements were in the papers did he learn that Henry was a self-made man; wealthy, but not a Rockefeller by any means, not descended from nobility, and he had not inherited a vast fortune from his father. That knowledge, gained from gossip in a poker game, sent Harrison Wentworth home early to call off the wedding. He felt Elizabeth could find a richer man who would probably be more willing to settle his debts.

Stunned by the news of Henry's ancestry but quickly realizing they would receive the strictures of society if the wedding was canceled, Katherine intervened. "Harrison Wentworth, have you lost your mind?" cried Katherine. "Elizabeth and I have kept this family going while you squandered everything with your gambling and wild schemes. I will not have my daughter or this family made a laughing stock by our friends. Our neighbors have no idea that our affairs are in such a deplorable state. Please don't blacken us further by revealing all of this to Henry and the whole city."

When Harrison remained adamant in his decision, Katherine fled the room in tears. Elizabeth, who had never questioned her father, felt compelled to take action. She found her father in his study with a glass of bourbon in his hand. Rushing in and clasping him in her arms, she tearfully pled, "Papa, I truly love Henry and he is wealthy."

Seeing that her father was at least listening Elizabeth continued, "He must have lots of money, since he wants to build me a house near Squirrel Hill. You said yourself that property in the Squirrel Hill area is worth a fortune. Besides, I'd just die if any of our friends should learn about our situation. Papa, they would even know why you want me to marry wealth. They all think that you are very wealthy and we would have no need for me to marry money. They also think, as I did, that Henry has inherited and is very, very wealthy."

Her father stared at her stonily and Elizabeth in tears begged, "Please, Papa, don't interfere. I'll tell Henry I don't want to live near Squirrel Hill. I know I can convince him, since that's the Jewish section and we don't understand their ways. I'll try to get Henry to just move in here. Then we can use the money here instead of on the house he wanted to buy for me."

Elizabeth was so distraught that Harrison relented, "All right, I'll think about it, but I'm not promising anything, you understand. So stop that crying and go wash your face." Harrison patted her on the shoulder and left the room.

Being desperate, Harrison did think about it and soon realized this would be the easiest way out and could solve many of his problems. He began planning a strategy to get

Henry to move into rooms upstairs, and with these thoughts in mind, he sought out Elizabeth and Katherine. With the two women seated comfortably in his office, Harrison explained, "Since Elizabeth vows that she loves Henry McCall, and I like all that I know about the young man, I'll agree, providing he is willing to live in a suite of rooms here at Wentworth House. After all, it will be cheaper and not so hard on me and Katherine."

"Oh, Papa! Thank you so very much. You must promise though to never say anything about this to Henry or anyone else. I'd just die if my friends knew of our situation, and Henry would be very angry," begged Elizabeth abjectly.

Once the wedding was over, Harrison felt free to gamble. He just knew his luck would turn and he would regain much of what he had lost. Thus, to the dismay of the family, his once weekly card games became almost nightly.

Elizabeth and her mother had practiced a frugality not known by anyone in the area, or even Harrison himself. Katherine Wentworth had a very wealthy sister living in Chicago. She was a couturier of design for women and prominent in that field. Therefore, all the elegant clothes that both Elizabeth and her mother wore were part of the largesse provided by her sister. The lavish gifts of money sent on birthdays and Christmas always went to pay the servants and do the social things that protected the façade of wealth.

Due to this pattern of pretense and deceit, Elizabeth grew up knowing she must keep up appearances at all costs. Thus, she wore an air of snobbish disdain around people of a lesser station in life. When she married Henry, she carried the pretense a little farther and bruited it about that Henry was the eldest son, with a substantial inheritance. Her explanation of her inheritance of the Wentworth estate as an only child satisfied her friends as to their choice of residence. As expected, Elizabeth and Henry started their married life in the stately mansion on the corner of Beechwood Boulevard, still occupied by her parents.

At first, Henry was bewildered and could not understand why Elizabeth did not want a new house of her own. "Elizabeth, that's a beautiful area and it isn't in Squirrel Hill, but on the outskirts. Anyway, I have a lot of Jewish friends and they are really nice. They are just like we are except they have different religious practices. Don't you want a new house, all your own to decorate?"

"Henry, I'd love any place as long as you were there, but Papa and Mama are getting old and really should not live in that big house alone. We can have a suite of rooms all our own and you won't even have to eat with them if you don't want to," reasoned Elizabeth. She was so distraught and pleaded so earnestly that Henry relented, and after the honeymoon, returned to the Wentworth mansion. Silently, he promised himself that he would wear Elizabeth down and they would eventually move.

Much to his chagrin, he shortly came to realize that his money was needed if the Wentworth estate was to be kept in the family. He often wondered if Elizabeth would have been so enamored of him had she known that he was not a billionaire. When he voiced these doubts to Elizabeth, she dissolved in tears.

"Henry, I wouldn't do you like that. You know I wouldn't. I love you very much. In fact, when Papa found out you hadn't inherited a fortune, he was going to call the whole thing off, but I cried and pleaded until he relented. Please believe me. I truly do love you."

Convinced, Henry took her in his arms, saying, "Sh-h, let's forget it. It's all right. I have enough money to take care of things, I hope." Still worried, but realizing he would upset Elizabeth, he tried never to mention the situation again.

Outwardly calm, he settled into the suite of rooms on the second floor that Katherine and Harrison Wentworth had set aside for them before the wedding.

Three weeks after the wedding, Harrison Wentworth had a massive stroke after a devastating loss in a poker game and died en route to the hospital. Once the funeral was over, Henry began the daunting task of clearing up Harrison Wentworth's numerous debts.

"My God, Elizabeth, this is going to break me. The old man pulled a fast one and I was fool enough to be taken in," grumbled Henry.

"You mean you didn't love me enough to marry me," cried Elizabeth in shock. "I didn't know Papa was so deep in debt, honestly I didn't."

"I'm sure you didn't and probably your mother didn't either, and yes, Elizabeth, I did love you and I do love you. The thing is, you and your Papa asked me to move in here because he and your mother were getting old and we could be of help. He also said it would help us financially not to have to keep up a house. I knew that was what you wanted also, and so I agreed. I see now, however, that he meant it would help him. God, what a mess! I may have to take out a loan to clear all this up," stated Henry worriedly. Harrison Wentworth had died owing almost a million dollars.

Elizabeth and her mother seemed to be concerned only about what their friends would think and making sure that the Wentworth estate remained intact.

To insure that their wishes were met, and because they were truly sorry for the situation Henry was in, they did join in the effort by practicing frugality in every way possible. Henry, whose spending habits had never been lavish, cut back on tennis, golf, and even bowling in his effort to pay most of the outstanding debts.

Even so, he remained financially strapped. When asked by his friends about his withdrawing from most of his once favored recreational activities, he rolled his eyes and grinned lasciviously. "I'm kept rather busy at home. Not that I'm complaining, mind you."

In a few years, with careful planning and some windfall investments, which had been put in his way by Joshua Washburn, his neighbor, Henry had paid most of the outstanding debts and had made the estate more beautiful than it had ever been.

Even before his father-in-law had begun his ruinous squandering, he had neglected the upkeep of the estate.

Katherine and Elizabeth were ecstatic with the improvements Henry had made in such a short time, and all without society's knowledge of their difficulties.

Henry had divulged most of the difficulties to his older brother, Howard, but with the assurance that it would never be discussed. He also knew that his lawyer and banker knew of the financial mess that Harrison Wentworth had left on his shoulders. Henry knew that private client information was sacrosanct with these people and thus felt assured that neither Elizabeth nor Katherine would ever find out that anyone knew.

Therefore, the only cloud on the horizon of the women in the Wentworth household was watching their nearest neighbors live in a much grander style than they could afford. The two women did not voice this to Henry, but they continually thought of ways to insure a constant upward movement.

Years later, during Jason's first stay in McDowell County, his father had fallen and was kept in the hospital for weeks. Until that time, Jason was unaware of this part of his father's life. During the first critical days, when there were questions about Henry's survival, Jason's uncle, Howard, told him of Henry's struggles in his early years of marriage. After discovering all this about his family, Jason often wondered if this was one of the reasons he felt closer to his father. In Jason's opinion, his dad had gotten a raw deal but didn't seem to mind. In fact, Henry did not even know that Jason had learned of the circumstances of his marriage, and Jason never revealed his knowledge.

When his mother really provoked him with her pretensions, Jason often wished he didn't know so much about her background. As it was, he always made excuses for her due to the history that he had uncovered.

## CHAPTER 5

While the Wentworth house was a beautiful, gracious Tudor mansion set in manicured grounds, it was far less opulent than that of their neighbors, the Washburns. The Washburn estate was almost regal in its grandeur. It contained its own private lake, stables and horses noted for their breeding, tennis courts, and a private conservatory.

Joshua Washburn, Henry McCall's neighbor, was a descendant of the Earl of Rothborn from Kent in the north of England. The Earl had inherited vast estates and had added to these acres over time. Joshua's grandfather continued to hold large boundaries, but Nathaniel, Joshua's father, was a fourth son.

Knowing he would not inherit enough to pursue his dream of being a magnate in industry, Nathaniel Washburn took the legacy left to him by his maternal grandmother and migrated to America. He was soon involved in the steel industry, building his own steel mill.

He became one of the first in pushing the Bessemer process, in which a blast of air burnt most of the impurities out of the molten pig iron, and soon became known for the quality of the steel his factories produced. Joshua stepped into his father's shoes and was just as innovative as his father by going to an open-hearth process for steel producing. He also lived the same affluent life style enjoyed by his family for generations.

The Washburn palatial estate abutted the Wentworth property on the east and south and the families had been friends since settling in America. Although they had met before, it was not until Henry McCall married Elizabeth and moved onto the Wentworth estate that he became really acquainted with Joshua Washburn, and they were soon fast friends.

Joshua, having connections to many banks, had known of Harrison Wentworth's financial disaster for a long time and he had admired and respected Henry McCall before he was really acquainted with him. Now, Joshua trusted Henry's judgment and put him wise to many profitable ventures that helped him financially.

Henry McCall was involved in the railroad industry and did the shipping of raw materials and steel for Joshua's company, making the two young men close business associates as well as neighbors.

To Elizabeth McCall's chagrin, Henry did not have the income that Joshua garnered, nor did he have the prestige and influence of Mr. Washburn. Regardless of income, however, Elizabeth was determined that society would see the McCalls as socially equal to anyone, especially the Washburns. Right after her marriage, she began to plan ways of uniting the two families more closely.

When she found she was pregnant, she wove a dream around her baby, which she just knew would be a girl. Her dream centered on her daughter and a Washburn boy marrying, which would further unite the two families.

She knew that Olivia Washburn was also expecting and was near time for delivery. Elizabeth never once thought but that the Washburn baby would be a boy. She was devastated when Olivia's baby boy was dead at birth. Elizabeth was ashamed when she realized she was as much hurt for herself as for Olivia.

Presently, Elizabeth became caught up in her own pregnancy and the many visits she received from both the Wentworth and McCall relatives. During this time, her social machinations were on a back burner. She found she really enjoyed the attention she received from her pregnancy and looked forward to the birth of her daughter.

After an eighteen-hour ordeal, Jason Henry McCall was born. On being told she had a fine baby boy instead of the girl she had dreamed of, Elizabeth began to cry. But once she saw and held her beautiful black-haired, brown-eyed son, she was ashamed of her outburst. Elizabeth found herself wanting to constantly touch and hold him.

Jason was a beautiful baby and easy to care for but his grandmother Katherine firmly insisted that they needed a nanny. Henry was astounded. "You mean that two women can't take care of one little baby?"

"Henry, what would our friends think? They have all had nannies to care for their children. We would be talked about all over the place." Elizabeth shuddered at the very thought of social ostracism

When Henry noticed the almost daily arrival of something new and expensive for the baby, he became very upset. "Elizabeth, we can't afford all these expensive things you want to buy, if you still feel like you need a nanny," stated Henry. He hoped this stance would cause her to dismiss the idea of a nanny. He had never, until now, openly voiced his opposition, but inwardly, he was disturbed by his mother-in-law's ploys which he had early learned were used to keep up with the Washburns.

Seeing that Henry was serious about all the new furniture and other things for the baby, Elizabeth relented. "All right, I'll take all this stuff back to Bloomingdales, but just a few at a time. I'm sure Mary Beth Hawley has a Jenny Lind cradle, crib bed, and bathing table for her baby."

"Does Mary Beth's husband pay thousands of dollars for debts he didn't make?" Henry quipped sarcastically. Seeing the hurt in Elizabeth's eyes, he was immediately contrite.

"Honey, I'm sorry. That was uncalled for. I know that the debts are not your fault. I really can't spend any more than I am now, though."

Elizabeth hugged him in gratitude because he tried so hard to help her keep up the façade of wealth. She knew how much Henry had sacrificed to please her. Her mother would have reminded her if she ever forgot it anyway.

In Katherine's eyes, Henry could do no wrong and Henry made sure she knew he appreciated her regard, even though he was often perturbed by her "trying to keep up with the Joneses"... or in her case, the Washburns.

Regardless, he did like his mother-in-law and was always kind and thoughtful, never forgetting her birthday, Mother's Day, or Christmas, and was always solicitous of her health.

Henry and Elizabeth now occupied the entire house instead of the rooms on the second floor. Katherine moved into the suite of rooms originally prepared for them. For Elizabeth this was the best of all possible worlds, living in the Wentworth house and having her mother living with her. It was almost like it had always been, except that now she had a husband and a baby and she did not have to worry about how much her father would lose in his next bout of poker playing.

Even though Henry McCall had not descended from royalty or the nobility, his ancestors had been shrewd businessmen and became tycoons in industry, accumulating vast fortunes. His grandfather, Prescott McCall, however, had lost most of the family fortune in the stock market crash of 1929.

Henry's father, Charles Henry McCall, had begun work as a fireman on the railroad and worked his way up to engineer, then manager, and kept buying shares in the company until, at the age of 59, he had a hefty portfolio of controlling stock and was a power to be reckoned with.

Henry had gone into business with his dad and learned his business acumen in on the job training. By the time his father died and he met Elizabeth, Henry had become very wealthy. Needless to say, he still remembered what it was to aim high and struggle for it and he wanted the same for his children.

Henry McCall truly loved children and wanted a large family. He hoped that his children would find work in the railroad industry. As his children grew, he was to be disappointed and recalled his own father's disillusionment when most of his sons chose different career paths. Having seen his father's anguish, he decided that he wanted his children to be individuals who would follow their own dreams.

When Elizabeth told him she was pregnant, he was elated. He took such good care of Elizabeth that she blossomed under his attention. She told him she wanted a girl and even though he wanted a boy, it was not a big issue since he thought they would have several children. Yet, when he paced the floor in a downstairs room until his son was born, he began to have second thoughts. When first seeing his son, however, all that went out of his head, leaving nothing but pure joy.

Katherine and Elizabeth were surprised at the attention Henry lavished upon his son. He often sneaked into the nursery, took Jason from his crib, and sat holding him. He loved this little boy so much and wanted the very best for him.

"Little fella, when you get big enough I'm going to take you to ballgames, movies, carnivals, and all kinds of things. We'll be best buddies, won't we?" asked Henry, as he tickled Jason under the chin and made funny faces.

Elizabeth often caught him lying on the floor with Jason on his arm. Both Henry and Jason would be fast asleep. She would have scolded him but they looked so sweet that she tiptoed out and left them for at least twenty minutes before she marched back in with the stern admonition, "Henry McCall, you get my baby up out of that germy floor. Do you want him to get sick?"

That was the first time she caught Henry. Soon it happened so often she learned to leave them be, but he never again lay on the floor without a quilt being placed beneath him.

Jason was only three years old when his little cousin Penny died. After that, he became passionate in his caring for others. Jason's uncle had been killed in an automobile accident one rainy night in 1927 at the bottom of Browns Hill.

Uncle Charles' wife, Juanita, had come to live with Jason's parents, bringing Penny, her infant daughter, with her. Jason was too young then to know why Aunt "Nita" had come, but he fell in love with little Penny. He crouched near her bassinet, playing with her toes and fingers, and brought her all his stuffed animals, which had to be removed from her crib on a daily basis.

He got a stern lecture when he put handfuls of live flowers in her bassinet, almost covering little Penny. He was told that things like that would make Penny sick and he was very careful after that about putting anything in her bassinet.

In spite of Jason's vigilant and solicitous care, Penny was found dead in her bassinet early one morning, two days before she was four months old. Doctor Nelson had come and examined little Penny but was not sure of the cause. He thought she had possibly smothered when she turned her head into the pillow. SIDS or Sudden Infant Death Syndrome had not been heard of at that time, and since he could find no other cause, smothering was the only explanation.

Jason was devastated and could not be consoled. He cried and had nightmares for weeks until his mother told him she was going to have a baby. Then he worried constantly about this baby, who turned out to be a little brother that he adored.

When Frank was born, Jason was nearing five and became more protective than a mother hen with her chicks. He kissed Frank before bed each night and checked on him first in the morning. His mother started calling him her little doctor, and the idea festered. From that time on, Frank, any animal, child, or adult that he could help in some way became the recipient of his caring.

Even though very young, Jason dreamed of being a doctor. At first, Henry was often the patient being treated from the toy doctor kit always found in close proximity. Henry delighted in his son's quick mind and intelligent questions. He began to take Jason with him to the doctor or hospital and often invited his friends from the medical profession home to dinner.

Elizabeth soon began to wonder if giving Jason free reign and encouragement about being a doctor at such an early age was good. When she found a neighbor child screaming, with his entire head swathed in adhesive tape, she realized something must be done.

The first step was to put a stop to his being taken by others on their visits to doctors and hospitals. The desire to be a doctor was already planted, however, and Jason was not deterred in his endeavors to help and heal people and animals.

To insure that no harm came to anyone Jason was not allowed in his grandmother's room unaccompanied. Katherine had contracted emphysema and was on various medications. Jason watched in fascination the measuring of dosages, which Elizabeth hadn't even noticed. Walking into her mother's room one morning Elizabeth found Jason upon

Katherine's bed. He had a spoon filled with liquid poised at his grandmother's mouth. "Here Grandmother, open your mouth. This is good for you. You want to get better don't you?" questioned Jason in a pleading voice. Katherine was shaking her head with her lips clamped tightly together. Needless to say, Jason now had Elizabeth's full attention. The possibility of Jason trying out some medicine on an animal or maybe even his playmates was a definite concern. With this possibility in mind Elizabeth and Henry made certain that all medicines were secured in safe places. This concern kept Elizabeth fearful and very vigilant in her watchfulness and few mishaps occurred.

Henry still invited doctors and nurses and even research scientists in for dinner on a regular basis. Jason was allowed to have his meals with them, now that he was six years old and had started to school. Henry was very proud of the attention Jason gave all his invited guests. The guests were also gratified to have such a rapt young listener and gladly talked about various cases. However, due to Elizabeth's concern, Jason was always cautioned that it was not safe to practice medicine until one was trained.

"You mean I can't even make my dog Jumbo, better?" questioned Jason. "He broke his leg and I splinted it up and now it's straight. He licks my face all the time, trying to thank me."

Dr. Nelson, the pediatrician visiting that night, was speechless for a moment and then replied, "I'm sure Jumbo was pleased but I think it was just luck that you set it correctly. You could have left him crippled for life. You would have felt really bad if that had happened, wouldn't you?"

Jason thought for a bit before he said, "We took him to Doc Sawyers and he said I did a grand job. But I could have messed it up, couldn't I?" Looking around the table he cheered up and said, "Well, I won't do that anymore until I go to college. Then I'll have those papers in a frame that says I can operate, won't I?"

Dr. Nelson reached over and ruffled his hair. "You sure

will, and then you'll be Doctor Jason McCall. How does that sound?"

Jason looked very solemn. "That sounds just right…Doctor Jason McCall with an MD after my name. You'd like that wouldn't you, Dad?" asked Jason, as he beamed at Henry.

Henry had been sitting bemused by his smart little six-year-old but now smiled broadly. "I sure would son. I'd be the proudest dad in the whole world." The other dinner guests smiled, realizing that Henry McCall would never be any prouder of Jason than he was at this moment.

## CHAPTER 6

Once, while Jason was five years old, he was walking beside Frank's stroller as he and his mother made their way down Beechwood Boulevard on the way to Frick Park. A little stray dog had been following them, and halfway down the block, the dog suddenly started across the street in front of the oncoming traffic. Jason dived into the street, leaving his mother screaming as horns blasted and cars squealed their tires, trying to avoid him. His only thought was to save the dog, but in his attempt was knocked to the street, tied up traffic for the entire block, almost gave his mother and a taxi driver a heart attack, and still did not save the dog.

Although he only sustained minor scrapes and bruises, he was under surveillance from that time on, especially around animals or children. Because of his insatiable desire for knowledge, his indomitable determination to help, and his embarrassing questions, Elizabeth tried to keep him away from clinics, doctor's offices, hospitals, and nursing homes if she could possibly do so.

When in those places, he picked up sterile instruments, tried out the doctor's stethoscope, and practiced with tongue depressors while constantly firing questions. "What's this do, sir? What kinds of things are you listening for? How do you know if a heart is beating too fast? What's blood pressure?" Being so young, he was pretty impressive but also a nuisance to busy doctors who soon felt that Jason was a discipline problem.

Not only his family but also the local firemen were instantly on the alert when Jason was seen in the vicinity of a fire. After a fire which had engulfed an apartment complex, they became even more watchful. The fire was on the east end of Shady Avenue, two streets over from Beechwood Boulevard. Jason and his dad had been to see Peter Pan at the Regent Square Theater and were on their way home when the fire engine sirens started. Seeing the fire engine behind him Henry pulled over to allow the fire engine and the trucks to get by him but then followed the trucks.

When Henry stopped at the scene behind the fire truck, Jason was out the door before his dad could stop him. Frantically Henry jumped out, running towards the fire, yelling, "Jason, Jason, stop, stop!" Luckily a fireman saw Jason and plucked him out of harm's way just as the mighty hoses began to spray.

After that, Elizabeth lived in a constant state of dread for she never knew when Jason would jump into a dangerous situation to help somebody or something.

"Jason, you are making me a nervous wreck," complained Elizabeth, only to have Jason run to the medicine cabinet in search of something for her nerves. Elizabeth loved her son dearly and was constantly in a panic that he would harm himself or someone else. More than that, however, was the worry that some of her friends would see her as not being a good mother.

"Henry," complained Elizabeth, "My friends already think Jason is strange or retarded. What are we going to do?"

Henry assured her that Jason was not retarded. "If anything he's too smart for his own good. Little devil," said Henry smiling proudly. Henry, however, was not the daily mediator when the results of some of Jason's doctoring ventures caused havoc in the neighborhood.

Jason's brother Frank and Janet Washburn, the next door neighbor, were often dosed, bandaged, salved, splinted and had their mouths rinsed, as well as given treatments such as hot packs for bruises or any imaginary, as well as actual, mishaps. These treatments also produced daily scenes which terrified Elizabeth and Olivia Washburn.

"Ouch! Stop! That hurts! I don't have a tumor in my froat. No, no, I told you my arm is not broken," were cries often heard, as well as dreadful gagging sounds from either Janet or Frank.

"No, Bruver! No! I don't want my tongue pressed," sobbed Frank, when Jason thought he had laryngitis.

Jason's close scrutiny of the doctor and nurse's procedures

when he was in for a check-up kept Elizabeth in a dread. "Henry, what are we going to do? I'm afraid to leave him with children a minute for fear he will try to operate on one of them. You need to be firmer with him. He is going to cause me to have a complete collapse," complained Elizabeth, at least once a week.

Henry's usual response was, "Now Elizabeth, have you ever known Jason to hurt anything, especially a child?"

"But Henry, he would think he was helping them. You know how he likes to make animals and people better," she complained, but to no avail, since Henry felt confident about his son's kind heart.

The entire family was torn when Janet Washburn's little brother Josh came down with polio. Josh had been a weak baby from birth, slow to crawl, walk, and still did not talk. Jason went to see him every evening after school and asked all kinds of questions about his care. Olivia Washburn thought Jason was sweet most of the time, but when Josh suddenly became very ill, she was short with Jason and sent him home.

"I don't have time to play games with you, Jason. Little Josh is very ill, so quit bothering me and go look after someone else," scolded Olivia.

Jason was not allowed to return, even when Josh was taken to the hospital and diagnosed as having infantile paralysis or poliomyelitis. Jason was then eleven years old and had already been studying medical books on his own. He found that there was no cure and no exact treatment of the disease. He was excited to learn that scientists were desperately doing research, in an attempt to find a vaccine to prevent this terrible, crippling disease.

Little Josh survived that long ordeal but had a long recovery. He was left with one twisted and shriveled leg and had great difficulty breathing. Jason, along with everyone else, was so thankful to have Josh alive that his handicap did not seem so bad. When little Josh was three or four years old and struggled so valiantly in an attempt to walk again everyone was so proud. Olivia Washburn had been told by the doctors that little Josh would not live to be grown but she kept that to herself. She was determined to prove the doctors wrong.

From then on, Jason, who was now in Junior High School, haunted the library near his home and in his school looking for articles and research on the disease.

Even when Jason entered high school, the hopelessness of the dreadful Infantile Paralysis, still lingered in the back of his mind. In his junior year, his best friend Lance Tolliver came down with polio and Jason once again turned to his thirst for knowledge about medicine and cures for illnesses.

By then, Jason had a steady girl friend, Judy Haskins, but she soon tired of going to lectures or to the library to do research when all her friends were going skating, to the movies, and to dances. She found someone else, which didn't bother Jason half as much as he thought it would.

When David Saults, another one of his classmates, was stricken with polio, in addition to Lance Tolliver, Jason was heart broken. Even though he was treated in an iron lung and underwent other procedures, David still succumbed to the fatal illness. It was then that Jason began thinking seriously about doing research, especially on poliomyelitis.

Both Elizabeth and Henry were worried that Jason was too serious and pushed him to get more involved with school affairs and his classmates. All his growing up years Janet Washburn, and his brother Frank, had been Jason's shadows, his playmates, and his friends until now. His parents had expected him to be like every other teenager but he was acting like a mature adult and him just a junior in high school.

After Elizabeth and Henry kept after him he seemed to do a ninety degree turn. To their consternation, he changed almost overnight. Now Jason styled his hair in a ducktail, donned pegged pants, steel heel taps, and all the other fads that made boys popular. All this now took precedence over school, his childhood playmates, and seemingly the Jason they had grown accustomed to.

Elizabeth went to Henry in dismay. Henry gave a heavy sigh and said, "I guess we got what we asked for, didn't we?"

Now, Jason played basketball with his school pals, went to movies, skated, and began vying for the attention of the prettier girls in his class. Jason still talked to Frank, and even Janet, while at home, but dared them to tail him when he was out with his pals. Both Frank and Janet were very upset and felt betrayed.

Elizabeth tried to smooth Jason's path with the youngsters, "Jason, still loves you kids. Honestly he does. It's just that he is in high school now and it's all different. He wants to fit in and be like his classmates. I'm sure his friends don't have two kids hanging on their footsteps, so try to understand how Jason feels. Once the new wears off, I'm sure you will have your old Jason back. Just wait and see," she said with an encouraging smile.

Instead of Jason returning to them, he became more involved in social activities and began dating lots of girls, at school functions and then afternoon movies. By the time he was a high school senior, Janet Washburn became just that kid next door. She had always been like a younger sister and Jason put her in the same cherished position as Frank. He still helped them both if they came to him with problems or most of the time he did.

For several months that year, Jason forgot about medicine and doctoring, and even research, and instead, started hanging out with a group of school pals from a different area. He, along with his friends, was a frequent visitor to The Linden Grove and Sullies to dance and listen to the music of the Four Lads, the Lettermen, and other groups.

Jason's group was a little noisier and bolder than some of the other teens who came there. He noticed this but at the time he seemed to be with the fun group. Soon he had his first beer, tried smoking cigarettes, and became sick at a party when he drank too much gin and tonic. Most of the parents of his friends were social drinkers and getting alcohol was no problem.

For some reason, Jason had never before imbibed and it hit him like a ton of bricks. Jason realized that he had gotten so sick because he hadn't eaten before the party but to barely make it to the bathroom was very embarrassing.

Later, after thinking he would surely die, Jason decided that he really did not like to drink alcohol. His friends all laughed and told him that he had to work into it gradually but he didn't see the point.

"Why in the world would I want to gradually learn to do something to make myself sick? Besides, alcohol is very bad for your health, in case you guys don't know it," said Jason knowingly. "Of course, I did know but drank it anyway. I guess that means I'm not too swift, doesn't it?" he questioned as he laughed.

"Yes, Doctor," laughed his buddies, as they finished off a six pack of Budweiser.

Being introduced to sex was a different story. In the crowd he was now hanging out with, it was standard practice to be involved in sexual activities. Some of the older boys in the gang wanted to play a joke on Jason and set him up with a girl most of them had been out with, but Jason did not know this. One Saturday night, they had driven to "Rosebud Lane," a teen name for a certain sheltered nook in the area of Schenley Park. They were into heavy "necking" and Jason was aware of where this activity was taking them but was so enthralled that he allowed Freda free reign. The euphoria of the experience lasted only a short time, however, and then he became very embarrassed and from a very red face he stammered, "I'm so sorry. I didn't mean for this to happen. I hope I didn't hurt you. I...I got way out of line." He couldn't look at the girl but she didn't have the same problem.

She grasped his chin and jerked his head up. Glaring at him angrily she said in a voice filled with cynical mockery, "What are you apologizing about and acting so saintly? Do you think you're the first one, big man? Well, you're not—and besides, you're not all that great."

Jason was embarrassed and hurt by her seeming insult, and once he had taken her home and got his emotions under control, began to worry about getting some disease.

Howie Stoots laughed when Jason voiced his concern. Howie and the other boys laughed uproariously at the joke they had played on Jason, which didn't do much for Jason's self-esteem.

Seeing that Jason was more concerned than ever when he realized the girl wasn't the innocent he had thought, Howie consoled him with, "Aw, you don't have to worry about Freda. We've all had her and we ain't got no disease. Man, you're going to have to wise up. Use condoms if you're afraid. You can't get a disease if you use protection. I thought you said you liked it," argued Howie.

"I did, but I don't want a disease. Besides, Dad and Mother would have a fit. They would probably send me to The Kiski School to board, or to a military academy," protested Jason.

"Don't tell them, Man. You don't have to tell your folks everything. How are you ever going to learn anything if you don't try a few things?" asked Howie.

Later, Jason wondered if he had actually initiated that sexual encounter but realized that regardless of who had actually started it, the memory did not make him feel good about himself.

Jason gradually broke away from that group of friends since he didn't seem to enjoy their company as much as he once had. He knew it just wasn't the things he had gotten involved in but it was this feeling of self disgust. He had found sex to be pleasurable but it was purely physical and he felt that it should be more than that. "I just want to like me and I don't right now. Besides Howie and the gang seem to think life is all fun and games," said Jason to himself as he left a party early. After that he failed to turn up when he was invited and gradually they stopped asking him.

Jason decided that he wanted to wait until he was older and could make wiser decisions about many of the things these young people wanted to do. His conscience bothered him since he knew better before he had ever gotten involved. "I must be an idiot," he chided himself since he now realized that he had never really liked some of the boys in that group.

After that he stopped hanging around with that crowd and once again became immersed in his studies.

## CHAPTER 7

Henry McCall had been so busy during Jason's high school years that he didn't spend as much time as he would have liked with Jason or with Frank. When they were younger, he was with them every weekend and they did all kinds of things together. He told himself every week that the next weekend would be different, but it wasn't. One reason was that Jason always seemed to be out with some of his friends or on the phone talking to some girl. Finally, Henry asked for a meeting with his sons.

"Boys, what has happened to us? We used to make every weekend special, but we don't anymore and I don't like it. Do you? How about keeping some time in your weekends free and I'll do the same, okay?"

Both boys agreed, and from then on, they always tried to plan outings like ball games, car races, horse shows or other things they could enjoy together. These were always fun activities and the future wasn't discussed.

Henry had heard Jason talk about being a doctor since he was three years old. He also knew that Jason had taken every science and chemistry class he could get in high school, but now Jason never mentioned anything to do with medicine. Henry was puzzled and wondered why Jason had changed. "If Jason has changed his mind," thought Henry introspectively "that may mean he will come into the office with me."

Finally he approached Elizabeth with the change in Jason saying, "Elizabeth, maybe Jason will come into the business like I've always wanted one of my sons to do. I could really help him," said Henry hopefully. Elizabeth agreed that Jason was different. "I haven't heard Jason mention medicine in a long time either," she said in agreement with Henry's thinking.

"Why don't you just ask him, Henry? If he has changed his mind it must have happened while he was running around with that gang from the south side of town," stated Elizabeth, also puzzled.

The next weekend they had together Henry did ask

Jason. "Son, have you changed your mind about a career in medicine?"

Jason gave his dad a startled look and warily answered, "We've been having so much fun Dad that I haven't thought about it much. Why?

"No reason except it just seems strange to not hear medicine talked about all the time," Henry laughingly said and slapped Jason on the back as they left the house to play golf.

Thinking Jason had really changed his mind, Henry hadn't pushed him to try to get into pre-medicine at any college. However, he was startled into action, when he met Dr. McClymonds, the principal of Taylor Allderdice High School, and was informed that Jason was trying to get into The University of Pittsburgh to take Pre-Medicine.

At first, Henry was shocked and disappointed, but soon realized that Jason hadn't forgotten his youthful dream of being a doctor. He also sensed that Jason hadn't told him for fear that he would be displeased.

After thinking through the reasons for both his and Jason's reluctance to mention any future plans, Henry saw the truth. He knew why he had not mentioned the subject to Jason. He wanted Jason to work with him and feared that he would not.

In the same light, he realized that Jason hadn't brought it up because he really wanted to be a doctor and knew that Henry did not want that career for him.

With this new insight, a very determined Henry, who had considerable influence, immediately started making phone calls to his many acquaintances. He left no stone unturned in trying to get Jason into pre-medicine at the medical school in Pittsburgh, but to no avail.

All the slots for the pre-medicine to medical school program had been filled unless someone dropped out. Jason had not applied soon enough. Henry had wanted Jason to get his degree in Pittsburgh because he knew so many people there who could help to further his career, especially if he wanted to go into research. Henry was very upset and asked for Joshua

Washburn's help, but that too, came to naught.

The president of the university suggested that Jason apply to West Virginia University Medical School, located at Morgantown, West Virginia, which also had a good reputation.

Henry had graduated with a degree in business from West Virginia University and knew it to be a good school for business majors, but wasn't sure about its medical credentials. He checked with the Mellon Institute and was told that West Virginia University was indeed a very good school of medicine. The school had a good research department and therefore would be especially good if Jason wanted to go into research.

It was almost a foregone conclusion in everyone's eyes that Jason would be a research scientist since he had taken a job in the research laboratory at Joshua Washburn's steel mill for the summer after graduation. After the bombing of Pearl Harbor in 1941, Jason and many of his classmates talked about being drafted into service. When he turned eighteen in 1942, Jason had registered for the required draft and expected to be called up at any time. However, without realizing it, when he took the job in the laboratory at Joshua Washburn's steel mill, it became the reason for his exemption from the draft. Research was deemed to be very important during World War II. Therefore, Elizabeth and Henry were very happy and relieved when he enrolled and was accepted as the last applicant for admission to the pre-medical program at West Virginia University in Morgantown, West Virginia in September of 1942.

For a while, both Henry and Elizabeth had thought that Jason had no plans for college and were very upset. Now, instead of being irate they were thankful, especially since he had been deferred.

Henry felt it was fortunate that Jason had gotten into a good school which was near his home. Morgantown, West Virginia was 75 miles from Pittsburgh; a possible two-hour drive if he wanted to pay a visit home. Elizabeth was also pleased that

Jason could get home on weekends and holidays, not having any idea what this would evolve into, and so it was settled.

If Jason's career went wrong they knew they would feel responsible and it would be hard to bear. Henry had many friends with ties to West Virginia University in both Pittsburgh and Parkersburg and each report received from these friends, lauding Jason's efforts, eased much of the worry.

In 1947, while Jason was in his second year of medical school at West Virginia University, he became aware of and fascinated by the work of Dr. Jonas Edward Salk, especially since it dealt with Poliomyelitis. Dr. Salk had become associated with the University of Pittsburgh's Virus Research Lab.

Often, when he should be studying, Jason daydreamed about meeting Dr. Salk and the conversations he would like to have with him. He felt that Dr. Salk's research would produce a major developmental treatment to prevent this dreadful crippling disease.

He was more convinced than ever after Dr. Wiemer, one of his instructors, introduced the class to Dr. Salk on a field trip to the University of Pittsburgh. Dr.Wiemer knew that most of his students were aware of and fascinated by the work of Dr. Salk. He especially wanted Jason to meet Dr. Salk since he had been so immersed in learning anything pertaining to infantile paralysis.

Meeting Dr. Salk would only further that interest and Dr. Weimer wanted his students to be interested in all aspects of medicine. Most of Jason's classmates stood back in awe at the introduction, but not Jason. "I'm so very pleased to meet you, sir. I've been fascinated by your work and eager to hear more about your findings. Have you published any definitive papers on your research? I would certainly be interested in reading them, if you have," probed Jason eagerly.

Dr. Salk was impressed with Jason's desire to know, "I haven't published my findings yet but I am preparing a lecture for the medical association meeting next month. Perhaps you could get Dr. Weimer to bring you along."

Dr. Weimer quickly agreed since he, and most of the other

instructors, felt that Jason would be a real asset in the field of research and they wanted to help him all that they could. After that, nobody was surprised when Jason began spending more time at his studies than anything else.

He volunteered to work in the research lab at the University, as well as helping out if there was an outbreak of flu in the city of Morgantown or in Pittsburgh. Jason felt that the more he learned about all illnesses in general, the better prepared he'd be to really help people.

With his avid interest and work in research, everyone was very surprised, shocked, and disappointed when, in June of 1949, Jason signed with a new pilot program to get doctors to practice in the coalfields. This was a collaborative endeavor between the coal companies and the university to insure medical help for the people in the coalfields.

Jason explained his reasons for signing on to the program and finally got the approval of Dr. Weimer and most of the others.

"I want to work with people and see them get better and know that I had a part in making that happen. I'm told that there are people in some parts of West Virginia that have had no access to a doctor their entire lives. I really think that's a terrible situation to be in. I can't imagine anything worse than seeing someone in your family linger on for years in dreadful pain. Maybe I can't help, but at least people will have some hope or feel like they have some one to turn to. If I were in research, I might be able to come up with something that would help people in the future, but if I were actually working with them I would be able to help in the here and now. Sure, research can find marvelous cures but it can't grant me the look in a mother's eyes when her child is saved," stated Jason with assurance.

It was then that his instructors realized that here was a doctor for the people. They all met together and discussed his record. Dr. Weimer who had really gotten to know Jason personally said, "He'd be good at research because he loves challenges but in his heart he wants to work directly with people. He's a "hands on" kind of person who likes to look at what he is working on and see the results of his labor"

They all finally agreed and reluctantly signed his forms to send him on his way, much to the chagrin of Elizabeth McCall and Janet Washburn.

Jason, who had once thought he wanted to do research, now did not know exactly which field of medicine he wanted to specialize in, if any. Therefore, he was eager to spend time as a general practitioner in this program which he felt would help him decide.

He laughingly told his classmates, "By the time I finish my stint down in West Virginia, I should be able to diagnose and treat every imaginable disease. I'm sure I'll get enough practice. Their description of the program has made me dream of becoming famous. Of course that may be because they are having trouble finding recruits."

His classmates thought he had "gone off the deep end," since Jason was the only one who had signed up. Jason smiled at their incredulous looks. "I'll be breaking new ground. You guys just don't have a pioneering spirit," he chided as he walked nonchalantly from the room.

However, that night Jason did worry and wondered if he had done the right thing. He felt it was a real opportunity and he somehow felt drawn to the program. There was a strange urgency in his desire to be involved that he could not understand.

Certainly, he would get hands on experience and learn many valuable lessons, but still there seemed to be something else. Something just out of his sight beckoned him.

"Maybe it's the challenge or maybe I'm just in a rut from so much studying," mused Jason as he tossed and turned. "Right now I only know I want to do this program. I don't really know the exact reason but I feel so sure about doing this. It has to mean something," said Jason aloud as he turned over and punched his pillow once again into what he hoped was a more sleep inducing shape.

Just before he dropped off to sleep he mumbled, "It just

seems like something I have to do."

This urge, or the seemingly fated circumstance that led to Jason's attending the West Virginia University Medical School, was slated to alter the pattern of life that both Elizabeth and Henry had always visualized for their son.

For a short while Henry had visualized Jason in the company board room making decisions that would affect the nation. Elizabeth, however, had a more personalized dream.

Since Jason had not gotten into the University of Pittsburgh Medical School, Elizabeth liked the idea of him studying at West Virginia University, because it was close enough to come home often. She was very upset, however, when Jason decided to go to that "god forsaken place" down among those illiterate people in West Virginia.

She wanted him to be a specialist, at home in Pittsburgh. She could see him in some plush office with the crème of society filtering in and out of his rooms on a daily basis. He would be a dermatologist or some other specialist that would free him on the weekends and holidays.

Once he was established in such a practice, he would then see the wisdom of marrying Janet, especially when he considered the likelihood of inheriting the Washburn palatial estate. That had been her dream and now Jason was throwing it all away.

Both Henry and Elizabeth knew that being a student in the medical school in West Virginia was the reason he was involved in this program and they therefore felt that somehow they had let Jason down by not starting early to get him into a different school.

Henry was unsure as to why Jason had chosen to enter that program. Most of the professors that Henry had talked with thought Jason would enter research. Elizabeth, however, was not interested in what program he entered as long as he did not leave Pittsburgh. She especially did not want him to leave Janet Washburn.

Many years later, Jason would look back and believe that divine providence, or maybe Aunt Sarie Lester's good Lord, had been directing his life. Had he gone to The University of Pittsburgh Medical School, he would never have been offered a place in the pilot project and he would never have gone to McDowell County, West Virginia. Also, he would never have met Lucinda Marie Harmon.

## CHAPTER 8

While Jason was in medical school and Janet Washburn was in high school Elizabeth wheedled and cajoled until Jason took Janet to a school dance. Before the evening was over, he realized that he had made a bad mistake.

Janet had stars in her eyes and instantly assumed that from then on they would be a couple. Jason told her that she was too young to go steady and that they were more like brother and sister or cousins. He left Janet crying and felt really bad but knew no other way to keep from being involved.

Elizabeth was very upset when she learned what had happened at the dance and scolded Jason.

"How could you hurt Janet like that, Jason? She has worshiped you from the time she could walk. You could date her. That doesn't mean you have to rush into marriage. She just thinks you are so suave and handsome."

"Mom, Janet is like my kid sister and I don't want to date my sister," said Jason in a joking manner. Besides, I feel embarrassed when a girl acts all moon-eyed over me. It is better to get it stopped before it gets started. I shouldn't have let you talk me into taking her to that stupid dance in the first place," grumbled Jason as he stalked out of the room.

This did not deter Elizabeth. She still schemed to maintain the family's position in the elite circle of Pittsburgh society and wanted a marriage between Jason and Janet. She knew this would not only insure their place but strengthen their position. However, seeing Jason's staunch refusal, she didn't say anymore about the incident.

From the time her sons could walk, Elizabeth had in mind this upward escalation in society through her sons. She was always vigilant to see that her sons went to the right parties, associated with the right people, and bought their clothes in the right stores,

Henry was different. He wanted his sons to know about the good and bad in life as well as people from all walks of life. In most instances Henry allowed Elizabeth free reign in rearing their sons but in this case he became very adamant.

"Elizabeth, don't you realize that our sons will not always deal with just their social equals, your term, not mine?" asked Henry infuriated. Nothing else was said and as his sons grew older, he took them on tours of the slum areas and the rural districts around Pittsburgh.

This caused many a rousing argument with Elizabeth, especially his unyielding demand that his sons attend public schools. Elizabeth resented this very much but Henry would not relent, and thus, Jason and Frank attended Taylor Allderdice High School on Shady Avenue.

Pushing this endeavor to broaden his sons' experiences, Henry insisted that Jason work for the railroad company during the summers. He allowed Jason to choose where he wanted to work and the type of work he would do.

"I'd like to be out on my own, Dad. You know, just to see if I could make it. How about letting me go to Uncle Howard's in Ohio? Could you work that out?" questioned Jason hopefully.

Henry worked it out and several summers Jason ended up inspecting the tracks and often doing manual labor when repairs were needed. Elizabeth was very upset with Henry and vowed that should he tell any of their friends she would never speak to him again. The boys were also threatened with loss of allowance, loss of vacation time, and movement to another school if they ever breathed a word about Jason's wasted summers.

When alone, Jason and Frank laughed hilariously as they imagined scenes in which it was blabbed in front of Elizabeth's Garden Club or her Wednesday Bridge Club.

"Can't you just see Mom's face when you tell Mrs. Hewlett how hard it was to set ties?" Frank had such a droll way of mimicking these society ladies that Jason roared with laughter.

All the neighbors and acquaintances believed that Jason summers were spent on his uncle's horse farm learning horsemanship and how to train show horses.

Jason laughed as he told Frank, "Mom doesn't know it

but mucking out stalls is just as dirty and hard as setting ties on the railroad. She'd have a fit if she saw me, and worse, smelled me after a stint in the stables."

Because of their parents differing viewpoints, Jason and Frank grew to manhood feeling that they were of two very different cultures. Their father's broadening interventions left them feeling that they had no biases. So, when Jason was offered the opportunity to go to a town in the so-called "poverty stricken" Appalachian region, he had no qualms about accepting.

Jason loved his mother but her rigid adherence to social etiquette and manners had always aggravated him. He went along with most of her desires, at least in public because he really did not want to hurt her feelings.

He remembered things she had done with him when he was small that were very endearing. Once she made a sweater for his dog, Jumbo. She also helped Jason put the sweater on Jumbo. They had a scuffle since Jumbo took exception to wearing clothes. On the maid's day off, Elizabeth took Jason into the kitchen where they made gingerbread men together. Those times were very special in his memory and he loved that mother.

Since he had grown-up he felt this adherence to etiquette and social taboos were like a drama fabricated in his mother's mind, even though it was real to her.

"I'm so glad I didn't inherit that trait from her," thought, Jason. Neither Frank nor Jason would ever challenge her or be disrespectful by confronting her with her bigoted way of thinking. Now that they were men, they didn't even tease her about it anymore but acted as if it was perfectly all right.

Henry McCall had impressed on his sons at an early age that their mother was to be respected and treated gently, and they had never broken his request.

When Elizabeth first learned that Jason was going to McDowell County, West Virginia to work it was almost like a death sentence had been issued. Elizabeth argued, cried, pleaded, and was actually sick but to no avail. Jason had already signed his contract.

After the clamor raised by his mother had slightly calmed, Henry asked Jason to drive up to Mt. Washington in the hills above the city with him. They drove along not talking but just enjoying the scenery, until they reached an overlook and pulled into the isolated parking area.

They stood looking out and down into the deep rugged valleys in companionable silence, broken by Henry's, "Jason, is this new venture something you've really thought through, or is it just the novelty of it? You know your mother is very upset. I want to help you get your education but you don't have to do this program. If you think I can't spare the money for you to continue your studies in research, you are mistaken. I've had an educational policy from the time both you boys were born, so don't do this for that reason."

"It isn't that, Dad. Interning in a hospital is the normal way of being certified, but that kind of training can't offer the hands on kind of knowledge to be gained by this program," explained Jason.

"Besides, you know how I am, Dad. This is a real challenge and anyway I learn better by doing. I'm truly excited about being a part of this kind of training."

They both stood leaning on the railing of the Lookout Station and gazing across the horizon as Jason continued, "Just think about it, Dad. If I've learned anything while I've been at the university it will show up in a situation like that. It really is an opportunity of a lifetime," enthused Jason.

Henry threw his arm about Jason's shoulder as he said, "I can see you're set on going so I'll say no more. You're right though; make it a challenge and you're sold," Henry finished with a chuckle as he dropped his arm and strolled back to the car.

As they drove home, Henry impressed upon Jason to take into consideration his mother's feelings. "She's never really been in areas such as where you are going," explained Henry and laughingly continued, "She believes everything she's seen on television and reads in the newspapers, and imagines you living without electricity, no indoor plumbing, and no telephone. In her mind every family down there is like Ma and Pa Kettle."

"No, now Dad, the real reason is she can't bear the thought of one of her sons living among and treating people who, in her mind, are backward and ignorant," stated Jason in an annoyed voice as he looked at Henry.

Henry nodded silently but begged for understanding. "She'll adapt eventually and end up being really proud of you. Just give her time to learn more about the situation."

Jason promised his dad that he would talk to his mother before he left and clarify some of her misconceptions about the area he was going to.

"In fact, I'll take her to see *Sound of Music* since I know how much she likes musicals. That should soften her up while I convince her that I'm doing something that will be very good for me," promised Jason as they reached the house.

The musical did not have the desired effect, however, for after spending hours with his mother, and using every enticement he could think of, Jason felt he had not made one bit of difference in her outlook.

He told his mother what a splendid opportunity this was to not only become a good doctor, but it would also help him should he ever decide to specialize in some field of medicine.

"But Jason, Joshua Washburn can get you into any kind of program you'd want to go into. You don't have to work way down there among those…that type of people. He'd be glad to do that. You know how much he thinks of you," argued his mother.

Jason had heard about the influence of Joshua Washburn from the time he was big enough to understand anything and now in exasperation he said, "Mother, for the last time. I do not want Joshua Washburn's help and I don't need Joshua Washburn's help."

Jason realized he could not change her mind or convince her that this was something he truly wanted to do. All the explaining in the world was not going to change his mother's mind. Neither did it matter that it was something that he truly wanted to do. "It isn't something she wants me to do," thought Jason and shut his mind to all her arguments.

Thereafter, he just quietly went about making the move. It was never mentioned to his mother again until the night before his departure. He planned to leave at six o'clock the following morning, so he told his parents good-bye the night before.

Elizabeth, who had kept a stony silence about it after that first wild tantrum, broke down and cried piteously. Jason hugged her without trying to reassure her further.

"I'll come back being one of the best doctors anyone has ever seen. You'll be so proud of me," reassured Jason.

Finally, Henry convinced Elizabeth to take a sleeping draught her own doctor had given her and go to bed. When she left the room, Henry shook his head worriedly. "This is very difficult for her. This may be the first time any member of her family has overtly gone against her wishes."

Jason looked at his Dad with compassion. He saw a man who had loved and given all he had to give. "He's satisfied as long as she is," thought Jason and hoped that when he fell in love it would be just the same for him.

Jason knew he would have to be on the job every hour, day and night, seven days a week, and no time off for holidays. Not wanting his Dad to be concerned he said, "It's a rough schedule but if one of you should need me, surely I can get someone to fill in for me. You know I'll get here some way," promised Jason solemnly.

Henry realized that this son had the makings of not only a good doctor but an honest, caring, and moral individual. Jason said good night and good-bye with his father's blessing and a fierce hug.

## CHAPTER 9

The next morning Jason climbed into his shiny, almost new car, which was packed to the brim with everything he thought he might need. His mother, visualizing no bath towels, no toilet tissue or Kleenex, had also added a huge box full of such things.

Jason laughed merrily. "Mom, I'm sure they have stores down there that carry those products. The coal company owners live there also, you know, and they are not going to do without."

Seeing his mother's distraught mien, Jason said, "Mom, please just think of the move in this way, it's the beginning of my actually practicing medicine. I'll get educated on the job. I'll be opening new frontiers. Hell, I'm a pioneer," he exulted. This didn't placate his mother and he was glad when he headed his car towards West Virginia.

He didn't know it then, but soon realized that he would be getting more than medical education; he would be introduced to a whole new way of thinking. Since it was a new program, Jason really felt like an adventurer.

Driving down through the hills for the first time was like a journey through sunshine and shadow. It reminded Jason of a poem by one of his favorite authors, Edgar Allen Poe. The poem, "Eldorado," had a line, "gaily bedight a gallant knight, in sunshine and in shadow," and Jason felt adventurous and enthralled.

Even if he wasn't a "gallant knight" he was embarking on an adventure, and was first driving under a hot, blazing sun and then dipping suddenly downhill into deep shadows, before climbing up another hill into blinding sunlight.

The tall, lofty peaks, deep ravines, meandering rivers, and the broad flat basins covered with scrub and every imaginable wild flower, were breathtaking. Jason stopped several times to take pictures.

When he reached Beckley, he pulled into a drive-in restaurant. Soon a cheerful young girl, uniformed in striped blouse, dark skirt, and a perky Army style cap was at his window to take his order. When she saw this handsome young man, she became more cheerful and flirtatious.

"What will you have, Handsome? You're not from around here, are you?" she questioned.

"No, I'm a stranger. Take pity on me and bring me a cheeseburger, fries, and a chocolate milkshake," Jason said, smiling.

"I'll make it myself. Is there anything else I can do for you," queried the girl suggestively.

Jason thought, as she left, that she was trouble in the making and he did not need trouble. He quickly finished his meal and soon was back on the road. He left Beckley thinking about the people he had noticed on the streets. They looked as prosperous as those in Pittsburgh and in many cases as stylish, or at least those he had seen did.

He left Beckley, taking Route 54, which was a fairly decent four-lane road, until he came to Maben and turned right on Route 97. This was a narrow two-lane road with one hairpin curve chasing the other up one hill and down the other side. There were no communities spread along this road. In fact there wasn't even a wide place to pull over for miles and miles.

When the urgent need for a bathroom arose, his only recourse was to stop on the edge of the road and go down in the woods that bordered the lower side of the road. The upper side of the road was cut into the hillside and was too high and steep to scale.

Suddenly, he came up behind a long string of cars and thought, "Oh no, a funeral procession." Cars were creeping along as far as he could see up the mountain. He shifted into low gear and crept along with the rest. Soon the cars ahead of him began to pick up speed.

Thinking they had reached the cemetery, he sighed with relief. That was not the case, however. A heavily loaded truck, which had been laboring to scale the hill, had finally found a wide enough spot at the top to pull over and allow all the other cars to pass.

As Jason passed, he saw the driver had taken off the radiator cap to allow hot steam to spurt high into the air.

Finally, he reached Pineville and pulled into a small place advertising "EATS." It had taken him an hour and a half to travel from Maben to Pineville over Route 97, if it could be called a route. It was paved, however, and that was some help. He went into the restaurant looking for a restroom and was met by a very short rotund man in clean bibbed overalls.

"Come in, Come in! Are you hungry? The Missus has just now got her famous beef stew off the stove. It's piping hot and we've got some homemade apple cider to go with it."

Jason wasn't really hungry, but the aroma was so tempting that he agreed and sat down at the bar.

"Sure smells good. Your wife must be a good cook. I guess I'll have some."

"One bowl of stew, Marge!" The pudgy owner yelled as he arose and poured a tall glass mug of cider.

Soon, one of the tallest, skinniest women Jason had ever seen poked her head into the room. She then shoved the door open with her hip and came on in, bearing a loaded tray. Jason noticed that her dark hair was stretched severely back in a bun, and the checkered apron was wrapped around her twice.

"That must be a family apron," thought Jason, as she carefully set before him a large bowl of steaming stew, and placed a huge square of cornbread beside the mug of cider.

Jason looked first at the woman and then back at the man. They certainly did not appear to be suited since she was almost a head taller than her husband. It reminded him of an old nursery rhyme that his Grandmother Katherine had told him in which Jack Spratt could eat no fat and his wife could eat no lean, but in this case it seemed as if the wife had "eat no fat," since it appeared that the husband had been doing most of the eating.

Jason smiled and thanked her before taking the first bite of the best stew he had ever eaten. He didn't know it then, but it would be another three hours before he reached his destination, and that he was now eating his final meal for the day.

As he drove out of Pineville he watched people on the streets. He saw several men in suits and some fashionably dressed women but noted that most of the people, although clean, were not very stylishly dressed. He assumed that this was due to the rural small town culture.

From Pineville, he left Route 97 and picked up Route 16 to travel in relatively flat land for several miles following the course of a river. Then Route 16 began the steeply twisting climb up and along Indian Ridge toward Welch, the county seat of McDowell County.

Nothing was said in his contract with Pond Creek Coal Company about the roads in southern West Virginia or McDowell County, but Jason now wished he had asked more questions.

"I should have asked for a stipend for tires and car repairs, since I'll probably have to travel a lot," thought Jason.

He was to be the company doctor for Bradshaw and the surrounding area, especially for the miners working for Pond Creek Coal Company. In return, the company paid him a salary while he was getting his training as a medical doctor in general practice.

Pond Creek and other coal companies had worked out an arrangement with medical schools in an effort to get more physicians into the coalfields.

Jason had not known where he would be sent when he agreed to work in the program, but wanted the experience of hands-on learning. He had heard about some places in McDowell County, such as Cinder Bottom in Keystone, and about the abundance of moonshine whiskey flowing in the area.

When he was told he was to practice in Bradshaw, where there was rumored to be a killing every Saturday night, he was filled with trepidation.

Before making the move, he had gone to the library and learned everything he could about McDowell County and especially about Bradshaw. The statistics he found did not verify the rumors of murder and mayhem. According to his findings, a large number of the people were without formal education, but were hard working, coalminers by occupation, and very few were brawlers or murderers.

When he crossed the county line between Wyoming and McDowell County, he didn't travel far before he saw the incorporation sign for Welch. There was also a historical marker describing the settlement of Welch. Several miles down the road, he saw a large neon sign flashing for The Sterling Drive-In and Restaurant.

A large number of cars were parked there and girls, called car-hops, were moving rapidly from one car to the other. Some of the girls bore trays loaded with food and some were going from the cars to the projecting window from which orders were given and taken to be delivered.

He drove slowly by, thinking the food must be good since so many people were eating there. He decided he would come back and try it out sometime. Since the hospitals were here in Welch, he could foresee the necessity of his coming to Welch frequently.

As he drove on toward the center of town, he again looked the people over and here they seemed to be in the forefront of fashion as they flocked to Blakely Field where a ball game was in progress. Cars were parked on each side of the road, making the narrow road almost impassable. He also passed an elementary school, a shoe shop, a car lot, and Roy's Club before he made an abrupt left, still on Route 16.

He passed the Welch Emergency Hospital on the right and their parking lot was well-filled. Soon he was on Main Street, which was shadowed on each side by two and three-storied buildings. Most had shops and restaurants on the street level and dwellings on the other floors as evidenced by flower boxes in the windows.

The sidewalks thronged with people dressed like most business and townspeople dressed, hurrying to and fro or just standing on the street talking. Some were dodging across the street between the stream of cars and trucks whose drivers were impatiently trying to make it through town.

This was a thriving metropolis in a county of 93,000 people, according to the West Virginia Blue Book. There were several restaurants, a pool hall, a music store, a Florsheim Shoe Store, and a Mens' Smart Shop, on the lower end of town. Then further along were the Corinne Shop, Beryl Shop, and a Chris Ann's, which displayed ladies apparel. On the left of the street was a Woolworth's and on up the street on the right was a Murphy's Five and Ten, and across the street was the Carter Hotel, situated on the corner of Bank Street.

When he looked up that street, he saw a large edifice with a sign advertising the services of the McDowell County National Bank, and farther away, a tall sign advertising the Citizens Drug Store. As he drove on up the street, he saw King Drug Company on the left, while on the right side was the Flat Iron Drug Store.

Almost at the end of the street, he saw a banner spanning the distance from one side of the street to the other, high overhead, advertising theaters. The Temple Theater was on the left and the Pocahontas on the right, just before he reached the Trailways Bus Terminal.

From there, he followed the same street that was also Route 16, since it ran along Main Street through Welch. He drove slowly between rows of houses that were located below the road and on the hill above it. Looking down, he could see a river far below and another street just above the level of the river to an intersection called Coney Island.

At this intersection, Route 16 merged with Route 52 leading south to Iaeger or north to Bluefield and Route 103 running east to Gary and the United States Steel operation and also the Sportsman's Club.

At first, Route 16 and Route 52 ran together following the course of the Tug River, but a short way up Premier Mountain, Route 16 veered left in the direction of War and Berwind with Route 52 continuing on toward Roderfield, Iaeger, and Panther.

Jason turned left on Route 16 at this intersection since his map indicated this was the closest way to Bradshaw. Once on Route 16, he had no other choice but to follow it because there was no room to turn around in order to go back. There were only two narrow lanes with very little berm on either side.

In places, the road was so narrow that it was positively scary when you looked down the mountainside to the bottom of the ravines. Gripping the steering wheel, he made the torturous trek around the hair-raising dips and turns of Coalwood Mountain.

Finally, he came off the mountain and down the long straight stretch through Coalwood, which was only a row of houses on each side of the highway. These were bigger and better houses than he had seen since leaving Welch.

Some of them looked like two houses pushed together since there were two front porches and a car pulled up to each porch. This community even had sidewalks, but it didn't look like a town. Surely there was more, but where, he wondered as he looked to the left and right.

He breathed a sigh of relief at seeing this long straight road ahead of him, but this only lasted about 4 miles and then he encountered the treacherous Caretta Mountain. Going up the mountain he met a long blue and white Trailways bus, and actually had to stop until the bus got around the sharply angled curve and passed him by with inches to spare. Now the road sloped downhill in a much straighter path and Jason began to notice the activity in the various communities he passed through.

In Caretta, all the houses were uniform in size and structure, made of wood, all one story, and well kept. The Caretta Elementary School sat on a corner lot across from the Post Office. It was a two-story structure of yellow brick with a large wire-fenced play area. The community was small but looked prosperous.

He saw miners walking toward the community with black faces, wearing hard hats, and swinging the standard aluminum bucket-shaped lunch pail carried by a bail or handle attached at the top. Some miners had something that looked like a light protruding from the visor of their hats. Jason knew that at one time miners used carbide lamps but now the light was on the front of the hard hats and had a cable or wire which ran down to a battery on their sides. These batteries had to be charged almost every night or day depending on which shift the miner worked.

Most of these men were laughing and joking as they walked along in pairs. He slowly drove around a curve and there was the coal processing plant and the shaft opening to the mine itself. There was a sign pointing right that said Shop Hollow, and Olga Coal Company Mine.

Trucks loaded with coal came out of the Shop Hollow road and turned right on Route 16 causing all the traffic to come to a crawl. Half an hour later, he was nearing the intersection of Route 16 and Route 83 which led to Bradshaw. Before he reached there, however, there was a loud whistle and a freight train cut directly across the highway pulling a long string of loaded coal cars. This entailed a protracted wait of twenty minutes as fine dust blew over everything within a mile radius of the passing train. Jason quickly cranked his windows closed to keep the soot and dirt from ruining the upholstery in his almost new 47 Chevrolet car.

The train passed and the traffic moved on down through Yukon, another small community. This community had a large company store, other stores and a doctor's office and the usual houses on stilts on the hillsides. The most noticeable thing about this community was the low hanging trestle railroad bridge which ran directly across the road.

This community, unlike Coalwood, had two facilities which proclaimed in bold signs that they were beer joints or saloons.

The first, which could be seen on the road going on to War, had a sign stating that it was the Cliffside Bar & Grill. The name was appropriate since it did seem to literally cling to a cliff. The other was on Route 83 just below the railroad trestle and was designated as Haskins Pool & Bar. Both seemed to be doing a thriving business.

After several more miles of winding road and small settlements like English, whose houses seemed to be built on stilts which clung tenaciously to the steep mountainsides, Jason arrived at Bartley. Looking over the edge of the road to a level plain near the river, Jason could see a large mining operation in full swing. Bulldozers and trucks were hauling coal and sludge as men waded the black muck which seemed very deep all around the shaft or mine opening.

Jason drove slowly in order to see as much as he could, but still knew he would come back for a better view. Pond Creek Company Store at Number 1 Bartley Mine sat on the lower side of the road above the river but fronting on the highway. One large two-story house sat on a hill above the road along with a dentist office.

To the left of the house, a steep rugged path or road angling up the mountain was designated Bartley Hollow Road by a makeshift sign at the mouth. The coal camp itself lay to the right across a bridge in the only piece of bottom land between the two towering mountains on each side. "These people don't live in valleys, they live in ravines," said Jason aloud.

After passing a long swinging bridge that spanned the Dry Fork River to reach the Atwell Community and further along, a small community called Raysal, Jason arrived in Bradshaw.

It was the edge of dark when he stopped at the bus terminal to inquire about the location of the Harris home. He had been assured by a Pond Creek Coal Company official that there was an upstairs room in the Harris home available for him. He was told the room had a bath and an outside entrance, and was conveniently located.

The lady behind the ticket counter in the terminal building pointed across the street to a store which showed a big sign proclaiming it to be The Ben Franklin Five and Ten Cent Store.

"That's the Harris building and they live upstairs over the store. Just go up the stairs there in front and knock on the first door."

She couldn't tell him anything else because people were

pushing to buy tickets and Jason wondered where all those people had suddenly come from. As he went out the door and looked across the street, he saw people still streaming from The Hatfield Theater and most of them heading for the terminal.

Thinking it must be a really good movie, Jason looked at the marquee which showed two feature films, plus cartoons, as tonight's attractions. The two features were The Lone Ranger and Tonto as the main feature and Hopalong Cassidy as the extra.

"Two-bit westerns," Jason said with a laugh as he went across the street and up the stairs.

His knock was answered by a small dapper gentleman who had a neat appearance, even in his shirt sleeves. Upon introducing himself as Joe Harris, he stepped aside and ushered Jason into the room, calling to his wife. Soon a pleasant little dumpling of a woman, with finger waved hair, came into the room. She eagerly shook hands and told Jason how much he was needed, proclaiming that she, as head of the United Methodist Women, had pressured the coal company to get a doctor for the town.

"Old Doctor Harrison died six months ago and we've had to go to Yukon to Dr. Hatfield since then. That's a long way and a lot of people don't have cars. Most of the people have had to go by bus but it only makes three runs a day.

Poor old Mary Shipley don't get home until nine o'clock at night, sometimes."

"Now, Mildred, let the man in before you want him to get out his pills," said Joe Harris, motioning Jason to a chair.

Jason declined, saying, "Really, Mr. Harris, I'd like to see the room and get my things unloaded. It's been a long trip and I am rather tired. If I'm to jump right in I'll need a good night's sleep." He smiled tiredly.

"I understand, Doc. Mildred, bring me that set of keys. We had two sets made so that your room can be cleaned while you're working. Is that all right with you?" questioned Mr. Harris.

Jason stared in bewilderment, his brain too tired to take

all this in tonight, "I guess so, Mr. Harris. Is this person who's going to clean reliable?" asked Jason.

"It's my sister, Doc. I wouldn't let some thief clean nothing for me," uttered a ruffled Mrs. Harris.

"I beg your pardon, Mrs. Harris. I did not mean to question your judgment. I'm just so tired that I'm not thinking straight tonight," Jason mumbled contritely.

"Oh shew! I didn't think nothing about that, but she is honest. You go on and get you some rest and if there's anything you need just holler down and me or the mister will bring it to you. I think I put everything in there that you'll need but I could of forgot something." Mrs. Harris smiled and patted his shoulder as he went out the door behind her husband.

Jason wearily climbed the second set of stairs on the little porch to be shown a really large room at the top of the house. It was furnished with a solid four-poster bed of some dark wood, a dresser, a chest of drawers, a night stand console, a small table with two wooden chairs.

There was also an upholstered reading chair with a floor lamp. In one corner, there was a chifforobe of the same dark wood as the bed, and to the right of that was another door that led to a bathroom with a new-looking claw foot tub, a lavatory on a stand, and a commode with a pull chain.

Blue speckled linoleum covered the floors of both the bedroom and the bathroom and was spotlessly clean, as if it had just been installed.

Going back into the bedroom, he noticed that dark blue drapes covered the two windows but had tiebacks that could be used to let in the light. He wearily sat on the side of the bed, which had a dark blue covering of some kind.

An hour later, he had all his gear in the room, his clothes hung in the chifforobe, and had taken a hot bath. He came back into the room and opened one of the windows facing the street.

His nose twitched, as he sniffed appreciatively. The aroma of hamburgers, fries, and fresh brewed coffee wafted across the street from the bus terminal. Jason longed for a cup of coffee but he was already in pajamas and decided he didn't want to get dressed to go back out. Since he had no way of making coffee in his room, he drank a glass of water and crawled into a clean and surprisingly comfortable bed.

# CHAPTER 10

He hadn't been in Bradshaw very long before he was able to verify by sight the validity of the statistics he had found about the people in McDowell County. It seemed that very few of the people coming into his office had gone to school further than the sixth or eighth grade, especially from off the mountains.

Jason had found among the books left by Doctor Harrison several West Virginia Blue Books and from the statistics found in them he noted that for the year 1949-50 the number of Elementary students was 16,588. In the same year the number of Secondary students were only 8,006; with only 755 of those students graduating from high school.

So truly, most of McDowell County's people only had a sixth to eighth grade formal education. "Somebody should be trying to improve the educational standards down here," grumbled Jason as he slammed the book closed and left the office.

In his mind, they were backward, rough, and uncouth, and he often laughed at their ignorance. At the same time, he realized that many were very intelligent and had quick minds but were certainly not worldly.

Even though he had always thought of himself as being fair and unbiased towards people, he unconsciously felt superior, but did not at first realize that. He later realized that many people, especially politicians, deigned to act as if they were on the same level as ones of lesser education but it was only an act.

Jason had always said that one person was as good as the next regardless of education, life style, religion, or race, and had always championed the cause of those less fortunate. Yet, in 1950, when he met Lucinda Harmon he was astounded when her mother made it clear that Burb Harmon did not want him or anyone else to date his daughter.

"I can understand him not wanting that beautiful sexy looking sixteen-year-old to date these crude yokels," said

Jason with a knowing smirk. "But I'm a doctor, and a well-educated one at that. That ignorant man should be proud that I even want to date her," grumbled Jason in exasperation.

This attitude of Burb Harmon's made him furious at first but after thinking about it he was more realistic. Even though Jason knew how to control his emotions he knew he could still be as easily aroused as these "so-called" yokels and was ashamed.

"I've got no reason to feel superior since libido is not ruled by education and culture," thought Jason solemnly. "But, I would never take advantage of a young girl or anyone else, that's for sure."

"I'm as much a bigot as Mom, after all. I need to come down off my high-horse and get to know these people better and I'll start now," Jason mumbled as he drove down the road.

Jason continued to soak up knowledge about the people and the area with the lingering thought in the back of his mind that he would eventually date Lucinda Harmon.

Then one evening in March, 1951 he followed a Trailways bus to War and found her getting on the bus to Welch. It was there in Welch where he finally found her again. He had met her in August, 1950 and hadn't seen nor heard about her from that time until he had seen her on a Trailways bus which had stopped in Bradshaw. After following the bus he knew she was working in Welch.

One Friday afternoon in April of 1951 he went to Welch to visit a patient he had sent to Grace Hospital for treatment. After visiting with the patient, he went down Main Street to stroll around.

He walked down one side of the street looking in the windows of the many stores and trying to avoid bumping into the throngs of people crowding the sidewalks.

The bumper to bumper stream of cars making their way along Main Street made it very difficult to cross the street. Finally he found an opening in the traffic just below Woolworth's Five and Ten Cent Store.

He made his way slowly back up the street toward the

Pocahontas Theater, thinking that he might see Kismet, which starred Howard Keel. As he passed Franklin's Dairy Bar, he glanced through the window and there, at a table in the window, sat Lucinda Marie Harmon.

Jason quickly went inside and seated himself in the vacant chair across the table from her. She gasped in surprise when she saw him and sat staring from a now rosy face.

"What's wrong? Did I scare you? You do remember me, don't you?" asked Jason.

"Sure, I remember you, but I'm surprised that you remembered me. I'm not covered with mud now," said Lucinda as she smiled, showing deep dimples in each cheek.

"No-o-o I didn't forget you, Lucinda Harmon. Not many men would. You are a very pretty girl, Miss Harmon," replied Jason as he looked at her in appreciation. Lucinda turned red but did not reply and Jason sat wondering if he dared ask her to spend the evening with him.

Never failing to face a challenge Jason asked, "What do you do for recreation besides dating all the men in town?" with a quizzical lift of his eyebrows.

From stormy glaring eyes Lucinda retorted, "I don't date all the men in town. I'm not that kind of girl."

"I was only kidding. Don't take offense! I know you are a decent girl," said Jason apologetically. When he saw her seem to relax he sat thinking of a way to make her more comfortable.

"I'd like some coffee if you will stay here long enough for me to drink it. Will you?" Jason asked. Lucinda agreed to sit with him since she had almost finished her meal. She refused the coffee he offered to buy for her but sat waiting.

Jason went to the counter and ordered the coffee and then he came back and sat across from her. "I'm not very familiar with Welch. Will you drive around with me and show me some of the sights?" he asked as he stirred milk into his coffee.

She didn't say no but instead said, "There aren't many sights to see, or at least if there are I haven't seen them."

"Well, go driving with me and we will discover them

together," urged Jason with a pleading look. He sensed that she wanted to but was either afraid or something since she was so hesitant.

Jason looked at her seriously, "I swear my intentions are honorable. You don't need to be afraid, if you are," he stated with a friendly smile.

That seemed to ease some of her apprehension and after more persuasion Lucinda agreed to spend the evening with him. Soon they were driving through Thorpe, Gary, Elbert, and Filbert.

They went to the Sportsman's Club, which was closed except to members, and then drove by the Golf Course at the Country Club before making the return trip to Welch. On the way, they passed Gary's United States Steel operation with its giant smoke stack, shooting fluffy clouds of white steam high into the air.

All the while, Lucinda had sat as close to the door as possible. Jason was afraid to mention her sitting position lest she decide to jump out.

They drove on out Browns Creek road to the Sterling Drive-In where the mellow voice of Nat King Cole sang "They try to tell us we're too young," setting a romantic mood.

They bought cheeseburgers, fries, and milkshakes and, while they were waiting for their order, the crooning voice of Perry Como further enhanced the mood with, "I hear singing and there's no one there, I smell blossoms and the trees are bare.........You're not sick you're just in love."

Jason didn't know how Lucinda felt but he was certainly in a romantic mood. When he looked at her, she didn't take her eyes away but sat starry-eyed as if under a spell. Remembering that she was very young, Jason silently cautioned himself to go very slowly in dealing with Lucinda Harmon.

Taking their food, they drove on to the little park at the edge of the city limits and sat together on a stone bench to eat. Placing their food on the stone table in front of the bench, Jason fitted the straws into their shakes and turned to give Lucinda hers but she jumped away startled.

"Did I bump you? I'm sorry. I was only passing your drink," explained Jason. Realizing how uncomfortable she was, Jason felt fortunate to be sitting this close to her and didn't try to push his luck.

They talked and ate, or at least Jason ate. Lucinda became more relaxed, and when she shivered from the cool breeze that had sprung up, Jason wanted to put his arm around her but was afraid to risk it.

Suddenly an owl hooted in the woods above the park and she jumped. In an effort to comfort her, he put his arm around her and she didn't move away. After that, they talked and talked, getting to know more about each other.

Jason found that Lucinda was very intelligent and really wanted to go to college but had no way of doing it. He told her of his contract with Pond Creek Coal Company, which had sold out to Island Creek since his arrival.

"I knew about Pond Creek being sold. My brother Gordon works, or did work for Pond Creek, and now he works for Island Creek. They are opening a mine at Beartown and Gordon will get to work there, he hopes," stated Lucinda.

They went on talking about mining being the major occupation for people in the county, especially for those living in the towns and coal camps. Lucinda seemed very thoughtful when they paused.

"I know that some company will always be mining coal in McDowell County until it runs out, and mining does create a lot of jobs for our people" Lucinda stated musingly. "But they are going to let Island Creek move the river bed to make a place for their slag dump so it will be closer to the railroad tracks. It will make it easier to load their coal on the cars," continued Lucinda as she sipped her milkshake. "That will help the company, but when it floods again the river will undermine the road. Daddy said we didn't have to guess who will have to pay to fix the road back. It will be the taxpayer who'll foot the bill."

Jason listened attentively and then interrupted, "Who's your nearest elected official? Seems like that's who you need to talk to if you want something done."

Lucinda's eyes took on a righteous glare. "Daddy heard from someone that Harry Pauley, who was elected to serve us, must be working with the coal companies. One of Dad's visitors said that Mr. Pauley could be returning the favor for that nice road he had built into Panther State Forest to get his coal out of there."

"You must be a student of local government to know so much about the situation," said Jason questioningly.

Lucinda smiled. "No, not really, but I do listen to people talk. A lot of people come to see Daddy. I always listen to them talk about things that happen in the county. I also read every newspaper Daddy brings home."

She sat thinking and then added, "I don't think I'm interested in political parties, but I am concerned when I know our elected officials aren't taking care of our interests. I can't do anything about it though, so I guess I should just keep quiet".

Listening to Lucinda talk, Jason felt a great swelling of pride in this beautiful young girl, who most people would assume had never had a serious thought in her head. He hugged her a little closer as he smiled, but at her immediate reaction, quickly relaxed his hold. He had a great desire to kiss her. He turned toward her, intending to do just that, but changed his mind. When he looked down into her innocent, trusting eyes, he refrained from doing so for fear of ruining a beautiful evening. When he took her home at 2:00 A. M., however, he forgot his fear momentarily and pulled her firmly against him. He proceeded to kiss her as he'd longed to do since he first met her. She melted in his arms and mumbling softly he kissed her entire face but when he buried his face in her neck she pushed against his chest. He lifted his head and seeing her frightened eyes he whispered "good night" and went down the stairs, leaving her standing on the landing below her room.

Jason knew he had shocked her but he also knew that she had liked it, and he went down the stairs whistling softly. He drove back to Bradshaw feeling happier than he had since arriving in Bradshaw.

They had spent ten hours together that night and Jason knew he would never forget it as long as he lived. He intended to visit her again there in Welch because Lucinda had said she could not tell her parents.

"Daddy will make me quit my job and go back home if he finds out I'm seeing a boy-uh-man, so I can't tell even Mommy. Jason you won't mention it to Aunt Sarie or any of your patients there in the area, will you? Daddy knows almost everybody, and somebody might tell him."

Jason assured her that he would tell nobody and he didn't. Inwardly he fumed at this needless secrecy. Again his superiority reared its head.

"You'd think Mr. Harmon would be proud that a doctor was interested in his daughter," Jason fumed in amazement.

"He has to realize that dating me would be a step up in the world. After all, how many girls here in this area get a chance to date a really educated person? He's just plain ignorant."

The longer he was in McDowell County, the more he understood that the mountain people had a fear of outsiders, especially when it came to their daughters. In their mind, he might be a fancy doctor but that didn't mean he didn't have the same nature as any other man.

Maggie Barker gave him a different perspective. "They've learned from experience. Mountain people have good reason to mistrust many of the outsiders who have come into the mountains," she stated knowingly. According to Maggie many outsiders came in and took what they could get, in any way they could get it. The coal companies had gotten most of their mineral rights for a pittance and bright promises. The company men and many of the workers for the coal companies and the railroads had taken advantage of their trusting daughters. Thus leaving many unwed mothers with money in their pockets, but ruined for life in the eyes of their neighbors.

A strong deterrent to his plan to date Lucinda was uncertainty of how to get past the strictures of her father, Burb Harmon. Her father wasn't the only deterrent however. A new policy had been put into place in the program he was working under, which required that he return to West Virginia University for a six- month training period on new procedures in the medical field.

Before he left in late April, 1951, Jason drove to Welch several times, even going so far as to check with her landlady on one occasion, to be told Lucinda was away. He seriously thought about going to the Harmon home some Saturday evening to ask her out but remembered the fear in her eyes, and refrained from doing so.

Now he had to go back to West Virginia University and did not know when he would get to see Lucinda Harmon again.

"I'm afraid this is going to be a long six months," groaned Jason aloud as he turned his car north on his journey.

He returned to Bradshaw the last day of October, 1951 to find she was no longer in Welch. When he visited Aunt Sarie, he learned that Lucinda had gone to Concord College in Athens, West Virginia. He still wanted to date her, but could not get away to drive to Athens. He became so caught up in his medical challenges that he only thought of Lucinda late at night when there were no calls on his time. He knew he would still like to date her but the likelihood of that opportunity seemed remote.

## CHAPTER 11

However, fate is capricious, and one evening in December, Lucinda came with her mother to see the doctor. Jason almost dropped his stethoscope when she walked in. He swiftly sucked in his breath and started to call her name but saw Lucinda's face and brief nod and stopped. Suddenly, he remembered Lucinda insistence that nobody from the area know that they had spent time together in Welch.

Quickly he put out his hand and said, "How are you, Mrs. Harmon? I see you've brought your daughter to the doctor."

"I ain't brought her," wheezed Nancy Harmon. "It's me that's sicker than a dog. She just come with me cause I've been so dizzy," explained Nancy before she began a wracking cough.

Jason checked her chest and listened to her lungs and bronchial sounds. Then he took her temperature and blood pressure before giving her a shot and presenting her with medicines to take home. Before Nancy Harmon left his office, he asked permission to date Lucinda. Nancy said she couldn't give permission, but told him to ask Burb Harmon.

Feeling it was useless to ask this seemingly overbearing lumberjack, Jason still took the chance and was rewarded for his tenacity. Unbelievably, Burb Harmon said yes.

Every evening at six o'clock Jason drove down Brushy Ridge road to the Harmon home to pick up Lucinda. The road was a narrow unpaved lane, riddled with ruts and mud so thick that all vehicles wore chains to traverse it.

Putting on chains was a twice an evening ritual since he needed chains to go down the ridge to get Lucinda and chains to get her back home, unless the ground was frozen. If they could have stayed out later in the evenings the ground would have been frozen on the way back. But Burb Harmon acted like something terrible would happen if she was out a minute past eleven o'clock.

"That is the most narrow-minded, stupid thinking I've ever heard of in my life," thought Jason.

Jason didn't like it one bit and fumed inwardly at such ignorance, but never let Lucinda know. He wanted to see Lucinda and would do whatever it took. Unlike his usual dates he had spent two evenings sitting through movies he had seen several years before. This was a little more than he wanted to endure.

"Lucinda, I know you like movies and I do too," said Jason "But we can't talk in a movie and I'm never going to get to know you. Can't we go someplace other than a movie?"

"I don't know, Jason. Dad would really be mad. If he found out, I couldn't go out with you again. Besides, there's no place else to go, is there?" questioned Lucinda worriedly.

Jason grasped her hand and arose, saying, "Let's get out of here where we can at least talk. It's better sitting in the car than in this dark theater."

As they walked towards the car Jason said, "Maybe we could drive over to Welch and eat at the Carter Hotel. I get tired of hamburgers, don't you? I'd like to take you to a nice place and show you off." When Lucinda looked at him questioningly he raised his eyebrows and grinned impishly as they reached the car.

After Lucinda was seated in the car she got very quiet as if studying or something. Jason tilted her face to look at him.

"What's wrong? Are you afraid I have some evil motive?" asked Jason. "I don't intend anything except to be able to talk to you and look at you. I can't see you in dark theaters."

Lucinda hesitated as if in doubt. "Jason, I know we seem like backwoods hillbillies to you, but we aren't stupid. Several girls that were in school with my sister Ellen had to drop out because they had gotten into trouble. Dad and Mom don't want that to happen to me. In fact, I don't really know why you want to date me, anyway."

Jason started to interrupt, but Lucinda stopped him. "No, wait, please. I'm thrilled, and pleased, and I've enjoyed our time together but you'll have to admit we're worlds apart. Don't you see how unlikely we are to have a serious relationship?" she asked looking at him in doubt.

Lucinda soberly continued. "All my family thinks you are just doing this because it was a challenge to get Dad's permission. My sister Ellen said...," Lucinda stopped and turned red.

"What did she say?" Jason questioned. "Lucinda, your sister doesn't know me. How could she know what my motives are?" but Lucinda wouldn't say anymore and became even redder as he questioned her.

Jason thought, "Her sister probably said something about being nice or that I would just take advantage of her." He knew Lucinda was certainly not ready to tell him something like that.

It was not quite dark yet and Jason turned, taking her face in both his hands, "Let me really look at you. I'll bring my camera tomorrow and get some pictures of you since I can't see you in a dark theater. Then if we have to go to a movie I'll still know what you look like." Jason said as he laughed merrily.

Looking at her intently, he ran his fingers softly over her face, tracing her brows and lips gently before leaning over and kissing her tenderly.

Lucinda reluctantly pulled away. "Jason, people can look right into this car. They'll think I'm awful and if anyone passing knows me, Dad will hear about this before I get home." Lucinda shivered and slid as close to the door as possible.

Jason stared in amazement. "Your Dad would get mad because I kissed you? What kind of thinking is that? Everybody kisses. Oh! You mean they only kiss in the dark," said Jason snidely.

"I...guess. I don't know," mumbled Lucinda. "I just know what Dad would say if someone told him I was seen on the street in Bradshaw kissing a man in public."

Seeing Jason's amazement, Lucinda blurted, "See there, I told you there is just too much difference in us."

Jason sat quietly for a few minutes. "Lucinda, are you ashamed to be kissed by me?"

"No," Lucinda quickly denied.

"Then are you embarrassed or ashamed because I want to kiss you?" questioned Jason as if trying to make a point.

"No, I'm not ashamed. I just feel uncomfortable when others see us, that's all," replied Lucinda quietly.

"Don't your parents kiss each other, Lucinda?"

"I... I don't know. I guess they do. They're old. What's all this about anyway? What difference does it make what Daddy and Mommy do?" questioned Lucinda.

Jason sat as if thinking. "I've just never run into this way of thinking before. If all the people on your mountain are like yours, I don't see how in the world all of them have such large families. But maybe they don't kiss, they just have sex," stated Jason philosophically.

When he saw the shocked look from Lucinda's wide blue eyes, he realized he'd said something wrong.

"What? Why are you looking shocked or scared? Which is it? Oh! I said sex. That is a bad word for you isn't it? Now, Lucinda, you are a grown woman, going to college, so don't you think it is time to grow up? Sex is a natural act and it is not nasty or evil... Here! What are you doing?" Jason quickly reached across Lucinda and grabbed the door handle to stop her from getting it the rest of the way open.

"You turn this door loose and let me out. I'm going home," stormed Lucinda and Jason could see tears brimming in her eyes.

Jason let out a long breath. "How are you going to get home? I can imagine how far you would get up that mountain before someone dragged you into their car and ran away with you."

Seeing the stubborn set of her jaw and the unbelieving glare in her eyes, Jason knew he had to ease the situation. "Lucinda, you are a beautiful woman and men are going to get ideas when they look at you," Jason stated affirmatively.

Seeing her disbelief he continued. "You won't have to do a thing but just be there. That is just the way it is and I didn't make it that way."

Lucinda spoke as if greatly puzzled. "Mommy said if girls acted right nobody would say anything to them." She hesitantly replied.

Sighing in exasperation Jason said, "She's wrong there Lucinda. Men like to look at you. I've seen too many of them doing it just since I've known you."

Lucinda gasped in shock and Jason grasped her hand where it was laying in her lap. "That does not make men bad Lucinda, they are just being men. That's the way the Lord made us. Men like pretty women."

Lucinda had settled back in her seat, listening but not looking at him. She sat as if puzzled. "So Mommy didn't know what she was talking about. Is that what you are saying?" asked Lucinda and Jason slowly nodded his head.

"Lucinda, I'm a doctor but I'm also a man and I'm telling you that men are going to like to look at you. Most of them will treat you with respect but some will not, yet all of them will fantasize. What I'm trying to tell you is that men like looking at you, and desiring you is just natural. You should be proud that you are admired. You like to be thought pretty, don't you?"

"Yeah, sure. I mean, I wouldn't want to be really ugly. It's just that I don't want men to think other things about me. It scares me and makes me feel dirty."

The doctor training took over for Jason as well as his more mature understanding since his teen years. "Who in the world got you so mixed up? Lucinda, sex is not dirty." Jason started to say more but stopped as he saw the color of Lucinda's cheeks.

"I don't want to talk about that and if you're going to, please just take me home," begged Lucinda.

"All right, I'll not talk about it, but if I bring you a book will you promise me you will read it? Really, Lucinda, you do need to know about human nature. Will you promise?" questioned Jason.

Lucinda mutely nodded her head and sat up straighter in her seat as if eager to go. Jason turned on the car lights since it had gotten dark while they were talking. He looked over at her and smiled. "If I promise to not talk about, uh, 'that word' and be really good, will you sit over here beside me. You know it is all right to be hugged, don't you?" Jason said with a winning smile.

Jason turned the car towards Bradshaw Mountain since he had to have her home by eleven o'clock. There was no chance of taking her skating or to Bluefield to a nice restaurant. Putting his arm carefully around Lucinda, as she hesitantly moved to sit beside him, Jason wondered how a girl lived in the world and yet had so little knowledge of life.

Lucinda was the prettiest girl he had ever seen and Jason was truly smitten. Her innocence was so appealing in one respect and appalling in another.

"How does one get past that fear and naiveté'?" wondered Jason.

He knew they would need a long courtship because her fears and inhibitions seemed so deep rooted that she would have trouble with intimacy. Even with that understanding, he still wanted to date her. It would be a long, hard, road but very challenging.

Jason thought, "Someday, I may want this beautiful little mountain girl to be my wife." Startled at this thought, since it had entered his head for the first time, he drove in silence almost to the top of the mountain.

He decided that he would bring the book tomorrow, hoping that once she read it some of the barriers would be removed. They were nearing the top of the mountain with Jason thinking back about the time he had seen her in Welch. He knew she was or could be passionate and she did like his attention. Jason looked down at Lucinda nestled in the circle of his arm and sighed.

"Slow and steady wins the race."

Lucinda looked up. "What? Did you say something?"

"Yes, I said, Let's go eat someplace," replied Jason.

"Let's go to the Sunset Drive-In. They have really good cheeseburgers," Lucinda said with a smile.

Jason pulled over in a wide section on a curve just before the top of Bradshaw Mountain and turned to Lucinda.

"You do know that I would never hurt you or mistreat you, don't you?" he asked.

Seeing trust in her eyes, Jason pulled her fully into his

arms and held her tenderly before he lowered his head and kissed her hungrily. Lucinda did not pull away or act scared because Jason had been so careful not to go any further than a kiss.

Jason felt relieved, knowing she wasn't afraid of him. She was afraid of sex though, and Jason doubted if she knew why she was afraid. She seemed to have very little knowledge about sexuality. He looked down at her upturned face and quickly kissed her eyelids and then her lips before he released her and pulled back onto the highway.

Looking at the time, Jason knew they would have to eat fast if he needed to put chains on the car, and was very thankful when he saw other cars turning to go down Brushy Ridge without chains. Still, he hoped they wouldn't have to wait very long for their orders to be filled. They didn't, and pulled up before Burb Harmon's house at exactly eleven o'clock.

# CHAPTER 12

Jason certainly had done an about face concerning the people of the area in a very short time. After spending a little over two years in the town of Bradshaw, he realized that the mountain people lived a separate life from those in the towns.

The town folks were more urbane and cultured than their mountain cousins. They lived in better or more modern houses with more conveniences and yet they were very charitable, nice people.

There was, however, an innocence and decency about the mountain people that he found appealing.

Also, they were so fiercely independent that they would never take charity of any kind. They were always willing to help a friend build a house, hoe a field of corn, butcher pigs, sheep, or cows, or help make molasses. However, they would be outraged to think that they were seen as "having their hands out" as if begging alms, as long as they were able to work. He further learned that the mountain people were vigorously against unions and any organization that told them what to do except the church.

The more he learned about these people the more he liked them. He would never forget Will Parks, a mountain man, from down on one fork of Stateline Ridge. His farm could only be reached by horse or a pair of horses and a wagon. Mr. Parks' wife Patty,was ready to deliver her seventh child and was having trouble.

A neighbor had come for Jason and followed him back up Bradshaw Mountain to stop at the mouth of Stateline Ridge. Jason gasped in astonishment and wondered where he was expected to go, when he saw Mr. Parks waiting with an extra horse already saddled. Luckily, Jason had spent many days in the summer on his uncle's horse farm. He swung himself into the saddle as Mr. Parks began to apologize for not bringing a better horse for him.

He arrived at the Parks home to find a big meal awaiting

him, plenty of coffee, and a bottle of moonshine whiskey to take back with him. Most of the mountain people were avid church goers and hated strong drink, especially the wives. However, some of the mountain men felt that they might as well get money for making moonshine as for the state to get it all.

So, while it wasn't every family that offered moonshine, the Parks family was known for theirs. It was made from pure corn with no additives and was very good, or so it was said. Anyway, to be given a pint of Parks' moonshine was to have earned respect.

If this had happened when he first arrived in Bradshaw, he would have refused the food and the moonshine, but now he knew better. These people didn't have much but they believed in paying for what was done for them, and they were honest in all their dealings.

To a mountain man or woman, a good meal was common courtesy, and the moonshine or some other prized gift would be offered to show appreciation. Some people gave home-grown honey or molasses and others gave gallons of cider or dried apples. Recognizing the honor, Jason thanked Mr. Parks and the moonshine was stowed in his bag, but the meal would have to wait. He went first to examine Mrs. Parks.

He could see a foot almost completely through the birth canal. He knew he would have to be very careful or the baby could be crippled, if it survived. He ground his teeth together in worry.

Looking at Mrs. Beavers, the midwife, he said, "It's coming breech and I'll need some help." Mrs. Beavers got up immediately and went out of the room.

"Hey, wait—I really do need your help. Don't leave—I'm going to have to go in there and get the other foot down, if I can," Jason said, and smiled in relieve as Mrs. Beavers came back in with a pan of water and several clean towels.

Digging in his bag, Jason came out with a bottle of alcohol and asked Mrs. Beavers to pour it over his gloves which he had already put on. That done, he told Mrs. Beavers to stand at the head of the bed and keep Mrs. Parks as still as she could.

Going near the head of the bed, Jason looked down at Mrs. Parks, "I'm going to have to help you and your baby. It's breech and there's no other way. Do you understand what I'm saying?"

Mrs. Parks mumbled through swollen lips and bulging eyes, "Do what you have to, Doc. I can't stand much more."

Jason clinched his fists as he went back to the foot of the bed. He turned to Mrs. Beavers. "Do you know any other way to do this, Mrs. Beavers? If you do please tell me, and I'll try it."

"No, Doc, I can't say as I do. I ain't never had a birthin like this un. Patty is plum wore out, so I thank whatever you're goin to do, you need to git at it." She looked at him worriedly. "I hope you ain't too late."

Jason began the daunting task of manipulating that small being still inside its mother's body. Patty Parks screamed and lost consciousness just as Jason manipulated the other foot down with the first one and gently pulled as the little body slid right on out, along with a gush of blood.

Mrs. Beavers was standing by, ready to cut the umbilical cord and take the baby out of the way. Jason grabbed the towels and stanched as much of the blood as possible. He then packed the birth canal with packing, before hurriedly checking Mrs. Parks' vital signs. Her pulse was weak but steady and her heart was slow but rhythmic. Worriedly, he turned to the baby who hadn't yet cried or made any response.

He began a careful examination and, on hearing a feeble heart beat, asked for a pan of water. He quickly plunged the baby into the water to be rewarded with a weak, whimpering cry. Smiling with relief, he transferred it back to Mrs. Beavers to be cleaned up before returning his attention to the mother.

He bent over the quiet figure on the bed and picked up her hand. "Mrs. Parks, Mrs. Parks, don't you want to see your baby girl?"

The pale figure moaned, tried to mumble, moved her head,

and slowly opened her eyes. When she focused on the face before her, she whispered, “What’s happened, Doc? Did my baby die?” Her questions were an almost inaudible murmur and Jason leaned down to hear her.

“No, Maam, you have a fat baby girl and as far as I can tell she is healthy. How do you feel?” asked Jason as he checked her pulse.

Mrs. Parks slowly turned her head searching and, on seeing Mrs. Beavers, whispered hoarsely, “Granny, can I see my baby?”

Mrs. Beavers stepped forward, offering the bundled baby as she answered, “You shore can, Patty. Honey, you shore have been through it for this un. I jest hope the Lord don’t send you no more. Seven is enough I think for any one woman to have.”

Jason turned to look at Mrs. Beavers. “Do you believe the Lord has a certain number of children for each woman to have?”

“I shore do, Doc. Don’t you? The Lord knows all things and if he meant for this baby to be here, it was going to get here. Another thing is, if it wouldn’t from Patty and Will Parks then it wouldn’t be this baby, now would it?” demanded Mrs. Beavers sternly.

Jason had run into this absolute predestination belief before and knew any opposition to it would only get people angry, so he said, “I was just wondering how you felt about it, Mrs. Beavers.”

Will Parks knocked and came hesitantly through the door as if he were trespassing, but his apprehension made him bold, “Is she all right, Doc? Did my Patty make it? I didn’t hear no more screamin and I figgered it was over one way or tother.”

Jason turned to him smiling. “Mr. Parks, you are one lucky man. Your wife is tired and weak but all right and you have a big baby girl.”

“Praise the good Lord. I was fretted near to death with Patty takin on so. She ain’t never done that afore and so I sent fer ye. Hope that didn't put you out none, Granny Polly, but I think a lot of my Patty. I jest wanted all the help I could get." He looked at the midwife with great pleading eyes.

Mrs. Beavers went over to him with the baby in her arms. "You never bothered me nary bit. I'se worried too, but this here young doctor feller knowed what to do. He was jest in time too. Patty couldn't uh took much more."

Will Parks looked down at the small bundle briefly and then made his way to his wife. "Patty, you shore give me a scare this time. I hope the Lord don't send us no more. It frets me nigh to death and it ain't doin you no good neither." He grinned as his big callused hand gently brushed the hair back off her forehead. He stood looking tenderly down at her and one tear rolled silently down his cheek.

Patty weakly lifted her hand and grasped his, mumbling, "Aw, Will, I ain't never seen sech a man as you fur frettin. I'm all right now. The Lord sent that doctor here right on time."

Jason was deeply moved by such humble displays of love. If I could find somebody to feel like that about, it would be wonderful, thought Jason, turning as not to embarrass Will Parks. "Would I have that kind of love with Lucinda Harmon?" questioned Jason silently.

Then he walked into the kitchen to get some coffee, thinking, "The Lord didn't send me. I wouldn't have been here if Will hadn't sent for me, but these people will never believe that."

A young woman came towards him as he entered the kitchen, "Set yourself down at the table, doctor, and I'll fetch the grub in jest a minute. I've kept it warm, since you didn't have time to eat afore." Jason sighed wearily and lowered himself into the indicated chair.

The room looked clean so probably the food was too, and the coffee was really good but very strong.

A plate of food was put before him just as Will Parks entered the kitchen. The plate was filled with soup beans, cabbage, cooked potatoes, a large piece of meat, which looked like pork, and a large square of cornbread.

"This is enough food for an army, Mr. Parks." Jason smiled as he took his first bite.

"Here, May, bring the Doc a glass of frash sour milk. It's cold, right out of the spring house. It'll go good with them vittles. Now there's plenty more where that come from, so eat that little bit and we'll fetch you some more." Will took a seat across from Jason and sat watching him.

Jason shook his head in amazement while relishing the delicious food. Somebody in this family knew how to cook. He had never tasted sour milk, thinking Mr. Parks must mean buttermilk, but felt sure he was not going to like it. Not wanting to hurt this kind, generous man, Jason took a tentative sip and thought, "Well, it is buttermilk and I've drunk worse." He continued his meal.

"Doc, I—well, I ain't got no ready cash but if you'se to tell me your charge I'd be sartin to pay you ever dime. Is that all right with you? I ain't been able to do none of my peddlin like I allus do for fear of leaving Patty and her might need me."

Looking serious, Will Parks said, "I ort to be able to pay you something by next week, or the week after, for sartin."

Jason finished chewing and then looked at Mr. Parks. "Sure, Mr. Parks, you bring in what you can. The bill is $35 and the company gets their cut out of that or I could charge you less."

"Well, pon my honor! You mean the coal company takes part of your pay? Why that ain't fair, is it?" blurted Mr. Parks.

Jason did not want to leave the wrong impression, so he explained, "Well, you see, Mr. Parks, I wouldn't have been here if the company had not hired me. They treat me right and I don't think they are being unfair. The company does a lot for the miners."

That seemed to satisfy Mr. Parks and soon Jason had checked Patty and the baby over again and prepared to leave.

"Here, wait jest a minute, Doc. You ain't filled out her birth certificate yet," said Mrs. Beavers, catching him in the front room.

"You're right, Mrs. Beavers. Thank you for reminding me. What are you going to name her, Mrs. Parks," asked Jason, going back to the bedroom as he fished a blank certificate out of his bag.

"Well, me and Will talked about it and was goin to name it Will if'n it was a boy, but since it's a girl, I guess we'll jest call her Wilma. Is that all right with you, Will?" she asked.

That much talk had been really hard on her and the last was a mere mumble.

"It shore is, Patty. That's a purty name and I hadn't even thunk of that. I wus plumb sartin it was goin to be a boy, but that's fine though, since you'ns is both here and all right," Will Parks assured her as he stroked back her damp hair.

So, Jason had another experience of McDowell County beliefs, values, and hospitality while performing a very unnerving medical procedure. It was also a quick insight into why there were so many Paula's, Charlenes, Jessicas, and Samanthas along with other derivatives of father's names.

## CHAPTER 13

In 1949 when Jason first came to Bradshaw, he was so busy he didn't even think of a social life. He dated a few girls in the area and once dated the daughter of Doctor Wilcox, who was a doctor working at Grace Hospital. Doctor Wilcox's daughter, Sarah, had been home from college and at loose ends, as was Jason. They had a couple of dates and then she went back to college and he forgot all about her.

He had been in Bradshaw almost a full year, when he first met Lucinda Harmon, in August, 1950. He immediately called home about that meeting. In the telling, he laughed uproariously about meeting this beautiful young girl sitting in the middle of a mud puddle.

By the next year, when Lucinda was still on his mind, his talk gradually became more serious, especially after that time in Welch. In his phone conversations he could tell by his mother's voice that it disturbed her.

"Jason, surely you aren't interested in someone from that kind of background, are you?" Mrs. McCall sounded amused as she questioned, as if it was some big joke.

"I mean, I'm sure you aren't going to stay down there without some kind of relationship with women, but she's young isn't she?" asked his mother.

"Yes, she is, and I'm not saying I'm interested in dating her," had been Jason's reply at first, but that had changed. It had not changed for his mother however.

When Jason had first mentioned her his mother had said, "Jason, that child is only sixteen years old and you know if she should get pregnant you would have to marry her. Please don't get entangled with that kind of people."

Jason was shocked at her prejudice even though he had at first had similar feelings. "What do you mean that kind of people? They are nice, decent, God-fearing people, and Lucinda is not the kind of girl that one seduces. Mom, I'm going to date her, if her dad will allow it," stated Jason firmly.

Mrs. McCall gasped in astonishment. "Jason McCall, have

you lost your senses? You are a doctor from an old and noted family. Does our heritage mean nothing to you? You're not really interested; it's just because you are down there in the sticks and she is the only girl available."

"You're wrong there, Mom," Jason stated strongly as he hurriedly ended the call. She didn't know Lucinda, but Jason knew that she wouldn't give Lucinda a chance if she ever met her.

Lucinda didn't have a pedigree linked to nobility and his mother only liked people from the "elite" classes. It wasn't so important for his dad, who believed that once his children were grown they had the right to choose their own lives.

From his studies and from life, Jason realized that all mothers seemed more protective than fathers for some reason; even with the animals the same held true.

"I think I'd best not mention Lucinda to Mom anymore," mumbled Jason as he left his room to go down to the bus terminal for his "supper," which was dinner in Pennsylvania.

Thinking that to not mention her would cause his mother to forget about her was only wishful thinking on Jason's part. His mother did not mention Lucinda either, but it did not keep her from writing Lucinda a long, condescending, and explanatory letter. In the letter Lucinda was told in no uncertain terms that Jason had a girl of his own class waiting for him when he returned to his own culture. She also hinted at the harm it would do to Jason's career should he marry beneath him. Elizabeth did not mail the letter but held it in abeyance until she thought it was necessary to intervene.

Later, circumstances played into Elizabeth's zealous hands. She did not have to mail the letter but had an added and more effective turn of events fall into her lap. Elizabeth never told anyone except Janet about her plan of action and she knew that Janet would not tell since she had the same desires as Elizabeth.

Just when Jason was dreaming about the spring break when he could see Lucinda again, he was called home. His dad had fallen and was seriously injured. He remained in the hospital for over a month during which time Jason had no contact with Lucinda.

All the family haunted the hospital waiting room until Henry McCall was off the critical list. Then Frank and Jason spent many hours with their dad. In fact, they took turns staying at night with him in case he needed water or anything else. Mr. McCall was in traction and could do nothing for himself at first.

Later, Jason talked to his brother Frank and his Dad about Lucinda and they listened. Frank laughingly said, "He's got a captive audience, Dad. You can't get away, and I won't leave you to his mercy. He's so wrapped up in Lucinda he's apt to forget all about you."

The fall had injured Mr. McCall's back, and he had a concussion which kept him in the hospital, but it did not cut back on his enjoyment of his sons.

While Mr. McCall was flat of his back, Frank and Jason were company and good therapy. They spent long hours talking to him and to each other. They discussed the terrible fighting in Korea and Jason told his dad that many young doctors were enlisting. "You don't plan to do that, do you Son?" questioned his Dad worriedly.

Jason grinned and said, "Well, not at the present. I'm fighting a losing battle where I am." Then Jason told them all about what he had found in McDowell County and the many things that needed to be taken care of that were ignored.

"I'll bet there's not a sewage system in place in McDowell County except for the towns like Welch, Gary, Keystone, and Northfork. I don't know that for sure, but I do know that many homes around Bradshaw run raw sewage into the Dry Fork and Tug Rivers" said Jason in disgust.

Remembering something else he said, "I was told that Island Creek Coal Company was allowed to change the river bed, which now undermines the road every time it floods and the state has to repair the road. Local residents say that companies are allowed to create slag dumps, damage the roads, and anything they want to do without any opposition from the elected officials."

"Don't the citizens complain?" asked Mr. McCall. "I mean, they do know they have a right to complain, don't they?"

"I don't know. They don't have much formal education but they do grumble and complain. But that's to me or to each other when they stop in one of the beer joints there in town." Jason said, meditatively.

"They complain, but I've never heard anyone say they were going to do something to change a situation. I guess they really don't know they can," Jason answered.

Frank leaned back in his chair, thrusting out his chest. "Well, I can see they need a good lawyer down there, a citizen's advocate, or something like that. I guess I'd better come down there and join you, brother. Then you can cure the sick and I can cure the citizenry. How does that sound?"

"You wouldn't last a week down there, little brother. Come Saturday night, all the drunks from Gus's place and the other joints would hunt you down. They'd be jealous, since all the women would be after you." Jason grinned as he gave Frank a playful jab on the shoulder.

Frank had been tagged the high school "heart throb" and was the butt of family jokes when it came to girls.

Jason didn't want to leave the impression that Bradshaw was a bad place because it really wasn't. Contrary to his first impressions, Bradshaw and Bradshaw Mountain were inhabited by the kindest, most truthful, and most honest people he had ever had the good fortune to meet.

His thoughts went to Aunt Sarie Lester, who had been one of his patients, and he told Frank and his dad about her wonderful faith and cheerful attitude. He also told them of how she coped with her illness for so long and explained about faith healing.

"We know that some men laying their hands on somebody cannot make them well, but honestly, I thought she would be dead in a very short time. Every time I visited her, she didn't seem to be any worse. She would not take morphine or anything except aspirin," Jason explained.

"Well, son, it had to be something. Perhaps believing

strongly does make a difference. We don't really know. Faith healing is a foreign concept to us, but do we really know anything outside our own existence?" asked Mr. McCall.

Neither Frank nor Jason made any comment since Mr. McCall seemed on the verge of sleep. They tiptoed from the room and made their way to the visitors lounge.

There they drank coffee from the pot kept ready for the families as they talked about their dad's condition. They both felt that he was on the mend and would soon be back on his feet.

"You don't have to worry, Jason. I'll be here to take care of Dad and Mom while you're finishing up down there. How much longer do you have?" Frank looked at Jason, who seemed to be off in some other place.

"Frank, you should see her eyes. I've never seen eyes that color of blue before. I was drawn to her the first time I saw her, even with mud all over her."

Jason laughed and continued, "No, that wasn't the first time. I saw her two weeks before that day walking along the road. I came around this curve and there before me was walking a girl with the sexiest walk I'd ever seen and so I stopped to ask if she wanted a ride." Jason laughed aloud.

"She wouldn't ride, of course, but then the next time... You should have seen those big blue eyes widen in shock and astonishment when she plopped back down in that mud puddle. She sprained her ankle that time—nice ankles too. Of course, I gave them a good feel while I was checking to see if they were broken." Jason looked at Frank, grinning lasciviously.

"Yeah-yeah, I know. She has a nineteen-inch waist, five-foot-two, blue eyes, dimples, long, glorious blonde hair. All I can say is, when you fell you fell hard, big brother. You may as well stake your claim even if she is just sixteen, or is she seventeen?" Frank could see that Jason felt more for this girl than any he had ever mentioned to him, even if she was from the sticks.

Jason sat thinking about how Lucinda felt in his arms,

"What—Oh, yes, she's seventeen now, but she'll be eighteen soon. She's also very intelligent. She would have to be to finish high school at sixteen."

Then they went on to talk about how their mother was holding up and about Frank's ambition to be a lawyer and start his own law firm.

"Frank, I'll help you, as soon as I finish up with my internship. You have to take your core classes anyway, in the first two years. Then I should be ready to bring in some extra money, if you need it." They both lapsed into a sleepy silence and Frank actually went to sleep.

Jason, however, had his mind on Lucinda. When he got back to Bradshaw, he was definitely going to not only date Lucinda, he might even consider asking her to marry him.

"I'm sure I love her and I'm almost as sure she loves me but she's so young and innocent," mused Jason worriedly.

Since their time together during her Christmas break from school in 1951, Jason, still in Bradshaw, and Lucinda, at Concord College, had written to one another faithfully twice each week and both professed that they were in love and wanted to spend their lives together. His mother would be very upset because she had planned his life around Janet Washburn.

"I'll just move to Welch and live there," stated Jason aloud and Frank jerked awake startled.

"What? Did you call me? Is Dad bad again?"

Jason patted his arm, smiling. "Calm down, Frank. Nothing's wrong. I just forgot and spoke my thoughts aloud. Sorry I woke you."

Every day that he had been in Pittsburgh he had cursed himself for not having the foresight to give Lucinda his parents' phone number. Still, every night he had written her a letter, but none of his letters were answered nor were they returned. Jason could not understand what had happened. His last letter from Lucinda was written the week he had left for Pittsburgh and Maggie had sent it to him along with his other mail. That letter had been the same loving and caring letter she had always written. In that one, she was anticipating the pleasure of the spring break so she could be home to see him again.

Then, there were no other letters and he just could not understand it. Although, Lucinda had told him that she could not receive personal calls except for family emergencies he did take a chance and call Concord College anyway saying he was the family doctor. He was told that Lucinda was unable to come to the phone but that he could leave a message. "Just tell her that Dr. McCall is trying to reach her," replied an exasperated Jason.

Each day he checked the mail sent on by Maggie but found no letters from Lucinda. Once he asked his mother, "Mom, I felt sure I would have some other mail. Is this all the mail that has come for me?"

Elizabeth hurriedly came in and looked all around the table in the foyer and on the floor. Innocently looking at Jason, she said, "I'm sure that's all unless Seymour dropped something. Why don't you ask him, Jason?"

Upon questioning, Seymour said that all of the mail was bundled together when he picked it up at the post office. "I put the whole bundle there on the table in the foyer like I have always done."

In a few more days he called the college again and a young girl answered the call. She hesitated for a moment and then snappily told him he was not supposed to call the students for personal reasons and immediately hung up.. That certainly sounded weird since he knew college students got and made personal calls all the time.

He wondered why the lady who took his message on that first call didn't say students could not receive personal calls. Jason was puzzled and worried. He knew that Lucinda could not write him at the Pittsburgh address until she had received his letters but he had written almost every night.

"Why is she not answering my letters? What is wrong? Could she be ill and not want me to know?" questioned Jason, and began to think about ways to get in touch with her at Concord College.

"I could say it is an emergency but if I gave them my name they would know it wasn't, since I gave my name as a doctor before and didn't get to talk to her."

Jason called Concord again and was told by a Mrs. Bodkins that Lucinda was in class but she took his number. "Tell her to call me collect," said Jason, thinking that now he would get an answer.

No call came, however, and he didn't know of anything else to do but wait until he was back in West Virginia. He possessed himself with patience until his dad was well enough to be taken home. As soon as Mr. McCall had recovered sufficiently for Jason to feel safe in leaving him, he returned to Bradshaw.

# CHAPTER 14

Sometimes fate steps in and changes the very fabric of our being and Jason was to be the recipient of fate's capricious moves. He had no way of knowing that his dad's accident would create a major wrinkle in the tapestry of his life.

He was eager to see Lucinda but didn't now how to accomplish that. He couldn't find out anything at the Harmon home. They didn't have a telephone and he had no excuse for visiting. There was no point in calling the college again since he had tried so many times to no avail. So, he waited, hoping to catch up on his patients before making a trip to the college.

Then one fateful evening, when he finally had time to look through his backlog of newspapers, his whole world fell apart.

As he had driven back to Bradshaw after his dad's recovery he thought, "I'll find out what is wrong with Lucinda. There must be something. I just know she wouldn't have stopped writing me without some cause.

Jason had been telling himself that his longing to hurry back to Bradshaw was due to his desire to see all those people he knew and liked. In his heart, however, he knew the real reason was and had always been Lucinda Marie Harmon.

He had made the trip back to Bradshaw full of hope and expectations, barely stopping for food. As soon as he reached his room and unpacked, he headed to the office. There he double checked all the mail, not taking time to look at the newspapers stacked on a chair in the corner of the office.

Patients, who had been waiting for his return, came pouring in and he was working around the clock. He also had to check up on all his critically ill patients, and that took an inordinate amount of time.

Two weeks later, he had time to go into his office and relax. It was Wednesday evening about eight o'clock, and he had just gotten back off Bradshaw Mountain, after delivering a set of twins, when disaster struck.

He took his equipment into the office and sat down to rest, and began to idly glance through the stack of newspapers. He only glanced at the front pages and occasionally turned to the obituaries, fearing to see that one of his patients had died. He was ready to trash all of them after he had glanced at ten or twelve, when the front page of the next one on the stack caught his eye.

"Local girl...," he started to read and then stopped, gaping at the picture there on the front page. There as bold as life was Lucinda Harmon in the arms of a tall black-haired man by the name of Jerome Petry. Jason crushed the paper in his fist.

"So, that's the reason she didn't write. I thought she was more decent than that. Here I am down here in this damn hell hole waiting for her to grow up. She's sure not waiting, is she?" He jumped up, kicked the waste paper can after he had thrown in the newspaper, slammed his chair against the wall, and went out the door kicking it shut as he left.

Jason climbed the stairs two at a time to his room and fished down in the bottom of the chifforobe for the bottle of moonshine given to him by Will Parks. He poured a tall tumbler half full and took a large gulp, grimaced, gasped, and then took another. After a few more drinks, he didn't feel so bad and decided to go down to the bus terminal to get something to eat. He went to the bathroom and didn't get any farther. He wasn't used to moonshine and was so sick that he sank to his knees and barely made it to the commode. Finally, he crawled back to the bed and plopped down, clothes and all, and soon was asleep.

He dragged himself out of bed the next morning and that picture blurred his view again. He was still angry, but decided he would go back and read what was being said about a local girl. "It was probably her engagement announcement by the smile on that guy's face," snarled Jason as he headed for the bathroom.

After shaving, brushing his teeth, and taking a bath he felt much better and headed to the bus terminal for breakfast. "I'll hunt that paper out of the trash. There is probably some reasonable explanation. I just got so mad because she didn't write me and I guess I just jumped to conclusions," thought Jason as he walked up the street to his office.

When he went in the office, Maggie Barker, his nurse/ receptionist, was already there straightening his desk. When he looked at the trashcan, it was empty.

"Did you already empty the trash, Maggie?" asked Jason.

"Yeah, and I threw all those old newspapers away. I saw you had been looking at them and had thrown some in the trash. I just dumped the rest. Why, was there something in them you wanted?" asked Maggie.

"I saw a picture of Lucinda Harmon in one of them. I wanted to cut it out. I didn't even get to read it. Do you know what it was about?"

"Oh! Gosh, I forgot. I was saving those papers for you for that reason. She and some man won something together when they spent a weekend in Huntington. I can't remember all of it, but I think it said something about a project. It was something that took several months to finish, I think."

"I'll go out and look in the dumpster. I might be able to find it," said Jason turning to the door.

"Sorry, the garbage truck ran just after I dumped our trash this morning. It would be like trying to find a needle in a haystack, even if you knew where the truck was taking it," said Maggie, smiling regretfully.

Maggie didn't know if Jason was seriously interested in Lucinda Harmon, but she did know that he had mentioned her off and on after the mud puddle incident. Maggie also knew that Jason had been receiving letters from Lucinda Harmon from Concord College.

"He must be writing to her," Maggie had mumbled to herself as she sorted the mail each day. In fact she had sent several letters from Lucinda on to Pittsburgh, while Jason was there.

Jason didn't want to tell Maggie how worried and upset he was, so he said, "Well, it can't be helped. Maybe somebody will tell me the next time I'm on the mountain."

Even though he asked several of his patients from

Bradshaw Mountain, he didn't get any relief. "You know, Doc, I ain't heard a thing about that girl cept that she was going some place with some people from the college, to get some kind of prize, I thank it was," related one woman seriously.

After that, he worked twice as hard and began to drink at night. Laura Blevins, a girl there in town, had been trying to catch his attention since he first arrived in Bradshaw. He had taken her to a movie once when he first came but hadn't repeated it again. She was out to get someone to marry her and she would do anything to make it happen.

One Saturday night, after having several beers in Gus's place, Jason called her and they went to Welch. They drove on to Bluefield to the LaSaluta Club and spent several hours dancing and drinking. They drove slowly back since Jason was still sober enough to know he should not be driving.

By the time they reached Welch Jason realized that he could not make it any further. They got a room with two beds at a motel at Big Four and spent the night. The next morning, Jason realized what a bad mistake he had made and rushed Laura out and straight back to Bradshaw. He felt very lucky that Laura was over twenty-one and he couldn't be forced to marry her.

Jason had hoped to shut Lucinda out of his mind and out of his dreams, but he realized that drinking and making stupid mistakes wasn't the answer. Now, he wished a thousand times that he had read the details in the newspaper story, but was too angry at the time. His prevailing thought was that he, Jason McCall, had been thrown over for a college kid.

"Who does that ignorant little hillbilly think she is, treating a doctor like that," fumed Jason angrily? Thus, his pride caused him to lose the thing he wanted more than anything in his life—Lucinda Harmon for his wife.

After about three weeks from the time he had seen the picture in the newspaper, he forgot his pride and called Concord. A pert young voice answered, "I've told you this before, Sir. Students may not receive personal calls except in family emergencies. Anyway, Lucinda Harmon is away on a school function and I don't know when she is expected back."

Jason quickly asked if he could leave a message. After some hesitation, the girl said he could. "Will you please tell her to call Jason McCall at his Bradshaw number. Tell her to call collect." Still not satisfied, he had written a short note, but it had now been two months and he'd had no answer to his letter and no phone call.

"Why don't you give up, stupid? The girl has found somebody else," Jason scolded himself. After that he tried valiantly to put Lucinda Harmon out of his mind entirely. He succeeded during the day, most of the time, but his dreams were filled with her image. Daily, he hoped that something would happen to completely erase her from his mind. Finally he began to long for the end of his contracted stay in McDowell County.

## CHAPTER 15

Daily he read the news and listened to the radio about the Korean War, now being waged thousands of miles away. He ached for those poor men who were involved. American soldiers had to have medical treatment and he knew that America would answer that call.

He had heard from many of his classmates of draft age who had been called up to fulfill that need. He also knew that some of them had gotten deferments because of the medical needs in the areas where they worked but others had gone without complaint. Jason suddenly thought that he would like to be one of those doctors.

He knew how desperately doctors were needed in Korea and he was so depressed and disillusioned that in this state of mind his reason for being in Bradshaw was no longer important. He often commented to Maggie that he'd be glad if he were called up. He also saw this as a chance to get away from all reminders of Lucinda Harmon.

"I'd enlist but I don't know if I can because of my contract with Island Creek Coal Company. They'd have to release me if I'm drafted, wouldn't they?" he asked Maggie.

Maggie didn't want him to go since the area needed a good doctor. "They would want you to get a deferment. You could, you know. Being a doctor in an area like this would certainly be grounds for deferment."

"Maggie, I don't really want a deferment. Besides, I was deferred in World War II, and the service won't let that happen again. Anyway, I'm no better than those poor men over there and the army must have doctors."

Therefore, when he received his draft letter from Uncle Sam, he felt a great sense of relief. He had lost his eagerness not only for his profession but for anything else. Now he could leave Bradshaw and never return and never think of Lucinda Harmon again, or so he thought.

His draft notice stated that he must report to Fort Dix, New Jersey within thirty days. He had to scurry around in order to leave by that time. He wanted to return to Pennsylvania early enough to have a week or two at home before his date to report to Fort Dix. Island Creek Coal Company offered to get him a deferment but he refused saying, "If those fellows can go over there and fight, I ought to be willing to help take care of them."

On the morning he left Bradshaw, Jason felt an aching sense of loss, like he was leaving something behind. It was a strange feeling and he wondered about it on the long drive back to Pittsburgh.

"Lucinda did not want to hear from me or didn't love me. If she did she would have written or called. She must have met somebody else," reasoned Jason aloud as he drove.

Once he almost turned around to drive to Concord College. "Maybe if I try my luck in person," Jason mused as he stopped the car and sat thinking,

"If I go there, I may not even get to see her. Even if I did see her and she tells me she is dating somebody else, it will just make me angry and right now, I'm just numb. If I saw her with that guy, I would probably beat the hell out of him and land in jail."

Jason pulled out and drove on through Beckley to pick up Route 19 towards Parkersburg before he pulled his mind away to think of what lay ahead of him. He wondered if he would have to go through basic training like an ordinary recruit or would he be sent straight over? He didn't know anyone or any other doctor who had been called up and would just have to wait until he reported for duty. He knew he would first go to Fort Dix, New Jersey. He wondered if that would be the jumping off place for his journey to Korea. "Well, it won't be long before I find out," mused Jason as he drove through Parkersburg.

When he pulled into the drive of the Wentworth Mansion at eleven o'clock that night, he realized that he had missed home. He had been dreaming of one day taking Lucinda all over the estate, showing her his favorite spots. Jason pulled his mind from that direction as he got out of the car and opened the trunk. Seymour, the chauffeur- com-butler, came hurrying out to the car smiling broadly.

"Ah! So the hunter is home from the hills, I see," teased Seymour.

"Yes he is, and with all his artillery with him," quipped Jason as he clapped Seymour on the shoulder affectionately. "You still got that secret fishing spot?"

"It is secret and it's going to stay a secret. I have to have some place to get you McCalls out of my hair? You people have too many things going on, so I can't get any rest here. You folks get me involved whether I want to be or not," stated Seymour tartly, and then grinned as he playfully slapped Jason. He followed Jason in, loaded with luggage.

Henry McCall crossed the hall from his study as he heard voices. "Ah, you're here. You made good time. We've been waiting on you." Henry smiled as he clasped Jason in a bear hug. "It's good to have you home, son."

Elizabeth came hurrying down the stairs, "Jason, Jason, you're home at last. I was afraid you'd turn into a mountain man down in those hills." She met Jason at the foot of the stairs to be engulfed in a bone-crushing hug from him.

"Good to be home, folks. I've missed you and the place. Where's Frank? I owe that young man a bout with those gloves he sent me last Christmas."

"Frank had to take some kind of exam this afternoon but he must have had something else to do. He should be here soon, though. He knew you were coming home," explained Elizabeth.

Jason, with Seymour's help, lugged all his paraphernalia up to his room. He then washed his hands and combed his hair before coming back down to eat the dinner they had saved for him. He met Frank coming in the door.

"Good evening, little brother," Jason said, looking up at the tall, broad young man who was his baby brother.

Frank grabbed Jason around the waist, lifted him off the floor, and swung him in a circle. "Who is the little brother, now?"

Jason grinned happily. “I reckon I am. How tall are you anyway? I’m six-two. So you must be what?”

“I’m six-foot, six inches in my socks and weigh 220 pounds. You didn’t take your vitamins, undoubtedly,” teased Frank as they made their way to the dining room.

Jason hadn’t really discussed his call with his parents but only told them he had gotten his draft notice and was coming home. Henry and Elizabeth had automatically assumed that Jason was going to try to get a deferment and would need their help. Knowing that he had influence in the city, Henry had stormed into the selective service office, complaining loudly. He was told to wait until Jason was home and then they would discuss it. Feeling sure he could get Jason a deferment, Henry made no further demands.

Jason was glad to be home so he could visit some of his instructors at West Virginia University and also his high school principal. When he did get to make the visits, they made much of him because of his willingness to serve. Jason had been feeling so down and this made him feel a little better.

He really didn’t know what was bothering him. He didn’t feel like he was afraid of the conflict but did dread the unknown. This didn’t account for his feeling of leaving something, which he just couldn’t shake. He finally decided that he just wasn’t over Lucinda and probably never would be.

“You’ll have to live with it, old man. That is just the way it is,” he chided himself.

The next evening, during dinner, Jason said, “Folks, I have to report to Fort Dix in seven more days.”

The silence around the table was like the aftermath of a storm. They were not surprised but were very upset. Thinking that Jason thought there was no way out, Henry blurted, “I’ve been to the Draft Board and you and I will go down there tomorrow. They didn’t talk favorably about a deferment since you were deferred in World War II, but there are ways to get around that. They just told me to wait until you came home.”

Jason looked upset. “Don’t you think you should have waited for my permission, Dad? I’m not a little boy anymore. I want to go. In fact, I would have enlisted long ago but I couldn't break my contract with Island Creek."

Although Henry, Elizabeth, and Frank begged and pleaded with him to get a deferment and stay out of the army, he refused. They went on and on about his ruining his life by not getting a deferment.

"Haven't you people been listening to the news? They need doctors badly. Those poor men are dying in droves because of lack of medical attention. I feel it is my duty and I wouldn't even think of a deferment," argued Jason.

The reasons given by Jason led to a long and vociferous debate, ending with his mother crying and his dad stalking off to his study. Finally, realizing that Jason fully intended to answer his country's call, they became subdued and tried to make his days at home as pleasant as possible. Knowing he could not make them understand that he just didn't care where he was anymore, he began spending more time away from the house until his time to leave.

Jason knew that patriotism was only one part of the reason he wanted to serve. He wanted to get completely away from everything that reminded him of Lucinda. He was now twenty-eight years old and he couldn't get that eighteen- year-old girl out of his head.

"She was probably right when she said our backgrounds were too different," thought Jason, remembering her innocence and beauty.

"I'll bet she isn't so innocent now. I gave her that damn book on sex. By the looks on that guy's face in that photo, she has learned a lot since we dated," grumbled Jason inside his head, but quickly jerked his attention back to the present with his mother's words.

"I can tell you are confused and bothered. Why don't you ask Janet to go for a drive with you? I'm sure she would, just as a friend," Elizabeth said with a smile.

"Why not?" thought Jason, remembering the last time he had seen Janet. Thinking she had probably grown up by now and wouldn't have expectations, he decided to call her. Janet's mother answered the phone and soon Janet was on the line, saying she would be ready in about ten minutes, but she would come through the hedge to his house. Jason wondered about this, but didn't say anything on the phone.

Jason went out to the car expecting to see a skinny dark girl with eyes too big for her face. When Janet came into the light beside the back patio, Jason stared in shock. The dazzling creature coming toward him was tall, willowy, and curved in all the right places. "Well, well, what have we here? Are you the Janet Washburn that I used to bandage, dose, and make gargle?" questioned Jason in amazement.

"One and the same, but don't try any of your medical procedures," said Janet, laughing as she gave him a friendly hug. They got in the car and drove into town, talking and laughing about old times and growing up. They ended up at the ice skating rink and spent an enjoyable hour practicing long unused skills. Jason learned that Janet had come to his house because she didn't want Olivia Washburn to know it was Jason she was going out with.

"She would be planning a wedding," said Janet. "You know how our mothers have always tried to throw us together. They just don't understand a friendship."

Jason smiled. "Yes, I know. For years all I heard was 'Why don't you ask Janet?' Or, 'Janet is free this evening. I'll bet she would enjoy the show.'"

The evening was enjoyable and Janet was available. Jason dated her for the rest of his time until he had to report for duty. He knew it wasn't fair to Janet. Even though Janet was trying to act as if she wanted to just be a friend, he knew it was more than that to her.

It wasn't fair, for he knew he could never really love Janet. He loved Lucinda. In fact, he cared so deeply that he knew if he was back in Bradshaw he would try to see Lucinda again, even if she had met someone else.

His mother planned a party for the following Saturday night and, of course, invited the Washburns, who had been their friends for many years. Janet, who had followed Jason around from the time she was in pigtails, was not only invited but was involved in planning the party, since she was so familiar to the McCall household.

The Wentworth Mansion was a second home to Janet and now it seemed natural for her to act as a hostess at the party. Toward Jason, she now acted pleasantly friendly but not possessive as she once had. She did not in any way act flirtatious, nor did she hang on Jason's every word. Jason was surprised that her presence did not make him uncomfortable as it had when she was a teenager.

"Some men may want a girl to have his coat ready before he asks, or his coffee poured before he gets to the table, but I don't," Jason said. "She's changed though and I couldn't be happier. I've needed someone to talk to."

Jason knew that his mother was encouraging an alliance between the Washburns and the McCalls; Jason and Janet to be the bond. In fact, he had always known what his mother had in mind but ignored it, since Janet just did not appeal to him as a girlfriend. She didn't before he met Lucinda and certainly not afterwards.

Jason had to admit, however, that she was good to look at, tall and curvaceous, with beautiful long legs. She had certainly changed from the skinny, freckled childhood shadow that dogged his footsteps over the years. Now Jason found she was not only nice looking but was also very intelligent. She and Jason had some lively discussions about many social issues, which he found enlivening.

They had gone to a movie, an opera, and ice skating and they had driven to Schenley Park, as if they were a courting couple like all the others parked there. They were not there to court, however, but instead, spent their time catching up on the happenings in each of their lives. Jason told about working in McDowell County but did not talk about Lucinda.

In fact, he didn't even mention her. That was just too painful and he didn't intend to discuss it with anyone.

The night of the party, Janet was the prettiest girl there and he danced with her several times and, after a few drinks,

Jason found himself inexorably drawn to her. They danced out on the patio and there, not exactly knowing how it happened, Jason found himself kissing her. It was very pleasant and arousing and Jason was surprised, since he had lost all interest in women after his disillusionment with Lucinda. So, with the drink and the moonlight, Jason found himself telling Janet that he was drawn to her. He promised he would write and asked her to write to him.

## CHAPTER 16

Jason left the next morning on a bus headed for Fort Dix and a year of an entirely different life. He arrived and, sure enough, he had his head shaved, was issued the usual olive drab uniform, and had to make the trek to the mess hall just like every soldier there.

His unit was put through a basic course of self-defense and use of weapons. This was to enable them to defend themselves and their patients should the need arise. Jason felt this to be the height of irony since doctors take an oath to heal the sick and save lives, but now he was getting instruction in how to kill.

That six weeks was the most grueling he had gone through in his entire life. Marching until he felt ready to drop and yet going on, wading through marshy, muddy fields, soaking wet, and rolling out of his cot all hours of the night for drill or inspection. This was about as rough as he wanted it and then some. He was too tired to write home or do anything but climb into the sack at the end of the day and hope he would be allowed a full night of sleep. Most of his buddies were looking forward to being shipped out.

"Surely we won't be expected to hike twenty miles in pouring rain," grumbled Sean Prescott of North Carolina.

"That's better than digging latrines for an entire unit or peeling potatoes for a squadron," Jason said, smiling tiredly. They all felt that regardless of what kind of conditions they had to practice medicine in, it would be better than basic training.

They left Fort Dix, crowded into an Air Force transport plane headed for Fort Ord, California, which was to be their "jumping-off" place. From there, they were flown in a much more comfortable plane to the Philippines. There, they had a three-day stopover, during which they were to rest. Rest wasn't on the agenda, however, or at least not for the doctors. In those three days, they were instructed in every aspect of what they should expect when they arrived in Korea. Close attention was paid to how they would react under pressure.

A week later, he arrived at his outpost about twenty miles north east of Seoul, the capital of South Korea. The compound was really a tent city or encampment. Tents even housed the company headquarters, but different tents than he had ever been in. They were sturdy, with both heat and air-conditioning, and very large. One long facility was the field hospital, composed of operating rooms, various offices and kitchen facilities. The next adjoining tent was the hospital, with wards that were really dormitories of closely spaced cots.

Like every other soldier, the doctors rolled out at six A.M. for roll call and then dashed to the mess hall in another tent. They even had a community room tent where they could shoot pool, play ping pong, and watch movies.

Jason knew he wouldn't get to spend much time there, after going through the hospital unit. Soldiers were constantly being brought in, patched up and flown out to a base hospital.

Even though he had asked Janet to write, Jason couldn't remember who had written the first letter, he or Janet, but he answered every one he received. Janet wrote amusing anecdotes of family happenings and intelligent comments about political and social issues, which Jason looked forward to reading. She also sent pictures, and his team of doctors and nurses were very struck by her beauty. Jason was pleased and wondered why he couldn't dream about her instead of Lucinda Harmon.

He didn't understand why, but since he had arrived in Korea he had begun thinking about the little church in McDowell County, West Virginia. In his mind he relived his visit to that little church. He had driven to Atwell and then turned left across the bridge and drove up Atwell Hollow all the way to the top to visit the Pruitt children. There the road leveled off into a long, narrow plateau. He drove along with his windows down. He came to a cemetery on the left of the road and as he passed it he suddenly he heard singing.

There just above the road was a little white church. The name above the door was Mount Zion Primitive Baptist Church. Children were playing at the side of the church under the shade of some giant maple and oak trees. He could see several mules and horses tethered to the bushes behind the church.

Jason pulled over and sat listening to the singing. He recognized some of the words as "It's that old time religion, old time religion and it's good enough for me."

He listened but heard no instruments. The true harmony of human voices raised in praise brought tears to his eyes. "What is this," he wondered since he was moved in some way that he had never experienced before.

"It sounds like everybody in the building is praising the Lord," he murmured in awe. Thinking that he'd never heard that in any church before in his life, he sat enthralled. Soon another song was started but he could not hear any words at first. Then he heard "and glory crowned the Mercy seat" and a female voice shouting, "Thank you Jesus." Again he felt tears on his cheeks but he wasn't sad. He had been there quite a while when some boys came running from behind the church house and stopped to stare.

He quietly shifted the car into gear and drove on down the hill. With that singing still clear in his mind, he drove on, not even thinking where he was going, until he saw another paved road. He then realized he had come out on Route 80 on the other side of Atwell Mountain which would take him back to Bradshaw.

He did not understand why the memory of that church and that singing had suddenly come to the forefront of his mind after all this time. Until he had arrived in Korea, the experience or feelings he'd had outside that old church had become a vague memory.

Now, however, he kept recalling how he had felt listening to their singing. The sound of that singing often floated to the surface of his mind at the most unusual times.

Like the time he and the team were operating and a bomb went off so close that all the lights went out and even the earth shook and trembled. He felt himself falling and things landing on him. The next thing he realized was hearing this singing,

"It's that old time religion and it's good enough for me." He got so calm and then somebody called his name and the singing stopped.

He began to wonder where he was, but wasn't afraid. He had several cuts, a concussion, and a badly bruised arm and shoulder. His team kept talking in amazement about his miraculous escape with all that medical paraphernalia atop him. Especially hazardous had been the resulting fire which had practically consumed everything around him while only his hair was scorched in places.

He didn't tell anyone, but he somehow had felt protected, and was puzzled by this reaction and the almost forgotten memory of a song in a church service.

Then not long after that, a young infantry man was brought in who had marched for miles. His leg was almost torn off by shrapnel. They had patched him up the best they could, but he was so full of fever and infection that he could not be moved.

Jason sat with him all that first night for some reason. He had told the nurse to take a break and didn't really understand it himself.

Later, he thought it was because he had found that the wounded man was a Davis from McDowell County, West Virginia. Anyway, sometime during the night, the young man began to thrash around and Jason had to restrain him.

Shortly, the soldier began to pray and then try to sing. It sounded almost like that same song, but was so low it could barely be heard. Jason began to sing the song himself and the soldier seemed to calm down and relax, then gradually drift off to sleep. The next morning he was so much better, the staff began to think he would survive and could soon be medi-vaced to the hospital in Tokyo, Japan.

Jason's buddies kidded him about having a miracle bedside touch since they had seen and worked with the soldier the day before and hadn't thought he had much chance of recovery. Jason didn't think about 'bedside manner' nearly as much as he thought of the horrors of war and its aftermath.

Days later a soldier from Iaeger, West Virginia was brought in with his head swathed in blood-soaked bandages. Jason cut the bandages free and the uncovered sight made him so nauseous that he had to walk outside for a few minutes. The soldier's left eyeball was protruding from its socket and the other was such a bloody mess that Jason first thought the eye was completely gone.

The nurse administered morphine and gave the soldier a pint of blood while waiting for Jason's return. As soon as his stomach settled, he went back in and asked the nurse to position a light at an angle that would give the best exposure. Then, he began the meticulous work of cleaning out the embedded debris from around the right eye before checking the nerves going to the bulging eye. He did not rest until he had cleaned both of the soldier's eyes as well as he could without doing further damage.

Jason's stomach had settled back to normal but he felt so much empathy, especially when the soldier began to moan and whimper in anguish.

"Poor fella. He's so young. I hope to God his eye can be saved," Jason said as he began the cleaning up after he had done all he could do.

When the chief doctor, Colonel Jared Franks, came and examined the soldier, he placed a curved plastic covering over his eyes and bandaged it securely around the soldier's head. Then Colonel Franks ordered the soldier to immediately be sent to the field hospital. Jason asked if he could go with the soldier in the ambulance since he had fluids being injected.

The Colonel agreed and Jason climbed into the ambulance holding bags of medicines aloft until they could be anchored to the fixed receptacles on the walls. They left the compound without lights blaring or sirens sounding. The enemy would target an ambulance as quickly as they would anything else and therefore even transporting the sick and wounded was hazardous. They arrived at the field hospital without mishap and quickly moved the soldier and Jason inside.

That soldier and that day became another major turning

point in Jason's life. The soldier was private Carl Justus from, Iaeger, McDowell County, West Virginia. He had a wife and three small children waiting for him at home. By the looks of his eyes, Jason wondered the entire trip if Mr. Justus would ever see his family again. He would be blind unless the doctors knew much more than Jason knew.

Fortunately, Dr. Randall Knowles was a doctor who had just finished his internship in ophthalmology at Johns Hopkins Hospital in Baltimore, Maryland, when he received his draft notice. Jason stood watching in awe as Dr. Knowles began the unbelievable task of sewing together the torn retina in the right eye before carefully seating the left eye more perfectly back into the eye socket. Then, Private Justus was again bandaged and put in a hospital ward to be later shipped to Walter Reed Hospital in the states.

Jason was so interested in the operation he had just seen performed that after discussing it with Dr. Knowles, he requested a transfer. Jason's commanding officer, Colonel Franks, agreed to the transfer and Jason spent almost all of his remaining time in Korea at the base hospital, working with Dr. Knowles.

Thus, circumstances led to Jason finding his true calling in the medical field. Private Carl Justus had been sent into his life for a season, but also for a very wonderful reason, in Jason's mind. The fleeting thought that, "Aunt Sarie Lester's Good Lord is in control of Jason McCall," came unbidden to his mind.

At first, Jason was with the group of doctors who were first responders because they were set up closest to the front lines of the battles. Further back there was a larger and better equipped hospital; still a tent however. That was where most of the amputations were done unless it was such a dire emergency that expediency was demanded and then Jason and his team did the amputation. This larger hospital was where Jason was now stationed since he worked with Dr. Knowles. Jason thought he would never have to return to the field hospital near the front but he was wrong.

One evening in late December of 1952, as Jason gratefully sank into his bunk shivering from the howling winds and extreme cold that had been with them for days. The sounds of much heavier artillery fire than the occasional noise of outgoing shells began and Jason covered his head and tried to ignore it. "Tomorrow will be busy," he sighed and snuggled deeper beneath his blankets. He finally dozed off to be awakened in a few hours and told to report to the field hospital. All personnel had been recalled as the wounded begin arriving. All through that night and all of the next day Jason and the other personnel were kept busy treating the many wounded which was the result of the heaviest battle aftermath that Jason had thus far experienced.

By late afternoon, trucks churned through the sludge and mud bringing in loads of men with severe frostbite along with other wounds and unloaded them at Jason's unit. All personnel was kept busy treating wounds an amputating toes and feet that were too badly damaged to risk gangrene. Every man had to have at least one of his toes amputated but most lost all their toes and sometimes a foot.

Jason was working on one young man, also from McDowell County, West Virginia, who had lost four toes and seemed so upset.

"Sergeant, it won't be so bad. Some people are born with only four toes," consoled Jason.

"Toes Hell! Do you think I'm upset because I lost some damn toes?" shouted the Sergeant. "My buddy gave his life so the rest of us could walk out of there. I'm not upset about me. We would have all been blown to hell and back if he hadn't been so damn brave." He was choked with tears as he continued, " I'm so damn sorry. It should have been me instead of him. He was one of the good ones," mumbled the soldier gruffly as he turned his head to hide the tears seeping from his eyes.

Jason didn't know what to say to such raw grief and compassionately squeezed the soldier's shoulder but moved on.

"Doctor." Jason was so full of compassion still that he did

not, at first, hear anyone speak. When "Doctor" was said the second time Jason was startled as he realized that he had been spoken to. Jason turned and seeing an officer standing before him, said, "Yes Sir."

"I am trying to locate Captain Jerome Petry and I was told he was here. Will you direct me to him?" asked the officer.

"Jerome Petry"...the man in that picture hugging Lucinda," Jason seethed as he began to look at the name tags on the end of each bed as the officer followed him. He stopped by the bed at the end of the first row and looking Jerome Petry full in the face for the first time, said, "An officer has come to see you Captain Petry." When the officer looked around as if seeking a seat Jason hurriedly found two chairs and sat down himself. He wanted to know why this 'Lothario' was getting special attention or whatever it was.

The officer introduced himself to Jerome Petry. "Captain Petry, I am Lieutenant Gray from the Division G-2 office. I need your after-action report. We usually wait until patients have been taken care of medically, but there are possible decorations in this case and , of course, there is the frostbite problem."

Jason looked up in amazement, and interjected, "Frostbite problem?"

Lieutenant Gray smiled grimly and explained. "Frostbite is considered a preventable condition. When anyone has it, he and his commander are in deep trouble and there is always an investigation. I've heard a lot about this case and I think the explanation is simple. However, I'm here to get the facts and that will enable the Division to preempt any inquiry from the top brass."

Jason found himself in rapt attention as Jerome Petry told his horrifying tale of the overwhelming Chinese attack. It had started about the time that Jason had heard the artillery fire. Jerome's Company A had been overrun by hordes of Chinese who broke through their final protective fire with heavy casualties but had kept on going to the rear. Company A had received light casualties even being run over but Jerome knew they had to move. His company was still connected by field telephone to Company C on the right and Jerome had decided along with the Company C commander to cross the small frozen stream between the two companies, and join forces.

Carrying their wounded they begin crossing the stream but the ice broke and plunged many of them into the waist-deep frigid water. Jerome ordered the others to seek a more shallow crossing but it too was knee-deep and over the tops of their boots. They had to make several crossings to retrieve their dead, their ammunition, and their weapons while on constant alert for an attack from up front or for the return of the enemy in the rear. Jerome had most of the men to dig in on the left flank of Company C facing the stream while he took a small patrol and went back across the stream to retrieve C-rations and blankets that had been left behind.

By now, Jerome and his men, were ready to drop and were suffering from frostbite but were steadily making their way when they had passed a Chinese soldier who they thought was dead. Just as the first line of the straggling, wounded soldiers passed, the Chinese soldier leveraged himself up on his elbow and with his remaining strength threw a grenade over the three or four feet separating him and the American soldiers.

"I didn't see a thing, but Staff Sergeant Jeremy White did. He threw himself atop the grenade, thus saving the rest of us. That 'dead' Chink died again in about three seconds."

Jason sat thinking, "Lucinda has found herself one hell of a man."

Lieutenant Gray kept taking meticulous notes as Jerome Petry told how the Chinese swarmed the front of Company C and tried to cross the stream in front of the repositioned Company A. The fighting was so heavy that the men had no time to warm up and shed their wet clothing and boots. It wasn't until later in the day that the snow, which had hindered vision all night, abated and they could call in directed artillery fire on the retreating Chinese from the fierce UN counterattack. The wounded and frost bitten men were then evacuated.

Lieutenant Gray closed his notebook and patted the bandaged leg outlined beneath the blankets and went on his way. Jason, who was already standing, gave Jerome Petry a penetrating glare, and then followed Lieutenant Gray out.

Jason thought he really hated the man but each time he made his daily rounds he found himself filled with pity and compassion for Jerome Petry and all the others.

"All these poor men have had to withstand this dreadful cold and still go into battle," thought Jason as he touched the cover on Petry's bed and moved on.

Jason thought of talking to Jerome Petry for several days. He wanted to know about his relationship to Lucinda, but he also realized that he should have been more professional. On his next round, Jason stopped by Captain Petry's bed and tried to converse with him as he was changing his dressing.

"I sure am looking forward to spring, aren't you, Captain?" asked Jason as he examined the patient's feet once again.

"Yes, Doc, I am. This winter will probably chill me as long as I live. I hope I can get past it but right now, I don't know if I ever will," replied the Captain forlornly.

When Captain Petry was on his feet Jason invited him to have a cup of coffee with him at the recreation center. They walked slowly along the few yards to the center chatting about the weather. Once seated with two cups of coffee and sweet rolls before them, Jason asked, "You are from West Virginia, aren't you?"

Captain Petry grinned broadly. "I sure am. How did you know? Oh! I guess you guys get all that information when we are brought in don't you?"

"Yes, we do get the basics. What part of West Virginia are you from?" questioned Jason and explained that he was a doctor in McDowell County before he came to Korea. He hoped this Petry fellow would give him the opening to find out about Lucinda, and his patience was rewarded.

Captain Petry sat for a minute, as if studying, then asked. "Did you know a girl named Lucinda Harmon? She was from

McDowell County—a place called Bradshaw?"

Jason felt the anger boil up in him but gritted his teeth and said with a grimace, "Yes. How do you know her?"

"I was at West Virginia University while she was a Concord College and there was a scholastic scholarship competition held in Huntington. Lucinda Harmon and I were selected to enter from our respective schools. She and I won. I won first place but she should have gotten it. She was much smarter than me. Her scholarship paid for two years of college for her though."

Captain Petry smiled and reflectively continued, "She was so shy, at first, that I couldn't get her to talk but when I told her about my girlfriend she really started talking. All she talked about was a doctor named Jason."

Suddenly Captain Petry opened his eyes wide in understanding. "Jason McCall! That's you, isn't it? Did you two get married?" asked Captain Petry as he looked but did not see a ring.

When he looked at Jason's blanched face and saw the astonished look, he asked, "What happened?"

Jason looked startled, "What do you mean? What happened? I never heard from her again after March."

"I don't understand that. I know she wrote. She told me that she wrote to you and her roommates kidded her because she wrote long letters every night," explained Captain Petry, looking puzzled.

"Do you suppose they got lost in the mail? Did you write her?" questioned Captain Petry. "She wrote me a short note after our pictures came out in the papers and said she still wrote to you but you were not answering."

Jason had been listening in stunned unbelief. "I had to go to Pittsburgh but I wrote her every day and even tried to call but somebody at the college switchboard would never let me talk to her," revealed Jason with a worried frown.

"After I went back to Bradshaw, I saw that picture of you and her in the newspaper and like a fool I didn't read the story. I just assumed she had dropped me for you, since I hadn't received any letters for months," explained Jason in bewilderment.

"Is that why you're here in Korea, Doc?" asked Captain Petry, with a knowing grin.

"Yes, and no," said Jason thoughtfully. "I had been really concerned about the lack of doctors over here ever since the war started. Then, when I thought Lucinda had thrown me over, I wanted to get away from Bradshaw as fast as I could. It was a great relief to get my draft notice."

Both men sat finishing their coffees, silently musing. "You mean you've never received any more letters at all from her since March of last year?" asked Captain Petry.

"No. I hadn't given her my parents address and she couldn't write to me in Pittsburgh but my nurse, there in Bradshaw, always forwarded my mail to me. I asked my mother every day but none came," explained Jason.

Neither man could understand what had happened but were both puzzled. Captain Petry was puzzled as to why Jason never got the letters which he knew Lucinda had written. Jason wondered the same thing not only that day but for many days and nights thereafter. He intended to talk to Captain Petry again about what he thought had occurred but two days later Captain Petry was sent back to the states.

After several weeks of worrying, Jason decided that since it wasn't Jerome Petry then something must have happened. He could think of no other explanation and decided to put it out of his mind.

Many nights Jason worked the night through, as did his buddies, when a battle was going on nearby.

Most of the time they were not in any danger from the actual battles, but once a woman came in with her baby who had a bomb concealed in its clothing.

Fortunately, it was found before it detonated. When the young woman was detained and questioned, they found that the baby wasn't her baby. Poor babies that were born to Korean girls and American soldiers were outcasts and nobody wanted them. This child was one of the outcasts.

When the army was made aware of this, the Red Cross was notified as well as several other charitable institutions. Soon an orphanage was started to try to take care of these poor helpless children until homes could be found for them. Jason and the other doctors and soldiers spent time playing ball and other games with these children.

Jason wrote Janet about the plight of these children and before long, there were requests for adoptions from people Janet had contacted. This made Jason so proud that Janet cared enough to work on this kind of project.

"She must not be as class conscious as Mother," thought Jason and was thankful.

Through their letters, Janet told Jason that she wanted children and wanted to take care of them herself, rather than have a nanny. Janet also revealed that she did not feel that living in the lap of luxury, as she always had, was a must for her happiness.

Even though this pleased Jason and made him feel even closer to Janet, he still had no thoughts of marrying her. Every letter he received from his mother made it very clear that she was elated with their communication with each other.

"You just don't really know Janet since she has grown up, Jason. She is an absolutely lovely girl, poised, educated, and very intelligent," wrote Elizabeth McCall.

"Mom is like a dog with a bone," mumbled Jason after reading her last letter. He had slowly reduced the number of letters to his mother until he only wrote about every three months. It did not stop his mother from writing him, however.

"Damn, Janet must be letting Mom read my letters to her. If she does, I'll stop writing her and I'll tell her so," stormed Jason when his mother had commented about the nice things he had said to Janet in his last letter.

Jason did complain to Janet and there were no further comments about anything he wrote to Janet.

## CHAPTER 17

When he left Bradshaw, the raw pain of Lucinda's betrayal was like an aching boil, needing a release. If Uncle Sam hadn't demanded his service and he had stayed in Bradshaw, Jason knew he would have tried to contact Lucinda again. It wouldn't have mattered if she had thrown him over for that other guy. She was just a kid and their time together had probably been puppy love for her, but not for Jason.

Sometimes he awoke in the night aching to see her dimples and shining blue eyes. He remembered her innocence, her honesty. If he had stayed in Bradshaw after that, he would have probably been a heavy drinker of that moonshine, which was so plentiful.

Here in Korea, it was in the long nights when he was off duty that he relived the first time he met Lucinda, and also the ten-hour period he spent with her, that one night in Welch. In his mind, Sterling Drive-In became a very special place along with the little park where they had sat on those cold stone benches and ate cheeseburgers and fries.

She hadn't eaten, though. Now, he remembered how she only nibbled on her burger and fries and then wrapped them both and put them in the bag. He hadn't thought about it then, but now he wondered if she had been ashamed to eat in front of him or was she saving it for next day.

"What if she didn't have enough money to buy food? She had lost weight," thought Jason. There was so much about Lucinda Harmon that he did not know and now never would know.

Tormented, he tossed and turned, to finally get up and hunt out a beer and take it outside to pace in the dark until the morning hours when he tumbled into bed worn out. When morning came, however, he put Lucinda out of his mind and kept busy doing the job he was sent to Korea to do.

Mail call was the highlight of the week for all the soldiers and Jason was no different .He really looked forward to the letters he received from Janet who wrote about the silly things that happened to people back in Pittsburgh that they both knew. Having grown up in the same place, they had lots of things to write about. He wished the letters were from Lucinda and often daydreamed that they were but then reality would set in and he cursed himself for being so stupid. To put it out of his mind he would write a long letter to Janet and in so doing grew closer to her.

Then, Janet got involved in helping find homes for the orphaned children and that gave them a project to work on together. He even called her several times from Korea about particular children but during the calls they talked about many other things. The more he got to know the grown-up Janet, the better he liked her and after a while, thoughts of Lucinda didn't bother him as much.

Jason, however, had never once thought of marrying Janet while in Korea, nor when he landed back in Pittsburgh either. But, Janet was so very pleased to see him when all members of the McCall and Washburn families met his plane and he was certainly glad to see her.

"It feels good to be welcomed back with open arms," Jason said beaming at all these people he loved so much.

He had to report to the military installations in Pittsburgh to be mustered out of the Army first and then he didn't have to do anything but rest and relax and somehow, he found himself spending most of that time with Janet. Jason didn't actively seek her out but it just seemed that she was there and they were together.

While in Korea, it was nice to get her newsy letters but it was different when he came home. He was weary and tired and it felt good that Janet seemed so very glad to see him.

She also had the ability to make him feel so important and manly that it was pleasant to be with her. Then too, she seemed to always be available when he wanted to talk or just drive around. One night, after having too much to drink and driving up in the hills, he proposed and was accepted.

The next morning he regretted it, but there was no backing out. Janet had told Olivia Washburn and his mother so the die was cast. Of course, both mothers wanted a big wedding and preparations were in full swing.

"Jason, if this bothers you, I don't have to have a big wedding," offered Janet. "As far as I'm concerned, we can sneak off and have a justice of the peace marry us."

"Our mothers would never speak to either of us again, if we did that. So, let's just let them have their way," Jason said with a sigh. "I'm going to be gone every day anyway. Did I tell you that I'm going back to school?" he asked.

Janet, who loved him very much, raised glowing eyes. "No, I didn't know. But it's all right with me. What are you going to study?"

"I, my dear, intend to become an ophthalmologist," Jason gloated as he stood at attention and saluted. When the families were told they were elated. This would mean that Jason and Janet would be living near Pittsburgh for at least one month, if not more, after their wedding.

Their fathers, Henry McCall and Joshua Washburn, got involved. As a surprise wedding present they rented a penthouse apartment for the newlyweds on Route 49 near Uniontown. The area was called Scenery Hill and was located on the outskirts of Pittsburgh. This would mean a shorter drive to West Virginia University where Jason would complete his studies before taking an examination in ophthalmology.

The wedding was set for April 1st to be held at the Shadyside Presbyterian Church on West Minister Place which was considered to be the church for weddings of the elite class. The wedding reception was to be held at Webster Hall at 5th Avenue and Bigelow Boulevard in the Oakland area of Pittsburgh. This was about a thirty minute drive from the church.

Elizabeth Wentworth and Olivia Washburn worked hand in hand and seemed to enjoy each other's company while working on this project. They were always friends but seldom did things together. Not since the death of little Josh Washburn had anyone seen them together so much.

When little Josh had died at the age of seven both families

were heart broken. During that time Elizabeth was the patient, caring, and thoughtful neighbor that Jason always thought she should be. He was very proud of her as was all the people who knew her. They had all hoped that this caring and compassionate attitude would continue.

A few months after the funeral, however, Olivia failed to include Elizabeth in an afternoon tea for some university ladies, and Elizabeth reverted to her old aloof, polite, and poised manner. She never mentioned her feeling that Olivia had slighted her but she never gave Olivia the opportunity to slight her again.

Jason and Janet were so busy from the day they became engaged until the day of the wedding that they had very little time together. Getting his scheduling and arranging his studies in ophthalmology at West Virginia University had kept Jason very involved.

While the penthouse was a fantastic gift for both of them, Jason was also surprised with a new car. Unwisely, Jason had complained about the damage all those muddy, rutted, mountain roads in McDowell County had done to his car. He was astounded, however, when a new car was waiting in the garage of the new apartment he and Janet were escorted to, after the wedding reception.

On the windshield of the car, Joshua Washburn had left a note stating that his son-in-law deserved a special present for his service in Korea. Jason's shiny black Chevrolet, almost brand-new when he went to McDowell County, was now a poor, dented, and scratched-up replica of the former show-piece, but Jason did not like feeling beholden to anyone, especially his father-in-law.

"Besides," Jason complained to Janet. "My old car runs well and I like it. I don't need two cars."

"I'll just tell Daddy that you don't want it, but it will hurt his feelings. He is so proud of you, Jason," explained Janet.

"No, don't do that, but I'll have to tell him not to give me expensive gifts. We need to learn to live on my income. That is very important to me," Jason said as he looked intently at

Janet. He did not want to hurt her but he wanted her to know how he felt.

Janet assured him that she understood and Jason was pleased that she tried so hard to fit into his way of thinking.

"I wonder if Lucinda would have been that easy to get along with," thought Jason and then gasped in astonishment.

"What is wrong with me?" Jason questioned himself. "I haven't been thinking about Lucinda, very much. Here I've been married just a few days and she pops into my head. I must be crazy."

## CHAPTER 18

Because of Jason's scheduled classes he couldn't be away very long and the honeymoon to Niagara Falls, paid for by their grandparents, lasted only five days. Jason promised a much longer trip at a later date.

"Just being with you, no matter where, is fine with me," breathed Janet twining her arms around his neck. Jason quickly disentangled himself since this kind of overture on Janet's part usually led to protracted delays.

"I'm sorry, Mrs. McCall, but I have to be in the classroom at WVU at eight o'clock Monday morning," explained Jason giving her one last lingering kiss.

Soon they were settled into the new apartment. Janet was engrossed in fixing up her first home and Jason was completely immersed in his studies. He spent every moment he possibly could at the university in order to complete his studies as quickly as it was allowed.

Jason and Janet grew close and enjoyed being together so much that Jason wanted to get his studies over with so they could have more time together. Janet couldn't wait for him to get home each night. She always had a nice meal cooked and was always dressed in a pretty outfit to greet him when he arrived.

Jason began to think he had been mistaken about loving Lucinda since he knew that he truly cared for Janet. He was able to talk to Janet about everything that occurred in his life except one thing. He did not mention Lucinda Harmon.

Before his six-week course of study was completed, however, they both had a taste of reality. Jason told Janet that he had to go back to McDowell County to finish up the internship he had originally signed to do. This upset Janet but since she knew how much Jason wanted to go she agreed; albeit reluctantly. That, however, was not the only fly in the ointment.

Janet started complaining about being sleepy all the time and she cried if Jason even looked upset. At first Jason suspected that she was using this to keep from moving to

McDowell County, but didn't know for certain. Finally, Jason insisted that she go to her family doctor. They were surprised when Janet was told that she was pregnant.

"How in the world did that happen?" fumed Jason. "I've used protection and we've also followed the rhythm cycle. Was the doctor absolutely sure?"

Janet ran from the room crying. Jason followed her into the bedroom and found her lying face down on the bed.

"What is wrong? What did I say that got you crying this time?" demanded Jason, whose nerves were also raw.

"You act like it's all my fault," moaned Janet without lifting her head from the pillow.

"All your fault! No, it is our fault, and I was just questioning how it could have happened when we have been so careful," explained Jason, sitting on the bed beside her.

"Come on now, quit crying. I'm not mad. We're just starting a family sooner than I had planned to, that's all," Jason said in a soothing voice as he massaged her shoulders.

Janet soon sat up and wrapped her arms around Jason. "Are you sure you aren't mad?" she questioned in an agitated manner.

"I'm not mad at you, Janet, so stop getting yourself upset. Come on, I'm taking you out to dinner," Jason said, pulling her to her feet.

"I have some pork chops thawed. What should I do about them," asked Janet on her way to the bathroom.

"Put them in the refrigerator. We'll have them tomorrow night. We'll go out and celebrate," Jason said with a smile. He was hoping that his show of pleasure would get Janet in a better frame of mind and it seemed to work. It didn't help his frame of mind, however, since he truly had not wanted a child, at least not for several years.

He and Janet decided that they would not tell their parents about the pregnancy until they were actually in McDowell County. They knew that both mothers would swoop in and put all kinds of stumbling blocks in the way of their return to McDowell County.

"I can just hear Mom now," said Jason. "'Do you mean that you want Janet to have her baby down in that horrid backwoods place? What is wrong with you, Jason? There may be complications with a first baby and then what will you do?'"

Janet laughed. "Mom would be the same. I guess they think that doctors in McDowell County don't go to medical school.

"They probably think you will only have a mid-wife to help you deliver," said Jason. "It wouldn't do one bit of good to tell them that Dr. Gavin Glovier is one of the best obstetricians in the Middle Atlantic States."

Jason was fearful that Janet would feel sick and one mother or the other would drop in during one of her nauseous bouts in the bathroom. That didn't happen, but one night Janet did feel faint during dinner at the Washburns, with the McCalls also present.

Jason gave Janet some cola with the explanation, "She visited the orphanage this week and probably picked up a virus from one of the children."

All the family members knew about both Janet and Jason's involvement with the orphans sent over from Korea, and assumed Jason was right.

Jason finished his course of study much earlier than it usually took most people, but he had worked constantly to do just that. Now, he was ready to return to McDowell County, West Virginia.

Jason had flown out to Korea in 1952 and returned in 1953 a more dedicated doctor. After what he had seen, and after the medical procedures he had been forced to use, the Hippocratic Oath had more meaning for Jason. He would be allowed to finish his contract as an ophthalmologist at Grace Hospital in Welch. He convinced Island Creek Coal Company that he would be fulfilling his commitment to them and to McDowell County by working at the hospital.

He explained that the training he had received and the skills he had acquired were to be used for the benefit of humanity. "By working in the hospital and treating the many eye problems in the county, I will be doing just that," stated Jason assuredly.

Even though he was eager to get started, he still had several details to work out. He called and wrote letters to Island Creek Coal Company officials about housing, salary, and numerous other details to be settled. He was informed that since he had asked to work in Welch, he would no longer be given free housing.

However, the company would rent living quarters for him until he could find permanent housing. Also, their furniture from the apartment had to be stored, until they found a permanent home. Then they could get a moving company to transport their furniture to Welch. They finally had their clothing and dishes packed, as well as the numerous details of a move completed. Early the next morning they were on the road to a much different life than Janet had ever lived before.

So now he was married, Janet was expecting a baby, and they were headed south to McDowell County. Jason was afraid the curves would give Janet motion sickness, and sure enough, she began to feel nauseous before they were out of Pennsylvania. He stopped and bought a coke and salt crackers, which had always seemed to help her, but as an extra precaution he took the curves very slowly.

Janet had also turned on the radio, which she said would lull her to sleep. Noting that Janet was nodding, he pleasantly passed the time as he drove along musing about his new position.

Suddenly the rich, mellow voice of Nat King Cole came through singing, "They try to tell us we're too young," and Jason quickly turned the dial as an image of wide blue eyes and honey blonde hair appeared.

"Damn," thought Jason. "There she is again and I thought that was all behind me."

He was almost at the Summersville exit when he thought, "I'd like to see Lucinda again. Maybe if I did I would realize that it was just infatuation, but then it might make it worse." Wrong or right, Jason knew that he would never find any peace until he saw Lucinda Harmon and then he hoped he could lay the past to rest.

From Summersville to Beckley, Jason pondered various scenarios as to opportunities to see Lucinda. As he drove from Beckley on down through the mountains, Janet awoke and was immediately carsick. Jason attended to her but his mind kept straying to Lucinda, wondering how he could meet her. He knew that his mind should not be on her, but try as he would, he could not stop himself from remembering.

He turned the radio low trying to soothe Janet back to sleep. This was a local station and the news was being given. Jason tried to concentrate on it. Presently it had his attention: a mine accident at Algoma, announced the newscaster. He knew that Algoma was north of Welch, but nearer Route 52 towards Bluefield. Probably the injured would be transported to one of the hospitals in Welch, or maybe on to Bluefield.

As he listened he could visualize the scene: black-faced men going in and coming out of the drift mouth bearing their wounded comrades on stretchers. They would be hampered by distraught relatives trying to get news. He had been called to Bartley to just such a scene the first time he was in McDowell County and he shivered at the memory. By the time he was in Pineville, he knew that twenty miners had been rescued and three men were still trapped but thought to be alive.

Janet had again drifted off to sleep and he drove on to Welch, trying to visualize how it would be to be married and living in Welch…thirty-four miles from Lucinda.

"Lucinda may not even be on Bradshaw Mountain. She's probably graduated from Concord and gone somewhere else to teach," argued Jason in his mind. He saw the historical marker describing the incorporation of Welch in 1893 and including the fact that it was named for Captain I.A. Welch, who led in coal development in the county and founded the city of Welch.

"McDowell County is coal. That's for sure," said Jason aloud.

Janet awoke with a start, saying, “What? What did you say?”

“It’s time to wake up and take a look at your new home,” said Jason with a smile, as he drove slowly down Route 16 into town.

He and Janet settled into the suite of rooms that had been rented for them in the Carter Hotel on Main Street. They were to stay there until they could find a house to rent. Jason parked in the lot behind the hotel and helped Janet out. She looked so tired and miserable that Jason was instantly contrite.

“I should be ashamed. Here’s my wife, carrying my baby, and I’ve been wondering how to see another woman. But I really just want to prove to myself that all of that is behind me,” thought Jason reasonably.

Their suite in the hotel consisted of a living room, bedroom, and bathroom and was nice and comfortable. When they requested dinner from room service it was brought up quickly and was good.

Janet smiled as she said, “Jason, this is really nice. My mother and yours will never believe this but I intend to tell them anyway.”

Much to Janet’s surprise the bed was very comfortable and the hotel was quiet. “I thought perhaps it would be so noisy that we would not be able to sleep, since it is right in the middle of town,” declared Janet as they ate their breakfast. Jason was concerned about leaving her all day but she assured him that she would get out and look the town over.

Jason walked the five blocks to the hospital and made his way to the administrator’s office. Mr. Phillip Rogers, administrator, greeted him at the door.

“Well, you made good time, Dr. McCall. Was your room all right?”

Jason shook the offered hand and took the seat indicated as he said, “The room was great and, yes, I finished up a little sooner than I first expected. I’m here now though, and eager to begin.” Mr. Rogers chatted for a few minutes and then the door opened to admit a small, narrow-shouldered man with sparse, graying hair. Mr. Rogers rose from his seat as did Jason.

"Dr. McCall, I want you to meet the Chief of Staff and backbone of this hospital, Dr. Charles B. Chapman, and Dr. Chapman, this is your new ophthalmologist, Dr. Jason McCall." Jason grasped the older man's hand in a firm handshake. He was very impressed by the intelligent eyes that gazed at him in an appraising manner.

"Welcome aboard, Dr. McCall. I hear you've just returned from Korea," said Dr. Chapman.

"Yes sir, that's right. I've been back a few months but haven't had time to think about it much. I went back to the university and finished up a course in six weeks. Of course, I had a lot of hands-on learning while in Korea," declared Jason with a smile.

Dr. Chapman studied him before saying, "I hope you don't mind but I called several of my friends at the university before I agreed to hire you. I believe in being right up front and I wanted to know if I was getting a good man. You wouldn't be here if I hadn't been assured that you were qualified."

Jason was momentarily stunned at this brusque statement, but then solemnly said, "I wouldn't have asked for the job if I didn't feel qualified to do it, sir."

"Good, good. Now that the air is cleared and all that is said and done, come along and I'll show you where you will be working," said Dr. Chapman as he walked hurriedly from the room with Jason right behind him.

Jason found his workplace was three rooms abutting the suite of rooms used by Dr, Chapman and immediately wondered if he was really trusted.

"I guess Dr. Chapman put me here so he could keep an eye on me," Jason mumbled angrily.

Dr. Chapman abruptly stuck his head around the door. "No, you're not here so I can ride herd on you. This wing has the best facilities except for the surgical wing and that is why you are here. You are starting a new service here and your office should be nice." Dr. Chapman suddenly gave a lopsided grin and asked, “Satisfied, young man?”

Jason smiled sheepishly. “Yes Sir, I am, and thanks for the explanation.”

From that terse beginning, Jason felt that he had found a wise counselor and a true friend. Jason worked three days with the help of Trudy Simmons, the nurse hired to work with him, and finally had his offices set up to his satisfaction.

## CHAPTER 19

Soon Jason was swamped with patients from all over McDowell County and Wyoming County. He even had people coming from Mercer and Mingo Counties. When Jason commented about this to Dr. Chapman his explanation was, "Until you set up practice, Dr. Blaydes in Bluefield was the only Ophthalmologist that these southern counties had access to."

In the evenings, Jason enjoyed the company of Kyle Bender. He first met Kyle when he came to the office to have his eyes checked. There seemed to be an instant rapport between them and they had arranged to go bowling together before the visit was completed. When Jason learned that Kyle was a lifelong resident of Welch and knew most of its citizens, he was extra pleased.

Kyle, through his acquaintance with Charlie Beamer, helped Jason buy the house which stood empty right next door to his own house. As soon as the deal on the house was settled Jason and Janet moved in. Their furniture from the apartment in Pittsburgh was shipped and they had three rooms completely furnished.

Soon Kyle and his wife, Rita, were not only next door neighbors but friends and mentors to both Janet and Jason. Since Janet was having problems with her pregnancy, Jason now felt easier about her. Rita was a nice, competent lady, who was five years older than Janet. To Janet this difference in years gave Rita an aura of wisdom that Janet felt she lacked.

Thus, a close bond of friendship developed between the two couples. Rita went shopping with Janet and introduced Janet to all her friends. Janet became a member of Rita's bridge club and the Methodist Church's Ladies Circle. Now Janet bragged about being a part of the town.

Jason promised Janet that they would look for furniture for the other bedroom and the den on the weekends. He felt that this would give him something to do and help to keep his mind off of what he was trying hardest to avoid—thoughts of Lucinda Harmon.

One weekend he asked Janet to drive down through the mountains with him, intending to go up on Crane Ridge and show Janet that little church. He would never forget the experience he'd had while listening to that congregational singing. He still remembered the feeling that had come over him, and the tears that had flooded his eyes as he listened.

There had been something about that church or that experience that drew him then and still did. He had experienced the same thing in Korea when that bomb exploded. Even thinking about that experience brought such a peaceful feeling to his mind. Jason had always wondered why and wanted to find the answer.

No matter how often Jason asked Janet to drive to Bradshaw with him, she always had some excuse. "Those hairpin curves make me so sick, Jason. I don't want to go down there anyway. It's just more coal and coal dust. I don't see any reason for you wanting to go, unless there's some girl down there you want to see," said Janet giving him a quizzical look.

Jason was momentarily stunned. Had someone told Janet about Lucinda, he wondered. He quickly tried to explain to Janet the experience he'd had listening to the singing he had heard outside Mt. Zion Primitive Baptist Church.

"Janet, I've never felt such peace. I don't know how to tell you. It was like I loved everything I saw," explained Jason as he groped for the words.

Janet either didn't want to hear it or something, since she replied, "Jason, you've always loved everybody. There's nothing new about that," she teased and then suddenly jumped up and ran to the bathroom.

Jason never tried to talk to her about that experience again since he detected a reticence on her part to hear anything good about Bradshaw or anywhere in that area. "There has to be some explanation for her attitude. I know I've never mentioned Lucinda to her. Mom could have though. It would be just like her to do something like that," thought Jason but still wondered if that had happened why Janet had never told him.

Since Janet was not having an easy pregnancy, Jason had finally agreed to let her put their wedding picture in the Welch Daily News. He did not see the need for it, but because she was so ill with morning sickness, crying jags, and constant nausea, he relented.

He didn't want that picture in the paper, not down here, but Janet insisted that his former patients would be happy to see it. He acquiesced, but still felt like it was wrong for some reason.

Soon they were all settled in and Janet was satisfied to stay home in the evenings because most of the time she felt so nauseous. Jason, however, was restless. He joined a bowling league and went bowling one night each week, but he was still on edge. Finally, he gave in to the urge to try to see Lucinda. This same urge had been drawing him since he first returned to McDowell County.

Each evening he would take a drive. "I had a meeting or I was tense and decided to drive around a bit. I had a rough day," was his explanation if he came home later than usual.

He first drove to the top of Premier Mountain. The next evening, he ventured a little farther and drove over to Coalwood. The following evening he drove to English, and finally by Friday, his final destination, which was Bradshaw.

Then he started driving to Bradshaw almost every week. He hadn't seen or heard anything about Lucinda but he still found himself going there each week. This week had seemed to last forever. He was anxious to get started to Bradshaw but what happened while there didn't help at all.

He arrived and made his usual rounds of the doctor's office and the bus terminal, ending up in the drug store. Today he changed his routine somewhat, and stopped at Gus's place, then the taxi stand and chatted with the deputy sheriff who stopped by there every evening.

Deputy Stevens was a friendly young man who remembered

him from his previous stay in Bradshaw. Jason was glad to see him. Deputy Stevens knew about everything that went on in the Bradshaw area and Jason hoped he would mention Lucinda Harmon.

Today, Deputy Stevens walked with him to the drugstore, telling him on the way about last peddling day. In the drugstore, Jason sat on a stool and ordered a fountain coke but felt on edge for some reason. He felt so restless that he got up to leave and the deputy rose with him. His exit from that place would be stamped in his memory for the rest of his days.

When Jason, with Deputy Stevens behind him, pushed the door open he almost knocked Lucinda Harmon to the pavement. Lucinda looked at him with wide, startled eyes, and mumbled "Jason" before slowly crumpling towards the asphalt. Jason reached to save her but was knocked almost off his feet by the strong muscular arm of a tall glaring red-headed man.

"Get your damn hands off my wife, you son-of-a-bitch," snarled the man as he lifted Lucinda into his arms and stalked down the street.

"But, I'm a doctor. I was going to help," protested Jason.

"I know who you are, damn you. You'd better get out of Bradshaw and stay out, if you know what's good for you," shouted the departing man.

Jason stood there in stunned amazement until Deputy Stevens said, "He didn't mean any of that, Doc. They're still practically newlyweds. He had a time getting her to marry him. She finally agreed about three months ago and he's been like an old mother hen ever since. Really, he's just so crazy over that girl that he was scared to death. He's a real nice guy."

Jason made no answer as he looked for his car, which seemed a mile away as he looked down the street. He clenched and unclenched his fists, knowing his face was the color of old bricks, as it always turned when he was angry. He lifted his hand in farewell but kept his teeth clenched tightly together and began his walk. His legs were like wet spaghetti as he tried to stiffen his steps into a march. He didn't want all these people to see him make a fool of himself. When he was inside his car, he frantically jabbed the key into the ignition.

"I have to get away from here before I go back and beat the hell out of that damn barbarian." Jason was almost screaming as he drove out of Bradshaw and up Route 83's winding road towards Bartley. He felt like the top of his head was going to explode as heat suffused his face.

At Atwell's swinging bridge he pulled over and got out. Taking deep breaths, he walked back and forth, trying to calm down. It was unthinkable that his sweet, innocent, beautiful Lucinda was married to that uncouth, red-headed hick.

"That stupid jerk almost caused her to fall flat on the sidewalk, just to push me away," fumed Jason bitterly. In his mind, Jason relived the entire incident from the time he came through the door at the corner drugstore.

"He said he knew who I was. Did Lucinda tell him about me...us?" Pounding the side of the car with his fist, Jason worked out his frustration. When he saw a dent in his car and his knuckles bleeding, he pulled out his handkerchief to wrap them. He remembered the deputy saying they hadn't been married but about three months. The deputy had also said that Lucinda wouldn't agree to marry him before.

Suddenly his own wedding picture flashed before his eyes. Three months ago Janet had won his reluctant approval to put their wedding picture in the paper. "Damn, damn...she tried to wait for me but I was too damn stupid to wait. That picture must have made her think that I hadn't cared for her at all. Because of me she married that...that red-headed idiot."

Jason walked around and around deep in thought and then climbed back in his car and drove slowly toward Welch. "I'll not be back to Bradshaw for a long time, if ever," he promised himself.

When he married Janet, he knew he didn't feel what he thought a man should feel to marry a girl. His mother was delighted and so was Janet. Now Janet was pregnant and he didn't really want a child. He couldn't understand it. He had always used protection and he just didn't see how she could have gotten pregnant, but she was. Everyone in both families was ecstatic, as was Janet. He should be happy too, but he was numb.

He knew he liked Janet. It was really more than like; he really cared about her. However, it was Lucinda that he had dreamed about in Korea and now he had started dreaming about her back here.

"She wouldn't have married that stupid hick if she hadn't seen that picture. Damn...damn," Jason fumed and then suddenly became quiet.

"What difference does it make, whether she is married or not. I'm married, so she might as well be. Jason, old man, you can shut the door on that daydream because it is not going to happen."

Jason made slow progress back to Welch, wondering all the way if he could stand to live in Welch, knowing that Lucinda was in Bradshaw. He knew he had to, since he had committed himself.

"I'll have to deal with it and I may as well get started by putting her out of my mind for good." He turned on the radio in an attempt to keep from thinking and was transported back with the words of one of their favorite songs. "I hear singing and there's no one there." and that long ago night with Lucinda flooded his memory. He quickly switched off the radio, rolled down the window, speeded up, and went racing around one curve after another, as if pursued.

When Jason first met Lucinda Harmon, he realized she was the most innocent girl he had met in his entire life. He had always thought that girls raised on farms were very knowledgeable about the physical side of relationships, but this was not true in Lucinda's case.

He recalled that time in Welch when he had taken Lucinda out and had kissed her passionately on the steps to her apartment. He realized then that she had no idea where that could lead. Her childlike innocence seemed to bring out a protective feeling and he abruptly released her. Whispering "good night" he went whistling down the steps.

Later when he had dated her every night for one full week, she had no idea what he was about when he tried to get a little more intimate. When he slid his hand around to cup her breast, she immediately jerked back with big startled blue eyes.

"What are you doing? I don't want you to do that. My sister, Odell, said nice girls didn't let men do things like that. I guess you don't think I'm a nice girl, do you?" questioned a puzzled Lucinda.

Jason was instantly contrite and apologized. "Lucinda, honey, I can't lie to you and say I don't want to do that and more, but that doesn't mean that I think you are immoral. I know you're a nice girl and I don't want to hurt you or do anything to make you feel bad. That isn't wrong though, between people that love each other."

He stopped at the shocked gasp coming from Lucinda. "I mean, after they are married, of course."

Now Jason looked back on that scene and smiled in amusement as he thought that many people think that dating is going all the way. Some of his friends argued that couples don't really know if they love each other until they've had sex. Jason knew that was untrue, however, because he knew he loved Lucinda and he certainly had not had sex with her.

"Lucinda must have read some of that book. She was more relaxed the last two nights we dated," reflected Jason.

"I should have just gone ahead and if she became pregnant, Mr. Harmon would have let Lucinda marry me, if he didn't shoot me first," mumbled Jason. These thoughts were too disturbing, and Jason jerked himself out of his reverie to get back to business.

Jason knew that he had to get all this off his mind and try to be a good husband to Janet. He now had positive proof that Lucinda was also married and probably pregnant, since she had fainted.

"Maybe seeing me in that unexpected way caused that kind of reaction," thought Jason. Knowing it would make no difference regardless of the reason he shut his mind to it and started thinking about Janet and the baby she was carrying.

After that, Jason felt guilty every time he thought of Lucinda, and he realized he had to do something to get himself straightened out. None of this was Janet's fault and he needed to concentrate on her. He thought that seeing Lucinda one more time would help, but he was certainly wrong. Now he knew he should never have gone to Bradshaw, but he had and it was over.

He wondered if Lucinda had finished college. He grimaced as he remembered that picture in the Welch Daily News that had destroyed his dream. She hadn't married that guy though. He had treated Jerome Petry at the field hospital in Korea. That poor fellow had lost his toes and Jason hated himself for being so quick to jump to conclusions.

Jason had learned the true story from Jerome Petry about the reason for that picture. Jason remembered Jerome saying, "Lucinda really should have won first place instead of me. She was much smarter. I think it was because she was so shy and did not want to look up when the camera was focused on her."

For some reason Jason had always believed she was right back in McDowell County and he didn't know why. Now he wondered if he had some sixth sense when it came to Lucinda Harmon.

He had left Bradshaw in 1952 and not knowing it then, was destined to return a year later to find that Lucinda had truly tried to wait for him but he hadn't waited for her.

His thoughts went around and around in the things he should not have done, like shutting his mind to the urge to try again to contact Lucinda, dating Janet, writing to Janet from Korea, but most of all he should never have doubted Lucinda without checking further. There would always be an aching empty spot deep inside that he could reveal to nobody; all due to his own lack of judgment.

"Aunt Sarie Lester would have said, 'You've made your bed and now you have to lay in it,'" Jason admonished himself.

"She would probably tell me to 'Look to the Lord and make the best of it' since that was her attitude about her cancer," said Jason resolutely.

By the time he arrived back in Welch he had already formulated a plan of action and that was to become a very community minded citizen.

"I'll join the Lions Club and the Chamber of Commerce. I'm already on a bowling team, and Janet and I need to become regular church attendees," Jason planned aloud.

The next evening he called across the hedge to his next door neighbor, Kyle Bender, asking if he and his wife, Rita, would like to attend a movie. Kyle was a nice man in his thirties and Janet liked Rita and their daughter, Katie. Rita was very helpful to Janet since she had already had a child and could ease some of Janet's worries about her pregnancy.

Although they had always attended the Presbyterian Church in Pittsburgh, he and Janet liked the Benders so much and also many of the people in their church that they started attending the Methodist Church to be with the Benders. They left their membership, however, with the Presbyterian Church in Pittsburgh.

"Mom would really be upset if she knew we were attending a Methodist church," said Janet as they sat talking one evening.

Jason grinned, "If you think your mom would be upset can you imagine what mine would say? People of royal lineage only go to well-established churches. I'm surprised Mom isn't a Church of England member."

Both Janet and Jason knew what an adherent to social class and etiquette Elizabeth was and laughed as they thought about her outrage.

"Mom's pretty bad," said Janet, "but Elizabeth is almost a fanatic. Isn't she?" finished Janet thoughtfully.

Soon Kyle had Jason attending city council meetings, school board meetings, and socializing with all the "movers and shakers" of the town. Jason gradually grew to realize that the leaders in the town were also the leaders in the entire county.

Kyle took him to a Forty and Eight dinner and there he met Harry Camper, Colonel Ballard, and Sam Christie. Soon, several of these men were including him in functions at the Sportsman's Club and inviting him to play golf. Jason did not have as much time to spare as most of them seemed to have but he accepted invitations as often as possible.

All these community and civic organization visits, plus the church activities and Janet's pregnancy, filled Jason's days so full that he thought of Lucinda less and less. In fact, about the only time he thought of her was when he had a patient from over that way, which wasn't very often.

Rita Bender's support and friendship were really appreciated by both Janet and Jason. Rita made their orientation into Welch society much easier. Kyle Bender had gradually gotten Jason involved in all the meaningful activities of the town. Also, he and his wife kept the McCalls supplied with fresh vegetables from their garden. In return, Jason and Janet tried to repay them by taking them out to eat or to movies or other recreational activities, as long as Janet was able.

When Janet's morning sickness had abated, Jason asked if she would like a trip home to see her parents. Janet, of course, was eager and so Jason made plans to take a trip to Pittsburgh. He felt that Janet's version of how civilized McDowell County really was might convince his mother to come down to visit. They had repeatedly begged both sets of parents to visit but they had always declined with some reasonable excuse.

"Janet, go to the Chris Ann or Beryl Shop and buy a couple of nice outfits to take home and make sure our mothers know where you bought them," ordered Jason when she planned a shopping trip with Rita Bender.

Janet laughed. "They will never believe it. I can hear Mom now saying, 'You stopped in Parkersburg, didn't you?'"

"I'm going to tell them that the only way they will get to see their grandchild is if they come on a visit. I'll bet that will do the trick," said Janet with assurance.

That is exactly what Janet told them when they were all having dinner with the Washburns. Elizabeth McCall looked across the table at Olivia Washburn, "I guess I'll take the chance if you will go with me," she said.

Olivia laughed. "We'll just all go. If Joshua and Henry go with us I'm sure those wild people won't bother us."

"Wild people! Mother, you should be ashamed of yourself. You have never met any of those people and you've already judged them to be wild," sputtered Janet indignantly.

"I think you will be very surprised, Olivia," defended Jason, who hadn't known before that Janet's mother seemed as biased as his own mother.

Trying to diffuse an escalating situation, Henry broke in with, "This is certainly good news. I've wanted to visit down there ever since Jason was there the first time, so set a time and I'll do the driving."

After that, the rest of the evening was spent in making plans for their future visit.

# CHAPTER 20

Jason was very pleased that Island Creek had released him from his original contract. After his Korean experiences and the required six weeks of extra training in vision problems, he just could not see himself going back into general practice.

Jason was very upset when he thought he would have to go back into general practice. He wanted to use his specialize training on eye diseases and treatments. He had sought advice from his instructors who told him to write to Island Creek Coal Company and they would also write. Each would ask for consent to finish out his contract in ophthalmology.

Jason had been informed that Grace Hospital in Welch wanted to start an ophthalmology service. Dr. Weimer, who was still a friend and mentor, suggested that he get Dr. Randall Knowles, whom he had trained under in Korea, to write a letter for him. With Dr. Knowles' letter, the instructors' letters, and one of his own, Jason was allowed to finish his contract with Island Creek by working at Grace Hospital in Welch.

Many people in McDowell County had diseases of the eye and heretofore had to go all the way to Bluefield to find any help. Now, Jason was very pleased with his new position and the opportunity to practice his skills.

There was a particular case of macular degeneration he had diagnosed that gave him concern. Jess Harper had come in saying he had gotten something in his eye at work. He had a small sliver of metal in his left eye but when Jason removed it, he found that Mr. Harper had an advanced stage of macular degeneration. Jason told him what he suspected and told him he needed to go to a Dr. Blaydes, in Bluefield, for further tests.

Mr. Harper sat stunned for a few minutes and then said, "I guess it's just meant to be, Doc. My wife has told me for years that something bad was going to happen to me if I didn't quit drinking, fighting, and cussing. I didn't pay no mind though cause I knew I was bound for Hell anyway. I'm fifty-five years old and don't figure I've got enough time to make up for the thirty-five years I've been carousing. I guess I'll just have to face the music now. How long do you think it'll be fore I go plum blind, Doc?"

"Mr. Harper, there are new treatments in the offing and I'm sure Dr. Blaydes can give you more information. Let's not think the worst just yet, and besides, you still have vision in both eyes. Let's hope Dr. Blaydes can treat you to slow down the degenerative process."

When Mr. Harper went back into the waiting room and told his wife, she was shocked at first and then Jason heard through the door which Mr. Harper had left ajar.

"Jess, we'll just go over to Mom's and get her to fix some of that fever bright that she used on Grandpa's eyes. That will probably do as much good as anything," said his wife with assurance.

Two elderly women, who Jason knew to be the Franklin sisters, were sitting to the side near the door, and raised their eyebrows knowingly.

Then Ruby, the elder of the two, said, "I'd rub a little butter on his elbow, if it was me, wouldn't you?" They both chuckled softly not to draw attention to themselves. However, like many elderly people, their voices carried more than they thought and they received a glaring look from Mrs. Harper, but a loud guffaw from Mr. Harper.

Unaware that they had been heard, the reply was, "One would do about as much good as the other, to my way of thinking. Our mother did use fever bright, though. You remember how she treated Uncle Charlie that time?" questioned Gracie of her sister.

This comment caused Mrs. Harper to shake her head smugly and say, "See there. Most old people know better remedies than these doctors do." Jason would have liked to listen further but another patient was waiting on him.

"What is fever bright?" questioned Jason aloud, and his patient turned startled eyes in his direction.

With each day and each new patient Jason gained another insight into the culture of McDowell County. Some ways and practices were provoking and thoughtful and others were hilariously funny.

He hadn't heard about tooth drawers until Jim Runyon from out of Bartley Hollow told him about his dad having a tooth taken out by a tooth drawer.

"Pa sent me to get this man; I think his name was Taylor, but I can't remember for certain. Anyway, when he got to the house, he told my mother to get the moonshine. We always kept some for medicinal purposes, and I swear, it seemed to me like he poured a half quart down Pa.

Then the tooth drawer pulled out these long handled things, exactly like a pair of pliers, and Pa jumped right out of his chair. Well, it took both of my uncles to hold him even after they tied him. Then, buddy, that feller got a good hold on that tooth and give a quick yank, and blood flew everywhere and that feller went right backwards. He landed on his ass against the door on the other side of the room." By this time, Jason and Mr. Runyon were both doubled over with laughter.

"You made that up didn't you, Mr. Runyon?" queried Jason.

"No sir, I didn't. I swear on the Bible that it's the truth. I was just a boy but I shore remember that and I've had a mortal fear of dentists ever since." Mr. Runyon smiled showing good solid teeth.

"See, I've brushed my teeth twice a day ever since. Back then, I'd have to put baking soda on a rag and scrub my teeth. It tasted awful but it was better than a 'tooth drawer,'" Mr. Runyon said, while laughing hilariously.

Mr. Runyon's tale kept Jason amused for the rest of the day since his images had been so vivid and graphic.

Later that evening, Jason's thoughts turned once again to the people and their habits and customs in these mountains. He had run into these home remedies, prejudices, and "old wives tales" here in McDowell County and was always amused and often puzzled.

He also knew that the many different religious denominations and sects had many different beliefs, but almost all of them here in the mountains believed in faith healing. It wasn't mentioned in the Methodist Church here in Welch, where he and Janet attended with the Benders, however. He thought that perhaps it was more widespread in the less populated rural areas.

"The tops of the mountains don't usually have the bigger established churches anyway," thought Jason, guessing that many of those churches had probably left the organized bodies such as Catholic, Presbyterian, and Episcopal faiths.

Jason also knew that even though many of these churches were small as to congregations, they were fiercely loyal to their beliefs. They had definite beliefs or doctrines which were fixed in their very souls, it seemed. There was a sureness in their speech when they talked of the "hereafter" or the "glory world."

Primitive Baptists like Aunt Sarie Lester very confidently stated that, "God is love and He ain't no respecter of persons. He loves everybody the same. It does my heart good to know that when I go on to the 'glory world' all the people I love will be there with me."

Jason also knew that people like Aunt Sarie were branded as "No-Hellers" and yet she was dearly loved by everyone who knew her. Jason had even heard other people say, "I hope Aunt Sarie is right but I can't see how in the world people can lie, cheat, and steal and still go to heaven when they die."

Aunt Sarie's funeral had been conducted in her home. Jason had learned that most of the funerals on the tops of the mountains were held in the homes. He had not been able to attend Aunt Sarie's funeral. She had died while he was away from McDowell County and he couldn't have gotten back even if he had known about it.

Since then he always tried to at least drop by the home when any of his patients died. Death and life were accepted and people got on with their lives but still it was traumatic, especially for children. He suddenly remembered Lucinda tearing up when she talked about the trauma of knowing about her grandfather being embalmed at home.

"When we get settled in good I'm going to do some research. I find this all very interesting," mumbled Jason when his thoughts turned to such things.

Religion wasn't the only strong belief among McDowell Countians. Practices in medical care also caused him much concern. Some of the old remedies and ways were not only painful but in some cases very unsanitary.

He had gone to deliver a baby up on Pea Patch, located on the top of Three Forks Mountain, and a midwife, called a "granny woman," was already in attendance. She had already dosed the mother with some kind of tea and given her a dose of Epsom salts. The woman was in terrible pain. When the baby arrived so did all the contents of the poor woman's bowels. That was the worst mess that Jason had ever encountered. He remembered that smell for days and could barely stand to eat.

Jason had also found some very different interpretations of biblical verses. Some churches did not allow their women to wear even a wedding ring but thought nothing about the dipping of snuff or smoking cigarettes. Also, he found it strange that dancing and playing cards were considered sinful, but cheating people in a trade was just good business.

One church on Panther Creek had a jockey ground (a place where trading of horses, dogs, etc. was conducted) right below the church house. The husbands brought their wives to church on their mules and horses, or sometimes in cars, but the husbands spent their time at the jockey ground. Often the wives found their rides home had been traded for a good hunting dog, a milk cow, or whatever their husbands had deemed to be the most attractive. Often the next morning when the effects of the moonshine had worn off, the husband was very upset because he had made such a bad trade.

Jason learned about the barter system which worked so well on the mountains and sometimes in the towns. If a man needed a heifer calf to raise for a milk cow, he would often trade work for the calf or offer some lambs, a fattening hog, or whatever the owner of the calf was willing to accept in trade. Most things that a family needed were acquired in this fashion except for flour, sugar, salt, flavoring, baking powder, baking soda, and coffee.

One time Jason made his house call to see Aunt Sarie Lester late in the evening and had found several men and women there. When he saw the crowd as he drove up, he immediately thought Aunt Sarie had died. On entering the house, he found she did seem worse but certainly not dead. The women were there to sit-up with the sick and the men were there to visit a spell with Uncle Jeb, her husband.

Once Jason had finished his treatment of Aunt Sarie, he decided to sit a while and soak up local culture. He soon learned that when someone died they were usually kept up three days. There was preaching two nights and then people stayed up all night two nights in a row. One night was a wake service before the funeral on the third day.

Most families would kill a sheep and all the neighbors would bring in all kinds of food, and everybody stayed to eat until the funeral was over and still they all came back to the house for a final meal with the family.

Whoever was the best carpenter in the community would make a planed wooden casket for the deceased and the women would line the casket with fine silky cloth if they could buy it, and if not, some woman would donate her best sheets, if the family didn't have any, to be used for that purpose.

None of the preachers were paid, but when one was sent for, he was expected to drop whatever he was doing and go to the bereaved family, preach both nights, and then conduct the funeral the next day.

Jason just could not imagine someone doing all that without pay. He was more amazed when he was told that most of these preachers worked in the mines, in timbers, or did carpentry as a full-time job. When they had a funeral to attend, they lost a day or sometimes several days of work and received less pay in their paycheck.

"There must be some kind of reward that I can't see and I certainly don't understand," thought Jason as he reminisced about his experiences here in the county.

Also, he had learned that either the men were fierce Democrats or just as fiercely Republican. This often led to fights during an election year. Most union sympathizers seemed to be Democrats and most non-unionists seemed to hold to the Republican persuasion, but there were a few mavericks who voted for the person.

There were not enough of these to make a difference in an election, and they were therefore ignored unless there was a really close election. Then the mavericks were the most sought after people in the county.

When he worked in Bradshaw, Jason often went into Gus's Place there in town and listened to these political arguments that sometimes led to fights, and then left when the fights broke out. He usually had to sew up a few heads and bandage a few cuts and bruises later that night.

He was always amazed to see the two combatants walking down the street or riding to work together that same week. It always reminded him of a big family who argued, quarreled, and fought but still loved each other. They would also turn on anyone else who tried to hurt a member of the family.

After Jason had been in the county for about a year, he understood the people a little better and had grown to really like most of them. While he was in Pittsburgh with his father he had actually missed many of the people and was glad to see them when he returned.

People greeted him on the street in a friendly but respectful manner. Many of the men from the mountain tops had invited him to hunt on their land. Jim Puckett had said, "Doc you work too much. You need to come up to my place and go hunting with me and the boys."

"I'd probably shoot my foot off, Mr. Puckett," said Jason. "I've never hunted in my life."

"Don't you own a gun?" questioned Mr. Puckett in amazement.

"Well, yes I do. I have a Winchester rifle and a Colt 45 handgun. I keep them clean but I can't remember when I have shot either of them," explained Jason.

He didn't tell Mr. Puckett but he had never been able to even think about killing anything. His guns were left to him by his grandfather and were therefore treasured. He and his dad had fired them at targets just to pit their marksmanship against each other.

Jason often thought with pleasure of the knowledge he had gained not just about McDowell County but about a proud and indomitable people. More and more he had thoughts about making McDowell County his permanent home.

## CHAPTER 21

Jason was becoming more and more interested in every aspect of McDowell County. He soaked up every bit of knowledge he could gain from people who had always lived and worked in the county.

One day while having lunch with Dr. Chapman and some other doctors, a discussion about county politics came up. "This is a solid Democratic county. You couldn't elect a Republican if he was as honest as Abe Lincoln," said Dr. Glovier the obstetrician.

"Is it because of the unions? I went to a rally and the union boss, uh—I forgot his name, but anyway you could certainly tell he was a Democrat. Since he was the head, I assumed that all the unions in the county were Democrats," said Jason.

"Yes, the organizations are mostly all Democratic but the individual union member may not be. I don't know if the union tells the men how to vote but most politicians really cater to the unions, especially if they are running on the Democrat ticket," responded Dr. Chapman.

Another doctor spoke up, "McDowell County is really corrupt politically. County jobs depend on your political affiliation and even some jobs that are not county jobs. Everybody seems to owe a favor to somebody. It certainly doesn't help a man financially, to be a Republican in this county."

"Why doesn't the Republican Party get organized and run some good people so they can have a balance of power?" asked Jason.

"Republicans used to run the show here until Roosevelt was elected and then the Democrats rode in on his coattails. They've been in ever since and I really don't see a change in the near future. Some people like Colonel Ballard, Harry Camper, the Falvos, and others still get candidates on the ballot but most of the time they lose," said Dr. Chapman solemnly.

Someone else spoke up from the end of the table just as they all begin to rise to leave. "The Democrats aren't any more corrupt than the Republicans were when they were in power. Their power brokers were running the show just like it is now, so I don't see why the pot wants to call the kettle black."

"Don't get your dander up, young man," scolded Dr. Chapman. "We were just filling Dr. McCall in on the history of McDowell County.

They all went their separate ways except for Jason and Dr. Chapman, who headed back to their offices which were next door to each other.

Doctor Chapman said with a wry grin, "I guess we'll need to watch what we say when we have a large group. Some people get really upset if anything is said about either party. I don't know what your affiliation is but as you heard inside, it would probably be good if you were a Democrat."

Jason grinned as he turned to enter his office. "I'll study on it Dr. Chapman," he said.

Dr. Chapman stuck his head around the door and stated, "Here's another bit of advice. If you're going to live in this county you almost have to believe in unions."

Jason laughed. "Not if I lived on Bradshaw Mountain. Those people sure don't believe in unions. Maybe a few, but I didn't meet many union sympathizers in all the time I was down there. Right in the town, yes, but definitely not up on the mountains."

"I've heard of Burb Harmon from over that way," said Dr. Chapman walking back out into the hall.

"He's the committeeman for the Republican Party in Sandy River District. He's pretty good too. His district always goes Republican, I think. Did you ever run into him over there?"

"Yes, I met him. He's a rough customer. Runs his family like he's king and everyone jumps when he speaks," Jason grimly replied.

"I take it you were not impressed with Mr. Harmon," laughed Dr. Chapman as he turned to go back into his office.

"We'll talk some more. I'd like to know the story behind your antipathy," he called over his shoulder and entered his door.

Jason entered his office and asked his nurse to send in the next patient as he closed his door.

"I hope he forgets to ask or at least forgets until I can cook up a plausible tale. I don't want him to know about Lucinda," thought Jason as he smiled at the elderly lady who came through the door.

That evening he attended a Board of Education meeting with Kyle Bender and was impressed and excited at the way they handled their business. He came away feeling that George Bryson, the superintendent of schools, wielded an enormous amount of power in the county. It was whispered that only Democrats were hired as teachers.

"Kyle, how many schools are in McDowell County?" asked Jason.

"I'm not sure but I can find out. Why do you want to know," Kyle asked.

"I just thought that the school system is a big employer and as such has a large power base," responded Jason

"Yeah, they are but not as big as the coal industry. The three major employers are the coal industry, the timber industry, and the school system, but I'd say the coal industry has the most employees," replied Kyle.

"If what I heard today about county politics is true, then the coal industry could almost choose who they wanted elected and it would be a done deal," said Jason.

"They could if it wasn't for the unions," Kyle said with a laugh. "You see either union members or union sympathizers are in almost every family since some of the family is usually employed by some coal company."

The rest of the week was taken up by patients, treatments, surgeries, and by trying to be a better husband to Janet in the evenings. He made sure that she rested, took her vitamins, and got any food she mentioned, even though he did not believe that cravings would affect the health of the baby.

At least once each month he took her flowers or some small gift, which he knew would please her. If she mentioned a movie she would like to see he made sure he was free to take her even to Bluefield if it was not showing in Welch.

Also, the more functions and meetings that he attended with Kyle Bender, the more he was drawn to the political arena. He was more interested in the school system for some reason.

"It's probably because I have more time to attend the board meetings," he explained to Kyle. "The more I attend, the more I want to get involved. What kind of chance do you think I'd have to run for the school board?"

Kyle grinned, knowingly. "Well, I'd say the first thing would depend on whether you are a Democrat or not. You are already living in the Browns Creek District so that is another step in the right direction."

"I was raised a Republican but I've always been more of an Independent. It shouldn't matter, the school board is non-partisan, isn't it," asked Jason.

Kyle, who had a droll sense of humor smiled as he said, "It is. You just ask anybody who serves on the board and they will tell you that they have no party allegiance. Those same people will show up at every Democrat rally and fundraiser. So, it isn't what they tell you but their actions that betray them."

"Well, it's early days, as far as an election is concerned, and I've a lot to learn it seems. Come on and let me beat you at the bowling alley," said Jason as he cuffed Kyle on the shoulder

Nothing else was said about running for office but Jason joined the Kiwanis Club, the Masons, the VFW, and the American Legion. Later, Jason joined the Rotary Club, which was a little higher classed, or so it seemed.

Sam Christie had invited him to join and Christie was the head of the Democrat Party in the county. Jason always attended school board meetings, city council meetings, and occasionally a county commission meeting.

"Pretty soon, some of these politicos are going to start wondering whose seat you are going to try to take," Kyle said with a laugh. "I'm sure Doctor Jason McCall is already discussed by both parties," added Kyle.

"Sam Christie invited me to play golf with him last week and the week before, Colonel Ballard asked me. Of course, I had to decline since it was in the daytime. I do have a really good excuse, don't I?" Jason asked with a knowing smile.

"However, I'm looking forward to being invited to sit in on one of their private poker games since they are nighttime affairs." Jason laughed merrily since neither he nor Kyle cared for poker.

"Did they tell you where they meet for these games? Their meeting place is supposed to be a well-kept secret," said Kyle grinning wisely.

"As a matter of fact one of them did ask me if I wanted to sit in, but he didn't say where," stated Jason slowly as it dawned on him that gambling was against the law.

"I don't want to run afoul of the law, so I don't think I'll be playing much poker. Did you ever play?" questioned Jason.

Kyle pulled out his wallet and revealed some one dollar bills.

"Does this wallet look like one that a poker player would be carrying? Their stakes are too high for me." He put his wallet back in his pocket and then said with a laugh. "Of course, if I made the bucks you do I might be tempted."

"I don't think you have to worry too much about the police though. Rumor has it that the police chief is one of the best players," offered Kyle soberly. Suddenly he grinned. "It could be a tale that one party or the other started to give the other one a bad name. I've known that to happen before. Or it could be that somebody doesn't like the police chief."

Jason smiled as he said, "This sounds like Tammany Hall. Who's the Ward Boss around here?

Kyle snickered mischievously as he replied, "Does sound a whole lot like that doesn't it?

As Jason became better acquainted with many people in the county, he could maneuver around without getting into very much political trouble. He only talked to Kyle Bender, however, about his true feelings and ambitions. He seldom attended a meeting without Kyle being present. Kyle professed to have no political aspiration but Jason felt he was very shrewd about the political climate in the county and especially in Welch.

"You're a good fella to have as a friend, Kyle Bender," said Jason as they came out of another meeting.

"Everybody knows who you are but they don't feel threatened by you, so they either talk to you or in front of you," said Jason with a wry grin.

"Oh, so you want to be my friend so I can fill you in on all the gossip, I guess," quipped Kyle.

"I'd probably want you for a friend anyway, but since you have that kind of clout you are especially valuable," teased Jason.

## CHAPTER 22

This period of getting his "feet wet politically" was good for Jason but, it was not a good time for Janet. She was getting more cumbersome every day and every day she seemed to become more easily irritated.

Jason didn't wake her in the mornings before he left but when he walked in the door each evening he was met with some complaint.

"Janet, I am so sorry that you are having such a difficult time. I do everything I know how to do. Would you like to go home to have the baby?" questioned Jason.

"No, I don't want to go home. This is my home," Janet stormed and then broke down sobbing.

"I wanted a baby, but I didn't know it would be like this. I wouldn't have had one so soon but your mother said you always wanted children," mumbled Janet through her tears.

"Mom said what?" gasped Jason in astonishment. "I have never discussed a family with my mother."

Janet sat up from where she had been lying on the bed.

"She said ever since your little cousin Penny died all you have talked about was children."

"My God! I was three years old. Sure I talked about helping children but I certainly didn't talk about wanting any of my own," stormed Jason.

Janet fell back on the bed and dissolved in another crying bout. Jason sat down beside her on the bed. "Janet, why are you doing this? You're going to make yourself sick and I don't know what to do to help you. Come on sit up and go wash your face and we'll go down to Franklins Dairy Bar and get an ice cream sundae. Come on...please," Jason begged.

With Jason's help, Janet rose clumsily to her feet and made her way to the bathroom. As she came out, she threw her arms around Jason and mumbled, "I'm sorry Jason. I don't know why I'm such a cry baby. I just feel so big, clumsy, and ugly."

"Honey, you aren't ugly. Sure you are big, but most of it is the baby. If I were carrying someone else around all the time, I'd be clumsy too," Jason said with a smile. "Just think you only have a few more months and then the baby will be crying instead of you."

Janet laughed and said, "You're not giving me much to look forward to, you know."

Sensing that she was in a better mood, Jason kidded, "After you've gotten up three or four times at night I'll get up the fifth time."

Janet gave him a shove as they went out the door saying, "Nothing doing, big daddy. I'll tell them to show you how to fix formula before we leave the hospital."

"Formula! I thought you were going to breast feed," said a surprised Jason.

"Well, I had intended to," said Janet before she continued cautiously. "The last time we were home, your mom and mine told me that nobody breast fed anymore. They also said that breast feeding causes sagging breasts and I sure don't want that."

"You wouldn't like that either would you?" she questioned as she looked at Jason narrowly as if expecting an outburst but he remained quiet.

She waited a few minutes before saying, "Well, go ahead and say it. I know you don't like it. But, you won't be the one having to do it."

Fearing that Janet would go into another crying jag, Jason said, "No, that's up to you. I didn't know you had been advised not to."

However, after that he often wondered how many more ideas Olivia Washburn and his mother would put into Janet's head. Thinking about it he suddenly remembered Janet saying she wouldn't have had a baby so soon, as if she could have kept from it. He wondered if she had just said whatever came into her head or what. Not wanting another crying episode he did not dare ask her about it, and it was soon forgotten.

Finally in November, before the baby was due in January, the Washburns and the McCalls came to visit. It was unexpected and Janet became very nervous. Jason calmed her by telling her they would take their visitors to the Carter Hotel for dinner that night and to the Sterling Drive-In Restaurant for breakfast.

"They'll think I'm lazy," sputtered Janet.

"No they won't. They'll just think we want them to see how civilized Welch is," assured Jason, which proved to be true.

During dinner at the hotel, many of Jason's newly acquired friends stopped by and were introduced. Colonel Ballard invited both Joshua Washburn and Henry McCall to the Country Club on Sunday afternoon for a session of golf, which they had to decline since they were leaving.

Earlier Jason and Janet had decided to take their parents to the Presbyterian Church, since that was the church both sets of parents attended. They had never revealed to their parents that they now attended the Methodist Church. Since both Jason and Janet knew many of the people who attended the Presbyterian Church, they felt safe in going there. After the service Sam Christie invited all of them out to lunch at the Carter Hotel restaurant.

"We'd be delighted," said Joshua Washburn, looking around the group. They all agreed and spent a delightful hour with Sam Christie and his wife.

As their parents were preparing to leave, Elizabeth McCall hugged Jason and whispered. "You see, Jason, Janet was the right wife for you. I'm sure she has helped you socially. The women in the church seem to adore her."

Jason smiled but did not reply since his dad and Joshua Washburn were urging everybody out the door.

When the door closed behind them, Jason drew a sigh of relief which quickly changed to irritation when he heard sobs coming from the bedroom.

"Janet, are you that homesick?" he asked.

"I don't know," she mumbled. "Mom told me about going to the opera and all my friends that she saw… it made me sad."

"Do you want to go back to Pittsburgh until after the baby is born?" questioned Jason.

"I'll not leave you down here. Why don't you try to get a job back in Pittsburgh? You know Dad would help you," pleaded Janet.

"Get a job in Pittsburgh! Now Janet, you knew how I liked working down here before we married. When we learned that Island Creek expected me to come back for a year you didn't act like this. I know I have a year to fulfill my contract but I want to live and work down here," stated Jason seriously.

"I'm in a new program, which is challenging. I'm providing a needed service and we both have made lots of friends. You've seemed so satisfied. Was it all an act?" questioned Jason staring in unbelief.

"I do like some of the people but Jason it is so –so provincial. You know it is. Besides, I thought you might change your mind. Your mother thought you would," whined Janet.

"Seems to me your mother and my mother did a lot of your thinking for you. If you are dissatisfied then maybe we need to rethink the whole thing," Jason angrily stated.

Janet got to her feet as quickly as possible and threw her arms around his neck.

"Jason, forgive me please. I am just upset to see Mom leave. I don't really dislike it down here. It's really not all that bad."

Jason pulled her arms from around his neck and taking her hand, led her to the bed and sat down beside her.

"Janet, I know it is very different from the way you have always lived but as you say, it isn't bad. I really like it here and will probably stay for a long time. I like the slower pace and quieter life style," explained Jason as he looked at her in anticipation.

Janet, seeing how serious he was, replied, "Jason, no, it isn't what I was raised with but regardless of how it is, if you are here I want to be here too."

Jason hugged her close as he realized that she truly loved him and meant every word she said.

"I wish I could love her like she loves me," he thought as he nestled her against his chest.

Janet clung to him in possessive urgency trying to get even closer to him than she already was.

"Jason, I need you and I love you more than anything on earth. So, if the only way I can be with you is to live down here in this...well whatever it takes, I'll do it," said Janet looking up at him with tears in her eyes.

Jason hugged her close and kissed her tenderly. "Why thank you Princess. That is the nicest thing a man could ever hear. After this baby gets here we will plan a second honeymoon to make up for the first one."

That seemed to please Janet. After that Jason saw no more tears nor heard any more complaints about not living in Pittsburgh.

## CHAPTER 23

Jason liked his practice, liked his neighbors, liked living in Welch, and liked most of the people he met. He was slowly becoming known in political circles even though he had not committed himself to a particular party affiliation.

Kyle laughingly told him, "Until you're wedded to one party or the other you'll be the 'Sweetheart of Sigma Phi'."

"Yes, I know I'm being courted by both parties. I kind of enjoy it. I know when I do decide, I'll be dropped like a hot potato by the losing side," Jason stated.

"Well, as long as you get invited to all these dinners and take me along, I hope you stay a sweetheart for a long time. Of course, Rita swears I'm putting on weight from all these dinners we attend," said Kyle, turning from side to side as if to check his weight.

Life moved pleasantly along until the cold night in January 1955 when he rushed Janet to the hospital. The next twelve hours were certainly not pleasant. Janet had hemorrhaged and had to be given a transfusion. Jason walked the floor in dread, blaming himself for not loving her like he should have.

"Lord, if you will just let her pull through, I'll be a much better husband," he earnestly begged. However, when his little daughter was brought to him, all other thoughts went right out of his head.

Jason couldn't see any resemblance to anybody but he thought she was beautiful. Soon the nurse came to take his daughter back to the nursery. He then went in to check on Janet who was sleeping. He was alarmed because she was so very pale. He questioned Dr. Glovier as to her status and being satisfied he went to his office and dialed Janet's mother.

"Olivia, you are now a grandmother. Your daughter has just delivered the most beautiful little girl in the entire world. She weighed seven pounds and four ounces and is sixteen and three-fourths inches long," bragged Jason.

Olivia interrupted his euphoric praise with, "How is Janet? Is my baby all right?"

Jason soberly said, "Janet is all right but she had a rough time. For some reason she hemorrhaged and had to have a transfusion. They had matching blood in the blood bank though."

"Oh my God! " gasped Olivia. "Let me speak to her. I've got to hear her voice."

"She's sleeping now, Olivia. I'll have her call you as soon as she wakes," said Jason and then, looking at his watch, said, "Well, it's one o'clock in the morning so I'll not wake her until at least eight o'clock."

"What if something happens before then? I want to hear her voice," demanded Olivia.

"I'm sorry, Olivia, but I would be thrown out of the hospital if I awakened her at this hour. You can expect a call around eight o'clock. Will you call Mom and Dad?" asked Jason. "They told me to be sure to call them."

Olivia agreed to call his parents but was very upset because Janet had been so sick. "I thought you said you had good doctors down there. Why didn't you bring her home like I wanted you to?" challenged Olivia.

"Olivia, she had a good doctor. That could have happened regardless of where she was. It was just something that happened," replied Jason soothingly.

"Well, I'm going to tell her to never have another one even if you do want more," stated Olivia belligerently.

"I want...Where are you all getting the idea that I wanted children? I didn't want any, especially not this soon, so why are you pointing fingers at me?" demanded Jason.

"Your mother told Janet that you would want a baby right off. That's why Janet tried so hard to get pregnant," snarled Olivia.

"My mother did what?" questioned Jason.

"Your mother told Janet that she should get pregnant as soon as she could after she was married to keep you more satisfied. I guess she thought you didn't really love Janet," sneered Olivia.

"If I had known about that I would have tried to stop Janet

from marrying you, that's for sure."

"Well, this is a hell of a time to be telling me since it's the first time I've ever heard anything like this," blurted Jason in amazement. "I can assure you of one thing, Olivia, and that is that having a baby early would not have made any difference to me. Also, I would not have married Janet if I hadn't wanted to."

A more contrite Olivia said, "Jason, I'm sorry. Please don't tell Janet what I've told you. She will just be upset."

"I won't ask her now, Olivia, but I assure you I will get to the bottom of this," stated a determined Jason. Even though he did not mention it to Janet, he wondered what Olivia had meant by "she tried so hard to get pregnant." Jason wondered how she tried or what she had done or not done to insure a pregnancy, but decided to put it out of his mind until Janet was much better.

Janet came home with the seven-day old Emily Elizabeth McCall. Jason held his beautiful little daughter every spare moment that he could. She had lots of silky brown hair and gorgeous, twinkling, brown eyes that seemed to smile. Janet was home but was very nervous and weak.

Through the help of Rita Bender, they found a nice middle-aged widow lady who agreed to come in each day to clean and help with the baby. From that time on, Hilda Bishop became a part of their household.

Jason hadn't planned to have a live-in housekeeper and nanny but that is what he ended up with for many years.

"Janet, do you think you could cope with caring for Emily and let Hilda come in about twice a week?" Jason asked after a month had passed.

"Please, Jason, don't stop Hilda from coming in. I get so scared if Emmy cries or spits up. I just go all to pieces," pleaded Janet.

So, Jason did not say anymore and after a while realized that his life was much easier with Hilda there. Janet did not have crying jags as she once had, but she became very upset if she thought she would be alone with little Emily.

Janet did not seem to mind that Jason was out with Kyle Bender, either bowling or attending some civic function. He could have even slipped away to Bradshaw and she would never have known. However, when she had been so ill at the birth of Emily, Jason had promised God that he would be a better husband, and he knew Lucinda had to be in the past.

They had made a trip to Pittsburgh in September after Emily's birth and both sets of grandparents fell in love with her. Janet was constantly sending pictures and calling her mother. Just as constant were the endless packages of toys and clothing for Emily and for Janet.

Jason resented this over-indulgence but knew that Janet would become very upset if he told her, so he tried to ignore most of it. However, he did get so upset when a sable fur coat and hat came for Emily, that he told Janet that they must be returned.

"You tell them that I can easily afford to feed and clothe my own family and I really resent such lavish gifts as well as the number. They may send gifts on birthdays and Christmas but tell them not to send at other times," demanded Jason angrily.

Janet cried, sulked, and begged but Jason would not relent until the fur coat and hat were finally returned. After that, Jason did not see new things every evening when he arrived home.

A year passed with Emily growing, walking, and jabbering and Jason was so proud of his beautiful baby girl. Janet too, became more relaxed with her as she grew older. Janet especially delighted in taking her to the shops and dressing her in all the latest fashions. When people on the streets or in the shops said, "That is the most beautiful baby I've ever seen" and "She looks a lot like you," Janet came home and immediately called her mother to gloat.

Jason was still attending Board of Education meetings and all the other functions Kyle had introduced him to, but he still had not united or become affiliated with either political party.

He knew and liked Sam Christie, Harry Camper, Colonel

Ballard, and also Harry Pauley from Iaeger. He remembered Lucinda Harmon repeating something she had heard about Harry Pauley building a road into Panther State Forest. At the time, he had not felt that Harry Pauley was someone he would like but later learned that Pauley was respected by most people in the Welch area. "I guess Lucinda only heard about one side of Mr. Pauley," thought Jason.

Listening to others talk it seemed as if Harry Pauley had become a very good statesman as he aged. One snippet of information that he had heard about was that Harry Pauley had been responsible for getting some public works going around the Gary area that helped many unemployed county residents and also that he was well thought of in most circles.

"I guess, that anybody in the public eye will have some negative things said about them, won't they?" Jason commented to Kyle Bender.

"Well, you know the old adage, 'If you make mistakes you must be doing something or trying, at least'," Kyle replied. "So, I guess that means Pauley has been doing something doesn't it?" "Some people did say that Harry Pauley had that road built to get out his coal. But if he did, he must have had legislative approval, since there was no hue and cry from the Republicans," finished Kyle.

Jason was still more interested in the functioning of the school system. Now, he had a daughter who would one day be attending the schools here in McDowell County. He wanted to make sure that the schools were the best they could be. George Bryson was a very knowledgeable and likeable man, even though he seemed cold on a first meeting. Jason had several very interesting conversations with Mr. Bryson about his ideas on education. They both agreed that good parents made for a good school system and good students.

In one school board meeting, Harvey Hendrix, a school board member, had stated almost the same sentiment as Mr. Bryson by saying that the parents with unruly children are the very ones who never show up at school unless they are noticed in. "I know for a fact that it's the biggest complaint from teachers. I visit the schools really often and I hear the same thing all the time," grumbled Mr. Hendrix.

Even with those comments, Jason knew that discipline was not a major problem in McDowell County. Teachers and principals could use a paddle if necessary and most children were respectful.

The biggest problem in McDowell County from Jason's perspective was the terrain over which children had to be bussed. Many of his patients had complained about the long bus rides their children had to make to and from the high schools. Jason thought that this was one of the factors for the high dropout rate in the county, especially on the mountains.

"It's not going to get any better either unless we get some good highways in here, is it Kyle?" Jason asked his friend when they discussed the problem. But most often this kind of thinking and discussions brought reminders of Lucinda Harmon's struggle to get an education and since Jason did not want to think about her he quickly changed the conversation to something else.

Little Emily Elizabeth McCall was an intelligent and mischievous two-year-old and the delight of her father's life. Everything she did was amusing to Jason.

"I love to see what that questing little mind is going to discover next," enthused Jason as he and Janet watched her.

"If you had to watch those questing hands every minute through the day I don't believe you would be too delighted," complained Janet good-naturedly. She now did much more with Emily and did not leave her with Hilda Bishop as often. Hilda would not have minded for she dearly loved the little girl.

"I'm here every day, Mrs. McCall, and Little Emmy don't bother me none while I'm cooking or cleaning. In fact, she keeps me company," Hilda said smiling. "I'll bet she asks 'Why' fifty times an hour. I swear that child wants to know everything."

Kyle and Rita Bender became Aunt Rita and Uncle Kyle to Emily and she went home with them at every opportunity.

"She always wants to go back home at six o'clock though," complained Rita. "I swear, I believe she can tell time. She will be playing and suddenly she will say, "Want to go home to Daddy" and it is always close to six o'clock."

Thus Jason's life unfolded and if he once in a while heard certain songs, or some name that reminded him of Lucinda Harmon, he resolutely transferred his thoughts to his daughter. He was ashamed that he could not erase Lucinda from his mind altogether but he could not. He thought it was unfair to Janet and tried to make up for his unruly thoughts by accepting whatever she decided to do, except one thing, and that was to take Emily to Pittsburgh without him.

"Jason, I don't see why Emily and I can't drive up and stay a couple of weeks. Both set of parents would be delighted. They don't get to see enough of their granddaughter," pleaded Janet again as she had for the last three months.

"No, no, no. Not unless I go with you. I don't want you driving that far alone. Besides I'll miss you all too much," explained Jason.

"You mean you'll miss Emmy too much. You could care less whether I'm here or not," accused Janet.

In the end, Jason took a week's vacation early and they all went to Pittsburgh. Jason had to admit that he enjoyed taking Emily about and introducing her to his old professors, and his numerous friends.

## CHAPTER 24

Nearly three years later, in May 1959, Jason was about to close his office for the day when the Emergency Room called up saying they were sending a patient up to see him. This was not unusual but it was rather late in the evening.

He switched the lights back on and donned his white coat just as the elevator across the hall swished to a stop and the doors opened. Jason had turned to his desk and did not look up until a voice said, "My little boy is hurt."

Jason stood bent over his desk without moving for what seemed like five minutes. He was so shocked that he turned slowly like a robot. That was the voice of Lucinda Harmon and now her beautiful blues eyes, filled with tears, was looking at him.

Lucinda Harmon, as beautiful as ever, stood in the door holding a small red-headed boy in her arms. She also looked as if she had been struck by lightning. She was deathly white, her eyes were round and staring, and he mouth was open. Jason hurried toward her fearing she was about to faint. Before he reached her she shivered, blinked, and spoke..."You", and stopped.

She clamped her lips together and without looking at him again said, "My little boy...he fell on a stick...his eye." A sob broke through as she stumbled as if she might indeed faint.

Jason quickly lifted the child from her arms and she sank into a chair by the door. Jason stretched the little boy out on a table and bent over him.

"What's his name?" asked Jason as he began to examine the left eye.

Lucinda got up and moved to the other side of the table.

"Danny...Daniel, " she replied. The little boy began to cry and reached his arms for his mother. Lucinda leaned over him just as Jason started to straighten up and their heads collided. They both gave involuntary jerks and together said, "I'm sorry."

"How old is he?" asked Jason as he remembered five

years ago and that incident in Bradshaw. He thought she was pregnant then, and now it seems she must have been.

"He's four years and three months old. Is his eye damaged? It bled but he stopped crying before I got here," explained Lucinda, who hadn't raised her eyes to his face since she walked into his office.

Using a strong light, Jason bent to probe more closely and Danny took violent exception to this treatment, screaming and flailing his arms. Lucinda scooped him up in her arms.

"Here Danny, Mommy's right here. You have to be big and tough. You can't be a cry-baby. The doctor just wants to look in your eye and see how badly it's hurt," soothed Lucinda as she gently placed him back on the table. She ruffled his hair and smiled down at him.

"Just think, you can tell your friend Joey all about what the doctor had to do. I'll bet Joey couldn't ever stand that."

Jason was amazed at the skill Lucinda used and the reaction from her son who looked up at Jason and smiled through gritted teeth. "All right, Doctor. I'll be still."

Once again Jason bent over the small quivering boy, but a boy that made no sound. Danny winced and stiffened as tears trickled from the corner of his eyes but he made no sound at all. Lucinda stood holding his hand in a firm grip with the other hand on his shoulder, also making no sound. When Jason raised his head again, he saw tears dripping onto the pillow from Lucinda's bowed head.

"I'm going to put some drops in his eye. I can't see anything that will damage his vision. I'll put in an antibiotic also to make sure it doesn't get infected. How did it happen?" asked Jason as he prepared the dosage.

Lucinda who had been standing ramrod straight relaxed her hold on Danny. With a trembling hand she accepted the tissues Jason handed her and wiped her face, after gently drying the face of her son.

"We were on our way home and Danny wanted to stop at Premier Cut. He likes rocks and things like that. Anyway, he was chasing a butterfly and tripped on a stone. I guess he must have fallen on a stickweed. I didn't wait to look after I saw his bloody eye," explained Lucinda.

Jason wanted to take her in his arms but knew he couldn't. He wished she would look at him but she kept her head bowed.

"I'm going to put a bandage over it so don't get it wet. Bring him back in three days and let me have another look. I think it will be fine but I want to make sure," he stated assuredly as he finished the dressing.

"You said you were going home. Do you live around here?" questioned Jason.

"No," said Lucinda and added nothing further but stood waiting to be told he was through.

"Lucinda," Jason began, to be stopped by her quick gasp and a raised hand, as if to block him.

"How, much do I owe you doctor?" asked Lucinda in a very formal voice as if she was speaking to him for the first time in her life.

"Nothing! You know I would never charge you," Jason said in surprise.

Seeing that she did not like that answer, Jason said, "You bring him back in three days and we can settle that."

"I don't know if I can bring him back. Is there another doctor who could check him?" questioned Lucinda worriedly.

"Oh! You mean it's too far to bring him back here?" questioned Jason. "Well, there is Dr. Blaydes in Bluefield and Dr. Wilkins in Beckley. Which one is closest to you?" asked Jason, thinking he could get some idea as to where she lived.

Lucinda lifted Danny off the table and straightened his clothes. "I'll take him to one of them if I can't get back here. Thanks again for taking care of him," said Lucinda as she grasped Danny's hand and moved toward the door.

"Wait! I need his full name for my records," explained Jason.

Lucinda stopped and started to turn but instead said, "Daniel Jefferson Marshall," and then went on out the door.

Jason stood shaken and staring as her rigid back retreated and, never turning, she entered the elevator to be swished away from him.

Once again he stripped off his white coat and automatically straightened the examining room before he switched off the lights and closed the door. He walked down the stairs at a slow pace, not even noticing Mary Jane, the cleaning lady who passed him at the bottom of the stairs.

"Hmm. I wonder what's wrong with the Doc? He always tells me 'Good night,'" mumbled Mary Jane as she shuffled her heavy body on down the hall. The grounds maintenance man got the same treatment, which also left him baffled.

When Mary Jane came outside to smoke, Jerry Helbert observed. "What's eating the Doc tonight? He always has something nice to say to me but he sure didn't tonight."

"Well, he looked right through me and anybody my size is hard to look through," Mary Jane said, laughing merrily. She then sobered. "I'll bet that little boy that came in last was hurt worse than he looked. If anything would get to the Doc it would be a hurt kid."

"Yeah," replied Jerry. "That must have been it. I ain't never seen a man as crazy over kids as the Doc. That little Emmy of his is the apple of his eye, for shore."

Jason left the hospital and walked slowly to his car, not noticing either of his loyal fans. He climbed into his car, slammed the door, and as quickly as possible pulled out headed toward Bradshaw. He drove fast and unthinking until he started up Coalwood Mountain and then suddenly realized what he was doing.

"Hell…damn, damn. I'm acting like a complete idiot. What's the purpose of going to Bradshaw? What's the use in any of it? It's over. Why in the hell did she have to show up in my office?" At the next wide place in the road Jason pulled over and stopped and sat in a deep study.

"Lucinda is not happy. She didn't look up after that first shock of recognition. Even when she first came in she looked drawn and tired." Jason wondered if she was just scared over her little boy or was there something else. He realized that she looked thin as if she hadn't gained a pound since she was sixteen years old, even though she was still as beautiful as ever. But there was something.

"Well, I guess I'll never know. Anyway, I hope her little boy gives her as much joy as my Emmy does me," said Jason aloud as he turned the car and headed back to Welch.

When he walked in the house, Emmy was crying, "I want my daddy. I want my daddy."

Janet was telling her to hush and was getting annoyed. "Emmy, I don't know where your daddy is. He could have at least called if he was going to be late. He knows how upset you get. Stop that crying. You're giving me a headache," admonished Janet.

When Emily didn't stop, Janet yelled, "Hilda, will you see if you can get Emmy to stop crying?"

Jason walked from the foyer into the living room saying, "What's wrong with Daddy's girl?"

The crying ceased immediately as Emmy ran on her short legs to reach Jason who swung her high in the air, as they both laughed merrily.

"I wanted you, Daddy. Where you been?" asked Emily as her arms tightened around his neck.

Jason held his breath making his face turn red. "Argh! You are choking me," he growled. Immediately the small arms loosened their grasp and Emily's soft hands began to rub and pat his face.

"I was just hugging you, my Daddy. I wouldn't hurt you," mumbled a very subdued Emily.

Jason began tickling her as he sat down on the sofa with her in his lap. "Well, you sure have a strong hug, little girl, but I'm not hurt."

"Where have you been, Jason? You know how upset she gets if you are not here by six o'clock," demanded Janet irritably.

Jason widened his eyes. "Who told her it was six o'clock? She can't tell time."

Jumping from his arms and off the sofa, Emily ran to the big grandfather clock by the door. "See, Daddy. When the long arm is on the top and the short arm is straight below it is the time you come home."

Grinning widely, Emily said, "I can tell time can't I, Daddy?"

Jason looked at Janet in amazement. "Well, princess, you can almost tell time. How did you know that?"

Emily stood looking from her mother to her father before saying mischievously, "I don't know. I'm just smart I guess."

Jason grabbed her up and tossed her in the air while she giggled merrily but Janet quaked in fear.

"Put her down, Jason. You know that scares me to death. What if you fell or accidentally missed her."

Jason lowered her to the floor and started towards the bathroom, to be stopped by Janet. "You didn't say why you were late," stated Janet suspiciously.

"A little boy was sent up just as I was ready to leave. He had fallen on some kind of stick and damaged his eye," Jason answered and went on to the bathroom.

Nothing else was said about the incident but it was still in the back of Jason's mind. He was looking forward to the third day when Danny was to be brought back.

"Maybe she will talk to me. She looked so fragile," mumbled Jason as he opened his office on the third day.

When Lucinda hadn't shown up by one o'clock, Jason thought that she had gone to one of the other doctors and tried to put it out of his mind. It came back to his mind with a wallop when at four o'clock, a tall red-headed man came striding through the door with Danny Marshall holding his hand. He hadn't waited for the nurse to usher him in either.

"I've brought my son back for his check up, Doctor," stated a belligerent voice.

Jason turned from the sink where he had just scrubbed his hands and looked up in a startled manner. "Hello, Mr. Marshall. I'm glad you brought Danny back in. How is he doing?" asked Jason while looking Lucinda's husband directly in the eye.

Jeff Marshall glared ferociously at Jason as he said, "He seems to be better. You can check him. Here, Danny, sit here on this table so the doctor can check your eye," he said, placing Danny on the table.

Jason loosened the bandage and laid Danny back on the table as he adjusted the light. Danny lay rigidly still as if petrified, not making a sound but looking at his father.

"Relax, Danny. I thought we were buddies. I didn't hurt you the other time did I?" questioned Jason softly as he carefully examined the boy's eye.

Then he raised up and turned to Jeff Marshall. "It looks fine but I think I'd better put another drop of antibiotic in it."

"Go ahead if that's what he needs," growled Marshall.

Jason administered the drops and patted Danny on the head. "See, champ, that wasn't so bad was it?" asked Jason with a grin, but Danny only looked at his father and made no comment.

Jason started to ask about Lucinda, but when he looked at Jeff Marshall, who was still glowering at him, he changed his mind.

"What's the bill for this treatment and the first time also? I'd like to know why you wouldn't let my wife pay when she brought him in here?" questioned Marshall, in a demanding tone.

Jason was stunned at his attitude. "I told her we would settle that when she brought him back," said Jason.

"No, you hoped she would come back, but you can get that out of your mind, doctor. You think I don't know what you're trying to do? You wanted to know where she lived and that's none of your damned business," stormed Jeff Marshall as his face became redder than it already was.

Jason stood staring but at a whimper from Danny, looked down to see a teary eyed, scared little boy. "Well, Mr. Marshall, let's not upset your son. I'll not cause you a problem."

"You're damn right you won't. My wife won't be back here anymore. You can count on that," roared Marshall as he took out his wallet. He pulled out a hundred dollar bill and slammed it down on the table before grabbing Danny's hand and striding through the door, almost dragging Danny behind him.

"Well, I'll be damned," sputtered Jason angrily. Trudy Simmons, his nurse came in ready to leave for the day.

"Good night, Doc… " She stopped short when she saw his face. "What's wrong, Doctor McCall? You look mad enough to bite nails," she stated curiously.

"I am. I'm mad enough to punch that barbarian out," stormed Jason furiously.

"You remember me telling you about that little boy that ER sent up here three days ago? It was after you had already left for the day."

Trudy studied for a moment, then said, "Oh! that Marshall woman who left without telling you where she lived."

"Yes, that's the one. Well, the husband came in with the little boy, who was rigid with fear. He wouldn't take his eyes off his dad for a minute. That little boy acted as if he feared for his life. It's no wonder though, for that man was like a wild man."

"I thought I heard loud voices, but some people talk loud," explained Trudy.

"You heard loud voices all right. He came in cursing and left the same way and I still don't know where he lives," stated Jason.

"He threw this hundred dollar bill on the table and said they would not be back here anymore and stormed out."

During this time Trudy was straightening up the office and as she and Jason went out the door, she laughed and said, "Well, at least, you won't have to be bothered with him again."

"No, I guess not, but I hope that little boy and his mother will be all right, living with that beast," said Jason worriedly as they got into the elevator.

They parted ways on the ground floor and Jason went on to his car thinking that it was no wonder that Lucinda looked wan and defeated and was so thin.

"If I had just gone to Concord and tried to find out what happened, she wouldn't be in this mess," mumbled Jason before he caught himself. But still he unconsciously begin praying, “Please, Lord, take care of her. Please.”

## CHAPTER 25

After that fiasco, it was many months before Jason heard anything else from or about Lucinda. He wanted to know whether Lucinda was ill since she had been so thin. Mildred Harris, his old landlady from Bradshaw, was a patient in Grace Hospital and Jason asked her about Lucinda.

"Oh! You mean that Harmon girl that married Jeff Marshall. They moved to Michigan, according to Jack Stevens, the deputy," explained Mrs. Harris.

"They don't still live in Michigan, do they?" questioned Jason.

"No. That's right. They moved back here somewhere, but not around Bradshaw," said Mrs. Harris. She sat propped up in her bed studying before continuing, "Somebody said they visit Mrs. Marshall's parents sometimes. They never stop in town though, or if they do I've not seen them."

Jason left Mrs. Harris thinking sadly about Lucinda and that hateful man she married. "I guess he's afraid to stop in Bradshaw. She might see me again," thought Jason as he left Mrs. Harris's room. "I'll bet she lives a miserable life," mumbled Jason sadly as he went down the corridor and opened the door to visit another one of his patients.

While Emily was still four and Katie Bender was nine, Jason and Janet made arrangements to not only take the Benders with them to Pittsburgh but to also make a swing through Amish country around Lancaster, Pennsylvania. They had waited forever it seemed before Kyle, who was an electrical engineer for U. S. Steel Corporation, could get the time away at the same time that Jason could also be away.

The four year-old Emily loved being with Katie. She called Katie "Sissy" and chattered the entire trip about all the things her "Papaw Henny" (Jason's dad) would take them to see. Emily liked Joshua Washburn but she loved Henry McCall.

Janet often complained, "Henry McCall acts like an idiot around Emily. He's too old to crawl around on the floor with her."

"Dad always loved children. You know how much time he spent with me and Frank and you also. When Uncle Howard's children visit he does the same with them. Leave him alone. If he enjoys it, I'm sure it won't hurt him," chided Jason

"Emily already feels she's the center of the universe and he makes it worse," replied Janet.

"Now, Janet, you know that Emily is a well-rounded little girl. She's too young to think about her place in the universe," Jason laughingly replied.

While in Pittsburgh, the Benders really seemed to enjoy going to the theaters, viewing all the historical places in and around the city, and the steamboat ride on Lake Erie.

It had been a very enjoyable trip for Jason and for the Benders, except in the presence of Elizabeth McCall and Olivia Washburn. Jason sensed a tenseness that he knew Henry McCall really tried to dispel, as well as Joshua Washburn to a lesser degree, but it was still a disquieting aspect of the visit.

Jason did not mention it and really hoped it was not brought up. He knew Kyle would give some kind of diplomatic answer if asked and so would Rita, but Katie was a different story. She would probably say just what she thought and Jason had a suspicion that his mother and Janet's were not high on her list of likeable people.

This was proven true as they were driving through Lancaster County to visit the Amish community. Katie and Emily were whispering and talking quietly until Emily spoke up.

"Katie does not like Grandmother Elizabeth. You don't do you, Sissy?"

Jason heard Rita's gasp of shock before Katie replied in a mumble. "I just said I didn't like how she talked about McDowell County. She thinks people from McDowell County are stupid."

"Now, Katie, you are just guessing. You don't know how she feels," chided a very embarrassed Rita.

"No, she's not guessing, either," piped in Emily, glaring stormily at Rita.

"We heard grandmother on the telephone, didn't we, Sissy?"

Katie looked at Emily in exasperation before she said, "We weren't trying to listen. We just accidentally heard her say... Katie hesitated and looked pleadingly at her mother.

'"What did she say that was so terrible?" asked Jason in a doubtful voice.

Katie looked at Rita who shook her head but when Jason insisted she replied, "I heard her say, 'They're leaving now. Oh! I didn't tell you that Jason and Janet brought some of the yokels to visit,' and she laughed."

Janet cut in quickly, "Katie, I'm so sorry you heard that but she was only kidding, I'm sure."

"Katie, she is Jason's mother and he loves her just like you love me and your dad. I think you need to apologize to Jason," stated Rita, looking steadily at Katie.

Katie dropped her head dejectedly and mumbled, "I'm sorry. That was not kind."

Emily pulled Katie's head up where she could see her face then looking her right in the eye said. "You're sorry that Daddy don't have a good Mommy like yours, I'll bet. Huh, Sissy?"

Everybody laughed and Rita was embarrassed, but the tension was relieved and the rest of the way was spent without awkwardness.

Talking to the people in the Amish community of Paradise, Pennsylvania and inspecting their goods made for a very pleasant day for everyone. Janet and Rita bought quilts and Rita bought a bread box. Katie and Emily spent their time trying to get the children to talk and play with them. One little girl was very friendly but her mother would not allow her to go outside the store.

"Her mother was mean. She took he girl away," said Emily when Jason asked why she was upset. "I asked that little girl if she wore panties under her long dress," said a curious Emily.

Jason, who was trying hard to keep a straight face, asked, "What did she say?"

"She didn't say anything. Her mother pushed her through

the door and left," stated Emily angrily. "She looked at me like I was bad. Was I bad, Daddy?" Emily questioned seriously.

"No, Princess, I don't think you were bad, but it was a very personal question. Sometimes it is best not to ask people about what they wear under their dresses," replied Jason with a smile.

Emily thought for a moment and then smiling, she patted Jason on the arm before saying, "Okay, Daddy, I won't do that anymore."

Kyle said he wished he had some way of getting one of the Amish buggies home. "I'd like to drive one of those through Welch, wouldn't you?" Kyle questioned as he laughed at Jason's amazed look.

"Kyle, there's a side to you that I didn't know existed. You like to shock people, don't you?" Jason raised his eyebrows in question.

"Oh, I like to operate out of the box on occasion," Kyle replied with a chuckle.

They finally climbed back into the station wagon, with Kyle taking over for Jason as the driver, and began their long drive back to McDowell County.

All the occupants of the rear seats went to sleep, which gave Kyle a chance to apologize to Jason for Katie's embarrassing remarks.

"Jason, I'm really sorry but you've known Katie since she was five years old and she is not very tactful."

Jason smiled. "Forget it, Kyle. You don't want her to lie do you? Mom's a snob. I've known that for years and I think she is the one with no tact."

Seeing Kyle was still troubled, Jason continued, "Really, Katie would never have revealed what she'd heard if my little chatty daughter hadn't blabbed."

"That's probably true and I don't think I've ever known a more observant child. Not one her age anyway," observed Kyle.

Jason laughed hilariously. "We have to watch everything we say and everything we do. From the time I enter the house until I go to bed I'll bet I hear 'Why' fifty times."

"If she carries things outside the house, when she starts to school, you may find yourself in trouble, my friend," Kyle said on a laugh.

"I'll bet her teachers will know more about you and Janet than you know yourselves."

This led to talk of recent school board action on expulsion of a student at Northfork High School.

"Looks like the school board would have noticed the parents in and have them discipline the boy," commented Jason.

Kyle shook his head in denial. "The parents won't touch him. They are as afraid of him as that boy he punched out. It won't do any good to expel him either. I believe the boy has some kind of mental problem."

"The parents should bring him in for testing. He would probably be eligible for special education," said Jason thoughtfully. "He may be so frustrated in a regular classroom that he just acts up to relieve his frustration."

"The school board's hands are tied. They can't make the parents discipline him and they can't allow the teacher and the students to be intimidated by his belligerence," explained Kyle.

"Is school board policy based on precedents, do you think? I mean, have they had this happen before and are acting as they did then?" asked Jason.

Kyle thought about this before he answered. "I'm not sure. I think some actions are mandated by the state but I don't know which ones. Are you still interested in serving on the school board?" quizzed Kyle doubtfully.

Jason grinned and scratched his head. "I guess I'm a glutton for punishment, but yes, I would like to sit on that board."

Kyle and Jason were still discussing the various actions of the school board as they left Route 19 to pick up Route 16 toward Beckley and Janet awoke.

"Hey, we're almost in Beckley, let's stop and eat. It's seven o'clock," stated Janet, to be seconded by Rita who was also now awake.

They pulled into a diner on the outskirts of Oakhill and shook Katie and Emily, who grumbled, but sleepily climbed out of the car.

"I need to go to the bathroom," began Emily as soon as she hit the ground.

So, a rumpled and tired group filed into the diner and asked immediately for bathroom facilities.

Janet came back from the restroom holding her hands out and, frowning, said, "Well, we're back in West Virginia. No towels in the restrooms."

"I'll bet restrooms in Pittsburgh occasionally run out, too," Jason said, trying to laugh. He heard the audible sigh of Kyle and Rita and saw them look to see if Katie was listening.

## CHAPTER 26

Jason became more and more embroiled in the affairs of Welch and the entire county as well as all state government activities. Most active people in both political parties knew Jason and liked him, but they were still puzzled and wary of his lack of commitment.

Four years later Emily was eight years old and in the third grade at Welch Elementary School. Jason and Janet were both active in the Parent Teachers Association and became chaperones at many school functions.

Realizing that things like this kept thoughts of Lucinda Harmon Marshall at bay, Jason became more involved than ever in town council meetings, Board of Education meetings, outings and play time with Emily, and taking Janet to movies and dancing when at all possible.

He also became interested in everything that Kyle and Rita's daughter, Katie, was involved in. She was now thirteen years old and was a cheerleader at the Junior High School and Jason never missed a game. Janet enjoyed doing things with Rita and Katie and now Emily was also always in attendance.

One evening as Kyle and Jason were returning from a Forty and Eight dinner, Jason said, "I'm going to file as a candidate for the Board of Education in this election."

Kyle looked at him in surprise. "You are. When did you decide that?"

"Tonight," said Jason adamantly. "After listening to that loud-mouthed Carlos Matthews, I just thought that anything would beat that. So, tomorrow my name will be in the hat."

"Are you also registering as a Democrat?" asked Kyle in wonder.

"No, I'm not. I'm going to truly be what a school board member should be—non-partisan," stated Jason with a grin.

"Well, good luck, for what it's worth," said Kyle as he pulled into his driveway. As Jason got out of his car and started across the lawn to his own house Kyle yelled after him. "You've got my vote."

Jason waved and smiled as he unlocked his door and entered his own house. Janet was watching television and did not look up as he came in and hung his jacket on the hall tree. As he made for the recliner, which he usually occupied, she switched off the television as the Milton Beryl show ended.

She looked up at him, saying, “Well, how did the meeting go? Are they still on to you to become a Democrat or are certain ones wanting you to be a Republican?”

Jason sat down, stretched out his long legs, and grinned at her before replying. “Yes, both sides still approach me but I think that may stop after tomorrow, or it may get worse.”

“Why tomorrow? What makes tomorrow different,” asked an alerted Janet.

“I’m going to file as a candidate for the school board. Charlie Simmons does not plan to run again and he is in the Browns Creek district. I’m filing to fill his place,” answered Jason solemnly.

“Are you the only one running for that seat?” questioned Janet.

“Lord no! There’s six more running. I just think it is time I threw my hat in the ring. I may not have a chance, but I’ll never know until I try,” Jason said with a smile.

Janet got up and came over to take a seat in his lap. “Well, I think I may vote for you,” she said as she kissed him and gave him a hug.

“Um. Well, that settles it. When women react like that to my announcement, how can I lose,” mumbled Jason nuzzling her neck.

Janet jumped up playfully. “Women! That’s just one woman’s reaction and it better stay that way too,” she quipped as she pulled aside the opening to her robe to reveal a long shapely leg. Then giving a decided twist to her hips she dashed from the room.

Jason gave chase, which ended up in the bedroom. From there she had no way to retreat, which was probably her intention anyway, since she did not put up much of a fight.

Emily came wandering into their room very early the

following morning, dragging her blanket behind her. "I'm cold, Daddy. Can I come into your bed?" she asked sleepily.

Sliding over, Jason made room by his side and, dropping her blanket, Emily climbed in. When she started trying to pull some cover up over herself, she said, "Daddy, your bed is all torn up. How in the world do you and Mommy get your covers all tangled up? You must have had a fight."

Janet was now awake and she looked at Jason, waiting to see how he would handle that.

"Well, we did have a sort of fight and your Mommy won. See, she has all the cover," Jason said with a mischievous look at Janet.

Janet raised her eyebrows suggestively before shifting the top quilt from under her and covering both Jason and Emily.

"Now, you two go back to sleep. It is only six o'clock."

Over breakfast, Janet said, "You know, Emily, you are a big eight-year-old now, so don't you think it's time you stopped climbing into our bed."

Emily looked shocked, "I may be big, but Daddy is still my daddy and you are still my mommy and I still get cold sometimes."

Janet smiled and replied, "I'm just saying that big girls don't sleep with their daddy."

"You're a big girl and you sleep with Daddy. I'm not near as big as you are. That's not fair. If I can't even come into his bed when I'm cold, I don't see why you can sleep with him all the time," argued Emily in her rationalizing way.

"But I'm his wife," responded Janet as if that should clear everything up.

"So…I'm his daughter and we've got the same blood. I heard you tell Aunt Rita that my blood and Daddy's was the same type," stated Emily reasonably as if explaining something to a child.

"Grandpa Henry says blood is thicker than water, and that means I have a stronger claim on Daddy than you do."

Janet looked at Jason expectantly. "Explain it to her Jason. She knows exactly what I'm talking about. She just wants to irritate me," complained Janet, but seeing Jason was ready to erupt with laughter, she sputtered, "It is not funny, Jason. You shouldn't encourage her."

Jason looked at his watch, rose from the table and looking at Emily, said, "We'll talk another time, Princess. I'll be late, as it is."

Looking down at Emily's upturned face; he stooped and kissed her cheek.

"You shouldn't tease your mommy though."

Emily threw her arms around his neck and said as she giggled, "I know, Daddy, and I'll try to stop but blood is thicker than water."

Jason gave Janet a quick kiss and went laughing out the door just as the school bus came to a halt at the edge of the pavement.

The bus driver raised his hand in salute as Jason went around the side of his house to the garage. Janet always came out and walked across the street with Emily. When Jason backed the car out, the bus had moved on with Emily on board. Jason had intended to tell Janet to send his suit to the cleaners but she either did not walk Emily to the bus or made a hurried trip back indoors. "I'll remind her tonight," thought Jason and then thought, "Maybe she didn't come out at all. If not, the driver didn't get out of the bus to watch Emily cross the street."

"That's something I will address when I'm elected to the school board," said Jason as he cautiously entered the street.

"That driver should have gotten out and escorted Emily across the road and into the bus." Jason considered this as he pulled to a stop at the flashing lights of another bus, and waited for children to cross the road and load. A mother was crossing with this group but in Jason's mind it was still dangerous.

Later that day, all of this erupted into actuality when Jason heard the shrill of the siren as the ambulance pulled into the Emergency Room bay. He looked out his window and saw a small child being wheeled into the hospital.

His scheduled patient was either late or not coming at all. He was reviewing the notes on a patient due for surgery the next day when his pager sounded.

It was the emergency room needing help with a child and Jason only waited long enough to tell Trudy Simmons before he was on his way. He realized it must be the child he had seen being brought in as he entered the service area.

Upon examination he told the nurse to call Trudy and tell her to get the surgery room ready as quickly as possible. Leaving the ER people to get the patient prepared and moved to the surgery facility, he took the stairs two at a time.

When he examined the mangled body, he realized that one eye could not be saved and he was heart broken.

"How did this happen?" asked Jason through his mask as he began the slow process of saving the eye itself if not the vision.

"A car passed a school bus when children were starting to cross and this child was thrown up in the air," stated the operating room nurse.

"I knew this was going to happen. The driver who picks up my daughter did not get out of the bus this morning. My wife walks her across the street but many mothers don't. That needs to be changed," grumbled Jason as he straightened his long back and shrugged out of his gown and cap.

Jason kept the child on his mind and that evening he told Kyle Bender about the accident, as they played their usual bowling game.

"Kyle, I'm going to start visiting the schools, town meetings, and every place where I can get an audience. We shouldn't wait for a child to be hurt before we think of safety," explained Jason.

"That's true and even if you don't get elected that issue will be before the public," said Kyle reflectively. "Of course, the other candidates may have already latched on to that campaign slogan."

Jason swung around angrily. "I hope you don't think I'd use an injured child to get votes."

Kyle looked startled. "Hey, don't get your dander up. I just meant that most candidates look for something that will appeal to the voters. I know that you are really concerned."

Jason looked at Kyle sheepishly. "Sorry, Kyle. I know you wouldn't think that of me." They changed their shoes and were headed out to the parking lot.

Jason said, "You know, you're right though. If anyone of the others thought about that safety issue they would jump on the bandwagon, wouldn't they?"

Kyle agreed and they rode toward home in companionable silence. As they reached their street, Kyle said, "It might be a good idea for you to think back on the issues which have come before the school board. Also, if you could send out a questionnaire to teachers asking about what concerns they may have."

"I thought about that," replied Jason. "It probably wouldn't be a bad idea to send out flyers to all residents of this district asking the same thing. What do you think?"

Kyle studied for a minute. "I think it is good but it may be cheaper to put it in the paper. Of course that will cost you also."

Jason agreed but felt that he could afford an ad in the paper. "Do you think Sam Sidote would interview me on the radio?"

"Nope! If he did he would have to interview all six candidates. He might consider a panel to question all of you," offered Kyle meditatively. "Have you ever heard of door to door salesmen?" Kyle asked.

"You mean like Fuller Brush men and Watkins Products?" asked Jason, looking puzzled.

Kyle laughed. "I'm not meaning to take samples. I just mean that I think it would be really helpful for you to go door-to-door and meet the people of your district. A lot of people don't know you. They know of you, but meeting you personally may make a lot of difference."

"You may be right, Kyle, but when would I have the time? Maybe an hour or so in the evenings is all I have," explained Jason

"What about Saturdays and Sundays after church? You could cover a lot of territory in that time," offered Kyle, thinking aloud.

"That's what I like about you, Kyle. You are very creative. Actually, I think a panel of candidates on the radio is a good idea," stated Jason. "I guess I'll run out to the radio station tomorrow evening."

Jason sat thinking as he pulled to a stop in his driveway. "How much would it cost me to get you to do some of this door-to-door hand shaking with me, old buddy?" asked Jason as he opened his door to get out.

"I don't know about that. I don't know how Rita would like that and you don't know what Janet will say either. Peace in my home is worth a lot to me," said Kyle as he grinned with raised eyebrows.

Undoubtedly both wives had agreed since Jason and Kyle spent the rest of their free time knocking on doors. One evening, the committeeman for the Browns Creek District, on the Republican side, went along with them when they campaigned.

A week later, Jason asked the committeeman on the Democrat side to go along with them. They stopped at roadside fruit stands, shook hands, and talked about issues. There were many concerns about school bus safety, consolidation, teacher requirements, maintenance of the buildings, and many other things brought up by the people they met.

Kyle grinned wryly after returning from campaigning with the Democrat committeeman, and stated, "I'll bet the County Commission will rake this committeeman through the coals when he finds that you haven't gone along with his ideas on consolidation."

Jason looked amazed. "Do you mean to tell me that the County Commission has a say in who is on the school board? I can see them working together but not picking the board members. I've heard that Mr. Whalen is a real party boss and rules the county but I didn't know he would go that far."

"He has his finger in every pie in this county, or so I'm

told," said Kyle. He continued, "I'm told he takes his orders from the State Chairman of the Democrat Party but I don't know if that's true or not. I guess you'll soon find out."

Since both the Republican committeeman and the Democrat committeeman had been with Jason, people were beginning to believe that Jason was truly an Independent and therefore he was gaining trust.

Jason was also on a radio panel with the six other candidates and seemed to do really well since he was more articulate than most of the other candidates.

Jason and Kyle campaigned until ten o'clock on the evening before the election. Election Day found them going from polling place to polling place, canvassing votes. They did this until the polls closed and then went home, sighing tiredly. Rita and Janet had supper ready for them before they set up the card table to play rummy while they listened to the election returns on the radio and watched it on television.

# CHAPTER 27

Election night was long and tiring for the McCalls and the Benders. When both families decided to call it a night, Bill Delp and Jason were running neck-and-neck. Jason arose from his seat to go to bed, thinking he had lost. "That loud-mouth Carlos Matthew from the Elkhorn District won handily," he stated grimly.

"Well, look who he had running against him. Not many people want a man who runs a beer joint and is a gambler on the school board, so I guess they chose the 'loud mouth,'" professed Kyle, and Janet and Rita agreed as the Benders left for home.

The next morning, Jason arose slowly, not eager to check the election returns but also wanting to know. He switched to WELC radio to hear Sam Sidote's voice giving the weather. He left the radio on and went into the bathroom, leaving the door open.

Before he had finished brushing his teeth, the telephone rang. Janet sleepily reached for the phone as Jason stepped to the bedside table to answer it. Janet passed the phone to Jason and fell back on the pillow. When Jason said hello, Kyle's voice came loud and clear. "Good Morning! Mr. School Board Member."

"You're kidding, aren't you?" questioned Jason.

"No, you really won. You had 2014 votes to Bill Delp's 1904 and he has conceded. I've been up since five o'clock," stated Kyle in an alert voice.

"Are you at work?" asked Jason.

"Sure, some of us have to really work for a living, you know," Kyle said with a laugh before cutting the connection.

"Well, Janet McCall, it seems that you are married to a school board member for Browns Creek District," said Jason, smiling.

Janet turned over, opened her eyes wide, and then asked, "Does that mean you'll be home more?"

Jason smiled as he started back to the bathroom. "I think

so. The campaign is over. I'll just have board meetings to attend, as far as I know."

Jason was delighted but also let down. He realized that he liked the challenge of running for office. He liked traveling all over the area and meeting so many people.

During the course of the campaign, he had visited every school in McDowell County briefly. He had seen that many buildings needed refurbishing and some actually needed to be torn down and rebuilt. This made him realize the burden for the County Commissioners. They were trying to ease the financial burden of keeping so many small schools open when they talked about consolidation.

However, Jason still felt that when a school was taken out of a community, it really hurt that community. Certainly there was the cost of maintenance for lots of buildings but when you put the buses, gas, repairs, and hazards to children on these mountainous roads into the equation, he felt keeping the buildings would win.

Jason had always thought that Lucinda may be teaching school in McDowell County but he now realized he was mistaken. "I don't know why I thought that anyway," he had chastened himself, but knew that thinking she was gave an extra impetus for his visits. Jason did not consciously want to think of Lucinda, but he still did not like going to Sterling Drive-In and he never passed the door beside Mountaineer Grill that he did not remember kissing Lucinda on the stairs.

All of this Jason guiltily kept to himself since he felt it was unfair to Janet. As hard as he tried, however, he just could not seem to keep Lucinda from popping into his thoughts.

When school started the next year, Emily was in the fourth grade and wanted to be in everything. She was an excellent student and was often called upon to participate in fundraisers and other school functions. The elementary and the middle schools had a spelling contest each year at each school. The winners in each school went to a county competition and the county winners went to the regional competition and finally to the state.

This year Emily was not only the school winner but the county winner and was slated to go to Beckley to the regional competition. Jason and Janet were proud and excited. Jason had gotten another doctor to stand in for him for a couple of days so that he could take Emily to Beckley.

The competition was being held at the Woodrow Wilson High School on Stanaford Street and each participant was told to be there early in order to rehearse the procedure. Jason had reserved a room at the Beckley Hotel, which wasn't a great distance from the high school.

Early on the morning of the competition, they had breakfast in their room and then took a taxi to Church Street. From there they walked slowly down the street, admiring the large church on the corner, and looking in shop windows on the way. Jason did not want Emily to be nervous and kept up a laughing monologue until they were almost there.

"Emily, you know that your mom and I couldn't be prouder of you than we are right now. Win or lose, that will always be the same."

Jason stooped and pulled her around to face him before asking, "You do know it will not make any difference in how we feel about you, don't you?"

Emily threw her arms around his neck and said, "Sure, Dad, I know that I'm your sun, moon, and stars. Hilda and Mom tell me that all the time." She giggled, "But, I'm glad you told me anyway."

They entered the hall and a small, short, attractive lady came over and asked their names. She then led them to a table where she selected a badge with Emily's name on it and pinned it to her dress. After explaining the procedure to all of them, she told Jason and Janet to go into the auditorium and find seats, then she took Emily through a door to the left and down a hallway.

Jason and Janet, wanting to be near enough for Emily to see them, went down the steps to a tier of seats near the stage and started through the row of seats toward the center when they came face to face with Lucinda Harmon, now Marshall.

Janet was in front and politely said, "Excuse me," and went on toward the seats. She took a seat and looked around to see Jason standing stock still in front of the woman she had just passed.

Finally finding his voice, Jason said, "Hello, Lucinda. Is your son in the spelling bee?"

Lucinda had turned red and dropped her head, but replied, "Yes. He won first place in the county."

Seeing Janet staring, Jason knew he had to do something and he said, "Janet, come and meet someone."

When Janet came back, they all stood there for a minute and then Jason said, "Janet, this is Lucinda Harmon...Marshall. I met her when I visited a patient on Bradshaw Mountain, when I was working in McDowell County the first time."

Janet stared at Lucinda hostilely and then said, "Yes, I know about Lucinda Harmon. Hello, Mrs. Marshall." Janet stressed the Mrs. as she stared at Lucinda.

Lucinda raised her eyes to Janet's face and tried to smile. "It's nice to meet you, Mrs. McCall. Do you have a child in the spelling bee?"

"Yes, we do. Our daughter, Emily, was the McDowell County winner," said Janet, putting stress on 'our daughter'." Then she asked. "Is your husband with you?"

Lucinda seemed to shrink as she said, "No, he had to work. He'll be sorry he missed meeting you." Then Lucinda said, "Excuse me please. I forgot to tell my son something." She went past Janet through the row of seats away from Jason and left the auditorium.

Jason had gone through this ordeal with thoughts tumbling through his mind. Why was she so thin? Why would she not look at him? Why did she want to get away so fast?

Jason knew that Janet's attitude had not been lost on Lucinda but felt there was something else also. Without saying a word, Jason followed Janet to the seats in the middle and sat down.

"I don't think she is all that beautiful," hissed Janet angrily as she turned in her seat to look at him. "You made a spectacle of yourself, standing there like you had been struck by lightning."

Jason looked soberly at Janet. "Will you please wait until this is over and we are home. You don't want to make a scene here, I'm sure."

Janet scowled fiercely and said, "Oh no, that would never do. Your sweet, innocent Lucinda would see what a terrible wife you have, wouldn't she?"

Jason rose from his seat. "I'm going to get something to drink. Do you want to come or should I bring you something?"

Janet rose also. "I think I'll go. There may be something more attractive than a soda out there."

They went into the hall again and found a soda machine at the end of the hall. Jason put a quarter in the machine and got out a Coca-cola, which he knew was Janet's favorite, before he got a Seven-Up for himself.

They stood drinking their sodas and had started back towards the auditorium when the main doors opened and several parents came in. Hurriedly they made their way inside and to the front row in front of the stage.

Soon the stage lights came on and the students filed in with their teachers. The local radio station announcer, Mr. Savage, was to conduct the contest. He asked each student to step up to the microphone and give their name and the county they were from.

Both Jason and Janet set tensely beside each other. Jason told himself that this could not have happened at a worse time. He knew that Janet would not hold her anger until they reached the privacy of their bedroom back in Welch.

Suddenly his eyes were riveted to the stage as a young red-headed boy walked tall and proud to the microphone and stated that he was Daniel Jefferson Marshall from Pineville, Wyoming County.

Jason remembered how he had cowered when his father brought him back in for his check-up. This boy looked full of self-confidence and was a very nice looking boy.

"He was just afraid of that damn barbarian," mumbled Jason and Janet gave him a hateful look.

"So, she's been living just over the line all this time," thought Jason and then turned his thoughts back to Emily, who now walked up to the microphone with a big smile on her face. "I am Emily Elizabeth McCall from Welch, McDowell County, and my daddy is right there on the front row."

There were gasps and snickers and some muted good humored laughs from the audience before they settled down to hear the other contestants.

After the first round, Mingo and Mercer Counties were out and Raleigh lost on the second round, leaving Wyoming pitted against McDowell.

Emily McCall and Daniel Marshall stood looking steadily at each other as each spelled their word correctly. The next word was omniscience and Emily looked at Daniel and smiled as she spelled it correctly. Daniel smiled back before he was given the word rendezvous but quickly sobered as he had trouble. He asked for a definition and when it was given he still misspelled the word.

Emily looked as if she was about to cry and Daniel looked so defeated. Emily ran to him and said something then patted his shoulder. Daniel looked at her and tried valiantly to smile.

Emily received a gold cup and two hundred dollars and Daniel received a silver cup and one hundred dollars. Emily grasped his hand and they walked off the stage together since they would both be entered into the state contest later that year.

Jason met them at the foot of the stairs where he gave Emily a hug and said to her opponent, "You did a good job, Daniel. That was a hard word."

"It sure was," said Emily. "I'm glad he got it instead of me. I would have probably missed it too."

Daniel looked up and recognized Jason. "You're the doctor who worked on my eye that time, aren't you, sir?" asked Daniel with an intent look.

"I sure am, Daniel, and I'm glad the accident didn't cause

permanent damage to your eye," said Jason with a smile as he reached out to shake Daniel's hand.

Daniel grasped his hand firmly and smiled as he said, "Thanks, sir. You are very nice, no matter what." Then seeming to suddenly remember something, he turned away.

"I think I see my mother, so I'd better go." He turned to Emily and smiled. "You're a good speller. I hope we meet again sometime."

Daniel almost ran up the stairs and as Jason watched him, he saw Lucinda standing at the door to the auditorium as if poised for flight.

## CHAPTER 28

Jason was right. Janet only waited until they were seated in the car. As soon as Jason started the engine she turned to Emily in the back seat and said, "Did you like that Marshall boy?"

Emily who was busy inspecting her gold cup looked up and said, "Yes, he was nice."

Then she giggled and said, "He's handsome too. Didn't you think so?"

Janet smirked as she said, "His mother was your daddy's girl friend before we got married."

"Janet," Jason stormed. "That won't make any difference to Emily. It has no bearing on whether she likes him or not. What if I said things about some of your past boyfriends?"

"Dad-dee, " Emily said with a giggle. "You had another girl friend and Mommy is jealous."

Emily tapped Janet on the shoulder, "Mommy, you're too old for that. My friend Amanda is jealous of Toby Atkins but she is in the fourth grade."

Jason grinned but kept his face turned to the outside window.

Janet looked as if she'd had cold water dashed in her face. To have her almost-nine-year-old daughter tell her she was acting childish certainly put a damper on her anger. She turned to look out the window and made no answer.

Emily sat quietly in the back seat until they were nearing Pineville and she read the sign. "Here's where he lives. He lives in Pineville, but I don't know which house he lives in."

Janet then looked around, "When did he tell you that?" Then she remembered the announcer saying, "Daniel Jefferson Marshall of Pineville, Wyoming County."

"The announcer told the audience which town we were all from, Mommy. Don't you remember?" questioned Emily.

"Sure, I forgot, Emily. Did you get to talk to him about anything else?" asked Janet.

"Yep. I asked him lots of things and told him lots of things,"

Emily chirped happily.

"He knows Daddy because he hurt his eye one time and Daddy fixed it. He and his mom were coming back from visiting his grandparents who lived somewhere around Bradshaw," continued Emily and would have gone on but Jason intervened.

"Emily, will you please stop? It gets your mom upset when you mention Danny's mother," stated Jason seriously.

Since Jason seldom used that serious tone with her, Emily immediately said, "Sure, Daddy, I'll stop, but Mommy did ask me if I knew anything else."

Nothing else was said and they rode on into Welch and pulled into their driveway before anyone spoke a word.

"Let me out, Daddy—let me out. There's Uncle Kyle and I want to tell him I won," said Emily and jumped out as soon as Jason unlocked the door.

Kyle Bender, stopped with a big smile on his face, as he saw Emily jump from the car smiling. "I think I see a winner. What's that you're bringing home, Emmy E?" he asked, using his pet name for Emily as she ran toward him with her trophy in her hands.

"It's my trophy and I got two hundred dollars besides. What do you think of that?" asked Emily proudly.

"Why, I think that deserves one of Rita's homemade chocolate pies and maybe some homemade ice cream," Kyle said as he hugged Emily fondly.

Emily turned to Janet. "Mommy, can I go with Uncle Kyle for some pie and ice cream?" she asked.

Janet nodded her assent from a stormy face and Jason raised his eyebrows as Kyle looked at him questioningly.

Emily followed Kyle across the lawn to his house as Jason and Janet went into their house. Jason made it to the kitchen before Janet hissed angrily.

"You knew that Harmon girl lived in Pineville, didn't you? Why didn't you tell me you had treated her son?"

Jason stood looking at Janet soberly before saying, "Janet, I didn't know you knew about Lucinda. How did you find out, anyway?" he questioned.

"Don't be stupid, Jason. Of course I know about her. Almost everybody in Pittsburgh knew about her, since Elizabeth was so upset. That was her cry for months," mocked Janet as she imitated his mother. "'My poor Jason is down there among that bunch of illiterates and is going to get in trouble. He's lonesome and is seeing some girl from down there. She'll end up pregnant and he'll marry that little nobody.'"

Jason was furious and Janet blanched as he turned a malevolent stare on her and through gritted teeth said, "I think we'd best leave this discussion until our tempers have cooled." He then stalked out to the car and roared away down the street.

Janet went through the house crying and ended up face down on her bed where she punched pillows and finally relieved her anger. Then she dialed the McCall house and spoke to Elizabeth.

Jason returned an hour later expecting Emily would be in bed and he would have to face one of Janet's jealous tirades. Instead, a calm smiling Janet offered him a cup of hot chocolate.

He found Janet and Emily seated cozily together on the sofa watching Sid Caesar and Imogene Coca. They laughed merrily just as he walked in the door and Emily jumped up and ran to him. Grabbing his hand, she drew him toward the sofa.

"Come on, Daddy. Finish watching the show with us. It will make you laugh."

Jason sat on the other side of Emily and Janet looked over with a smile, and said, "I made hot chocolate. Do you want a cup?"

Jason looked up and, seeing no anger on her face, decided that she had gotten past her fit of temper. He smiled and nodded yes. Janet quickly left the room and Emily snuggled close to his side and said, "This is nice isn't it, Dad? I mean, the three of us together and not mad at each other."

Jason hugged her close. "It sure is, Princess. I don't like

to be angry," he murmured, just as Janet came back with the chocolate. She also had a plate of cookies, which she placed on a table beside him

Jason looked up at her and smiled as he said, "Thanks, Janet. This is nice and a most welcome surprise."

Janet smiled in relief. "You are welcome, sir. I can be nice occasionally, you know, even if Hilda did make the cookies."

Jason reached over and grasped her hand. "You are nice most of the time, Janet. You really are and I'm proud of you."

Janet leaned behind Emily and kissed Jason on the cheek. Emily craned her neck around and said as if disgusted.

"Well, that's the end of watching television if you two are going to smooch."

They all three burst out laughing and Jason said, "It's pretty hard to get in the mood to smooch with a little nosy daughter watching every move we make."

The show was soon over and Janet looked at Emily, and started to speak, to be forestalled by Emily's, "Yes, Mom, I know. It's bath time."

Then she grinned wickedly before saying as she went, "It is more likely to be smoochie, smoochie time."

Jason laughed and threw a cushion at her as she went through the door into the hall. She looked back and giggled happily and yelled, "Ha ha! You missed me."

The next day Jason wondered what had brought on the sudden change in Janet. When he had slammed out of the house she was bent toward a jealous, angry tirade but an hour later she was totally different. He was afraid to question her about it since he felt that any mention of Lucinda would have the same result.

His most prevalent thought was that his mother had painted a very biased picture of Lucinda and all the people in southern West Virginia. He would have liked to be able to talk to Janet about the situation but feared bringing the subject up. Therefore, they both steered clear of any talk about the spelling bee and they certainly did not discuss Lucinda Harmon Marshall.

Jason kept himself busy and became more and more involved in community life. Representative Harry Pauley was reported to be trying to get the legislature to fund another works project in the county and Jason was interested.

"I think I'll get better acquainted with Mr. Pauley. He sounds like a man that gets things done." Jason said to Kyle when he read about the project in the paper.

"Yes, it does seem that way. I don't know him. I just know of him and most I've heard has been good, if you can say a politician is good," Kyle said.

"I guess politics is like anything else...some good, some bad, and a few that don't know what they're doing. It's the same in everything," stated Jason reflectively.

"Some teachers are excellent, some mediocre, and some shouldn't be allowed to enter a classroom. It's the same with doctors and all professions."

Kyle listened closely before saying, "Sure that's true, but when the voter doesn't know how to pick the good ones, his tax dollars still pay for the duds. That's what makes people angry."

Jason grinned in agreement. "That's life, my friend. It's like a hand of poker. You either hold them or fold them and take your chances."

"My God, what kind of attitude is that?" exclaimed Kyle. "Life's not a poker game. Educated people should make wise choices."

"Kyle, how many people do you think we have in McDowell County who are educated? I mean, educated in the workings of government. They should be but they aren't," stated Jason with concern.

They had been having lunch at the Mountaineer Grill and were now finished. Jason paid the bill and they walked into the street.

Suddenly Kyle said, "You're on the school board, so why don't you get the county to start a series of classes on government?"

By this time they had reached the car and Jason unlocked

the door and got in, waiting until Kyle was settled. He turned to look at Kyle as the engine roared to life. "Classes for whom? Civics is taught in schools already, but it must not be very effective."

"No, I meant citizenship classes as evening classes, or something like that," Kyle suggested.

"Hmm, I don't know Kyle. How many do you think would attend?" asked Jason curiously.

"Probably none, unless you paid them," grumbled Kyle. "I wasn't thinking. Some of these people don't care what happens as long as they have money in their pockets and a roof over their heads."

"I suppose they've made it all right so far and they just don't see the need to get involved. Most people vote for the same party that their parents voted for whether they know the candidate or not. I'd say that two-thirds of the voters go in the booth and vote a straight ticket, wouldn't you?" questioned Jason.

Kyle nodded yes and sighed in exasperation as they pulled into Jason's driveway, then smiled as he opened the door and said, "Well, thanks for helping me solve the political problems of this county."

"Sure thing. Just call on me. I have all the answers," said Jason as he slammed the car door and threw up his hand in farewell.

## CHAPTER 29

Everything seemed to be moving along in an even tenor for the McCalls and the Benders. They spent many hours together without ever having any kind of disagreement. However, Kyle sensed that in the last few years something had happened in the McCall marriage but did not know what.

One evening they had all returned from Beckley, where they had gone to see a movie. After the McCalls went home, Rita plopped down beside Kyle on the sofa. She put her feet up and heaved a sigh of contentment.

"Kyle, there's nothing I can really pin down to say it's this or that. I mean on the surface everything seems the same. Yet I feel an undercurrent between Jason and Janet that wasn't there before," said Rita curiously.

"Yeah, I sense it too. The only time I remember either of them being really upset though was when Emily won that spelling bee in Beckley," replied Kyle reflectively.

Rita thought about that. "You're right. I remember she barely spoke when they returned and Jason was very tense. They let Emily stay over here a long time that evening."

"Well, Emmy-E was happy enough for both of them. I'll never forget her hugging that trophy like it was a million dollars. But normally she would have been all over Jason, wanting him to take her to the Sterling for a treat, wouldn't she?" questioned Kyle.

Rita went toward the kitchen but stopped about halfway. "I wondered about that at the time but in a few days forgot all about it. But you are right. Jason isn't as relaxed as he once was, especially if we go to Beckley."

Kyle laughed. "Well, they're still together and that was four or five years ago. That must not be the problem. We're probably just seeing something that isn't there."

Rita pursed her lips. "Well, maybe, but there's something about Beckley and Pineville which grabs Janet's attention. Remember when you and Jason were talking about some business man in Pineville asking Jason to set up a clinic over there? Janet had the strangest look on her face.

Kyle got up stretched and yawned. "I don't know about a look but she was certainly against it. I remember that quite well."

Rita got up too. "So do I, and if you recall Jason made the fastest decision I've ever known him to make about eye care." They both went to bed still wondering about the McCalls.

Several months later, Rita, Kyle, and Katie went to Beckley shopping and to spend the day out. They were going down an aisle in Hills Department Store looking for new curtain material to redecorate Katie's room when they came face to face with a girl they hadn't seen in years.

Lucinda Harmon gasped in pleased surprise. "Rita Gilmer! Oh my! What a surprise, and Kyle Bender also. You got married, didn't you?"

Lucinda threw her arms wide and gathered Rita close in a big hug. Suddenly she looked beside Kyle and there stood a young version of Rita and Kyle combined. She had Rita's gentle eyes, curling hair, and nice complexion, but Kyle's chin and saucy grin as well as his mischievous gray eyes.

Rita and Kyle began at the same time. "Where have you been?" Kyle stopped and Rita continued, "I thought you had died, girl. What happened? You went away to college but then we lost touch. Where do you live?" questioned Rita as she took Lucinda's arm and started toward the front of the store.

"Kyle, you and Katie go ahead and find what Katie wants and then Katie can come for me. I want to talk to Lucinda."

The two old friends spent a very pleasant half-hour catching up. They exchanged phone numbers, promising each other to call occasionally and keep in touch.

In the car going home, Rita went on and on about how little Lucinda had changed as to looks. "She looks sad though. Didn't you think so, Kyle? Her eyes looked so…I don't know… forlorn. Didn't you notice?" questioned Rita.

Kyle admitted that he, too, thought Lucinda didn't seem that bubbly, happy girl they had known, even though she laughed and smiled.

That evening they invited the McCalls over to grill burgers with them and both Rita and Kyle scurried around getting everything ready. Katie, now ready to graduate, had a date and Emily, now in the eighth grade, was down the street playing volley ball with her friends.

"I'll call Emily when the food is ready and save a cheeseburger for Katie," said Rita as she carried condiments to the picnic table. Katie had often told her mother not to save food for her, but Rita's reply was always the same. "I'd feel awful to fix something I know you like and not save some for you."

Kyle often wondered how hard it was going to be on Rita when Katie married and moved out.

Jason had served two terms on the school board and was now contemplating a run for the County Commission. The pros and cons of this action were discussed, and Janet quipped. "Well, Rita, I suppose we may as well forget about having our husbands home for more than two or three hours each day. We will only see them after ten o'clock at night when all Jason's constituents are in bed."

This was said good-naturedly and the conversation continued on in this peaceful camaraderie as they settled back in lawn chairs to enjoy their burgers.

Suddenly Rita said, "Jason, I met an old friend today. You may know her, Lucinda Harmon from Bradshaw. Did you ever meet her when you worked over there?"

Jason sat silent and Janet gasped aloud. Rita looked at them in amazement. "What? Did I say something wrong? I used to work with her at the insurance agency. She left and went to Concord and I never heard from her after that." Rita stopped suddenly as she sensed something had upset Janet.

Janet spoke first in a strangled voice, since she had taken a drink of coke which had gone down the wrong way. "Yes, we both know her, don't we, Jason?" giving dagger glares at Jason as she spoke.

"Yes, I met her when I worked at Bradshaw, but I haven't seen her but once or twice since," replied Jason as he looked at Janet beseechingly. "Her son won second place in the spelling bee that Emily won in Beckley."

Rita looked at Kyle with raised eyebrows and an "Uh-Huh" imperceptible nod. They had thought the trip to Beckley had caused something to happen to the McCalls.

"We didn't know she had a son, or was even married for that matter, until we happened to bump into her in Hills Department Store there in Beckley," supplied Kyle, trying to ease the tension that had suddenly arisen.

Both Rita and Kyle, sensing that Lucinda Harmon was not a good subject to discuss, got up from their chairs to start cleaning up just as Emily arrived.

"There you are, Emmy-E. I don't know if we have anything left for you," teased Kyle as he looked around for a plate.

Emily settled on one of the chairs to eat and looked at each person in turn as she bit into her burger. "It was awfully hot when I was down there playing, but a cold spell has blown in here. What's up? Did you folks have a falling out?" asked Emily in wonder.

"No, Miss Emmy-E, we've not fallen out. We've been discussing whether your dad should run for County Commission this year and you know politics can dampen any party," said Kyle, laughing.

"Don't do it, Dad," said Emily as she munched. "If we don't have people like you on the school board, we will never get a new high school and by the time I graduate, we'll be holding classes in the hallways."

"It's too crowded already," cut in Rita. "Nancy Smaltz, who teaches math over there, said she had thirty-five students in four of her classes and twenty-nine in the other two. She says it makes for bad teaching and I'm sure it does."

Jason spoke up, "I know for a fact that overcrowding in the classroom creates discipline problems. Every teacher I've talked to in the last few years has expressed similar concerns."

He sat studying for a few minutes before patting Emily on the head. "Okay, Princess. That settles it. I won't run for the commission. I'll start in tomorrow working to get a new high school built before you graduate. How does that sound?" asked Jason, with a big smile on his face.

Emily jumped up and ran to Jason and plopped down on his knee. Looking around she said, "I've got this man wrapped right around my little finger," then held her little finger up in the air as she laughed merrily.

Everybody but Janet was back to normal and the atmosphere was much more relaxed, until Janet got up, saying she was going home to lie down, that she had a headache. She walked across the Bender's lawn, telling Emily and Jason to help Rita and Kyle clean up as she went.

When Janet had crossed the lawn and gone into her own house, Emily piped up. "Okay, which one of you guys said something to set her off? I know Mom. If she gets upset she lays down with a headache."

"I guess she got upset because I was talking of running for the county commission," answered Jason, while giving a warning glance over Emily's head.

"Okay, if you say so, but I think it was something else. She'll tell me. She always does, you know," Emily warned Jason with a knowing smile.

Jason got up and began cleaning the barbeque pit, then said, "Kyle, what am I going to do with this girl? She has ESP."

Kyle laughed. "Are you just now finding that out? I've known that since she was two years old and started telling time."

Jason lingered as long as he could, cleaning and chatting, since he dreaded what he might encounter when he went home.

Finally, he grasped Emily's arm and said, "Come on, little mind reader, let's go home."

Emily hugged both Kyle and Rita and thanked them before scampering behind her dad as he strolled toward his front door.

When they went in, Janet was seated at the dining room

table with a sheet of paper in front of her. She looked up as they entered but did not speak.

"Is your headache better, Mom?" asked Emily, putting her arm around Janet's shoulders.

Janet patted her hand before saying, "Yes, Emily. It's almost better. Did you enjoy your game?"

"Yeah, I did. My team won. It always does because I choose the best players," Emily said with a laugh. "I swear Mary Ann is so dumb. She still doesn't know how my team always wins. She picks her friends and none of them are good players. You'd think she'd catch on after a while. She knows I can't stand Harry Stoots, but I always choose him."

"What don't you like about Harry? I think he is a nice boy," asked Janet.

Emily thought for a minute before she replied. "He's fat and sweats a lot and his eyes are little piggy eyes. That's probably because he's so fat and he always wants to pat on me," Emily continued as she shivered in revulsion.

"I can see why you don't want him to pat you, Princess, but try not to be unkind. Okay?" asked Jason as he patted her on the head and went towards the bathroom. Once inside, he breathed a sigh of relief thinking that at least Janet was not going to make a scene in front of Emily.

Jason knew he had not heard the last of the news that Lucinda was a friend of Rita and Kyle, but he didn't know how the information would be used by Janet.

Several days later, he knew the direction she was going to take when, right out of the blue, Janet said, "Jason, wouldn't you like a bigger house? Emily is growing up fast and we need a room where she can bring her friends and have maybe sleepovers and things like that."

Jason had never heard Emily say one word about being dissatisfied with where they lived. In fact, he was pretty sure Emily would not want to move, but he went along just to see what Janet would say.

"It's hard to find houses in this area, Janet, and there's certainly not much land for sale around here," answered

Jason. "You're not thinking of moving out of Welch, are you?"

"If I could just talk some sense into you, we could move back to Pittsburgh. I've lived fourteen years down here with you and I don't see why we can't live where I want to live for a change," complained Janet.

"Janet, I can't retire now. Men in their forties don't retire and besides that, I like, no, love-my work. I'd go nuts if I retired," Jason adamantly stated.

"I didn't say retire. You could go to work in one of the hospitals in Pittsburgh. You know you could and Daddy would help you. I'd love to move back to civili…I mean I'd love to go home," said Janet wistfully.

Emily came prancing through the room to show off her new cheerleader outfit. "Who wants to go home? Not me. I'm already home and I love it, love it, love it," gushed Emily as she spun around showing off her flared skirt.

"How do you two like my new outfit? Isn't it the most?" asked Emily, too alive to be still.

Jason turned to his exuberant daughter with a smile. "Princess, you do a lot for that outfit. You make it happy just like you make me happy. Come give your old Dad a big hug," said Jason, spreading his arms wide. Emily catapulted into his embrace, almost knocking them both to the floor.

Janet stood looking on. Seeing how happy Jason and Emily were seemed to give her pause for she said, "I guess my idea doesn't merit attention after that endorsement of this place."

She smiled at Emily and in a resigned voice said, "All right, you little minx. You know how to turn people up sweet, don't you?"

Emily pulled out of Jason's embrace and ran to Janet. She threw her arms around Janet and looked up at her, smiling as she said, "I want you to be happy like me, Mom. I really do. You are, aren't you?"

Seeing something in Janet's face that puzzled her, Emily said, "What is it, Mom? You have friends here, and you said you liked the house, so why do you want to go back to Pittsburgh?

That can't be home to you now. Home is here."

Janet smiled and hugged her daughter as if she feared she'd suddenly be gone. "I don't know, Honey. I think I must be tired. Sometimes I remember things from there and it makes me homesick, I guess."

## CHAPTER 30

From that day forward, week after week and month after month, there were subtle hints and some not so subtle about moving back to Pittsburgh. Even a year later she was still at it. Janet knew that Emily did not want to move and Jason certainly did not want to move.

Privately, Jason thought that Janet only wanted to move as far away as she could get from where she thought Jason might have an opportunity to see Lucinda Harmon.

Lucinda would never be Marshall to Jason. He just could not think of her with that rude, belligerent man. Jason tried to be fair and think that he might be a nice man because Lucinda had married him, but his two encounters with the man had left a strong negative impression.

Regardless of Janet's hints, Jason put it out of his mind. He had a goal in mind and all his concentration was bent in that direction. He wanted a new high school for Welch and the surrounding area.

Now Jason and Paul Christian, another member of the school board, were working closely with Pierce K. Martin, the present Superintendent of Schools, in an effort to get the new school. Jason felt that he had helped the students and the teachers during his tenure on the school board.

Now the bus drivers could only pick up and drop off children on the right side of the roads. This kept children from having to cross the roads in front of oncoming traffic. Now, there were also school patrols, to stop traffic around schools when the buses were loading or unloading, especially in the towns.

When George W. Bryson had retired, J. E. Batten had served for a short time before Pierce K. Martin had taken over. Jason liked Mr. Martin but he felt that George Bryson had wielded more power and had more influence in the county. Some said that he had enough power to control the entire county, but Jason had only met a nice, intelligent, and dedicated school superintendent. George Bryson and Pierce K. Martin were both honorable men and Jason worked well with both of them.

Now, it seemed different, however. Instead of the school board controlling the county, Jason felt that the county commission was taking control of the county. Even the school board appeared to heed whatever was dictated from the county commission.

"Kyle, I see the need for county agencies to work together, but it seems as if only one is calling the shots," stated Jason as they returned from a Kiwanis Club meeting.

"Yeah, and it has gotten worse since Bill Bishop became Clerk of the County Court," stated Kyle assuredly.

Jason grinned wryly, "Who do you suppose is pulling his strings?"

"Somebody told me a certain state senator was instrumental in getting him elected to the Clerk position," replied Kyle grimacing in disgust.

"Was that the same somebody who told you to see if you could get me to register Democratic last year?" questioned Jason as he smiled broadly.

"You're getting real warm, but guess again. You'd be surprised where that information came from," stated Kyle seriously. "In fact, I keep trying to figure out what his purpose was in telling me."

Jason stopped the car in his driveway and sat with the engine running before turning to Kyle. "Somebody knows that if many more of these shenanigans take place, I will finally get disgusted enough to try to take a certain delegate's job. Now, that, good buddy, is what I've been hearing." Jason switched off the engine and opened his door as Kyle stepped to the sidewalk.

"Well, well, that explains a lot of things. When did you figure that one out?" asked Kyle in amazement.

Jason walked around the back of the car and lifted the trunk lid to retrieve the groceries he had stopped to buy.

He looked at Kyle and asked, "Wouldn't that be your thinking, if a member of the County Commission had informed you that you would make an excellent member to the House of Delegates?"

Kyle raised his eyebrows in surprise. "I certainly would, if Henry Samper is the one who told you that. Why he almost lives in Senator Fleming's pocket."

"Yeah, I know," said Jason with a smile. "It does look mighty suspicious. Now why would Henry Samper say that to me? There must be a reason," he said turning toward his own door.

Kyle chuckled and with raised eyebrows, turned to go as he replied, "I think you're beginning to see what I see, Doctor. Good night!" He then entered his own house.

That night after everyone else was asleep; Jason stole from his bed, and taking a ledger pad from the desk in the den, made his way to the kitchen. Here he wouldn't be disturbed since it was farthest from the bedrooms. He wanted to really concentrate on these political lures, hints, rumors, and innuendos and he did not want to be disturbed. He got a soda from the refrigerator and sat down to do some thinking.

He began to number things in numerical order of their happening and his result was very enlightening.

1. Both parties wanted him to be either a Democrat or a Republican.
2. Both parties offered him help the first time he ran for the school board.
3. Neither party overtly opposed him on his second run for the board.
4. Then he had done some campaigning against Wade Dotson in his run for county commission and Dotson was a bosom friend of Delegate Henry Paulson.
5. Since Paulson, Samper, and Senator Fleming were all Democrats and yet opposed each other, it appeared that there were two factions forming or already formed in the county and probably the state Democratic Party
6. Since Bill Bishop was Clerk of the County Court and Kyle had heard that the County Commission was running the school board (behind the scenes of course) then who was Bill Bishop aligned with?
7. Were Paulson and Bill Bishop working together, or was

Paulson only using Bishop to take control of the school board?
8. Or was Bill Bishop really working with Senator Fleming, while leaving the impression he was with Paulson?
9. Was Samper sending out feelers to see if Jason would take a side or would even register as a Democrat?
10. It appeared to Jason as if Senator Fleming and Samper wanted him to run against Henry Paulson for House of Delegates.
11. Was the rumor true that Delegate Paulson had been working on some projects to help McDowell County with the Republican senator, Jacob Rivers?
12. If that rumor was true, then Senator Fleming and his cronies may want to oust Delegate Paulson.
13. Did someone think he had a chance to take Paulson's seat?
14. If this were the case, then Jason would know for sure that there were definitely two factions of the Democratic Party in the county and they were already at "daggers drawn."

"What a mess," said Jason aloud as he stood up, stretched, and yawned before putting his soda can in the garbage can.

"I'm not getting involved in that mess if I can help it," thought Jason, but at the same time knowing that he certainly did not want the school board controlled by anyone except the people. He shook his head sleepily and tiptoed back to the bedroom and eased quietly into bed.

He awoke with Janet shaking him. "Jason, wake up! Jason, turn that clock off. It's going to wake Emily. What's wrong with you? Are you sick?" questioned Janet worriedly.

Jason opened blurry eyes, ran his hand over his face and sat up. "Sorry! I didn't get much sleep last night," he said tiredly. "I'm not sick though. Kyle told me something last night that kept me awake."

"I guess he ran into their friend, Lucinda, again," Janet sneered.

Jason gasped, instantly awake, "Janet, do you think Kyle or Rita would ever mention that woman's name again after your reaction the first time?"

Now, Jason knew for certain why Janet wanted to move. She no longer trusted Kyle and Rita because they were friends to Lucinda.

"You don't see them as friends anymore, do you Janet?" questioned Jason as he gave her a probing look.

Janet hesitated before saying, "I still like them. It's just different since they met that woman."

Jason, who was already standing, reached down and pulled Janet into his arms. He looked at her steadily and then released her to sit on the bed beside her. "Janet, please believe me. I know that if Kyle or Rita had known that I had ever met Lucinda Harmon and it would upset you, they would never have mentioned her. That's been almost a year ago. Can't you just forget it ever happened? I can assure you they will never mention her again."

Seeing that Janet was still upset, Jason kissed her tenderly before saying, "Janet, I have not seen her since we met her in Beckley and that was almost five years ago. You know I haven't. Can't you let it go? I don't know what Mom must have told you, but please don't let it destroy us. Emily needs both of us."

Janet buried her face in his shoulder and hugged him tightly. "I'm sorry, Jason. I truly am. Now what did Kyle tell you?"

"I think he is being questioned as to whether I would register as a Democrat. I don't know if Kyle was asked to talk to me or not, but he wouldn't anyway. Kyle is like me. He respects a person's privacy."

"Why do they care whether you are Independent or a Democrat?" asked Janet.

"I'm not sure. That's what kept me up last night. It was hinted to me that I would make a good member of the House of Delegates," stated Jason in a puzzled manner.

Janet arose from the bed and headed for the bathroom but stopped and asked, "Were you thinking of running for that seat?"

Jason shook his head negatively. "Never entered my mind. I'm having so much trouble trying to get us a new high school that I don't have time for anything else."

He looked at the bedside clock. "I don't have time to do anything but get to work right now. Unless you want to share a shower with me, you'd better get your hinny out of the bathroom."

Janet laughed as she left going toward the kitchen. Jason quickly showered and shaved and then headed for the kitchen. He stopped at the door and stared in surprise at what awaited him. There on the table was orange juice, coffee, scrambled eggs, toast, and bacon, which was unusual, since Janet was usually too busy helping Emily get ready for school to make breakfast for him.

Jason smiled. "My, this looks good. Is it for me or Emily?"

Janet looked shocked. "You don't mean you could eat all that by yourself, do you? That is for all three of us."

Janet moved around the table to get juice glasses from the cabinet. Jason noticed her running her hand along the edge of the countertop as she went.

"You're still half asleep, Janet. You have to hold onto something to get to the cabinet." Jason laughed and then fearing he had hurt her feelings he said, "This is really sweet, Janet."

Janet turned with the glasses and came back to the table. Jason met her halfway and leaned in for a kiss. As he pulled away Janet suddenly crumpled toward the floor, sending the juice glasses in all directions.

## CHAPTER 31

Jason grabbed her just as her bottom hit the floor and was able to shield her head from injury. He lowered the rest of her gently onto the floor and checked her pulse, looked at her eyes, and felt for her heartbeat as she slowly moaned.

"Janet, Janet, speak to me. Please speak to me," begged Jason in panic as he patted her face gently.

Janet opened her eyes in amazement. "What is wrong with you and why am I lying in the floor?" She started to get up but Jason pushed her back.

"Lie still a few minutes, Honey. You fainted," ordered Jason calmly as he got to his feet, maneuvered a chair into place to receive her, and then grasped her arms to pull her up. Before he had moved her, however, Emily bounced into the room, sniffing in antic pantomime.

"Umm," she sniffed. What's that good smell…Mom, what are you doing sitting on the floor?" questioned Emily and broke into a giggle.

Jason gave Emily a dark angry glare. "Emily, your mother is sick. She fainted and is just now coming out of it." By this time, Janet was on her feet and was being helped into the chair.

Shocked speechless, Emily stood staring until Janet said, "I'm all right, Emily. It's all right to laugh if you want to. I guess I do look funny."

Emily went around the table and bent down to look into Janet's face.

"What's wrong, Mom? You've never fainted before. You're never sick either, so why did you faint?"

Janet was still clinging to Jason's hand, which she now squeezed as she said, "I don't know, Emily. I don't feel sick. I guess I just wanted to see what kind of reaction I would get."

She looked up at Jason and winked then looked at Emily who stood gaping in astonishment. "You fainted to see how we would react? Mom, people can't just faint anytime they want to, can they, Dad? I think you'd better go to see a doctor," said Emily before she realized that her dad was a doctor.

Seeing that Janet feared upsetting Emily, Jason forced a grin. "Well, that certainly puts me in my place, doesn't it?"

"Oh Dad, don't be silly. You're not that kind of doctor. She needs something besides her eyes checked," stated Emily seriously. "You'll make her go won't you, Dad?"

"Yes, Princess, I will get her in to see Dr. Chapman today and he's the best," promised Jason as he used a dust pan and broom to sweep up the broken juice glasses.

Janet pulled her hand away from Jason's and stood up. "Now, listen you two. I am not sick and Dad can't make me go to a doctor. I don't know why I fainted but I feel fine."

Jason and Emily kept insisting until Janet relented and Jason called Dr. Chapman's home number. "Charles, this is Jason McCall and I'm sorry to bother you so early but can you see Janet this morning? She fainted and I'd like you to check her out."

Doctor Chapman agreed, and everyone started to renew their daily routine, except nobody had time to eat the big breakfast that Janet had so happily prepared.

Emily ran out the door with a piece of toast in the hand that was also waving good-bye as she ran. Jason put all the food away and cleared the table, while Janet was dressing.

He would be late but he had already called Trudy Simmons. Trudy was not only a very good nurse but she managed any crisis that came up with a cool poise that Jason could always rely on.

"Don't worry, Doc. I gotcha covered," chirped Trudy at his request to make some appointment changes.

As they drove down Browns Creek toward town, Jason asked, "Janet have you been hurting, having unusual aches, heart palpitations, or anything like that?"

"The only thing that's bothered me is backache. Sometimes it wakes me at night, but it isn't a steady ache. It's more like sharp pains that come and go occasionally," explained Janet.

"It's embarrassing, Jason, but I am a little concerned about a vaginal discharge that I've been having. I think it is a yeast infection."

Jason glanced sideways at her in concern. "How long have you had that? You never mentioned it."

"I told you that it was embarrassing to talk about, you know like diarrhea. Nobody wants to discuss that," said Janet chuckling.

Jason drove on into town, made a left off Main Street onto Wyoming and then right on Elkhorn Street to park behind Grace Hospital and as they got out, he said, "I wish you had told me about that discharge and the backaches."

"Why? Does that mean there's something wrong?" questioned Janet in a concerned voice.

"No, I don't think so, but it always pays to check anything different out. It's probably nothing or Dr. Glovier would have caught it on your last check-up," assured Jason.

"When was your last check-up anyway?" asked Jason as they started into the hospital.

Janet grasped Jason's arm. "I've not had a check-up in two years," she blurted as if afraid he would be angry.

Jason had reminded Janet to call for an appointment six months before but she was feeling well and had forgotten all about it.

"I forgot to call and get an appointment. I know—I know, you reminded me, so don't get upset, okay?" begged Janet as they made their way into the elevator and pushed the button for the second floor.

Jason went with Janet into Dr. Chapman's waiting room and signed in, but when the nurse looked up she immediately ushered them into Dr. Chapman's office. Dr. Chapman came from behind his desk to shake Janet's hand as he said, "What's this I hear about you fainting, young lady?"

Janet sat down in one of the chairs beside Dr. Chapman's desk and turned in her seat to look at Jason.

"He says I fainted. I guess I did. I cooked breakfast and had it all on the table and when Jason came in everything just suddenly went black and I felt myself falling. Jason caught me before I did much damage, except to my dignity," Janet explained trying to laugh it off as nothing.

Dr. Chapman began asking probing and personal questions, such as regularity of her monthly cycle, breast tenderness or swelling, bloating in the belly, backache, nausea, and other symptoms or problems. Janet answered each question with a negative except for the backache.

Jason said, "Charles, she has been having a discharge. Tell him about it, Janet. He needs to know."

Janet turned red and gave Jason a glowering stare since she hadn't intended for him to tell her personal problems.

Dr. Chapman's eyebrows went up. "Yes, Janet, don't leave anything out. We want to find out what caused this fainting spell."

Once all the questions were answered, Dr. Chapman said, "Well, we are going to get Dr. Glovier to do a pelvic, and we'll do some x-rays and see what we can find out."

He turned to Jason. "You may as well go to your own office, Jason. We'll let you know if we need you."

Jason smiled and said, "Okay, Doctor. Take good care of her for me." He bent over and kissed Janet. "I'll see you in a little while. Be a good girl and mind the doctor."

The morning hours seemed endless as Jason waited on one patient after another. In the back of his mind was the dread that something was wrong with Janet. This brought to the forefront of his mind the depressing guilt he felt because he could not forget Lucinda Harmon.

It wasn't Janet's fault that he couldn't forget Lucinda but she had lived with only part of his love. He had been faithful to Janet except in his heart and it wasn't fair to her.

Suddenly Jason remembered Aunt Sarie Lester and that feeling he'd had outside that little church house on Atwell Mountain. He remembered the peace he had felt and silently began to pray as had that soldier he had tended in Korea.

"If the Lord would give me just a little of the faith of Aunt Sarie, I'd feel much better," Jason mumbled aloud.

Trudy, his nurse said. "What? I didn't understand you."

Jason turned, startled that he had spoken aloud. "Forgive me, Trudy. I was thinking out loud, I guess."

Trudy walked over, patted his shoulder, and said, "The worst is the waiting. Most of the time the things we dread the most never happen, you know."

Jason grinned worriedly. "I know, Trudy, but Janet has never been sick. Well, if she has I've never been told about it," stated Jason, now in doubt.

He knew that Janet had tried to be a good wife to him and she had been. Their only problems had been after they met Lucinda in Beckley. Since then, Jason had felt like he was on a tether. The easy, comfortable feeling had slowly slipped away to be replaced by a wariness on Janet's part for any stray word or mention of Lucinda Harmon.

There was also a dread on Jason's part, fearing that he could accidentally run into Lucinda again and Janet would hear of it. They didn't run in and out of Kyle and Rita Benders house as they once had, either. Their knowing Lucinda Harmon seemed to have changed their relationship in Janet's eyes

Jason now realized that his mother must have told Janet about his dating Lucinda, on his first stay in McDowell County.

"That shouldn't have caused the effect on Janet that meeting Lucinda did," mumbled Jason. He began straightening his desk, but twirled around as his door opened and Janet came in. Janet looked stunned and right behind her was Doctor Chapman.

"What's the matter? What did you find, Charles?" demanded Jason as fear almost choked him.

Doctor Chapman smiled grimly before saying, "I hope you two did not want more children. We're going to have to do a hysterectomy. Her ovaries are enlarged and tender and the discharge is infection."

Jason wrapped his arms around Janet and held her close. He tilted her face up to his and smiled saying, "We don't want any more children anyway, do we, sweetheart? Emily is enough for three families." He kissed Janet tenderly. "Thousands of women have hysterectomies, don't they, Charles?" stated Jason, using Dr. Chapman for extra assurance.

"Janet, I know you would rather not have surgery, but it is not a complicated operation and not a long convalescence either. If everything goes well, you should be able to cook breakfast every morning for the next fifty years," stated Dr. Chapman with a twinkle in his eyes.

Janet seemed to move in closer to Jason even though he already held her tightly. "Well, if I have to have this operation, when do you want to do it?" asked Janet as she let out her breath in a long drawn sigh.

"Ralph Glovier and I talked it over while you were getting dressed. He will actually do the surgery but I'll be there. Today is Wednesday and we'd like to do it about seven o'clock Friday morning," said Dr. Chapman, looking from Janet to Jason for approval.

Janet looked up at Jason and he stood waiting. Janet grimaced. "Okay, but I want my mom to be here."

Jason looked over her head and nodded to Dr. Chapman. "That's it then. I'll call Olivia and Joshua this evening and they can drive down tomorrow. I thank you for not keeping her waiting," said Jason as he looked steadily at Dr. Chapman.

Dr. Chapman dropped his head and turned to go. "All right, I'll see you two, bright and early, Friday morning. Jason, you know, of course, that she is not to eat or drink after ten o'clock Thursday evening, don't you?" asked Dr. Chapman.

Jason assured him that he would take care of it and then, with his arm still around Janet, he walked her to the elevator and then out of the building to the car. Once inside, Janet broke down and cried and Jason sat holding her without speaking, but trying to pray to Aunt Sarie Lester's God.

# CHAPTER 32

Olivia and Joshua showed up on Thursday night and once again Jason had to be strong and console Olivia. Just as he had to do with Emily, Jason let Olivia have her cry and then calmly explained exactly what was to be done and why it had to be done. Even though both Emily and Olivia had eventually calmed down, there was a gloomy stillness about the house that made everyone want to tiptoe.

Olivia and Joshua had thrown a tantrum when they first arrived because Janet was to have the surgery in McDowell County. "You know that our trusted family doctor is there at the university hospital, don't you?" Joshua questioned Jason. Even though Jason explained how well-trained and knowledgeable Ralph Glovier and Dr. Chapman were, Joshua Wentworth was not satisfied.

Janet interrupted his diatribe with, "Daddy, this is not Jason's decision. It is mine and I want to have it here. I trust these doctors and I don't want you blaming Jason about the decision I made."

They were silenced by the doorbell and dropped the topic altogether when Kyle and Rita Bender were admitted. They had come over to greet Janet's parents since they already knew them. Jason soon filled them in on what was to occur on the next day and Rita looked at Janet and blurted in a shocked voice,

"You're having surgery! I've never known you to be sick, except for headaches, in all the years I've known you. What happened?"

Janet explained what had happened and that she was to have a hysterectomy. Rita hugged Janet and told her not to worry since many of her friends had gone through the same surgery and felt better for it.

"You'll be a little sore and achy but you'll soon be back as good as new. I'll do anything you want done here while you are recuperating," promised Rita.

Olivia, not to be outdone said, "Oh, we're staying until

she is home and feeling better. I wish she would go home with us for about a month. Why don't you plan to do that, Janet? You wouldn't mind would you, Jason?" asked Olivia in a challenging tone.

Jason had been watching various expressions flitting across Janet's face and thought she would be better satisfied just to be alone with him.

"It's up to Janet, Olivia. Emily and I would miss her terribly but if she wants to do that, I'll not hinder her," Jason said as he looked steadily at Janet.

Janet laughed as she said, "Sorry, Mom. My wedding vows were that I would stay with him until death parted us. So, unless I die, I'll just stay with Jason."

Olivia shivered in dread. "My goodness, Janet, don't talk such morbid talk. I only meant for a visit."

Janet laughed merrily as she turned to her dad, saying, "Would you look at Mom's face. She still can't take a joke can she?"

Joshua smiled but said, "Your mother is always serious when it comes to her children. I guess that's what makes a good mother."

After that the conversation was on generalities and events in both Welch and Pittsburgh that everyone felt were noteworthy. Soon Rita and Kyle left, saying that they would be at the hospital in the morning to wait with the family through the surgery.

On Friday, Emily missed her first ever day of school. She was almost ready to complete the ninth grade and had never missed a day of school, a record of which she was very proud. Today, records went by the wayside, and Emily climbed in the car with her mother on the trip to the hospital.

Janet was wheeled into the operating room at exactly eight o'clock that morning and was in recovery by nine-thirty. Dr. Glovier and Dr. Chapman both came out and told the family that she had done really well through the surgery and should be moved to a regular room in another hour. Before they left, they told Jason they would like a word with him and he arose and followed them into Dr. Glovier's office.

Having worked with Dr. Chapman closely, Jason knew that the spouse was only called in if something serious was found. He felt that he might faint himself as he made his way behind the doctors. He was very thankful when he could sit in the proffered chair. Dr. Glovier went behind his desk but did not sit down.

Dr. Glovier moved a few papers around and then said, "Dr. McCall—Jason, your wife has ovarian cancer.

"Cancer!," gasped Jason, his eyes wide in shock.

Dr. Glovier looked at Dr. Chapman, grimaced and then continued. "It had spread. We hope we got it all."

Jason arose from his chair and walked around the desk, looked out the window, seeing nothing. He turned back to the two doctors. "What can I do? I mean, surely there is some treatment or something."

"We wanted to make certain so, we have sent a sample to a lab in New York. If it comes back positive we suggest that you take her to some university hospital or to the cancer treatment center at the Mellon Institute," said Dr. Glovier seriously.

Jason sat down stunned speechless. Tears came to his eyes and he wiped his face with both hands as if to push any feelings away. "Are you absolutely sure? I mean sometimes things are not as they seem, are they?" asked Jason in anguish.

Seeing his anguish, Dr. Chapman clapped him on the shoulder, "I'm so sorry, Jason. Ovarian cancer is known as the silent killer. Janet had no signs of being ill. In fact, she told me she had even been feeling good," consoled Dr. Chapman.

Dr. Glovier interrupted. "By sending some of the tissue off to a lab we're trying to be absolutely sure but I have no doubt, myself. I've seen too many cases lately."

"Did you tell her?" asked Jason as he looked at Dr. Glovier. "I'd rather she didn't know for awhile. How long do you think she has? I—I mean..." mumbled Jason brokenly.

"No, we haven't told her and I can't say for certain how long she will have but usually six months or maybe a little longer is about the length of time for most patients," said Dr. Glovier. At Jason's startled gasp he quickly continued. "That's why Dr. Chapman and I feel that you need to take her someplace else. A dtate-of-the-arts research center may have some new treatment."

Dr. Chapman was sitting in a chair beside Jason and now looked at him intently before saying, "Mellon Institute has a good research center and if anything can be done, they will know about it. We, Dr. Glovier and I, have talked it over and we feel that should be your next move."

All three men sat pondering the situation. "I'll have to get a leave from the hospital. Do you know of another ophthalmologist who could fill in for me while I'm away?" asked Jason in a benumbed voice. He arose from his chair with robotic actions and went back to the window and then turned to a table with magazines. He picked up one magazine after another and laid each one back down in the same place.

Dr. Chapman, realizing that Jason was overwrought said, "That's one worry you won't have."

Jason stopped his meaningless shifting of magazines and stood very still. "What worry? Oh! you mean about finding someone to work for me?"

Dr. Chapman arose also and strolled towards the door. "I've been dreading to tell you this, even though you and I have talked about the decline in population; and the corresponding decline in patients coming into the hospital. I imagined you had given it some thought but, I didn't give you the information I've been getting," said Dr. Chapman wearily and added. "This may be a good time or, who knows, it may be a bad time to tell you but, you won't need to worry about leaving patients without care."

Both Jason and Doctor Glovier were looking intently at Dr. Chapman and he quickly continued with, "Today, is the first time I've mentioned this, and you two doctors are the first to hear it. This hospital will be closing in six months. You would have had to leave or go to Stevens Clinic and I don't think they need anyone. Now you can go back to Pittsburgh and let her be seen at the Mellon Institute as if you are only taking her there for a check-up. Lets all hope they have some new treatment that can kill cancer cells in their tracks."

Both doctors look stunned momentarily and then Dr. Glovier spoke. "You both knew I had already applied for a job in Tennessee and this will free me and also give Jason the freedom he needs."

Jason rubbed his face with his hands once again and mumbled, "It's all happening too fast. I can't even think straight. I don't want to tell Janet now. She's too weak having just come through surgery."

Dr. Glovier broke in. "Why not take her home in a few days and not tell her anything. We need to wait on the results of the test unless she goes drastically downhill. She is still feeling good and if she should feel worse it can be blamed on the surgery."

Jason, in spite of all his will power, still felt tears slide down his cheeks and dropped his head in despair. He wondered if Janet's jealousy could have activated the cancer cells. "Maybe the doctors were wrong," thought Jason.

In an agonized whisper he said, "I really can't think straight right now." He looked at Dr. Chapman. "Charles, what can I do? I…I don't know if I can go back in there and act normal. Can you cover for me for an hour? "

At Dr. Chapman's nod of agreement Jason arose from his chair. "I'd like to get away by myself for a little while to gather strength. I'm not just thinking of myself. I know I need to show calmness and strength in front of Emily and Janet's parents. Thank God, you didn't tell Janet. At least she can gain a little strength before we tell her, can't she?" asked Jason.

Dr. Chapman looked at Jason with penetrating eyes. "You're in no shape to talk to her now. Besides she will be asleep for several hours, so why don't you get away for a bit."

Jason had sat back down and now looked up at his mentor in appreciation and then stopped. "I can't run off and leave Emily like this. She would be so hurt."

Jason still sat with his head in his hands. "The Benders are there also. They will think I'm an unfeeling brute. I'll have to go back and be with them," he mumbled miserably.

"I'll tell the Washburns, Emily, and the Benders that you have to do something while they go out and have lunch. They can't see Janet anyway," said Dr. Chapman.

When Jason arose but hesitated, Dr. Chapman gave him a little push toward the door. "Go on. Take a drive or something and pull yourself together."

Jason hurriedly left the room and, taking the back stairs left the hospital, got in his car, and went spinning out of the parking lot. He didn't know which direction he was taking but he was only getting away from the site of his anguish.

When he came upon a sign that said Pineville, eight miles, realization hit him. "What am I doing, going to Pineville? God, I must be the most heartless man that you ever created. Here I am going to where Lucinda is, and my wife lying in Welch diagnosed with cancer."

At the next wide place he stopped the car and got out. He was really puzzled since he did not know where Lucinda lived and, therefore, it made little sense to go to Pineville. He walked around the car and then down the road a little way deep in thought.

"Could it be that I know Lucinda trusts in the same God that Aunt Sarie Lester did and I am looking for some reassurance?" he questioned.

He remembered Aunt Sarie saying that her elders knelt when they prayed and also Lucinda talking about a Preacher Hiram kneeling to pray.

Still thinking this, he made his way down the hill from the road on a little path that he suddenly saw. It must have been there all the time but he hadn't noticed it. Now he had a great desire to follow that path. Soon he came to a sort of hollow, cleared of brush, and there he knelt also.

Later Jason could not remember anything he had said, but he felt as if the Lord had heard him because he came back to the car with a sense of peace. All the way back to Welch, he begged the Lord to make him strong and able to do what needed to be done. He had only been gone an hour but it seemed like a lifetime.

Jason did a lot of soul searching as he drove slowly back to the hospital. “I can’t help how I feel about Lucinda but I married Janet and I do love her. She has been a good wife and I certainly don’t want to betray her in any way. Lord please help me. I’m so weak. Give me strength, please,” begged Jason as he pulled back into his parking place.

He went back to the hospital, stopping by Dr. Chapman’s office first, before he planned to go see Janet. Dr. Chapman had just finished with a patient and seeing Jason, motioned him in.

“Well, I told a lot of lies for you today,” Dr. Chapman said with his usual wry grin. “You’d better talk to your friend, Kyle Bender, before you do anything else, since I lied on him also.”

Jason’s pale face wrung the heart of Dr. Chapman. He felt that something had happened to calm Jason down, but he did not know what.

“I didn’t know what I was going to tell your folks, but I met Kyle Bender and his wife in the hall and they said they were going home. That left Emily and the Washburns. I told them you had to leave because Kyle stopped on his way home to see if everything was all right at your house and found a leak in a water pipe and you had to run home to help take care of it before it ruined the floor,” said Dr. Chapman now wearing a raffish grin.

“It’s a good thing I saw the Benders first and knew they were going home,” said Dr. Chapman solemnly. “Is that good enough for you, Doctor?” he asked and smiled at Jason.

Jason’s slow appreciative smile and his heartfelt thanks was uttered along with, “Pure genius, Charles. You’ve missed your calling. You should have been a politician.”

In reply Dr. Chapman pointed to the phone and said, “Call your buddy before we both get caught in this deception. Anyway, he said they wouldn’t be back until this evening. I want him to know before he comes back here.”

# CHAPTER 33

Three days later Jason took Janet home with the admonition from Dr. Glovier that she was to have at least three weeks to make a relaxing recovery.

"No cooking, cleaning, shopping, or anything tiring," Dr. Glovier said and then grinned at Janet's gasp of surprise. "Oh! You mean you don't get tired shopping, Mrs. McCall?"

"Get tired shopping! Are you married, doctor?" asked Janet as she laughed merrily. "The cleaning and cooking I think I can forego, but shopping…no, that's just too much."

Olivia settled herself in one of the spare bedrooms, prepared to stay the three weeks Janet had been given to recover. This left Jason to carry on just as if everything was fine. He already had planned how he would work it all out.

Kyle and Rita Bender were in on his plans and agreed with him, even though it saddened them to know they would lose him as a neighbor and friend. It was especially trying to know that Emily would not be around to bounce in and out of their home with good news of any kind.

As he and Kyle Bender sat out in Kyle's backyard near the creek, Jason told Kyle, in confidence, that Grace Hospital, now called Doctor's Memorial, was to be closed within the next six months.

"We've lost so many people here in the county that I had been suspecting something like this would happen in the near future," explained Jason before continuing. "We both know how school enrollment has dropped. We talked about parents educating their children to leave the county, remember?"

Kyle nodded affirmatively, deep in thought, "If things don't pick up, Stevens Clinic will close too. Hospitals have to make money to stay in business and since many of the big coal producers have moved on, there's just no money to be made."

"It's too bad that our elected officials didn't use the Business and Occupation taxes to diversify the business base in the county," stated Jason reflectively.

Kyle agreed and then added, “What business would want to locate here though? It would be a hard sell since we don’t have good roads, clean water, or county-wide sewer systems.”

Jason studied quietly as he scooted his chair to a position of more shade, then said, “It’s a damn shame that someone in this county didn’t ask for some good roads for this county or a county-wide water and sewage system instead of a federal judgeship when Kennedy made his offer. After all, McDowell County helped to get Kennedy into the White House.”

Kyle grinned knowingly, “With the help of Chicago, though.”

Jason rose, and aiming a mock punch at Kyle, said with a laugh, “Well, I guess they helped a little bit.”

He then turned toward his house, telling Kyle that he would keep him informed of his plans as they were worked out. Jason had already made an appointment for an evaluation for Janet at the Mellon Institute on the 25th of June.

Yesterday, he had contacted, by phone, two hospitals in the Pittsburgh area for possible jobs. Jason intended to work, regardless of where he lived, since he had a great need to be constantly involved in doing something.

Jason had told his dad the dire news, with the promise from his dad to keep it confidential for the present time. He also had his dad quietly scouring the area for an appropriate house for the three of them.

“I will put Emily in a private school, I think,” said Jason. “The Alderdyce School was very good and I’m glad I graduated from there, but since Emily has always been in a small school, I believe a private school would be better. What do you think, Dad?”

Henry McCall was worried but wanted to help Jason. “Emily has another week of school doesn’t she? Well, it seems to me that there are more pressing things to be concerned about right now, Jason. I know you are trying to make everything as easy as possible for everybody concerned, but go a little slower. Just treasure every day you have,” cautioned his dad.

Jason tried to take his dad's advice, but there seemed to be so much to do and every time he looked at Janet, guilt and shame overwhelmed him. He felt so bad because he had not loved Janet with his whole heart and now it was too late.

"I shouldn't have married Janet. I knew I hadn't gotten over Lucinda. I couldn't and I don't guess I ever will. Sometimes I almost wish I had never met Lucinda Harmon," moaned Jason, rising again to pace the floor as he had almost every night since he received the news about Janet. Janet knew nothing of this, however, since he presented a smiling, cheerful, and attentive mien in her presence.

In the second week Janet was home, Jason received a call from The Wyoming County Vocational School in Pineville. He was asked to be one of the speakers from the medical profession for their regional Career Days program.

He started to refuse but the lady calling pleaded with him, saying the doctor who had promised to be there had cancelled. "He only cancelled this morning and I'm desperate. I dreaded asking you or anyone at the last minute, but I know you are really interested in students and the schools," said the persuasive voice on the other end of the line. Jason finally agreed to be there the next morning at nine o'clock.

Since Janet always reacted so strongly against him being in the Pineville area, Jason only told her that he was going to present at a regional career day function. He was a little worried about leaving the numbers where he could be reached, since she might recognize it as a Pineville number, but he wanted to be notified if Janet should need him.

Since Olivia was there, Janet did not seem to pay as much attention to Jason's activities as she normally did. Janet, not knowing of her dire diagnosis, was planning a trip home to Pittsburgh as soon as her convalescent period was over and Emily's school was out.

Jason talked everything over with Kyle that evening when he went to visit. "I just need some advice and some help," stated Jason in a troubled voice.

"I'm going to tell her about the hospital closing next week.

She and Olivia will be on cloud nine when I tell them I'm going to move back to Pittsburgh."

"Yeah, I know Janet will," said Kyle. "But you have to think about Emily. I don't think she is going to like it very much."

Jason grimaced in pain as he said, "No, she won't. Neither Emily nor I ever wanted to live in Pittsburgh. I may have to tell Emily the truth. What do you think, Kyle?"

"I think that you had better let her spend the night with us when you tell her. She will certainly be upset," said Kyle solemnly.

Kyle stood looking down at the floor before stating adamantly, "She can handle it though. That girl has more sense than ten girls her age. I swear, to hear Emily and Janet talk, you would almost think they were sisters instead of mother and daughter."

Jason grinned sadly. "It's a lot to throw at her, I know, but I just don't know what else to do. I'll not only have to tell her that she may lose her mother but also that she has to leave the only home she has ever known."

Kyle smiled and added, "And don't forget her Uncle Kyle and Aunt Rita. She loves us as much as we love her. She feels almost as dear to us as our own Katie. Actually, having her here has helped us bear having Katie away in college all this time."

Jason clapped Kyle on the shoulder. "This isn't why I came over here. I came to tell you and Rita that I am going to the Vocational School at Pineville tomorrow to present at Career Day. I didn't tell Janet where I was going, since she has an aversion to Pineville, but I brought the numbers to you in case I'm needed. I left them on my desk also, hoping she doesn't know the exchange for Pineville.

"Why did you agree to go?" questioned Kyle in amazement, since Jason had long ago revealed his previous relationship with Lucinda Harmon.

"This lady called and said that the doctor they had scheduled to present had cancelled yesterday. She laid it on thick about how she knew of my interest in schools and students," said Jason with a smile.

"Besides, I don't think there's any chance of Lucinda being there since it is for high school students. There's no reason for parents to be present," Jason explained.

Kyle agreed and took the list of numbers Jason handed him and placed the paper in his wallet. They talked a few minutes more, but when Jason saw Rita returning from visiting Janet, he left through the back door and walked across their backyard to his own house.

The next morning he arose at his usual time, checked on Janet, who was sleeping peacefully, and went quietly into the kitchen to find Emily already dressed and at the table. She had a bowl of cereal in front of her but sat staring off into space, lost in thought.

"Good Morning, Princess! What fantasy are you hatching in that fertile mind this morning?" questioned Jason, as he went to the kitchen counter and turned on the coffee maker.

Emily looked up and quietly studied her dad's face before asking, "Dad, did Doctor Glovier send off a specimen or something for testing when he did Mom's surgery? If he didn't, how would he know that only her ovaries were bad?"

Emily's worried expression wrenched Jason's heart and he really did not know what to say. He had always been and wanted to continue to be truthful with his daughter, but he didn't know how much to tell her.

"Yes, Emily, Dr. Glovier did send samples of the tissue off to a lab, but as of yesterday, he had not gotten the results. He knew the ovaries were enlarged when he took them out. That could have caused the infection, so he put her on Streptomycin, which is an antibiotic."

Emily seemed relieved but still troubled. She spoke quietly, "Dad, I think Mom feels like there is something else wrong."

"Why do you think that, Emily? Has she said something to you," asked Jason in a concerned voice.

Emily drank the milk from her cereal and got up to place the bowl in the sink before coming back to the table. She sat down beside Jason and leaned her head against his shoulder.

"Yesterday, she got out her jewelry box and went through

it telling me about each piece, especially the pieces you have bought her. She said, 'Emily, if anything should happen to me you can sell all these other pieces but these that your dad has given me, please don't sell them.' "

"I thought at first she was going to cry but then it was like she got angry. She said, 'And don't you allow anyone else to have them either.'"

Emily looked solemnly at Jason with her soft brown eyes and asked, "Wouldn't that make you think she is worried, Dad?"

Jason felt that Emily was right but didn't want her to worry so he said, "I guess so, Princess. But, in your Mom's case it may be that some of the medicine she is on is making her depressed. I'll ask Dr. Glovier about it today, so don't you start worrying needlessly, okay?"

Emily looked at her watch, jumped up, gave her dad a hug and ran for the door, just as the school bus came to a stop before the house.

Jason was almost relieved because Emily was already suspicious and now she knew that sample testing was being done, so when the results came back, he could just tell her the whole truth.

"My poor little Princess," mumbled Jason as he got up and poured a cup of coffee and put a slice of bread into the toaster.

Just then Olivia walked through the door. "Did I hear talking? I thought Emily had missed her bus," she said looking around.

Jason smiled. "No, she didn't miss it but she had to run when the bus pulled to a stop. But you probably heard me mumbling to myself. I must be getting old, since I often catch myself voicing my thoughts aloud."

Olivia poured a cup of coffee and looked out the window before she seated herself across from Jason.

"You are coming to Pittsburgh with Janet and Emily aren't you, Jason?" asked Olivia as she stirred sugar into her coffee.

"Olivia, right now, I'd go to the moon if Janet asked me to, and I could. It really bothers me to see Janet ill. She has been the mainstay of this family, so yes, if she goes I'll certainly be with her," stated Jason seriously.

He then glanced at his watch and arose from the table, saying, "I'll go in and check on her before I leave, but I put the numbers where I can be reached on my desk." He had told them the night before that he was doing a career day program. Neither Janet nor Olivia asked any questions since they were so engrossed in their plans to go shopping in Pittsburgh.

Janet was still asleep and Jason tiptoed out of the room and quietly closed the door.

## CHAPTER 34

As Jason drove across Indian Ridge and started down the other side into Wyoming County, Janet was heavy on his mind. The guilt he was carrying seemed to be sucking the very marrow from his bones.

Suddenly, he thought of that place he had found the day Dr. Glovier had given him the bad news. He started looking on both sides of the road searching for that stretch of wooded road. He remembered driving around a curve and stopping in a wide place on the right hand side.

Up ahead was a curve and sure enough there was a wide place on the side. Jason got out and went along the edge of the woods bordering the road but there was no path.

"This must not be the place," mumbled Jason as he looked around. He started back to the car thinking that it certainly looked like the place where he had gone to pray. "I'll just keep looking. It has to be along here somewhere," he muttered as he opened the car door and slid behind the wheel.

Although he stopped on every curve between there and the incorporation sign for Pineville, he could not find a curve with a path running down into the woods. Jason felt stupid since he knew he had gone down into some woods along this road and prayed. "I couldn't have made it that day if the Lord hadn't blessed me to pray. I know that path is somewhere but I don't have time to find it this morning."

He arrived at the Vocational School on Route 97 and was overwhelmed by the crowd. If a young attendant had not been directing parking he would have been later than he already was. Another young man helped him unpack the materials he had gathered for his presentation and helped carry them into the main lobby.

They soon located a table with Jason's name across the front in bold black letters. Jason thanked his helper and started getting his things in order when from behind him a voice said. "Thank God, you made it. I thought you had cancelled also."

Jason turned to see a pleasant middle-aged woman

standing about two feet away from him. He smiled and reached out to shake hands as he said, "Sorry, I'm a little late. I had to stop a few times before I got here."

The woman grasped his hand and with a warm smile said, "Well, you're here now, so let me know if you need anything. I'll be going from one table to the other all day so you won't have any trouble finding me."

Jason looked around at a vast array of occupations displayed and then asked, "Do I present here or do I go into classrooms?"

The woman, who introduced herself as Mrs. Lillard, looked down on the large ledger pad held in her arms and studied it.

"Let's see...Dr. McCall in the auditorium at eleven o'clock, and I don't see...oh yes, here you are also scheduled for another presentation in Classroom F1 at two o'clock. The rest of the time you will be here to answer questions and visit with students."

Mrs. Lillard raised her head and smiled in a harassed manner before saying, "The auditorium will have a big crowd but that's the only way we could get it all in."

Jason assured her that it did not matter to him whether he needed to talk to a large or small number of students and she went on her way relieved.

Many students and some of the teachers,came by and looked at the plastic model of a large eye and also a cross section of an eye that he had on display, as well as the many drawings and charts which discussed the various diseases and problems with the eyes. He also had pictures and material about the various careers associated with eye care.

He had little handout bags with sunglasses, eye drops, lens cleaners, and the most sought after item, a key chain with an eyeball dangling on the end of a miniature slinky toy which looked like a real eye.

At first Jason did not realize what the attraction was to his table until the key chains with the eyeballs began to show up on belt loops, on hair ribbons, on the arms of glasses, and other unusual places.

Mr. Carpenter, who ran a tax service, had a table next to his and they struck up a conversation. After a crowd of youngsters had just left his table, Mr. Carpenter stepped over. "If the crowds you are garnering are any indication, we have a budding crowd of ophthalmologists."

Jason laughed as he told Mr. Carpenter, "Wait until they come back around and you will see what the attraction is. You'll be surprised, I think. At least I was."

The auditorium was just as crowded as Mrs. Lillard had said it would be. They came in like all teenagers, laughing hilariously, but when Jason walked to the podium and began his presentation, everyone settled down and listened attentively. He talked about the years one spent in school, what classes one needed to take. He expressed how challenging and helpful a career in ophthalmology was, while also stressing its benefits to humanity.

As soon as his presentation was finished the noise level rose to a crescendo as once again the students were on the move. They pushed and shoved their way out into the corridors, dispersing in various directions.

Jason wondered if perhaps teachers were not stationed in each tier of seats, which would account for the seeming attention of the students.

Mrs. Lillard appeared like a genie from a bottle to guide the presenters to the dining hall. At first, she could not be heard above the noise, but soon her voice came through very loud.

"If you will please, follow me. We have lunch set up for the presenters." When she realized she was almost screaming, she blushed hotly and stammered an apology.

Jason enjoyed lunch sitting between Mr. Carpenter and Mr. Richards, who was manager of the local IGA store. Even though accountants and people who worked with taxes are assumed to be "dry as dust," Mr. Carpenter was an exception. He was gregarious and full of jokes, which kept Jason and Mr. Richards laughing the entire time.

When they arose, Mr. Carpenter said, "Well let's get back to our stalls. I want to see what new use these kids are going to find for Jason's eyeballs."

This was said in a serious manner and Mr. Richards looked puzzled, and asked, "What do you mean? Is this another joke?" He had his answer when a boy with long hair came by with the eyeball on a keychain hanging almost in his eyes.

When Mr. Carpenter saw him stare in amazement he said, "There you are Richards. See what that kid did with Jason's eyeball," then laughed uproariously.

Jason kept looking at his watch hoping that his second presentation time would soon come and then he could pack up and go back to Janet. He hated feeling guilty and he had felt that way ever since her surgery. Today he felt worse since he knew how she felt about him being anywhere near Pineville.

Two o'clock finally rolled around and Jason made his way to F1 classroom. There again, noise reigned supreme until he walked to the lectern and then as if a switch had been flipped off, all the noise stopped. This time, Jason allowed the students to pass around the huge model eye and the cross-section and ask questions as they studied the display. Several students were truly interested and wanted to linger as the session was ending.

He thought that perhaps the room was needed for another presenter and he had to be briefer than he really wanted to be. They finally all drifted away and he was left alone to pack up his material. Just as he finished and started for the door, it was opened from the outside and a nicely rounded derriere came backwards through the door.

Jason's breath caught in his throat because he knew before she ever turned that Lucinda Harmon had shown up. She finally got the huge box she was carrying through the door and turned to put it down.

When she saw Jason she turned deathly white and not only dropped the box but sank into a chair herself. She raised enormous blue eyes to his face and stared in stunned silence.

Jason couldn't speak. He stood numbly thinking, "She is so thin and she looks so…lost." He wanted to pull her into his arms and ease whatever was giving her this haunted look, but then guilt took over.

Instead of what his heart felt he heard himself say, "Why don't you stay out of my life? I don't need you in it."

Lucinda dropped her head and from trembling lips whispered. "I'm sorry. I didn't know you were here." She tried to get up but she seemed to have no strength. Jason, still buoyed by his overwhelming guilt, started for the door with a harsh glare from his eyes.

He turned at the door and gave her an angry stare. "You could have answered my letters. Why didn't you? Now it's too late…Just too damn late."

He walked on out the door, slamming it behind him. He marched swiftly down the corridor to the main hall and, with the help of two students, soon had all his material packed up and in his car.

He had to force himself to get in the car and start the engine. Then he killed the engine and opened the door to get out, then slammed it again, started the engine, and pulled out. Jason hated himself. His wife was probably dying with cancer and here he was broken-hearted because another woman looked so lost.

"What kind of man am I, anyway? Oh God, if you are really there, help me to do the right thing. I've made Janet's life miserable, and by the way Lucinda looked, she's miserable too. She's married and I couldn't help her even if Janet wasn't sick," Jason groaned aloud.

Still in his mind's eye he saw her stunned tear filled eyes. He remembered what he had said. "Why don't you stay out of my life? I don't need you in it." Looking back on that scene, Jason remembered her looking at him as if all hope was suddenly gone. It was almost like a shadow of death stole slowly over her face. Jason swung off the road, put the car in park, and then cried until tears wet his shirt.

Finally, Jason pulled out and drove on into Welch, but stopped at the Sterling Drive-In and went into the restroom and washed his face. Something was wrong in Lucinda's life and she had looked at him as if he had cut the only lifeline she had been clinging to.

A sudden image popped into Jason's mind and because of it he made up his mind to go to the Primitive Baptist Church up on Atwell Mountain. He knew he had found true peace there for a few minutes. Maybe the Lord would hear him if he went there again. He decided he would go the next morning. He walked out of the restroom and drove on home.

# CHAPTER 35

Once, when they were first married, Jason had tried to explain to Janet the experience he'd had outside that little church on Atwell Mountain. Although Janet listened, he knew it really meant nothing to her and he never mentioned it again.

The next morning after his trying day at Pineville, and an almost sleepless night, Jason checked on Janet, saw that Emily was all right, and then drove to the hospital. Trudy Simmons, who now knew the hospital was to close, had been busy transferring Jason's patients to a Doctor Paine in Bluefield as well as the Stevens Clinic Hospital in Welch.

When Jason went in, Trudy took one look at his gaunt cheeks, and troubled eyes, and dejected manner. She grinned.

"I've gotten rid of all your patients for today. Why don't you take the day off and go fishing?" She laughed hilariously since she knew that of all sports Jason disliked fishing the most.

With a sad smile, Jason answered solemnly, "Even that would be preferable to what I'm going through right now."

"Don't be so pessimistic, Doctor. Everything that seems so bad to us may be the purpose of the Lord to move us to the next phase in our lives," theorized Trudy, almost as if the idea had suddenly sprang into her mind.

Jason looked at her in amazement. "I didn't know you were religious, Trudy. You're just full of surprises, aren't you," questioned Jason as the idea seemed to fixate in his mind.

Trudy gave him a puzzled look and said, "Would you believe that I have never thought of something like that before? I really don't know where that idea came from."

Jason knew where it came from and he knew that Aunt Sarie Lester's Good Lord had sent it for him, but he said, "Now confess, Trudy. You do have ESP, don't you?"

"ESP! What's that? Oh! You mean extra sensory perception," mused Trudy aloud. "No, at least I've never had it before."

Jason patted her on the shoulder and turned toward the

door, saying, "Well, whether you have or not, I'm going to take your advice and go fishing."

He went on out of the door and into the elevator, leaving Trudy staring at his back.

She was surprised when the elevator swished to a stop again and Jason stepped back out into the hall. She went to the door laughing, "That was a quick trip. How many fish did you catch?" she asked as he came back in.

"Trudy, if anyone calls could you say that I'm not in my office right now, and ask to take a message?" asked Jason while he waited for her answer.

Trudy assured him that she would. "Go on and try not to worry so much."

She felt that he wanted to get away by himself, but he didn't tell her that. She just sensed his need for some peace.

Jason drove down Route 16 to Yukon and then turned right on Route 83 until he came to Atwell Hollow Road. There he turned right across the metal bridge and took the narrow meandering road to the top of Atwell Mountain. Once he reached the top and started along the high plateau that ran along the ridge, he accelerated.

He was anxious to get to that little church. When he arrived, it looked as if nobody had been there for a long time, but the grass around the building was mowed. He drove into the yard and got out of his car.

"I'll just look in the windows since the door will be locked. I didn't go in that time I was up here and I've often wondered about what it looked like," thought Jason as he went toward the front window.

When he stepped onto the porch, he, for some unknown reason, tried the door and it swung open. He jerked back in alarm, thinking that someone was inside and was coming out. When that didn't happen, he cautiously walked inside. There was nothing there to make it special, only rough wooden benches in two rows down the sides, and a wide aisle in the middle.

This led to a stained wood pulpit in the front with a long

bench behind the podium. The only pictures on the walls were a calendar, and some framed photographs. In the first was a man and a woman (perhaps his wife), thought Jason as he studied them, the second was a group of men dressed either in suits and ties, or white long-sleeved shirts. A third picture was another man and probably his wife and Jason noticed that there was writing beneath the picture.

Since there were no lights on and the building was dim on the inside he could not see to read the writing. Jason looked around for a light switch but when he looked overhead he saw that there were no lights in the ceiling.

Jason was still restless and wasn't finding what he had hoped to find by coming here. "I'll just sit down on one of these benches and pretend I hear that singing again," thought Jason as he took a seat on the front row. He sat there thinking about that one time he had been here and the peace he had felt, and then a quiet peace stole upon him.

Jason was carried back and he sat listening to that singing while tears ran unheeded down his cheeks. From somewhere it seemed that a voice came to him saying, " Stand still, and see the salvation of the Lord."

Jason could not say how long he sat there, but finally he got up, and going to the podium or whatever it was called, he rubbed his hands over it as if to carry something away with him.

Then he walked quietly out, closing the door gently behind him, and made his way to his car. He thought,"I wish I had a camera but a camera could never capture what I have found here today." He did not react the way he had the first time, aimlessly driving down the other side of the mountain as if he had lost all sense of direction.

Instead, he slowly shifted into gear and drove down the same road to the mouth of Atwell Hollow in such peace that he had arrived on Route 83 before he even realized it. "I don't even remember coming off that mountain," thought Jason as he turned left and began his trip back to Welch.

Jason arrived back at his office at two o'clock to find Trudy still there. She was packing things into boxes and cleaning out the office. It suddenly hit Jason like a ton of bricks that Trudy would not have a job either.

"Trudy, I'm a selfish brute. You're losing your job, too, and I have been so wrapped up in my problems that I haven't even thought of you. I'm so sorry. Please forgive me," begged Jason contritely.

Trudy put down the load of files she had just taken from a drawer, wiped her hand across her forehead, and smiled warmly. "Well, I'm not facing cancer and a major move in my life, you know. I'm going to work for Dr. Burger at the Stevens Clinic Hospital. I thought you already knew that. In fact, I did tell you, but you've been so torn up I felt you had either not heard or forgotten it."

Jason then remembered the conversation he'd had with Trudy about what would take place in his life. She had told him she was going to work at the Stevens Clinic Hospital located on Route 52 towards Bluefield. He smiled. "Yes, now I remember. I'm glad, if that is what you want to do."

"It is. Jess and I don't want to move away from our children and grandchildren. I only have about twelve more years and I can retire, so this works out fine for me," Trudy explained.

"You must have caught a lot of fish today," Trudy said with a laugh. "You've come back a different looking man than the Gloomy Gus that left here this morning."

Jason smiled a glowing tender smile and said, "I caught the big fish today, Trudy. I've been trying to catch him all my life and didn't even know I was looking for him."

Being very perceptive, Trudy replied, "Sometimes the right time has to come along when our hearts are set on fishing."

Jason nodded and grinned in acknowledgement as he realized that Trudy knew what he was talking about. He didn't want to describe his day in words and he hadn't had to with Trudy, she seemed to understand.

After that, they worked together without much conversation but with peaceful companionship until every file had been transferred to labeled boxes. These would be left for the movers to transfer to whatever destination was marked on each box.

Jason went into Dr. Chapman's office to see if he could be of help there but was told they were progressing really well.

"You go on home and cheer up that wife of yours," ordered Dr. Chapman with a smile.

"Did she call?" questioned Jason worriedly. "Trudy did not tell me if she did."

"No, not that I know of," said Dr. Chapman. "I was just thinking she would like to have you around."

"She does, but her mother is with her and that is also good for her right now," replied Jason as he left to gather his personal things from his office to take to his car.

When Jason arrived at home, he was met with delicious smells coming from the kitchen. "Um-m, what is that. Gosh, whatever it is smells really good or I'm starved to death, one or the other," said Jason with an appreciative sniff. He followed his nose into the kitchen where Olivia and Janet were working together.

"Janet, what are you doing? You shouldn't be out here working," scolded Jason as he went toward her.

Janet looked up from the salad she was putting together and said, "Don't come near me. You haven't washed your hands and I don't want my masterpiece contaminated."

When she saw Jason's concern, she looked at him with adoring eyes as she said, "I've not been in here very long. I've only put the salad together and I've been sitting the entire time. So, don't get all worried. I haven't hurt myself."

Jason stood looking at her with a different look than she was accustomed to, like he was seeing her with new eyes or something.

"What? What are you looking at me like that for?" Janet questioned.

"I guess I just didn't realize how very beautiful you are, Janet, and I love you, you know," stated Jason solemnly as he swiftly bent and kissed her questioning lips.

The happy mood was contagious and soon Emily, Olivia,

Janet, and Jason were seated around the dining room table, laughing and talking. The meal was the most pleasant Jason could ever remember having with his family. They had always had good meals but there was a happy peaceful atmosphere about this setting that Jason hadn't found before. Jason was so thankful for what he'd received today. He wished he could share his experience with someone but knew that neither Janet nor Olivia would understand

Suddenly Jason said, "Well, I think this is the right time to tell you all some news." Then he thought of Emily and decided not to tell them all of it straight out.

"What is it, Daddy?" questioned Emily, who wasn't known for patience.

Jason sat looking around the group trying to decide the best approach. Finally he said, "I'm out of work."

Every eye was staring intently at him and Janet spoke first, "You're a doctor. How can you be out of work? What do you mean?"

"This is not how I intended telling you, Janet, but since we've had such a pleasant evening, I thought it would be a good time. I've known this since the day of your surgery but I've waited until you felt better. Doctor's Memorial Hospital is closing its doors," uttered Jason with dread, thinking of the various reactions.

Janet reached across the space between them and grasped Jason hand. She squeezed his hand gently before saying, "It's sad for you, isn't it? I'm so sorry. I know you love your work. You'll be able to go to Stevens Clinic, won't you?"

"I don't know right now. I thought I would wait until we make the visit to Pittsburgh before looking for anything else. Don't you think that would be best?" he asked, looking at Janet.

Olivia spoke up with, "I think it's a good idea. It might take a while to find something or you may be asked to come for interviews, which would hinder you from going."

"But, Mom, if Jason wants to find a job first, I can wait to go home," said Janet seriously. "Jason loves his work and he loves it down here in the ...in this area. I've never stood in the way of his work and that will not change just because I am sick. I don't want to ever stand in his way."

Jason got up and sat down beside Janet and, putting his arms around her, exulted, "This is the best woman in the whole world. There is no way you're going to miss going to Pittsburgh. You've let me have my way long enough," Jason continued as he cuddled her close.

"How long are we going to be gone, Daddy? Cheerleading practice starts the first of August and I am the Captain," bragged Emily as she looked at each person in the room.

Janet and Jason both looked stunned since they knew that Emily had wanted to be captain in the eighth and ninth grades but hadn't made it. "When did you find that out, Princess," asked Jason.

"Well, Dad, you were not the only person in this family to come home with news. I was saving mine until the right time just as you did," said Emily with her twinkling smile.

Still looking at her dad, she demanded, "Well, how long will we be gone?"

Janet smiled, "We don't know for sure, Honey. If Dad had a job we'd only stay two weeks but now…" she rolled her eyes as she said this as if to leave the return time open.

When Jason looked at Emily, and saw that she was getting very upset, he quickly said, "Don't worry, Princess. We'll work out something. Right now though, let's you and I drive to the Sterling Drive-In for a sundae. Want to?" asked Jason with a pleading look.

Olivia blurted, "You're wanting a sundae when you've just finished this huge meal! I can't believe what I'm hearing."

Janet who had realized how upset Emily was about leaving Welch understood Jason's ploy. "Mom, those two can eat a sundae regardless of how much they've just eaten."

# CHAPTER 36

Emily, who could always tell when her dad wanted to talk to her, quickly said, "Sure, Dad. I've inherited your sweet-tooth, along with your other bad habits."

She grinned at her mother when she said that and her mother winked and nodded in agreement as they left.

Jason drove to the drive-in and ordered the sundaes and while they were waiting, Emily said, "Okay, Daddy, what is it? Have I done something wrong?" she questioned as she gave him her "you can't fool me look."

About that time, the car-hop came back with their order. When the tray was removed from the window, Jason asked, "Why don't we go up to that little park and eat? I can't drive and eat and I don't want to be disturbed."

Once they reached the park and were seated on the stone benches, Emily sat waiting on her dad to speak. Finally he said, "Emily, we may have to move to Pittsburgh permanently."

"Move! Oh no, Dad! No! I won't move. I love it here. You know I do," cried Emily. "It's Mom, isn't it. I just knew she'd wear you down," blurted Emily defiantly.

Jason reached over and picked up her hands, and with his heart in his eyes, he pleaded. "Emily, there is something I have to tell you and it really hurts to do it, but ...Well, you remember those samples from your Mom's operation that Dr. Glovier sent off?"

Emily nodded numbly. Jason said, "Princess, the one that came back was positive. The other one hasn't come yet, but we know that your mother has cancer. We have to move back so she can get treatments at the Mellon Institute."

Emily sat stunned for a minute and then she hurled herself into her dad's arms, crying, "No! Oh God, No! Dad she has always been so alive. I can't stand it. I just can't stand it." Then she crumbled into a quivering sobbing heap, moaning and lamenting about all the things she should have done for her mother.

Jason lifted her head and she saw tears in his eyes also.

"Princess, I know how you feel. I think I can't stand it either until I think about your mother. Then I know I have to be strong for her and for you. We can't think about ourselves right now."

Emily looked at her dad through eyes awash with tears but nodded her head mutely. Jason quietly pulled her back against his shoulder and rocked her back and forth.

"We can't tell her yet. I've talked it over with Dr. Chapman and Dr. Glovier. They think it best to tell her that they have gotten her an appointment with a doctor at the Mellon Institute for her first check –up since she will already be in Pittsburgh."

"Are they never going to tell her, or do they think they can help her?" asked Emily sadly.

"Dr. Glovier said they treated her kind of cancer with radium, which burns the tissues but sometimes stops the growth of new cells. I don't think it really cures the cancer though," explained Jason as he held Emily close. They were both trying to draw comfort from each other.

When Emily lay her head down on the little table and cried as if her world had dissolved, Jason allowed her to cry. When she finally seemed to be spent, Jason pulled her around to face him. "Emily, do you remember me telling you about Aunt Sarie Lester from Bradshaw Mountain?"

Emily nodded but looked at Jason as if he had lost his mind, but before she could say anything, Jason put his finger on her lips.

"She talked to me a lot about her Good Lord. She had cancer also and she was as cheerful the day she died as she was when I first met her. I want to tell you what she told me once. I asked her how she stayed so cheerful since she knew she had an incurable disease. She said, 'Why Son, the Good Lord helps me.'"

"I asked her if she prayed and she answered, 'I don't know if I've prayed or just done a lot of begging.' She said that the Lord heard the beggars too."

"She still died, Daddy," muttered Emily brokenly.

"Yes, she did, Princess, but she died happy. You see she believed that the love people have for each other never dies.

She thinks we leave our love here to help those we leave behind," said Jason, now speaking with a softness and reverence that was new to Emily.

"Did you believe her, Daddy?" questioned Emily, desperately wanting something to hang on to. She looked up at her dad's face and it was different. There was a peace and calmness about him now that wasn't there before. But when Emily thought back, it seemed as if he had been different all evening.

Jason smiled a beautiful sweet smile and his face was suffused with a rosy glow as he said, "Yes, Princess, I believe her. Honey, I met Aunt Sarie's Good Lord today and I know she was right."

Emily looked at him, seeking an answer, and asked, "How did you meet Him, Daddy? God is a spirit, or that's what the Bible says."

"You're right, Princess," said Jason before he continued with assurance, "I guess His spirit came to me because I've been begging and seeking Him. I've tried to pray but like Aunt Sarie, I guess I've been begging. I guess that when we get to the place where we can't handle something any longer, the Good Lord gives us peace"

Emily sat quietly now, holding her dad's hand. Neither of them spoke for several minutes and then Emily asked softly, "Daddy, will you beg the Good Lord to help me?"

Jason hugged her close again as he said, "I certainly will, Princess, and maybe you could do some begging too."

Emily looked up at her dad and then nodded, "Yeah. I guess you're right, Dad." Then Emily sat staring off into space and absently eating her sundae, as did Jason.

Emily said, "Daddy, I don't believe I can go back home and act natural around Mom. Do you think it would be all right if I stayed with Aunt Rita and Uncle Kyle tonight?"

Jason looked amazed as he exclaimed, "Emily, Kyle and I talked and he suggested that when I told you, it would be a good idea if you spent the night with them. Isn't that strange that you should suggest the same thing?" asked Jason in a stunned manner.

Emily grinned. “Maybe the Good Lord is already beginning to help me. I hope He is, but I still think I should stay with them tonight. I’m going to ask Aunt Rita to pray for me also. They’re really good people, Daddy. You know that though, don’t you?” questioning, yet already knowing how her dad felt about the Benders.

Jason and Emily were both puzzled when they realized they had both eaten their sundaes.

“I don’t even know what it tasted like,” giggled Emily before turning guilt ridden eyes on her dad.

Knowing that Emily would give it all away if she couldn’t still be her old giggly, bouncy self, Jason cautioned her. “Now, Princess, you can’t load yourself down with a load of guilt. That won’t help Mommy. You try to be your same old giggly self, for after all, you did not do anything to cause this. It is just something that happened.”

He sat thinking and then said, “Aunt Sarie said, ‘the rain falls on the just and the unjust and they all get wet.’ ”

Emily, who had turned fourteen in January, nodded wisely as she suddenly remembered Mary Leonard’s mother getting killed in a car accident. She told Jason about how torn up Mary had been.

Wise beyond her years, Emily philosophized. “I’m no better than Mary. At least I’ll have Mommy a little while longer or maybe even more. Mary came to school one day and when she went home that evening her Mommy was no longer there.” Emily shivered as she remembered her friend’s grief.

When they drove back, Emily jumped out of the car and ran into the Bender house, which wasn’t unusual, and Jason went on into his house.

After about an hour, the phone rang and Rita asked if Emily could spend the night since she wanted her help in making a stuffed teddy bear. Janet knew how much Emily loved to help with Rita’s projects and so happily agreed.

Jason knew that Emily was very upset about her mother but also about having to move and was feeling guilty because she did.

"My little girl certainly received a double dose of anguish today," thought Jason forlornly. He hoped Rita and Kyle could help her, and more than that, he hoped the Lord would help her.

Knowing that guilt could be such a burden to carry around, Jason hoped they could help Emily. He himself had carried guilt since the day he married Janet. He couldn't forget Lucinda Harmon and he had married Janet knowing that. He felt that his suffering was justified, but little Emily had no reason to suffer; she was just one of the innocents that got caught in the rain.

Jason had been sleeping in the other spare bedroom to keep from disturbing Janet until she had recovered from surgery, and he was still using that room. He hadn't been sleeping very much, but felt that since his visit to the church, he would be able to sleep.

He was wrong though. While he went to sleep almost as soon as his head touched the pillow, he was suddenly awake from a dream of pure torment. In the dream, he was walking down a narrow path that led to that little church house and as he walked he heard crying. It wasn't happy crying, but crying in suffering and despair. He began to hurry in order to help whoever it was, and when he reached the place where the crying was coming from, he saw Lucinda Harmon caught in the branches of a tree. She seemed to be too weak to move or free herself and had given up.

Jason began to break branches and brambles in an effort to reach her, but when she saw him, she looked at him as if someone had died. "You told me you didn't want me in your life, so it's all right if I can't get out."

Jason jerked awake almost screaming, "No, No. Lucinda, I didn't mean it."

He sat up shaking, with sweat running down his chest, while he gasped for breath. He finally got out of bed, praying that nobody heard him crying Lucinda's name.

"Oh! Lord, please help me and help her. I shouldn't have said that to her. She'll never be out of my heart and I cannot help it. I've tried so very hard," thought Jason as he went into the kitchen to get a drink.

Once there, he sat down at the table and dropped his weary head into his hands as he moaned softly. Suddenly, he arose and went to the living room and picked up a Bible that Janet always kept on a table behind the sofa. He'd never seen Janet reading it but it had always been there. He hadn't read it either, or not very often anyway. When Jason sat down with the Bible in his lap, it fell open and when he looked down, Psalm 121 was there in front of him.

He began reading, "I will lift up mine eyes unto the hills, from whence cometh my help. My help cometh from the Lord, which made heaven and earth. He will not suffer thy foot to be moved; he that keepeth thee will not slumber."

Jason stopped reading as the surety of that message sank into him. "That's what I'm supposed to cling to, I guess. There's no other reason for the Bible falling open to that Psalm."

He went back into his room and knelt by his bed and softly begged the Lord to help Janet to get well, and to help Emily adjust to all this trauma in her life, and to help him learn to live with the guilt he carried around, and finally he begged the Lord to not let anything bad happen to Lucinda.

"Lord please let her know, somehow, that I was just distraught. I didn't mean those awful things I said to her, please, Lord. She's not the guilty one, I am. I'm willing to pay, Lord, but please spare her," he begged silently lest someone hear him.

When he went back to bed, he finally fell into an exhausted sleep and did not awaken until the sun crept through the curtains to shine on his face.

Emily came home the next day, seemingly the same cheerful imp that had always been such a blessing in their lives.

Jason planned to talk to Kyle and Rita as soon as he could. He wanted to hear their thoughts, as to how all this was affecting Emily. He also needed to talk to Kyle and get his agreement to look after the house and see about anything that cropped up. "You can call me collect if something comes up that I need to know about. I really can't make any definite plans until we find out more about the progress of the disease. We may get to come back and we may not. If that happens then I'll need a lot of help from you."

Jason smiled when Kyle said, "It'll cost you." His usual twinkle appeared but he soberly said, "You just ask. I'll do anything I can."

Thus, Jason spent his time in clearing up the numerous things that had been such a part of his life for nearly sixteen years. He went to a school board meeting and told them he would have to resign and asked that they please still work to get a new high school built for Welch. Paul Christian, his buddy on the school board, assured him that he definitely would "hold their feet to the fire" on that issue.

## CHAPTER 37

Janet did not seem to be gaining her strength back as quickly as they had thought she would and Jason called Dr. Glovier. Jason explained Janet's tiredness and the doctor asked to speak to Janet. "I think we need to try you on a bigger dose of streptomycin. That infection really got a big hold on you, Mrs. McCall, and it doesn't want to let go."

Janet complained but agreed to try it, however, she still felt that the streptomycin was making her feel tired. "It must be that, Jason, because I seldom felt tired before I started taking it," she argued. Jason assured her that the infection was making her tired and the antibiotic was fighting the infection.

Emily seemed to want to be out with her friends all the time and Jason didn't refuse her, but Janet fussed. "Jason, she is out too much. I know school is out but she isn't getting enough rest. I'm afraid she'll get sick."

Jason thought that it was because she knew she would be away for a while and she hated to leave her friends. That was the explanation he gave Janet but according to Rita and Kyle, they had told her to do just that, since she was afraid she couldn't keep up that cheerful façade.

One day, she called from a friend's house and asked that her dad come and pick her up. Jason thought this was unusual since her friend usually brought her home. He picked her up out at Maitland and seeing her face, decided to drive on up Route 52 with her before going home. He drove up to the old Leatherwood building and then pulled over and stopped. He turned to Emily and she threw herself into his arms, crying.

"Dad, help me. I just can't make myself leave here. I want to be with Mom but I don't want to live in Pittsburgh, Dad. I've hated it every time I've gone there. Can't Mom get the treatments down here closer so we can stay home?" she questioned in heart wrenching whispers.

"I thought about that, Princess, but the Mellon Institute is a research center and has the latest procedures for almost everything. I want the very best for your mom," explained Jason.

"Now, I can't tell you that I know how you feel because I didn't have to move at your age nor have my mother be ill, but there are some very nice people in Pittsburgh. In fact, your Uncle Frank's Kim will be coming to stay with Dad and Mom while you are there. You liked her, didn't you?" asked Jason hopefully.

Emily grimaced, "Yeah, Dad, I liked her but I haven't seen her in over a year. She's not like Kitty and Marsha. We're like sisters. I just don't know if I can tell them good-bye or not," moaned Emily. She began to cry even louder as she blubbered. "I worked so hard to be captain of the cheerleaders and now...I can't."

Jason didn't know what to do to console his distraught daughter. "Emily, you and I have gone along doing exactly what we have wanted to do. We've always assumed that what ever we do will be fine with your mother. We're both guilty," said Jason looking at Emily intently.

"Yes, but Mom seemed happy as long as we were. She really didn't mind, Dad," said Emily still crying.

Jason shifted in his seat and pulled his daughter close. "Don't you think that this one time in our lives we could stop thinking about ourselves? Your mother needs all of our caring and attention. She is a very sick woman and we need to see that she gets the very best care we can get and that is at the Mellon Institute's Research Center," Jason stated adamantly.

"I'm sorry, Princess, but in this instance your mom comes first. Neither you nor I want to go to Pittsburgh but we have to forget about our wants, at least for awhile." Jason begged for understanding.

"I know that this is a special time in your life, but would it be so special if your mother can't enjoy it with you," he asked.

Emily had stopped crying and at least had shown some interest. Jason waited hopefully.

"Can we come home as soon as Mom has her treatments? I mean, if everything goes well, of course," finished Emily looking expectantly at her dad.

"Let's just take it one day at a time, please, Emily. I don't want to promise you something and then have to renege on it. We will come back if it is at all possible. That, I promise," stated Jason with assurance.

Emily seemed relieved but still sad. "I can at least tell Kitty and Marsha that we will be back soon…if it is at all possible, can't I?" she asked.

Jason hugged her close and kissed her cheek. "That you can, Princess, and I do keep my promises, you know," said Jason as he started the engine.

As they drove home Jason started to tell Emily to concoct some kind of plausible story to tell Janet and Olivia but then thought better of it. Emily was wise for her age and he felt sure she could handle it. So they drove on home in companionable silence and with a sense of peace.

When Janet wanted to know why she needed her daddy to come for her, Emily explained that suddenly knowing she wouldn't get to see her friend for a whole month was just too much and she needed to get away.

Janet looked at Emily sadly and said, "I know just how you feel. I felt the same way when I left Pittsburgh to come down here, except I knew I wasn't going back. Well, not for a long time, if ever. I left all my friends, my parents, and all that I knew and loved behind, except your daddy."

Jason and Emily both stood in muted silence since they had never known that Janet had suffered that much by her move. Jason went to Janet and knelt down by her seat on the sofa. Taking her hands, he said, "Janet, I am so sorry. I wish you had explained all this to me. I thought you were satisfied in the beginning. Of course, after that meeting with ….Well, since then you've wanted to move."

Janet dropped her head and answered in a saddened voice, "Yes, I know, Jason, and I was unfair. I should never have said anything to you. I am sorry," and her look of anguish almost broke Jason's heart since he felt so guilty over Lucinda already.

"Honey, you don't need to feel sorry for a thing. You've

been a better wife than I've deserved," mumbled Jason as he hugged her around the waist and lay his head against her breast.

Emily hugged her mom also. "Thanks, Mom! You've really helped me but I also feel pretty rotten. I've been moaning and groaning because I have to move for a while and you left your home and lived here all these years."

Emily looked so sad but suddenly she hugged Janet again and giggled, "I guess you are just tougher than me."

Janet looked first at Emily and then at Jason before she smiled and said, "No, honey, I just found something that I wanted more than anything on earth—your dad." Then she dropped her head and mumbled, "I did everything in my power to get him, even some things I shouldn't have done."

A few days later Jason climbed behind the wheel of a new station wagon he had bought especially for Janet's comfort. When Emily watched him come up the drive she ran to the door, thrust it open and stepped into the carport just as he stopped. "Well, where did you get this fine looking carriage, Sir?" she questioned impishly.

"I shall take your mother home in all the comfort of a royal carriage, Princess. She deserves one that is gold-plated but they are so-o hard to find," Jason beamed as he opened the doors and showed Emily the nicely padded back seats, which let down to make a bed. "See, if she gets tired we can stop and make her a bed."

Janet came to the door just then and stared in amazement. "Jason, where did you get that beautiful station wagon?" she asked as she stepped out onto the carport.

Jason bowed and put his arm out in a wide sweep and said, "Your carriage, Madam. Would you like to take a drive?" he asked, smiling broadly.

Janet did not hesitate but immediately went to the passenger side and stood waiting for Jason to open the door. He hurried around the hood of the car and opened the door with a flourish, saying, "Step right in, Madam, and you will be whisked away to wonderland."

Emily jumped in the back where the seats were still down and stretched out as if asleep. "Don't mind me, I'll be Sleeping Beauty while you're taking Cinderella to the ball," she chortled as Jason and Janet happily went along with her pretense.

"Are you the kind of princess that snores, I wonder," teased Jason. Then looking at Janet, as they recalled the game they once played with a younger Emily, he said, "Do you think we should put a clothespin on her nose, just in case?"

Janet said, "Yes, let's do. Here I have one in my pocket." Janet looked at Jason and smiled since they'd played this game hundreds of times.

"No, you don't," said a wide awake Sleeping Beauty who was also reliving her past delight in their little game. She was not only awake but up on her knees in the back seat. When Jason and Janet looked around at her she was laughing merrily and Jason started the engine and backed out of the drive.

They drove around for almost an hour going to Kimball, stopping to take a picture of the Leatherwood building and then the Stevens Clinic Hospital, before coming back into town to take a picture of Doctors Memorial Hospital.

Emily spoke up, saying, "Let's take a picture of the high school because when they build the new one this one will be history, won't it."

By this time, Jason had begun to notice Janet frowning occasionally and knew that he should get her back home. He could see that she was relieved when he turned up Wyoming Street, saying that it was time to go home.

Their scheduled date to leave Welch was June twentieth and even though Janet had not felt well since the drive they had taken two weeks before, she still wanted to get started.

The morning of June twentieth finally arrived, and it was then, for the first time since the day she had fainted, that Janet became nauseous when she tried to eat.

"You're not used to eating this early," said Jason since they had gotten up at six o'clock in order to leave by at least seven-thirty. Janet agreed that being so early was probably the reason, so they decided they would stop somewhere about nine o'clock and get something to eat. "Here, take this coke and sip it along. It helps with nausea most of the time," said Jason, putting a bottle of coke into her hand.

Jason tenderly helped Janet into the car and checked with Olivia and Emily to see if they were comfortable in the back seat and had not left anything. Then he went back to check that everything was locked up, before honking his horn three times to let the Benders know they were on their way. They had decided on this way of saying farewell since they all felt it would be easier on Emily, and in fact all of them, if they did not have to see each other before their departure.

Jason took the curves up and over Indian Ridge very slowly but before they had gotten into Pineville, Janet was sick and they had to stop. Jason helped her out of the car and walked with her along the road until the sickness wore off. Then they resumed their journey.

However, from there to Beckley they stopped five more times until Jason finally gave her a shot of Phenergan for nausea and made her a bed in the back of the station wagon with Olivia beside her.

After a few miles, Emily looked back and Olivia motioned that Janet was sleeping.

"Dad, she's sound asleep. I'm sure glad. There's nothing worse than being carsick. But she was sick before she got in the car, wasn't she?" spoke Emily, questioning the meaning of what was happening.

Moving across the seat, Emily leaned close to his ear and whispered, "Dad, could that disease be causing her to be this sick?"

Jason shook his head and put his finger in front of his lips to silence Emily, fearing that Janet might be feigning sleep and could hear them. Olivia didn't know about the cancer either and Jason did not want her to hear them. Emily understood and they fell silent as they drove on.

Once Jason was outside of Beckley and could get on a four-lane highway, he put his foot down and really moved the big car along the highway. He and Emily talked very little since they were concerned for Janet and did not want to wake her. In about three hours they were in Morgantown and Emily whispered that she was hungry. Janet was still fast asleep and Olivia was also dozing, but awoke just as they decided to stop for food.

"I'm hungry as a bear," whispered Olivia as she tried to stretch without waking Janet.

Jason pulled into a drive-in and quietly ordered sausage and egg biscuits, two coffees, and a carton of milk. He did not shut off the engine for fear of waking Janet.

They quietly ate and were soon on the highway again. Now, they were nearing Washington, Pennsylvania and would soon be home, but just then Janet awoke and felt sick. Jason hurriedly pulled to the roadside but Olivia was already holding the waste can they had put in the back floor board. Finally, Janet fell back completely exhausted.

"Janet, honey, we're almost there. Can you make it a little farther or do you want me to take you to the hospital here?" asked Jason in a worried voice.

Janet looked at him from a pale face and told him to go on home. "I want to go home, Jason. Please take me home," she mumbled weakly. Olivia, wide awake and very alert, sat beside Janet holding the waste can as Jason pulled back out into traffic.

Not very long after that, they pulled into the drive leading to the Washburn Estate. "You're home, Janet," whispered Olivia as the mansion came into view.

Janet seemed to revive and even sat up as they drove up to the front entrance. "Oh Mother! How I have missed this place. I've really come home at last, haven't I?" murmured Janet.

Olivia leaned over and kissed her cheek, saying, "Yes, Baby, you're home." When Jason looked back at them he saw tears in both their eyes and again he felt a stab of guilt.

"Why didn't I realize how much living here meant to Janet? I've been so selfish," he chided himself silently.

## CHAPTER 38

Before they were out of the car the front door of the mansion swung open and Harvey, the butler, came out to carry the luggage inside. Once inside, the housekeeper, Mrs. Fiske, and Elsie, who had taken care of Janet's needs before she married, were waiting to take Janet to her room.

Jason trod up the stairs behind this entourage fearing that Janet would be sick again. Once he saw that she was ensconced in the room that had been hers from childhood, he left quietly to call the Mellon Institute and get an appointment for Janet

When he mentioned his name to the switchboard operator, she immediately connected him with a Dr. DeBouran.

"I've been waiting for your call, Dr. McCall. Your man in Welch, Dr. Glovier, called me yesterday to apprise me of the case. How did your wife make the trip?" he inquired in a concerned voice.

"She became nauseous when she tried to eat this morning and she has been sick all day. After numerous stops from her being sick, I gave her a shot of Phenergan and she went to sleep but when she awoke she was sick again. That was this side of the town of Washington," stated Jason worriedly.

Dr. DeBouran seemed to hesitate before saying, "I think you should bring her in as quickly as possible. From what Dr. Glovier told me, her cancer is the fast growing kind and we need to begin treatment as soon as possible."

Jason was shocked. "Fast growing! Dr. Glovier didn't tell me that. I came here on the assumption that you people had new treatments that could possibly help her if not cure her," he said in bewilderment.

"I'm sorry, Doctor. I thought they had told you everything before you left with her. We do have some promising treatments but when a disease is so rampant...we have no guarantees," stated Dr. DeBouran with sympathy.

"Would in the morning be soon enough, Doctor? She is so glad to be in her childhood home again that I hate to spoil this one evening for her," said Jason, remembering her tears and then her smiles as she entered her old room.

"Sure, I don't think one night will do too much harm, but have her here by eight o'clock tomorrow morning prepared to stay," Dr. DeBouran replied briskly.

"Come to the emergency entrance and there will be someone waiting there with a wheelchair. They will know where she is to come. Good night, Doctor," said Dr. DeBouran brusquely and broke the connection.

When Dr, DeBouran hung up, Jason sat pondering how to break the news to Janet when his father-in-law, Joshua Washburn, came through the door. "Sorry, I didn't mean to intrude," he said, and turned to leave the room, but Jason's plea stopped him.

"Wait, Joshua. I need your thinking on something," said Jason, and proceeded to explain Janet's condition and also what Dr. DeBouran had just told him.

Joshua Washburn stood still in shock before wiping his hand across his face in a swiping manner, as if to wipe something away. "The doctor said she has cancer! Does Janet know she has cancer?" asked Joshua in dread.

"No, and neither does Olivia. I had to tell Emily since she had guessed something more was wrong anyway," replied Jason, and asked if Joshua had any ideas how to get Janet to go into the hospital without telling her.

"Lord, Son, it's hard enough for me to take right now," said Joshua, who had sat down heavily in the nearest chair.

"This has hit me right between the eyes and I don't know what it will do to Olivia and to poor Janet. Oh God! My poor little girl," moaned Joshua miserably.

Jason felt really bad that he had blurted it out to Joshua in such a fashion. He had thought that his dad had told Joshua when they first learned about it. Jason got up and went to the sideboard and poured Joshua a shot of brandy and brought it to him. Joshua looked up and then grasped the glass and drank it down. "Thanks! I needed that," gasped Joshua as his ashen face slowly regained its color.

"I'm so sorry, Joshua, but I thought Dad had already told you. I told him not to tell anyone else but I assumed he would tell you," said Jason as he patted Joshua's shoulder in compassion.

"I've been out of town for two weeks. I left right after she came through her surgery. I haven't seen Henry to talk to since then," explained Joshua.

Jason poured a small amount of scotch in a glass and sat sipping it as he pondered what to do, when Olivia came in, saying, "Jason, there's something else wrong with Janet. She keeps vomiting and she hasn't eaten a bite today. I got her to eat a salt cracker just now and she was immediately sick again."

Jason looked at Joshua, who nodded his head in agreement before saying, "Sit down, Olivia, we have something to tell you."

He looked at Jason solemnly and said, "I think you'd better do this. I don't think I can."

"Tell me...What is it, Joshua? Why are you so pale?" she questioned in an agitated state.

Jason got up and went toward a small sofa, and taking Olivia's hand he pulled her with him to sit together on the sofa. Then he said, "Olivia, I have to tell you something and I don't know how to make it easy." Jason looked so miserable. He was thinking, "What if someone told me something like this about Emily?" He didn't think he could bear it.

Olivia looked almost ready to cry but then checked herself and grimaced. "I know, Jason. I've known all along that Janet has cancer. She does, doesn't she?" She asked as if to confirm her suspicions.

"How did you know? I haven't told anyone except Dad and Emily. Oh! Emily told you, I guess," spoke Jason questioningly.

Olivia shook her head and sighed in despair, but said, "No, Jason, nobody told me. I just knew from the time I looked at Janet. It was like something told me. I've not said anything to anyone, hoping that by not saying anything it would not be true," finished Olivia with tears creeping slowly down her cheeks.

Joshua hurried across the room, sat down beside his wife, and pulled her into his arms. "I should have been with you down there, Olivia. I'm sorry, I wasn't."

They sat holding hands as if to reassure each other until Jason spoke, "Well, I've just talked to a Dr. DeBouran at the Mellon Institute and he wants Janet at the hospital by eight o'clock in the morning. Actually, he wanted her to come tonight but I just couldn't tell her tonight. She was so glad to be home," mumbled Jason in a voice choked with tears.

He looked at Joshua and Olivia in a pleading manner. "How am I going to tell her?"

Olivia got up and found some tissues, wiped her eyes, and stood looking out the window. She turned. "Let's just tell her we are taking her in for her check-up that Dr. Glovier told you to get for her as soon as she arrived here."

"Olivia, she has to be told. If we don't the doctors will, you know," said Joshua looking at his wife with great sad eyes.

Olivia turned with a jerky motion to hide her tears, "I know that, but let her have a few more hours of hope. If we tell her now she will not even get to enjoy being home," mumbled Olivia and swiftly left the room. Joshua got to his feet and followed her.

Jason sat with his head down, as he silently begged the Lord to help him be strong for all of them. He could empathize with Joshua and Olivia since he had a daughter of his own.

Jason longed to be back on the top of Atwell Mountain. There he had felt wrapped in love and peace while sitting on that hard wooden bench, in a silent empty church building. Aunt Sarie Lester had said that the Lord was everywhere and now Jason prayed, "Lord, if you are near, please hear me. I need help and I need some peace, but Lord, not just for me but Janet, her parents, and our little Emily. Help us, Lord. We need your presence so very much," he begged as the door opened and Emily came in.

"What are you doing sitting here in the dark, Dad?" asked Emily as she came and put her arm around his shoulders. Jason looked up and then stood and hugged her close.

"Emily, I received a call from a Dr. DeBouran at the Mellon Institute and he wanted me to bring your Mom to the hospital tonight. I asked him if it would be all right to wait until tomorrow since she was tired and was so glad to be back in her old home and he agreed." Jason looked down at his daughter, debating whether to tell her what he had just learned.

Finally he said, "Emily, Dr. Glouvier hadn't gotten that final test when we left so he didn't tell me the worst. Emily, your Mom has the rapid growing kind of cancer."

Emily's facial expression did not change but from a solemn face she asked, "Does that mean that nothing can be done?"

Jason ran his hand, with fingers splayed, through his hair and tiredly said, "Yes Princess, unless they have something brand new that I'm not aware of, there's nothing they can do."

Then Emily turned her face into her dad's shoulder and began to cry. When Jason tried to console her, she erupted. "I didn't mean this to happen, Dad. I've been so selfish. Oh Daddy, I've been praying for something to happen so that I could go back home. Now God answered me like this. I've caused this." Emily whimpered as tears coursed down her cheeks.

Jason drew a long breath as if pulling in knowledge before he said, "No Princess, this is not because you prayed for something to happen. In the Bible there's a story about a man called Joshua who was trying to take Jericho for Israel and he prayed for the sun to stand still to help him in battle. Now we know that the earth revolves around the sun but Joshua prayed for what he knew at that time. The important thing is that God knows the intents of our hearts and he hears our cries. So, don't feel guilty, Honey, the Lord knew what you wanted. Besides, this had already happened before you prayed," Jason finished solemnly as he patted Emily's hair.

Emily raised swollen red eyes to her dad's face. "I didn't know you read the Bible, Dad. I mean, I know you have always gone to church and tried to be honest and good to people, but I have never seen you reading the Bible," she stated in a curious, questioning voice.

"I'm ashamed to admit it, Princess, but I have read very

little in the Bible. I don't really know how I knew about Joshua unless it was from Sunday school or maybe some of the sermons I've slept through," Jason said with a sheepish grin.

Jason sat holding a silent Emily until she said, "Dad, maybe Aunt Sarie's Good Lord sent that story to you to help me. He could do that, couldn't He?" questioned Emily solemnly.

"Yes. Princess, I'm sure he can. God can do anything," Jason stated firmly and then mumbled, "He might even forgive a selfish brute like me."

Emily reached up and patted his cheek, "Dad, you're not really selfish. You're just like me. You would rather have had things another way and you feel guilty because you wanted it."

Emily arose from the sofa and turned to her dad, and in a maturity beyond her years she said, "Remember what you told me, Dad. You said we need to quit thinking about ourselves so much. So now we need to be thinking about Mom and how to make her last days the best we can make them. Don't you think it's time we started doing that?" questioned Emily.

Jason arose also and tilted Emily's chin, searching her face, "Princess, I think the Lord is giving you wisdom to help me," stated Jason as he patted Emily's shoulder before letting her go. "Let's go up and just tell Mom that in the morning we are taking her into the Mellon Institute," Jason said while looking at Emily for her approval.

"She'll want to know why we're taking her there, Dad. Mom knows that Mellon is big into research," began Emily and then continued with, "What are you going to tell her when she asks?"

"I'll just tell her the truth…or at least part of it," said Jason tiredly. They were walking up the stairs and when they reached the landing, Jason said, "I'll tell her that I'm concerned because of her nausea and that I want the most knowledgeable doctors to check her."

Emily and Jason looked at each other and then both nodded and made their way down the corridor to Janet's room.

## CHAPTER 39

When they entered, Olivia was just easing Janet back on her pillow as a maid took away the receptacle she had just used. "Jason, she's been sick three times in the last hour," said Olivia worriedly.

Jason bent over the bed and kissed Janet's forehead, which felt cool and damp. He slipped his arm behind her and sat down beside her on the bed,

"Sweetheart, let me take you to the hospital tonight. They can give you something to stop this vomiting and you can get some rest," begged Jason as he tenderly patted her arm.

Janet looked up at Jason imploringly, "Please, Jason, don't take me tonight. Can't you give me another shot? It helped and I slept most of the way here," she begged weakly.

Jason looked at Olivia and Emily who were both nodding their heads. He sighed helplessly and said, "All right, Sweetheart. I'll give you another shot of Phenergan, but in the morning, bright and early, I'm taking you to the hospital."

Janet reached out her hand to Emily who came to the bed and sat down by her mother. Janet patted her hand where it lay on her arm, "I'm so sorry, Emmy. I wanted to bring you home and show you all the delights I remembered," whispered Janet, looking lost and bewildered.

Emily swallowed before bravely replying, "Just wait until you get in that hospital. They'll have you out running foot races with me." She leaned down and kissed Janet's cheek before she realized that Janet was crying.

"Mom, please don't cry," begged Emily, looking around for her dad, who was standing at the foot of the bed. Jason hurriedly came to the bedside.

He sat down beside Emily before he also saw the tears running down Janet's cheeks. "What's the matter, Janet? Please, Honey, don't cry. Are you in pain?" questioned Jason in an anguished tone.

Janet wiped her face with her fingers before Olivia pushed a box of Kleenex within her reach. She took one and wiped her face but couldn't stop crying. "I know this sounds foolish but I don't feel like I'm going to get better," Janet cried brokenly as Jason gathered her in his arms.

"Sh-h Sweetheart. Don't even think like that. You're just tired and worn out by the trip," Jason assured her. He looked at Olivia, who had turned her back and was looking out the window.

Jason knew she was crying, as was Emily, who had gone to stand beside her. He looked down at Janet and then tenderly kissed her lips, saying, "I love you, Janet. Please don't talk like that. Emily and I need you so very much."

Janet put her arms around his neck and leaned her head against his shoulder, but she was still crying. "Jason," she mumbled, and then broke down and cried even harder.

"Go down to the study and get my bag, Emily. She needs another shot and something to make her rest," said Jason as he held Janet gently, making soothing sounds to calm her.

After administering the shot and a mild sedative, Jason sat holding Janet close until the crying stopped. She lay back on the bed, smiling up at Jason as she squeezed his hand. "I've loved you too much. I wanted you more than anything this life had to offer," she said and gripped his hand tightly.

Janet stopped talking and lay looking at Jason intently. She started to say something else but Jason put his finger over her lips as he said, "Sh-h, go to sleep, Honey. You can tell me in the morning."

Soon Janet was asleep and Jason left the room, followed by Emily and Olivia. They didn't talk but went quietly down the stairs and entered Joshua's study before anyone spoke. Olivia found a chair beside a window and sat down resignedly. "She knows, Jason. She already knows," Olivia said in a bemused voice.

Joshua had not risen from his chair on the other side of the window when they came in, nor had he indicated in any way that he realized they were there, but now, he jerked around and almost shouted. "How could she know unless you told her? All of you said she hadn't been told. So, how could she know?"

Jason had not taken a seat at all but stood beside the bar with Emily by his side. He picked up a glass and poured himself a drink from one of the decanters present and then turned to say, "I don't think she really knows, but I do think she senses something. Don't you think so, Emily?" Jason asked his daughter.

Emily looked tired and beaten but spoke clearly, "Yes, Dad, I too think she senses something, but no, Grandfather, she doesn't really know."

Jason and Emily then went to sit on the sofa and each person filled the room with their gloomy silence until Jason said, "I think I'll let Dad know we are here," and went to the telephone. Joshua arose and said, "Well, we may as well go to bed. Sitting here grieving as if she is already dead won't help the situation." He turned to Olivia, "Come on, Dear, you need to keep up your strength. I fear that there's worse to come."

When the Washburns had left the room Jason sat with his head down until he felt Emily's arm steal around his shoulders. He turned to look at her.

"Princess, remember that we talked about help coming from the Lord. Well, I think we both need to find some private place and beg for help for all of us. Your grandparents are taking this hard and I can understand why," finished Jason as he hugged Emily close to his heart.

Emily hung onto Jason as if he could spare her the grief she was experiencing. "I don't know how to pray, Dad. Since we talked the other day I've been saying, 'Lord, please help us. Please have mercy on us and help Mom,' but that's not praying is it?" asked Emily.

Jason stood holding his daughter and wondering how to answer her. How did someone who had just recently felt the true presence of God, tell another person how to call on Him? "Emily, if you truly wanted God to help you, I think you did pray. I think God listens to the heart," said Jason solemnly.

Emily stepped back from Jason's embrace and said, "I hope you're right. I wish I had known your Aunt Sarie. I'll bet she would have helped me too. She helped you, didn't she, Dad?"

Jason stood remembering things that Aunt Sarie had said and also what Lucinda Harmon had said with such assurance. "Yes, Emily, Aunt Sarie helped me and so did someone else. I think when people truly trust in the Lord it shows."

Emily went over to the sofa and sat down. "What do you mean it shows? Do they look different?" asked Emily curiously.

"No. It is just that everything they do seems to be connected with the Lord. I mean, like Aunt Sarie saying the Lord helped her bear her pain. She truly felt that the Lord was her help and because she was so sure it made me believe that there must be some higher power. I guess true believers have a confidence or sense of security that the rest of us don't seem to have," said Jason in an effort to explain.

Just then Olivia came back into the room. "Jason, don't you think that you and Emily should go to bed. We'll have to be up early and tomorrow is apt to be a rough day."

Jason immediately arose and turning to Emily, said. "Your grandmother is right, Emily. Let's go to bed. We can't do anything for your mother tonight."

Emily went over to Olivia and put her arms around her. "Grandmother, I'm not just sorry for me and Daddy. I'm sorry for you also. Mom is your baby, isn't she?"

Olivia gave Emily a convulsive hug. "Emily, your mother holds all the tenderness I have left in my heart. Part of my heart died with little Josh. The rest was given to Janet." Olivia turned abruptly and went hurrying out of the room.

Jason and Emily turned out the light and closed the door quietly as if they had left someone in the room. Then together they mounted the stairs and tiptoed into Janet's room.

They stood quietly by her bedside. She was sleeping but there was a frown on her face as if something was bothering her. "Is she in pain, Dad?" whispered Emily.

Jason bit his lip, fighting the tears that were trying to escape. "I don't know Emily. I hope to God she isn't," he whispered as he turned Emily and together they left the room.

Out in the hall they hugged each other tightly. "Mom, is so beautiful, isn't she, Dad?" asked Emily.

"Yes, Emily. She was my pin-up girl while I was in Korea. Most of my buddies were halfway in love with her," said Jason proudly. Jason kissed Emily's cheek and said, "Good night, Emily. Let's try to pray. Maybe she'll feel better tomorrow."

# CHAPTER 40

When Jason arrived with Janet at eight o'clock the next morning, two nurses were waiting for her just as Doctor DeBouran had promised. Jason, Olivia, Joshua, and Emily followed the wheelchair into the elevator, which whisked them to the third floor. The nurse behind the wheelchair started to explain that this floor was exclusively for terminally ill oncology patients, but Jason broke into a spate of questions which prevented this disclosure.

Olivia, Joshua, and Emily were ushered to the family waiting room, while Jason followed Janet into Doctor DeBouran's office. "Good Morning! So you are Mrs. Janet McCall, I've wondered what you looked like," spoke Doctor DeBouran as he picked up Janet's hand and shook it. He then turned to Jason and asked, "Have you explained everything to your wife, Doctor McCall?"

Jason turned red and hesitated momentarily but then stated firmly, "No, I haven't doctor. The family and I discussed it but felt that she should have another night of peace and rest. We hoped that she could accept it easier coming from you."

"Accept what?" exclaimed Janet. "What did you need to explain to me, Jason," asked Janet from a blanched white face, her voice choking.

Doctor DeBouran gave Jason an angry glare before pulling up a chair in front of Janet. After taking both her hands in his, he squeezed her hands and smiled gently before saying, "Mrs. Mc…May I call you Janet?" When Janet mutely nodded, he continued, "Right, well Janet, what your husband failed to tell you is that when you left West Virginia, Dr. Glouvier hadn't gotten all the results of the tests he sent off after your surgery. He received the final one after you left, so he called me. Janet, your ovaries were riddled with cancer," finished Dr. DeBouran solemnly.

Janet gasped and turned to Jason, who quickly took her in his arms as best he could with her still in the wheelchair. Janet didn't cry aloud but shook silently with heaving sobs.

Both men sat and let her cry for a few minutes and then Jason looked at Dr. DeBouran in muted appeal.

When Dr. DeBouran saw the anguish on his face, he broke in with, "Now, Janet, you know that crying will not change anything. Many women have been given the same news. What we have to do now is determine the best treatment we can give you. We would like for you to be able to discuss your treatment with us. Are you ready to do that?" questioned Dr. DeBouran.

Janet raised her head from Jason's breast and turned to the doctor nodding slowly, "I don't have much choice do I, Doctor?" she asked feebly.

"Well, you could refuse treatment or discussion but I don't think either would be a wise choice, do you?" asked Dr. DeBouran.

Janet sat silently for a moment and then straightened her shoulders and said, "All right, Doctor, what do we do first, and can Jason stay with me?"

Dr. DeBouran explained that she would first have to have a thorough examination, during which Jason would be present. "After that, we will sit down with you and Jason and decide on what to do next. Is that satisfactory?" he asked with a smile.

On Janet's nod, Dr. DeBouran beckoned his nurse who took Janet into an alcove to undress, leaving Jason with him. Dr. DeBouran went behind his desk, sat down, and motioned Jason to the chair on the other side. "I was angry with you at first for not telling her last night, but after seeing her and watching her reaction, I think you did the best thing."

Jason smiled wearily, "I didn't know what to do, but after discussing it with her parents and our daughter, I went along with their wishes to give her another night free of worry. She was so sick anyway that I don't think she could have stood much more last night. I finally gave her Phenergan, and a sedative."

The nurse then came to the door and both men went into the examination room. Jason stood by holding her hand and talking calmly to her the entire time. When she was told she had to go to X-ray and that Jason could go to the door but could not go in, she did not demur but smiled up at Jason and squeezed his hand.

Jason looked down on her as she lay quiet and completely still. He was torn by the blankness in her eyes. "All the life seems to have been pulled from her," he thought. He gripped her hand tighter and only released it as they wheeled her into X-ray.

When she came back from X-ray, she was helped to dress and wheeled back into Dr. DeBouran's office to sit with Jason and wait for the results and then their talk about treatment.

An orderly came in with coffee and doughnuts, which Dr. DeBouran had ordered, but as soon as Janet caught a whiff of the coffee she became nauseous again and the nurse hurried to her side with a receptacle.

Dr. DeBouran and Jason darted looks at each other and quickly moved the coffee and doughnuts into another room and came back into the office. After about twenty minutes, the nurse came back with the X-rays, followed by the radiologist.

Dr. DeBouran arose and came around the desk as the nurse clipped the X-rays to the wall-mounted viewing space. The radiologist was introduced as Doctor Townsend to both Jason and Janet before the three doctors stood with their backs to Janet, studying what the X-rays revealed. The doctors mumbled and pointed to various places on the x-ray while gravely nodding their heads.

Then Jason and Dr. Townsend came back and sat down in the two chairs on each side of Janet and Dr. DeBouran sat down in a chair he had placed directly in front of her. He looked at both doctors before saying, "Janet, the cancer had spread before you were operated on and that makes it more difficult, but we have had good results with radium."

He again looked at the other doctors as if to confirm what he had said and Dr. Townsend nodded and said, "I think you should decide quickly and get it done. The quicker we get started the better. Don't you think so, Dr. McCall?" he asked, turning to Jason.

Jason sat as if turned to stone, but when his name was called, he flinched and quickly said, "Yes, I'm sure you're right, Doctor. Really, we should start today, I think," he finished adamantly.

"Why ask Jason?" demanded Janet belligerently. "I'm the one with cancer," she almost shouted, and covering her face with her hands and bending toward her knees, sobbed loudly.

Jason arose and knelt before her and began in a soothing voice, "Honey, I know you are hurt, disappointed, and ...," he couldn't continue for Janet jerked back and looked wildly around the room.

"Hurt! Disappointed! Oh yes, go ahead and use all the platitudes you can spout, but they won't help. How would you like to be told you were soon going to die?" shrieked Janet as she frantically tried to get out of her chair.

She was too weak but in her frustration she managed to fling herself out of her chair. Jason caught her before she hit the floor and scooped her up into his arms where she clawed and scratched weakly, managing a long scratch down his cheek.

At this point, Dr. DeBouran had a hyperdermic ready and administered a sedating shot. He motioned for Jason to lay her on the examination table, saying, "She's taking it hard but I've seen worse reactions. She'll be calmer when she awakens. Now we need to put her into a room."

Jason handed her over to the nurses, who had rolled a gurney in, and they soon had her ready to be moved to the next floor. "Where are you taking her? I want to go with her," said Jason, wiping his hand down his cheek.

Dr. Debouran stopped Jason with, "Let me look at that scratch. Fingernails can be potent weapons. We'll clean it and put some antibiotic ointment on it. We don't want you getting sick." He smiled as he swabbed the scratch. "She didn't break the surface but it will be sore."

Jason appeared to care less what was happening to him, but seemed to be in shock himself. "I'm glad Emily and Olivia did not see that happen," he said softly. "If you don't mind I'd like to tell the family about the X-ray results and the proposed plans for immediate treatment."

"I'll go with you," offered Dr. DeBouran. "None of you will be able to go to her room for about an hour anyway. She'll probably sleep until we take her to start the radium and she has to agree before we can do that," he stated worriedly.

Seeing Jason's bewildered look, he explained, "The faster we can begin fighting the multiplication of those cancer cells the better chance we will have."

They had been walking down the hall and now reached the waiting room door where Dr. DeBouran stopped and turned to Jason, asking, "You do want us to try radium, don't you? It has had better results than anything we've tried so far."

Jason stopped and quietly said, "Could we discuss it as a family before I give the go ahead? They will want to know the side effects and the chances of cure. It's only going to delay the inevitable, isn't it?" questioned Jason with a grimace.

Dr. DeBouran nodded, but before he could speak, the door opened and Olivia started out, stopping when she saw Jason. "Where is Janet? Has she been put in a room already?" she asked.

Jason took her elbow and together they went back into the waiting room. Jason looked around and almost every seat was filled with waiting families.

"Dr. DeBouran, can't we go back to your office for our family discussion?" asked Jason. He felt the family reaction needed to be private.

Jason was right in his supposition. Olivia fainted, Joshua turned deathly white and began to gasp for breath, but Emily stood like a zombie, not saying a word. Henry and Elizabeth McCall had arrived during the examination and now, they too were in shock.

Both Jason and Dr. DeBouran worked with Olivia and Joshua and finally gave both of them a mild tranquilizer. Emily had sat down on a chair and still sat silently, not moving or crying, but looking straight ahead in a fixed stare.

Jason pulled up a chair and sat down in front of her, "Princess, are you all right? You know it's all right to cry if you want to," he said softly as he squeezed her hands between both his own.

She looked at Jason and then tears rolled down her cheeks before she slumped against his chest. "Daddy, is this for some kind of purpose? Does God send this kind of pain just to satisfy some whim? What kind of God would do this to Mom and to us? We've not been bad people, have we?" questioned a troubled Emily.

Jason cradled her in his arms, like he had when she was much younger, while he rested his chin on the top of her head. "No, no, Princess. Please don't get angry with God. Remember your friend whose mother was killed in that car wreck. She was a good person too."

"But Daddy, why...why...why?" questioned Emily brokenly.

"I don't know, Princess. I just know that we aren't any better than anyone else and that all humanity suffers. I guess that if we never felt sad we wouldn't recognize joy," mused Jason aloud, in trying to find some answer to help his daughter and himself.

Over an hour later, Olivia, Joshua, Emily, Jason, and his parents were ushered into a room on the fourth floor to find Janet propped up in bed with her hair combed and looking very pretty.

She smiled when they went in and reached out her hand to Emily, "Come here, Baby. Mommy wants a big hug," she said as she spread her arms wide.

Emily ran to the bed and threw her arms around her mother's neck and gave her a strong hug. She leaned back then and smiled as she said, "How's that for a hug? Can you stand about fifteen of those?"

Jason was amazed at the strength and courage of his almost fourteen- year-old daughter. She was acting so natural when Jason knew she was aching inside. He sat down beside Janet on the bed and asked how she was feeling.

She smiled mistily and said, "Much better now that I know the worst." She looked at Jason and seeing the long scratch on his cheek, opened her mouth in amazement,

"Did I do that to you, Jason?" she asked in embarrassment. Jason smiled and explained that it was an accident.

"You didn't mean to hurt me, Honey. You were just lashing out at fate," Jason said with a smile. "I've had patients do worse than that."

Once assured that Jason was all right, Janet looked to where Olivia and Joshua were standing, as if waiting for admittance, and asked, "Have you told Mom and Dad, and your folks?"

Jason nodded that he had and then beckoned Olivia and Joshua to the bed. "Janet, Dr. DeBouran told me about a new treatment. Did he discuss it with you?" asked Jason, looking steadily into her eyes.

Janet shook her head no but then said, "He said he wanted to discuss treatment with us, though. I don't know if I want any treatments, Jason. There's no guarantee that it will help."

Olivia looked ready to cry and said, "Oh Janet, honey, please don't refuse to take any help you can get. Please, please! If Dr. DeBouran says it has been used successfully before, then there is a chance it will help," begged Olivia in an urgent plea.

Dr. DeBouran came in then and stood by the bed to explain what they wanted to do. He explained the procedure and then said, "The worst part is that for a period of days you will be in isolation. We will leave you plenty of reading material, the television, and a telephone, however, so you won't be completely cut off from your family."

After discussing possible side effects and the treatment, Janet finally agreed, and after more tears, the family went away as Janet was once again placed on a gurney and wheeled out of the room.

## CHAPTER 41

Jason checked with the doctors and talked to Janet by phone three or four times on the first day after the radium was implanted, as did Olivia and Emily. After that, however, Janet was too sick to talk, which had the entire family upset. Jason talked to the doctor and was told that the treatment was really working on the malignant cells and they were doing everything in their power to keep the sickness at bay.

Still, for three more weeks Janet was unable to talk to any of them. Later they learned that the phone had been taken out of her room because the ringing seemed to agitate her too much.

After the fourth week, Jason was allowed to put on a lead apron and go into the room, but just inside the door and not any closer than ten feet to Janet. Janet looked as if flesh had dropped from her. Her eyes were sunken, her cheeks pale, her hair listless, and she looked at Jason with such sad eyes that he had to leave. Outside, he slid down to the floor and, dropping his head onto his knees, gave way to his grief.

In four more days, Janet was moved into another room but was still semi-isolated. Jason could go in and sit in a chair about four feet from her bed and talk with her, which he did every day. Olivia, Joshua, Emily, and the McCalls were allowed to come to the door and speak to her.

On the second day, when Jason was allowed to go into the room to sit and talk, Janet, at first, lay listening to him and then interrupted.

"Jason, I know I'm not going to recover from this. I knew before I took the treatment. I did it for all of you but I don't want anymore. The odor, I know you smell it. I can't stand it. It makes me feel ashamed."

Jason stood up to go to her but Janet stopped him saying, "No, Jason! Don't come any nearer please. I've hurt you enough already."

Jason gaped in amazement. You've hurt me! No, Honey, I've hurt you. I should have known how you hated West

Virginia…" He was stopped by Janet telling him to be quiet.

Janet drew a long breath and then continued, "Jason, there's something you need to know but I can't tell you. I couldn't stand it to know…to see you hate me," she whispered from blistered, swollen lips.

Jason was filled with compassion and thought she didn't know what she was talking about, so he said, "Honey, you couldn't tell me anything that would make me hate you." He smiled as he gently patted the hand that lay twitching on the coverlet.

"What did you do, take all our money out of savings?" he questioned in a tragic voice.

Janet closed her eyes wearily as if talking was making her tired, but just as Jason started to leave so she could rest, she stopped him. "There's a metal box on the left–hand corner of the shelf in my bedroom in Mom's house. It's locked. Nobody knows it's there."

Janet paused to gain strength before going on, "I'll leave you a note about where the key is, and after I'm g-gone," she began gasping for breath as tears squeezed out from tightly closed eyes. Jason quickly hit the light for the nurse, who seemed to have been just outside the door since she was there so fast. Jason was shooed out of the room and not allowed to return that day.

Fearing that their talk had caused that reaction for Janet he didn't want a repeat. Therefore, on the next day Jason brought Janet flowers and made sure nothing serious was brought up. The other family members were now allowed in to see her and talk to her. They did not stay for long periods, however, since it was so difficult, due to the odor.

The sores around her mouth and nose were almost well, and her hair had been washed, but the entire room still reeked with an awful odor, even though it was sprayed twice daily with a deodorizer.

Jason knew this was from a terrible vaginal discharge, which was one of the side effects of radium implants, but still he never ate before he visited. Dr. DeBouran had told Jason and Janet that the odor would subside after several weeks if the treatment worked and they both waited patiently.

Nothing else was said about Janet's mention of a box and Jason tended to think it had all been in her imagination. Thus, he told nobody else about that conversation and put it right out of his mind. Now, his major concern was trying to keep Janet happy and cheerful. Emily joined him in this endeavor but not until the stench had abated.

One day on the way home from visiting Janet, Emily rolled down the window and let the wind blow her hair. Jason looked over and asked, "Don't you mind having your hair blown all over the place?"

"I'm trying to blow away that odor. I think that I'll never get that smell out of my nose. I don't see how she stands it, Dad," said Emily in a choked voice.

"Mom was always so clean and constantly cautioned me about body odor...and now she has to live with...." Emily stopped to keep from crying.

Jason reached over and rubbed her arm gently, "It bothers her so very much, Princess, but she knows she can do nothing about it. The radium killed off those cancerous cells and at the same time, it sloughs off the surface of surrounding tissues. It is painful and it has a horrific odor, but I guess she is willing to stand anything if they tell her it will make her well again," said Jason, smiling sadly. "She's having a hard time of it, Princess, and I don't know if it's helping or not. The doctor is to give us his evaluation in another week. I hope it's good."

"I do too, Dad," whimpered Emily as she slid across the seat and lay her head against his shoulder.

They drove on to the house in silence. Both of them knew that Pittsburgh, as nice as it was, could never feel like home to them, but also knew they would be here as long as Janet wanted to stay. Right now, she had no choice, but even when she was better they knew they would never mention going back to West Virginia unless she wanted to.

After that, one day led into the other, with a heavy dread hanging over the entire Washburn Estate. The doctor's evaluation was not good but he did say that the cancer cells in the treatment area were gone.

"We fear the cancer has spread to other areas, however. We won't know for certain until we do further testing. I'll let you know," assured Dr. DeBouran.

Nine days later, Dr. DeBouran called Jason to set up a family meeting for eight o'clock on Monday morning.

Everyone in the family was on pins and needles anticipating the findings. Janet seemed some better but was bone thin, very weak, and often too nauseous to eat, but seemed to always be cheerful when she was able to see them at all.

Dr. DeBouran did not have good news, however. "The radium killed off the existing cancer cells but it had already spread to the spleen, pancreas, and the colon before the radium was implanted. I'm sorry that I can't give you better news," stated Dr. DeBouran sadly.

"There is some good news though. I believe it won't make any difference if she goes home for a few days. She talks about her own room all the time and I think she will feel better just to be in it," he continued.

"Won't she have to have treatment and care?" asked Olivia, who wanted her daughter home but felt she needed care that she would not know how to perform.

"We'll send a nurse home with her. In fact, there are two nice ladies who do private nursing and both, I think, will be glad to help out," informed Dr. DeBouran.

Impulsively, Emily hugged Dr. DeBouran and then realized what she had done and stepped back embarrassed and said, "Excuse me, Doctor. I'm just so happy that Mom can go to her home for a few days."

Dr. DeBouran smiled and patted Emily's shoulder as he said, "That's all right, young lady. I have two daughters your age and I'm used to hugs."

Jason had been standing as if an observer of a play, but suddenly said, "Dr. DeBouran, I am going to be deceitful and tell her that she is doing better and will be allowed home for a few days. Do you have any objections?" asked Jason hesitantly.

"No, I don't, for in a way she is better. Her platelet count has been up for the last few days. I'm hoping it stays up. As you know, should we have to operate with such a low platelet count, it would be very bad," explained Dr. DeBouran.

Jason looked relieved. "I'm glad. I hate to deceive her but I was going to anyway. I've never lied to her since we've been married, but now I can truthfully tell her she is better. That will give her some hope, won't it?" he asked, looking hopefully at Dr. DeBouran.

The doctor looked at Jason, whom he had grown to respect. From the time Jason had first arrived with his wife, Dr. DeBouran had seen Jason change from a strong robust man to a much thinner, sadder human being. Dr. DeBouran had noticed Jason's almost daily weight loss. He looked so much older now and Dr. DeBouran felt such compassion for this man who cared so very much.

He clapped Jason on the shoulder and said, "Yes, let's go together and tell her the good news."

Dr. DeBouran walked out of his office, trailed by Jason, Emily, Olivia, Joshua and two nurses as he turned down the corridor toward Janet's room, but stopped halfway there.

"None of you are to discuss this with anyone else, you understand. Others may think we are less than truthful with our patients."

As he looked from one face to the other, they all solemnly nodded in agreement and then they all turned with a smile to enter Janet's room.

# CHAPTER 42

Even though Janet could not get up, she was thrilled to be back in her childhood room again. As soon as she was settled and everything was arranged to the nurse's satisfaction, Janet asked that her maid, Elsie, be sent to her.

Jason thought she would want him to stay so he sent Emily to summons Elsie but when Elsie arrived, Janet said, "I want all of you to leave. I want to talk to Elsie alone."

Knowing that Elsie had always held a special place in Janet's life, they all smiled and trooped out of the room and down the stairs. At the bottom of the stairs, the housekeeper met them to say that a late lunch was prepared in the dining room.

They all sat down around the table and Jason realized that this was the first time he had seen Joshua, except in passing and today at the hospital, for over a month. In fact, Jason had not seen Joshua at all, except for the night he had revealed what Dr. DeBouran had learned from Dr. Glouvier. Until they had gotten back to the house, they'd not had a chance to talk.

"I've not seen you in weeks, Joshua. Where have you been?" asked Jason.

"I've had to be away. I'm sorry," apologized Joshua without looking up from his plate. Suddenly he stood up, pushed his chair back, and walked briskly from the room.

Jason and Emily sat with mouths agape in surprise until Olivia said, "Joshua can't stay around when something like this happens. Do you remember him being away all during little Josh's final days?" she asked of Jason.

Suddenly, Jason remembered a conversation he had heard between his parents. "Henry, I don't understand Joshua Washburn. He has left poor Olivia all alone to bear this grief," stated Elizabeth in bewilderment.

Now he looked at his mother-in-law with compassion as he said, "Yes, I remember."

Olivia looked straight ahead of her and in a choked, pain-filled voice said, "He loved little Josh better than his own life, but with all his power and influence he could not save him. I thought it was just because little Josh was his son, but it is the same for Janet. I guess when someone is used to fixing things and they run into something they can't fix, they become lost."

Emily got slowly up, and going around the table, put her arms around her grandmother and for the first time truly felt close to her.

"Grandmother, I am so sorry. I forget that Mom is your little girl and she's the only child you have," whispered Emily as she hugged Olivia again.

Olivia hugged Emily tightly and said, "Thanks, Emily. I guess you've always thought of me as the 'cool and poised' lady of the manor and I've cultivated that veneer. I've had to be strong. Joshua needs me to be strong."

Then pushing back her chair she said, "Excuse me, children, I must go see how he is," and walked sedately out of the room.

While Jason and Emily finished their meal, they discussed the things they had learned about Janet's parents, which neither had known until that moment.

"I really thought Grandmother did not want me to hug her or sit on her lap or really be around her. The only time I saw her act like she had any feelings was around Mom," said Emily.

"Your grandfather was always portrayed to me as a 'man of steel' who could get anything he wanted, fix any problem, and was hard as nails when it came to business," explained Jason as he drained his coffee cup.

He arose from the table as he said, "I guess everyone has an Achilles Heel. Do you know what that is, Princess?" asked Jason as they walked into the sitting room.

"Of course I do. I read the Iliad and the Odyssey, you know. It means some kind of vulnerability," said Emily smugly.

Trying to lighten the atmosphere she quipped. "Who do you think you're talking to anyway? I'm pretty smart for a fourteen-year-old hillbilly." She looked at her dad, who had changed so much and smiled.

Jason smiled broadly as he strode to the window. "Don't be calling yourself a hillbilly in front of your Grandmother Elizabeth, though." He raised his eyebrows and gave Emily a knowing look.

"Gosh no, I wouldn't think of it. She would be scandalized." Emily impishly grinned. "I really don't like her very much, Dad. I'm sorry, but it's the truth. It's almost like she's this bright, shiny, prim façade because her actions only seem prim and superficial, almost like there's no heart behind what you see. Does that make sense?" asked Emily, pondering.

"You're pretty accurate, Princess. Mom really believes in keeping up appearances but never gets involved in anything unpleasant. Although she's been here almost every day, she's only gone up twice to see Janet," said Jason sadly.

"You know, Princess, Mom acts almost like she is afraid of Janet or something, doesn't she?" asked Jason.

Emily realized that Jason was hurt at his mother for her uncaring actions and tried to make him feel better.

"I think she feels like you have too much on you to be bothered with her and Mom can't really talk to her. Mom doesn't want to talk to her either," said Emily thoughtfully.

"Remember the last time when Grandmother Elizabeth came? She said she wanted to talk to Mom. But Mom refused to allow me or Grandmother Washburn to leave the room when Grandmother Elizabeth was there," stated Emily curiously. "Don't you think that is strange, Dad?"

Jason sat pondering before saying thoughtfully, "I was in the room the first time Mom came and Janet had a viselike grip on my hand and would not let go. She told Mom then that she didn't want me out of her sight. Mom stayed a little while but seemed agitated and soon left," said Jason, looking steadily at Emily.

"Then the same thing happened when you were there. What do you suppose is behind that?" asked Jason, his brow wrinkled in concentration.

Emily thought about it and said, "Well, Dad, it may not be anything, but I did notice it and wondered why. Mom's too sick to ask about it so I guess we will never know unless she tells us."

Emily yawned and said she felt like taking a nap. "I think I'll go up and see Mom and then lie down for an hour. You should too, Dad. You haven't slept an entire night since we got here," she stated as if she was the mother.

Jason grinned at her grown-up attitude and said, "Okay, Little Mother. I'll go up as you go and check on your mom first."

Together they mounted the stairs but when they arrived at Janet's door and turned the knob, they found it locked. They looked at each other in astonishment and then Jason tried to turn the knob again but it was definitely locked. He then knocked on the door and waited and then knocked again. It was cracked open by Elsie, who whispered that Janet was asleep. She started to close the door again, but Jason stopped her.

"Why is her door locked, Elsie?" demanded Jason irately.

"Miss Janet was doing something that she wanted to be private about. She'll be finished after she rests a bit. The door will be unlocked in another hour, or before, if she feels ill, I promise," said Elsie seriously.

"I know all of you folks are worried but I wouldn't do anything to harm Miss Janet. She's like my own daughter," said Elsie with tears in her eyes.

Ashamed of his thoughts, Jason backed away and smiled as he said, "I'm sorry, Elsie. I've just been so worried. Please forgive me," he begged.

Elsie patted his shoulder saying, "Don't worry about it, Mister Jason. I know how you always tried to take care of everybody when you were just a little boy. I know you're worried."

Jason smiled his appreciation and patted her arm. "Emily and I are going to nap for about an hour. But if Janet should awaken and need us before an hour is up, you will call us, won't you?" he asked, and when Elsie nodded, he turned and went on down the corridor to the room given him when they first arrived.

An hour later, Janet's door was open and she was sitting up in bed chatting with her mother when Jason awoke and went to see about her. She stretched out her hand for him as he entered the room and smiled up at him.

"Elsie told me that you were about to kick the door in while I was asleep. I'm sorry I worried you but I had something I wanted to do and not be disturbed," Janet explained quietly.

When Jason started to protest she continued with, "Now, Jason, you know that some of you pop in every few minutes. I knew I couldn't concentrate with all that traffic so I told Elsie to lock the door, but I'm sorry you were upset."

Jason leaned down and kissed her forehead and said, "It's all right, Honey. I understand. It's just that your door had never been locked before and it scared me," explained Jason.

Emily had awakened and was now in the room. She piped up with, "What were you doing that's such a big secret, Mom? Were you writing a secret love letter?" she questioned, laughing merrily.

Janet looked shocked for a moment and then said, "Yes, Baby, I was writing your Daddy a love letter but he's going to have to wait a while to get it. It isn't finished yet," she looked up at Jason with such burning love in her eyes that he found tears in his own.

He sat down on the bed beside her and took her in his arms. "Janet, I know I never have appreciated you as much as I should have, but I do love you. I loved you like a little sister when we were kids, but now I love you as my wife, my companion, and the mother of our beautiful Emily," whispered Jason as tears ran down his cheeks.

He sat thinking how awful he had been to carry Lucinda Harmon around in his heart and head when this woman had been so much to him and he felt so sorry. He hugged Janet tighter and said through his tears, "Oh, Janet, I never meant to hurt you. Please forgive me."

Janet wound her thin arms around his neck and said brokenly, "Jason, Jason, you don't have anything to be sorry for. You have been all I ever wanted in my life. If I couldn't have you, I didn't want anything else," she stated firmly.

She pushed him away until she could look into his eyes then said, "Please remember that I always loved you more than life. You have been my life, Jason." She then started crying so forlornly that Jason didn't know what to say.

Emily came over with tears in her eyes and sat beside Jason on the bed. "There you two go again with all that romantic moonshine stuff. Before it becomes too mushy, can't you two have a little disagreement or something, please," Emily begged in mock horror, but with tear drenched cheeks and got them both in a different frame of mind.

## CHAPTER 43

Janet got to stay home three more days. These were days during which she felt well enough to talk and laugh with her mother, Jason, and Emily. Joshua, her father, would stop in each morning long enough to ask how she felt and if she needed anything, and then he would quickly leave.

When Olivia voiced her concern to Janet over Joshua's seemingly uncaring attitude, Janet told her not to worry about it. "I remember how he was when little Josh was ill. Daddy just can't handle sickness, can he?" she questioned with a tired smile.

Jason and Emily stayed in Janet's room as much as possible, only leaving to eat or while Janet napped each day. When she was awake, she seemed so much better that they all began to hope the radium had really worked. On the fourth morning, however, their world fell apart again.

Janet awoke with a high fever and was soon vomiting. Jason called an ambulance and they soon had her back in the hospital with numerous doctors and nurses in attendance. After a while she seemed to have calmed down. She looked around and began calling for Jason. The doctor went to the door and summoned Jason, who was just outside anyway.

When he reached her side, she grasped his hand with a weak but determined grip and, looking up at him, mumbled, "Jason, don't leave me. Please don't leave me. I love you so much." She looked so anguished that not only Jason but the nurses were shedding tears.

Jason kissed her scorching forehead and said, "I won't leave you, dear. I'm right here. Please try to relax."

Her agitation appeared to ease, but as the nurse came to put ice packs around her, she suddenly started vomiting blood. The nurse who was working on her called for help and soon the room was filled with doctors.

Janet was quickly placed on a gurney and wheeled out of the room. Jason, realizing the enormity of the situation, walked beside the gurney, and taking Janet's hand, squeezed it. When he saw Janet looking at him beseechingly, he leaned down and whispered, "I do love you, Janet. You've been a good wife." He felt a faint weak pressure from her hand, but just then she was rolled into an elevator and Jason was told he could go no further.

The rest of the family was in the waiting area except for Joshua. Jason was pleased that his mother and father had arrived by this time. Someone, probably Elsie, had called Henry when Janet had been taken away in the ambulance.

They all sat in silent dread after Jason had explained what had happened. Emily came over to the window where Jason stood looking up into the hills behind the hospital. She put her arm through her dad's and leaned her head against his shoulder and whispered, "Dad, do you believe that Mom will live again if she dies?"

Jason looked down into her white face desperately wanting to help her. He remembered Aunt Sarie Lester saying that she wasn't afraid to die. In his mind's eye he could see her glowing face when she talked about Jesus.

"Jesus was an example for us. He was alive, he died, and he rose from the grave and walked and talked. Now, Son, if he was an example he weren't just part way but every way. So, if my Jesus rose from the dead, then I'm a goin to as shore as you're standing there right now."

Smiling gently he spoke with assurance. "Yes, Princess, Jesus died for us and arose for us, and I believe that is what we will do."

Emily looked steadily in dry-eyed thought. Looking up at Jason she solemnly said, "If Mom can't get better, then I hope Jesus takes her. Because she won't have to suffer anymore and we'll get to see her again someday, won't we?" questioned Emily very seriously.

Jason turned and hugged her to him, "Yes, Princess, we will, and I was thinking the same thing. It is so hard to see her in so much pain and agony," said Jason softly as he pulled her head more snugly into his shoulder.

About an hour later, a white-coated Dr. DeBouran came

into the room and, looking around, saw Jason and strode toward him. Jason noted the serious expression on his face and knew the news was bad, but it still shocked him when Dr. DeBouran said, "I'm sorry, Dr. McCall, but we couldn't save her."

When Jason just stood, not speaking, nor moving, the doctor looked at Henry McCall with a plea in his eyes. Henry stepped beside of Jason and asked, "Jason, do you want to sit down?"

Jason seemed to suddenly realize what had been said and like a robot he put out his hand to the doctor, shook his hand, and said, "Thank you, Dr. DeBouran. I know you've done all you could."

This was said in a monotone, which revealed no emotion, and then Jason turned and walked to a chair and sat down. His face was still the same, he didn't cry, nor make any sound until he looked at Emily who was reacting the same way. He arose and went to his daughter, who flung her arms around his neck and dissolved in tears.

Henry stood quietly talking to the doctor. Olivia and Joshua had fled the room and soon Elizabeth followed them. Henry told the doctor that Jason needed some time before he could be calm enough to talk about arrangements. The doctor agreed with Henry. He went away leaving Henry to get back with him, once some decisions had been made. "We'll get back to you no later than sometime tomorrow," promised Henry.

Jason sat in white-faced numbness. A daily part of his life for almost sixteen years was gone forever. He groaned in agony and recrimination. "I didn't do right by Janet. I wish to God it had been different," he mumbled incoherently.

Henry came and sat beside him. Emily was still snuggled close to Jason's side, silently weeping. Now she looked up. "Dad, you were good to Mom. Everybody always said they were envious of how good you were to her."

"That's right, Son. We all know you were good to Janet. Don't do this to yourself. Janet loved you better than anything on earth," said Henry McCall as he patted Jason's knee.

Jason jumped up from the sofa and pounded his fist into his hand. "I know she loved me more than anything on earth. That's what hurts so damn bad."

Henry wanted to talk to Jason but when he saw the anguish on his son's face and the stricken look in his eyes, he instead went to sit beside Emily. He put his arms around his granddaughter and hugged her close.

Olivia, who had gone out of the room with Joshua after Dr. DeBouran left, came back in. Her eyes were red and swollen and Joshua was no longer with her. Elizabeth had gone to see about her and now followed her into the room.

When the two women saw Jason they came to a dead stop. Olivia went to Jason and put out her hand as if to touch him but said instead. "Jason, you have to pull yourself together. This won't bring Janet back and Emily needs you."

Jason pulled away from Olivia. "You don't know anything about it. I think I'll hate myself the rest of my days."

Elizabeth gasped in astonishment. "Jason, what is wrong with you? You were good to Janet. She told me you were so good to her."

"Like Hell, I was. I've got to get out of here. Dad, take care of Emily for a while. Will you?" asked Jason and on his dad's nod he almost ran to the door.

Jason went to his car and drove aimlessly until he found himself at the lookout area on Mount Washington. He pulled to a stop and got out. He stood looking out to the horizon, his thoughts in chaos.

"I just never could get Lucinda out of my head and heart. That's what's killing me. I tried so damn hard, but she was always there. Oh, I bought Janet anything she wanted, took her anywhere she wanted to go, but I never gave her my heart." Jason put his arms on the railings and then dropped his head onto his arms and cried brokenly.

Finally, he began to beg for forgiveness. "Please Lord, forgive me. I tried but I couldn't forget Lucinda. I couldn't give my heart to Janet because it had already been given away. Please, please, forgive me and give me some peace. If not for me, Lord, do it for Emily. I need to take care of her," he begged softly at first and then almost howled.

From the corner of his eye, as he raised his head, he saw somebody coming up the path. He straightened up and turned toward his car. The man came on up and said, "Hello! Are you leaving? I always come up here when I'm troubled, and before I leave I feel better. Of course, most people just come for the view. It is beautiful, isn't it?" he asked.

Jason smiled and agreed with him before going back to his car. As he opened the door the man said, "Life is hard sometimes. I do hope you will soon feel better."

Jason was embarrassed. "That man must have heard me making a fool of myself," he thought but turned to the man and said, "Thanks, I hope so."

He drove slowly back to the hospital. "I'm not the only person affected by Janet's death. I have to handle this better than I am now," mumbled Jason as he pulled into the parking lot. Feeling much stronger now he got out to enter the hospital and met Henry, Elizabeth, and Emily at the entrance.

"We decided to go home, Jason. We left word for you at the desk," Henry said, looking steadily at Jason.

"I'm sorry, Dad. I haven't been acting like much of a man. I…I didn't expect this so soon. I…well, anyway I'll take over now. Thanks for all your help and support. You and Mom have been great." Jason put his arm around Emily who had walked over to him and stood by his side, waiting.

They climbed into Jason's car and drove to the Wentworth house. Jason called Olivia and Joshua, telling them that he and Emily would spend the night with his parents. "We'll be back over there tomorrow to discuss what needs to be done, if that's all right with you and Joshua."

The next morning Henry and Elizabeth went to the Washburns with Jason and Emily. After much discussion they all finally agreed with Olivia's wishes. "All the Washburns have been laid to rest in the same mausoleum since the first Washburn arrived in America," pleaded Olivia when Jason complained. Jason also gave Olivia free reign in selecting the church, the minister, and the funeral parlor who would embalm Janet.

"Dad, Janet was the only child Olivia had after Little Josh died. I feel that in this she should be allowed some comfort, don't you?" Jason asked of Henry, who agreed with him.

Jason thought, "I would like to hear that song sung that I heard on top of Atwell Mountain, but if I mentioned that, all these people would think I had lost my mind."

For the next several days people walked around like wraiths, speaking softly as if their voices could awaken her, and going about their daily activities in slow motion, or so it seemed to Emily and Jason.

"Dad, this all feels to me like I am watching a play without the main character present. The stage is all set and every person does this at a set time and then something else at another time; like a wedding without a rehearsal," murmured Emily rebelliously as she and her dad were walking about the grounds.

"Yes, it seems that way to me too, but I think your Mom would have liked this. It is the way she was raised and, it is the correct way for her. You see, Princess, your Mom lived down in West Virginia, but her heart was always in Pittsburgh," explained Jason solemnly.

Since he had first found out that Janet had terminal cancer, Jason felt constant guilt because he had refused to leave West Virginia.

"Thank God, she never knew the real reason," thought Jason as he tried to deal with his guilt.

Jason and Emily followed the directives of Olivia in stoic compliance all during the planning and the carrying out of the funeral, not really talking about any of it. When the casket holding Janet had been shrouded in a silk mantle and the last words said over her by the minister, they walked out of the mausoleum in a daze.

They climbed into the back seat of the limousine, with darkened windows, that they had ridden to the church and on to the cemetery, thankful that it would all soon be over.

"Dad, let's go for a drive up into the hills," said Emily, coming into his room several days later dressed in jeans and a sweatshirt. She saw that Jason must have had the same idea, since he too had donned jeans and walking boots.

He looked around with a grin and then looked down at her feet.

"If you're going with me, you'd better get some walking shoes on. I feel like walking for miles."

Soon they were in the family station wagon speeding toward Mount Washington. Jason turned on the radio and they went humming along until he heard, "I hear singing and there's no one there." He reached to turn it off but Emily stopped him.

"Don't turn that off, Dad. That's pretty and has a nice tune to it, even if it is old," said Emily, who turned it louder and sat listening.

Jason was listening too, but he was transported back to a moonlit night in McDowell County, and that wonderful dream that never came true.

"God, what kind of man am I? I've just buried my wife of almost sixteen years and just a line of a song makes me think of another woman. Oh, Lord, please forgive me and help me to forget," he begged silently.

Emily looked over at him and said, "Dad, you're sad aren't you? I am too, but thinking about it won't bring Mom back."

She sat thinking before adding, "To be truthful, I don't want to bring her back in the condition she was in, do you?" she asked as if perhaps she was wrong to feel like that.

Jason jerked his thoughts back to Emily and answered, "No, Princess, I don't wish her back into the misery she was living in. I do wish I had been better to her, however."

Emily rode along not saying anything for the longest time and then she said, "You may have thought you weren't good to Mom, but she thought you were. She told me that you were the best husband that ever lived and much too good for her. So, quit beating up on yourself. If she thought you were good to her, then that's what counts, isn't it?" she questioned wisely.

## CHAPTER 44

They drove on to the top of the mountain, parked in the "lookout" area, locked all the doors and took the hiking trail that led up and through the woods. They climbed steadily until they reached the crest of a small hill. Sweating and panting for breath, they both plopped down in a bed of leaves beneath a giant oak tree.

"Whew! That's enough to blow the cobwebs away," said Jason with a laugh, before stretching out full length to look up at the sky.

"This is the best I've felt since we left Welch, Dad. I'm homesick, are you?" questioned Emily hopefully.

Jason sat up, dangling his hands between his knees. "We have to make some decisions, don't we, Princess. You've missed several weeks of your sophomore year already and you have to get back in school," stated Jason in a determined voice.

He looked at Emily thoughtfully and continued with, "I know you want to go back to Welch and finish up, don't you?"

Emily didn't bat an eyelash. "You bet I do. I didn't mention school up here for fear you would make me enroll in some school and I'd have to stay. Honestly, Dad, I think I would have been a dropout if you had done that," she stated firmly.

Jason knew that his parents, as well as Janet's parents, expected him to stay in Pittsburgh permanently. He didn't have a job down there anymore but he still had a house, good neighbors, and lots and lots of friends. Lucinda was there somewhere, but after what he had said to her that day in Pineville...God, why had he lashed out at her like that?

In his mind's eye he saw her blanched cheeks and eyes, which suddenly looked lost when he had said, "Get out of my life. I don't want you in it."

"Dad, where are you? I've been talking to you and you didn't hear a word I said," said Emily shaking him by the arm.

Suddenly he had made up his mind. He was going back, even if he never got to see Lucinda again. At least down there he might hear of her once in a while and know she was all right.

So, he rose to his feet and stretched, then looking down at Emily, he said, “Rise up, fair maid, and come away with me, I’m going to West Virginia.”

Emily let out a yell of pure joy. “Oh Dad, thank you, thank you! You’ve made me the happiest girl in the whole world,” she exclaimed and started down the trail at a fast clip.

Suddenly she stopped and turned. “No, Dad. I’m not the happiest girl in the world, not with Mom gone. It’s just that I think I can handle it better down there with Aunt Rita and Uncle Kyle and all my friends.”

“I know, Princess. We’ll miss your Mother as long as we live,” said Jason and then cautioned her to slow down since they needed to discuss the best approach to keep from hurting both sets of parents.

“I’ll call Kyle tonight and ask him about the house. I hate to be devious but I’ll tell him to call me about the middle of next week. I’ll tell him to say someone wants to either rent or buy the house. That would sound reasonable, wouldn’t it?” Jason asked, looking at Emily for approval. “Is that soon enough for you?” asked Jason as if in doubt.

Emily was swinging down the trail in front of him but yelled back, “I’d pack tonight and leave in the morning if you would. The sooner, the better, for me!” enthused Emily, stopping to wait until he caught up.

Jason explained that there were insurance papers, bills, stocks, and business things that would have to be cleared up. “We don’t want her folks to think we want away from all reminders of her. You know we’ll have to sort through her personal things, don’t you?” asked Jason as he stopped to rest.

“She already told me she wanted me to have her rings and all her pictures. I don’t really want anything else, so do I have to be there when you do that? I don’t really want to…It’s too soon for me, Dad. I’m sorry but I really just can’t,” said Emily as two tears rolled down her cheeks.

Jason was instantly sorry that he had expected so much from this fourteen-year-old child/woman. He had always talked to her as an adult and she was so perceptive, but this was dealing with her mother's personal belongings. After all, they had only buried Janet two days ago.

"I'm sorry, Princess. I'm a sorry excuse for a dad. I'll not put that on you. I'll get Elsie to help me if she can bear to do it," Jason said as they reached the bottom of the hill and walked toward the car.

"Poor soul, she is really torn up, isn't she?" opined Jason as he unlocked Emily's door and went to the other side of the car.

The next morning, Olivia asked about Emily's schooling. "Jason, have you decided about a school yet. Also, if you would like some help in finding a house for you and Emily, I'm sure Joshua can help," she offered helpfully. "Of course, you are welcome to live here as long as you want to. We'd be glad to have you both," she stated sincerely.

Jason assured her that he understood and appreciated her offer and that he was working on getting their lives organized. At that moment he decided he would ask Olivia about something that that had puzzled him since before Janet was taken to the hospital that last time.

"Olivia, how long has Mom been dropping in like she has in the last several days? I didn't know she was someone who would do that," said Jason, looking curiously at Olivia.

Olivia thought about it, "You know, Jason, she has acted out of character. She and I have always been friends but not bosom buddies, so her frequent visits have been rather unusual.

Elizabeth had been dropping in and asking if there was anything that they needed from Janet's room and once she had asked Elsie if Janet had left any message for her. Elsie shook her head. "No, Mrs. McCall she didn't leave you a message." When Olivia and Jason looked at her in surprise, she said, "We were so close. We shared secrets and did girl stuff together. I…Well, I thou…no, hoped she would leave me a word or something," she confessed miserably.

Both Jason and Olivia felt sorry for Elizabeth and consoled her by saying that Janet probably intended to, but the sickness acted so fast that she was just overwhelmed.

But after Janet died, Elizabeth still wandered in and out at unexpected times as if looking for something she had lost.

"Olivia, do you suppose Mom is having some kind of emotional problem?" asked Jason.

Olivia assured him that if that were so she was not aware of it. "I think this is the first death that has been this close to her, and Janet did go over and make cookies with her and things like that, especially while you were in Korea," explained Olivia.

Jason didn't think any more about it, but went about meeting with Joshua to settle any financial matters that had to be taken care of. He and Emily had dinner with his parents and Frank's family one night, and soon Tuesday of the next week had arrived.

Tuesday was the day Jason had set aside with Elsie to go through all of Janet's things and do something with the things Olivia or Emily did not want. After breakfast that morning, he and Elsie walked into the room, which now looked just like it did before Janet's illness.

"I guess we should take one drawer at a time, Elsie, and pack everything into boxes. Do you know of a charity that would like most of her clothes?" asked Jason as he lifted one drawer from the dresser and placed it on the bed beside Elsie.

Elsie assured him that she would take care of that but her voice sounded muffled and she wiped tears from her eyes. "Elsie, if this is too much for you, I can do it myself," offered Jason with compassion, but Elsie shook her head, saying that Janet would have wanted her to help.

By lunch time, they had everything packed and labeled except the small closet on the right side of the room, and Jason had decided that it could wait until after lunch. They were both tired and some of the things had brought back such painful memories. Janet seemed to have kept everything that Jason had ever touched or written. Jason found the corsage he had given her when he had taken her to that high school prom. It had been dried, pressed, and sealed in a plastic container, and marked "the first corsage Jason ever gave me."

Jason was seeing a girl who had felt as if he belonged to her from the time she was a kid. Everything pointed to her ownership, in her mind, of Jason McCall. He shook his head in amazement, thinking how well she had kept that side of her nature hidden.

He dreaded finishing up after lunch since he feared more of the same memorabilia of adoration for a man who didn't love her like he should have. It was making him very depressed but he knew he had to complete what he had started.

Elsie seemed to be slower mounting the stairs and she also seemed depressed. "Elsie, there's no need for you to put yourself through this, really. I can manage the rest of it by myself," offered Jason.

Elsie looked sadly at him, "No, Mister Jason there is something I have to do but I don't really want to. She pulled a chain from around her neck with a key on it and reached it to Jason.

"My sweet Miss Janet told me that I was to keep this until she died and then give it to you. It opens a box that's up in the left-hand corner of that shelf," Elsie said as she pointed to the shelf inside the small closet.

Suddenly those words Janet had spoken in the hospital when he thought she didn't realize what she was saying, came back to him. "There's something I need to give you. I'll write a note...and something about a key," Jason remembered part of it.

Jason was very puzzled since Elsie seemed so upset, but he took the key and walked inside the closet and looked at the shelf, not seeing a box.

"Are you sure, Elsie? I don't see a box?" questioned Jason, to be moved aside by Elsie as she started throwing out pillows and two stuffed animals.

"There it is. I knew it was there. I put it there myself that day she had me lock the door and you got upset. You remember that, don't you?" asked Elsie, smiling grimly as she brought the box down and handed it to Jason.

Jason sat down on the bed, clasping the box in his hands, but before he inserted the key, Elsie said, "Now, I don't think you need me anymore. I'll just go to my room and lie down if you don't mind."

Jason assured her that he would be fine on his own and waited until she quietly closed the door. Then he viewed that seemingly gold-plated box, which appeared to be "Pandora's Box" in his mind. He couldn't imagine what she could have kept so secretive. He was almost afraid to open it especially since Elsie had dreaded giving him the key.

He slowly inserted the key and heard the click as the lock disengaged, and then lifted the lid. A half-folded sheet of paper covered the contents and he slowly picked it up and unfolded the sheet to see Janet's writing. He had been so tense that his nerveless fingers let the letter slip through them and it was then he saw the packet of letters tied with a ribbon.

He picked up the bundle and the first thing he saw was Lucinda Harmon, Room 301 Sarvay Hall, Concord College, Athens, WV in the upper left hand corner and the letter was addressed to Dr. Jason McCall.

## ACKNOWLEDGEMENTS

In this the second book of a trilogy about West Virginia and particularly McDowell County I must first, give thanks to my almighty God. The scriptures declare in Psalm 92 that: *"It is a good thing to give thanks unto the Lord, and sing praises unto thy name, O Most High"*: I therefore, dedicate this work to the gift given of God. I did not earn the gift to write; it was given freely from the almighty hand of my loving Savior.

Many, many people have used their gifts and talents in bringing this work to fruition. All the help I have received, whether in editing, making contacts, in advice, and in encouragement I truly appreciate each and every person who helped.

Again I must mention my precious brother and sister-in-law, Giibert Horne and his wife, Edna. They have given me insight into what it is like to be a coal miner and a coal miner's wife. I thank them so very much. They have always been there for me.

Jerry K. Horne, my nephew, who allowed me into his home and also allowed me to pick his brain as to aspects of the political climate of McDowell County. He patiently answered the many phone calls and responded to numerous emails when I was in doubt. Thanks Jerry, I will never be able to repay you.

A another young man and long time friend Randy Osborne, left his busy schedule to spend several hours discussing Bradshaw and the surrounding area with me. I owe you my friend.

Thanks to my husband and two sons, John and Jonathan for putting up with a wife and mother who has been seemingly glued to the computer for many hours each day and far into the night. I'm glad all of you still love me. Thanks for your patience.

Many, many thanks go to my two best friends, Mike and Jo Osborne for keeping my computer going, and helping me untangle the many pitfalls in technology that I frequently encounter. Also thanks Jo for finding just the right answer to literary questions which you seem to know just where to find.

To my dear, dear McDowell County friends, Reba and Claude Banner who have helped me from the outset of writing this trilogy. I'll always remember the visit my son John and I made in their home. Thanks for the hospitality. You have both been friends indeed.

Carol Addington, who teaches nursing at the Russell County Vocational School, answered every call about medical matters with such graciousness and kindness, even with her busy schedule. Thanks Carol.

Dr. Brian Easton, of C-Health in Lebanon, called me from his home and on his leisure time to answer a question that only a doctor would know. Thank you so very much Doctor Easton.

I owe a debt of gratitude and thanks to Dr. Jerry Beasley, President of Concord University, located at Athens, West Virginia for not only writing the Introduction to my first book, but putting me in contact with Dr. Ross Patton. Thank you so very much Dr. Beasley.

I will be forever indebted to Dr. Ross Patton, M.D., Professor, Joan C. Edwards School of Medicine, at Marshall University, Huntington, West Virginia who agreed to write the introduction to this book. Only a doctor who has worked in the coalfields of McDowell County could have his depth of understanding about the culture. Through our telephone conversations I feel that I now have a wonderful new friend. Thank you so very much Dr. Patton

Thanks to Dr. Robert J. Higgs, Professor Emeritus of East Tennessee State University, Johnson City, Tennessee who is a font of knowledge about literature, especially Appalachian literature. His encouragement, comments, and friendship mean more than mere words can convey. If one wishes to learn about Appalachian literature he/she would do well to read some of his works such as: *The Machine In The Garden In Anes Station*; *Southern Humor: The Light and the Dark*, and *War in the Stadium*. He graciously wrote a review of *Lucinda's*

Mountain and also a blurb for this book. Thanks so very much my good friend.

Many, many thanks are extended to my precious friend and famous Appalachian writer, Lee Smith. Some of her titles are: *Fair and Tender Ladies*, *Family Linen*, *Agate Hill*, *The Last Girls*, and *Black Mountain Breakdown*. There are many more works by Lee Smith which speak to the heart of any person who ever struggled to overcome stereotypical snobbery. Any person who aspires to bring honor and dignity to a part of this country which has historically been seen as backward and uneducated must read Lee Smith. Dear friend I owe you a debt of deep appreciation for your comments on my books and your encouragement not just by words but by example.

To Greg Horne, English Professor, Southwest Virginia Community College, Richlands, Virginia for his encouragement in my writing and his comments on this book as well as the first one.

I am deeply in debt to my friend and fellow writer Kathie Mokwa for all the information she provided about Pittsburgh, Pennsylvania. Thanks very much Kathie.

My two editors, Rachel Riggsby and Matthew Asbury have been honest and forthright in their critiquing of this book. Matthew made the book so much better by the numerous rewrites he forced me to do. Rachel just as diligently rephrased sentences, checked grammar, time lines, and any part of this book which needed work. These two people are editors who want a book to be the best it can be. They both have my undying thanks.

Last but not least is my precious friend Dr. Thomas Keats McKnight, Professor of English Southwest Virginia Community College. He is also the founder and instructor of the Reminiscences Writing Project and a friend to any and all writers. His unstinting encouragement and faith in all my work has meant more than I could possibly find words to express. Dr. McKnight, a very talented writer himself, is an emissary to all writers and would-be writers passing along his expertise and knowledge of good writing. Thanks Tom.